BEYOND
ALL
Doubt

PETER A. MOSCOVITA

Beyond All Doubt
Copyright 2025 @ Peter A. Moscovita

Library of Congress Control Number: 2025915528
ISBN: 978-1-968069-31-5 (Paperback)
        978-1-968069-37-7 (Hardback)
        978-1-968069-32-2 (Ebook)

The views expressed in this book are solely those of the author and do not necessarily reflect the views of the publisher, and the publisher hereby disclaims any responsibility of them.

Olympus Story House

CONTENTS

This second book has been written as a sequel to The Following Storm.

Once again, I have turned to the people who helped me with the first book. Their encouragement to continue writing is greatly appreciated.

To my wife Martine, again, my appreciation for the countless hours helping with the draft.

Your tireless encouragement is the drive behind all that I do.

Thanks to our close friend, Mary Storsteen, for again helping me with the draft.

**To all the
Men and Women
who served their countries
in times of war.**

INTRODUCTION

The thrilling sequel to *The Following Storm* throws Karl Vita, the main caricature, once again into the dangers of a world now at war, starting with the evacuation of the British Expeditionary Force off the beaches of Dunkirk France, May 27th-June 4th, 1940.

Although this story is fictional, it is based on many events that changed and scarred the countries in Europe. This book starts in 1940 and continues through to 1944. As a British Intelligence Officer, Karl Vita is deeply involved in the planning and implementing of intelligence missions into occupied France. These hazardous operations leave him injured on several occasions. Recuperating, he becomes romantically involved with several ladies but no wedding bells until he buys a car and an exciting new romance flourishes from that purchase, opening the door to lasting happiness—assuming he can survive the dangers of being a spy.

CHAPTER 1

In Harm's Way

England can be damp and wet in the early summer, and this day was no exception. Lieutenant Karl Vita stood in the crowded aisle of the double-decker bus, holding onto a leather strap hanging from the ceiling, heading to his job at the military camp outside of Slough Berkshire, England. Hearing the conductor announce his stop, he moved to the open platform at the rear of the bus. Squealing brakes brought the old double-decker bus to a shuddering halt; like a flood, the passengers inside pushed toward the platform in a hurry to get off, heading to their places of employment. Another workday was about to commence.

The war was not going well for the English Expeditionary Forces in France. The combined German blitzkrieg forces were driving the English, French, and smaller divisions of Belgium's and Canada's forces toward the English Channel and the long, open beaches of Dunkirk, their survival now questionable. Over three hundred thousand English troops and approximately another hundred thousand plus French troops, along with their equipment, were now in jeopardy of total annihilation.

The drizzling rain made the short walk miserable for Karl, his umbrella not really shielding him from the blowing rain. "Excuse me, Sir, may I share your umbrella?" asked a pretty ATS (Auxiliary Territorial Service) sergeant.

"Of course, you can, young lady. I'm heading to the camp; I'm assuming you are going that way as well?" replied Karl, noticing how striking she was in her khaki raincoat.

"Excuse me for asking, Sir; are you one of those international chaps stationed here at the camp? There seems to be an awful lot of you. By the way, my name is Gwen Phillips," said the young ATS girl, looking up at the handsome lieutenant. At the main gate, they presented their ID's to the military police guard, then proceeded toward building B-3, located on the left side of the compound.

"This is where we must part, Sergeant. Keep the umbrella; I'm sure you will return it one day soon," said Karl as he started walking away from Gwen.

"Sir, how do I find you, and who do I ask for in this building, to return the umbrella, that is?" asked Gwen as she stood under the umbrella, hoping that their brief encounter would not be the last.

"Just ask for Lieutenant Karl Vita," replied Karl, continuing to walk briskly toward the entrance of the building marked B-3 in large red letters.

Once inside, he was greeted by the receptionist, "Good morning, Sir; you look rather wet," said the jovial receptionist.

"You are so right," replied Karl as he took off his raincoat. "Jean, would you get me the briefs for today and an updated schedule?" asked Karl as he headed to his small cubicle at the end of the row of workstations. Jean returned with a large steaming mug of coffee and a stack of briefs for Karl to review.

"Major Knight sent his compliments and asked for you to join him at 0930 hours in the main conference room and to remind you to bring the latest aerial photographs of the beaches at Dunkirk," said Jean, making sure her boss would not forget anything prior to the first meeting of the day. Karl arranged his briefs, then placed them under his arm; he stopped momentarily to look at the framed photograph on his desk of his deceased fiancée, Kitty Johnson, killed on a mission in Germany almost two years ago. This he did every day without fail.

The German military van she and another British intelligence officer were being transported in was deliberately rammed by a resistance fighter's lorry in a brave attempt to rescue them before the dreaded Gestapo could interrogate and torture them for information. He picked up the picture, kissing it tenderly; his love for Lieutenant Kitty Johnson was still that strong. It would be very difficult to let someone else into his broken heart even after all this time. On the opposite side of his desk, Karl looked at the ship he had served on as its first officer back in 1936. With war on the horizon, he had deserted his post to escape to England with his mother, sister, and nephew and a new life as an officer in the British Intelligence Service.

"Morning, gentlemen; please, be seated," said Major Knight as he entered the conference room. "The news from France is now critical. As of this morning, all leave has been canceled, and you are confined to base until your assignments have been issued. Is that clear? Any and all persons having prior experience with boating and seamanship are to report to this room at 1300 hours as we are desperately short of skilled seamen.

"Operation Dynamo will commence on May 26th from ports around the southern coast of England. Our boys in the British Expeditionary Force (BEF) are with their backs to the sea. Prime Minister Winston Churchill, has directed all branches of the armed forces to aid in the evacuation of our troops back to England.

"Gentlemen, this is a monumental undertaking. Vice-Admiral Bertram Ramsey has been charged with directing the evacuation. Every seaworthy civilian vessel is to be requisitioned for this operation. As of this morning, all private boats, yachts, ferries, and merchant ships, along with every available naval ship, will gather to sail to Dunkirk.

"Lieutenant Vita and Lieutenant Armstrong, both of you have prior experience as senior merchant officers; you will both be given temporary command of armed trawlers being reactivated from the reserve fleet. You will leave for Lowestoft after the meeting here at 1300 hours. On your arrival, you will be met by naval personnel, who will brief you on the operation and direct you to your command. Your crews are all Royal Navy chaps.

They are already working on the trawlers to make them seaworthy. When we adjourn after this meeting, return to your quarters and pack a kit bag for at least one week. As for the rest of you, your orders will be assigned when you assemble here tomorrow morning at 0630 sharp. More than likely, you will be assigned to a boat or dock support, so do the same. Pack lightly; is that clear?"

Lewis Armstrong looked at Karl, fear and shock across his face. "My God, this is unbelievable. There are somewhere near 400,000 troops on or near those beaches. How on earth can we rescue them all before the German forces capture or kill them out in the open like that? They are almost defenseless, with no place to take cover or defend themselves while they wait to be evacuated."

Lewis was reacting in a state of panic. Karl knew instinctively he must calm Lewis down, "Lewis, get ahold of yourself, man; you are an officer in a room full of junior officers and non-commissioned types, not a good way to set an example. Some of these chaps could well be with you on one of those trawlers. How confident will they be in your leadership after seeing you like this? Now, straighten up."

Karl's leadership was showing through. With a look of approval on his face, Major Clive Knight was watching this interface, thinking, you can always rely on Karl to take charge. Back in his cubicle, Karl ran quickly through the briefs that needed his attention, then called Jean to file them until he returned. If ever. "Jean, I'm in a rush. Please have a staff car brought over from the motor pool. I have to pick up a few things from my flat; it looks like I'll be out of town for a while."

Karl started feeling exhilarated at the thought of returning to sea. He savored the idea of having his own command, even though it was only a tired old armed trawler. Outside the building, Karl walked quickly toward the staff car waiting by the curb. The roads were quite congested for this time of the morning.

Karl asked the driver if there was a quicker way to get to his flat and back again to the base. "Not really, Sir, never easy this time of the morning. I think it should be better returning, though." The driver could see the lieutenant in the back seat was becoming very anxious. At his flat, he packed a field uniform and essentials such as socks, underwear, and a toilet kit, then packed his trusty compass from the desk drawer. Taking a last look around, he returned to the waiting staff car.

Back at the base, they showed their IDs at the gate, followed by Karl instructing the corporal, "Drive me straight to Command." Almost jumping out of the car before it came to a stop, Karl thanked the driver. He grabbed his kit bag from the back seat and entered the Command Center; half running, half walking, he covered the distance to the meeting room at the end of the long hallway in record time.

To his surprise, he found the meeting room still full of military types milling around waiting for Major Knight to return. Karl yelled out over the group in a loud, authoritative voice, "Has Lieutenant Armstrong arrived back yet?"

"Over here, old man. Are you all set to go?" replied Lewis. The door opened, and in walked Major Knight along with two other officers.

"Vita and Armstrong, with me over here—we need to go over your roles in Operation Dynamo very quickly as the convoy of lorries will be leaving within the hour for Lowestoft. Once you arrive, you will have only a day and a half to get your crew and trawlers ready to sail for Ramsgate to rendezvous with the flotilla of boats being assembled that are heading to Dunkirk. Your assigned vessels are both Naval Admiralty Trawlers from the reserve fleet; they are about as ready as they ever will be, so don't expect too much when you first see them. Here is a folder on each vessel; try to read them on the way to Lowestoft. The operation details are on top, so familiarize yourselves with the rendezvous points, traffic lanes in and out of the beaches, and other information you need to familiarize yourselves with before the start of the rescue operation.

"Your crews are mostly Royal Navy reservists and regulars, about thirty-five in all. They are, as we speak, getting the boats ready. It is going to be up to you to whip them into shape before casting off. Is that clear enough for you? This armband and cap band will identify you as the ships' commanders; put them on now and keep them on until this evacuation is completed. Both Lieutenants stood, saluting their commanding officer before turning toward the exit. "Good luck, chaps. May God keep you safe."

"Lieutenant Vita, a word if you please," said Major Knight. Karl turned and walked back to Clive, standing by the desk. "Karl, my dear friend, please be very careful. The word from the Admiralty is they are expecting heavy casualties and heavy losses to the rescue vessels. Karl, make me this promise: you will not do anything reckless. I know you have a chip on your shoulder against Germany and especially the ones that caused the death of Kitty." Clive was showing genuine concern for the welfare of his close friend.

"Don't worry about me, Clive. Once this evacuation is over, you can send me back into Europe where I can really get my revenge," replied Karl, being his usual sarcastic self. "Get out of here, you crazy Austrian," said Clive, laughing. Karl turned, then adjusted his cap to one side as a seaman would do. He was returning to sea duty after all.

CHAPTER 2

LOWERSTOFT AND THE HMT REESE

Outside, there seemed to be much confusion about who was in what lorry. "This is ridiculous," said Lewis to Karl as they stood waiting for further instructions. "Sirs, please follow me; you will travel with these other officers in that bus at the head of the convoy," said the sergeant major as he guided them toward the bus. On board, Lewis and Karl introduced themselves to the other officers before sitting down together.

"Well, old man, I was getting worried we would be traveling in one of those drafty lorries, so this is so much better," remarked Lewis. The journey of one hundred sixty miles would take about four to five hours with a quick stop halfway. Karl opened his folder and started to memorize the operation details; he was not in the mood for further talk.

The sun was still high when the convoy reached Lowestoft. Pulling into the shipyard, they were totally surprised by the gathering of all types of boats and ships, from civilian cabin cruisers to merchant ships. *HMT Reese* and *Twain* were dockside with smaller boats rafted on the freeboard up to four deep. "Well, Karl, that's mine in front of yours, the *Twain*, so I guess the *Reese* is the one behind. There's a skippers' meeting at 0530 hours tomorrow morning, so let's meet up dockside at say 0515 hours, shall we?" asked Lewis.

"Sounds good to me," replied Karl. Walking down the dock toward the *Reese*, Karl was thinking out loud as he got closer, "My God, what a difference to the *Tristian*."

A loud voice announced, "Captain arriving aboard," came the command from the ship's first officer, standing at the top of the ramp with an ordinary seaman piping Karl aboard.

"Thank you, Lieutenant Adams, pleased to make your acquaintance. Would you kindly assemble the crew on the fantail, so I can introduce myself and outline what I expect from them over the next few days? After that, you can show me around the boat; considering her size, that will not take long. My main concern at this point is the state of readiness of this boat and its crew," said Karl, finally realizing that this was his command; he was no longer a first officer. "Mr. Adams, tomorrow morning you will join me at the flotilla operational meeting. I suspect this will take about two or three hours."

Karl followed Adams to the stern of the *Reese*, mentally taking note of the condition of this old trawler. The crew of thirty-five men formed up in rows on the fantail, all in work overalls. Some were covered in grease and rust from working on the old triple expansion steam turbine engine, while others in standard dark blue overalls were working on servicing the armament and deck equipment.

The last ones to join the assembly were the seamen working on the outdated bridge equipment. The crew stood apprehensively, waiting to hear their new captain give them his orders. Adams spoke quietly to Karl as they approached the rail on the fantail, "Sir, over the last four days, these chaps have been frantically trying to get this old girl back into a state of readiness and, believe me, it shows. They are a terrific bunch of chaps, as you will soon find out."

Lieutenant Adams approached the rail ahead of Karl. In a controlled voice, he ordered the crew to attention.

"Thank you, Number One," replied Karl as he placed both hands on the rail. He deliberately stood silently, looking from left to right at his crew mustered below for what must have appeared to be an eternity to the crew. In a loud voice, Karl started to speak, "Gentlemen, please stand at ease. We are all in this same boat, and it will make our work so much easier if we dispense with naval formalities.

"Up until two years ago, I was an officer in a foreign merchant service but never served in any Navy. My accent, as you can tell, is not English; it's Austrian. And being a sailor was all I ever wanted to do until Adolf Hitler changed my career plans. For the last two years, I have been active in British Military Intelligence. I hope this will not deter you from following my orders as we make ready for a perilous but essential mission to save our troops.

"We have less than two days to get this old lady ready for that lifesaving mission. The British Expeditionary Forces and those of the French Army have been pushed back to the beaches of Dunkirk. With their backs now to the English Channel, they have no place left to retreat. This makeshift Armada being assembled has many types of vessels made up of merchant ships, tugs, all ferryboats that can float, privately-owned power boats, sailing yachts, and yes, we will be towing navy lifeboats.

"Gentlemen, we have only one objective: to get to Dunkirk on May 26th to rescue as many troops as we can. Hopefully, it will be all of them; God willing, we can make this happen. We depart for Ramsgate along with *HMT Twain* and the rest of the flotilla on the afternoon tide two days from now. Most of the vessels in the flotilla are unarmed. They will be under the protection of thirty-nine Royal Navy Destroyers with added French and Norwegian Naval units. We will also provide screening to those unarmed vessels throughout the operation. Any questions before we map out the operation?"

"I have one, Sir. How many vessels will take part in this rescue?" asked one of the stockers.

"Good question. What is your name?" asked Karl.

"Chief Petty Officer Charlie Brice, Sir," answered the seaman. "Glad to know you, Charlie. From what I have been told, it could be close to eight hundred or so; that is the number we have been told." Karl scanned his crew as he gave them this information.

"Crikey, is there enough room for all these boats converging around the Dunkirk beaches?" asked another seaman.

"What makes you all believe the bloody German Navy and Luftwaffe are not going to do their best to sink the bloody lot of us?" asked another seaman.

"The Royal Navy and Royal Airforce are mustering every available ship and fighter plane to protect us. Hopefully, they can keep the Germans at bay. Our biggest challenge right now is to get as many of those troops as we can off the beaches before the Germans force them into surrendering." Karl was trying to make his crew understand that if this Army were forced into surrendering, England would more than likely be forced to negotiate a conditional armistice. "This plan was the brainchild of Prime Minister Winston Churchill. All of us must give him our one hundred percent. Let's give him something to be proud of; what do you say, boys?" Karl was now speaking more like a politician than a military officer.

A loud cheer came back from all the crew. "We're with ya, Skipper," yelled Charlie. This was the answer Karl was looking for.

Another crewman, Marvin Brown, with an authentic Cockney accent, yelled out loud, "They better not mess with Winnie; he'll have their guts for garters." To this, the entire crew started cheering out loud; sadly, this seaman would be the first fatality on the *Reese* off the beaches of Dunkirk on May 26th.

"Before dispersing the crew, Number One, I would like to go down onto the deck to shake hands with each one of the crew. After that, you can give me a tour of the old girl." Karl was now starting to feel good about his new crew. Meeting the crew took over thirty minutes. There was genuine excitement and acceptance for their new foreign skipper. "Okay, Number One, show me around this old gal," said Karl.

Sailors on the forecastle were busy servicing the single 12-pound gun; other sailors were installing antiaircraft guns on either side mid ships. Two more were mounted on the stern for additional protection. Depth charge racks mounted on the stern gave them a limited four spread capability. "Better not waste those four charges if that's all we have. What's next?" remarked Karl to Adams. On the bridge, two seamen explained the steering station and the limited, outdated instrumentation. The radio shack only had room for one operator; it looked like an afterthought squeezed into the rear of the pilothouse.

Scotty, the chief engineer, waited patiently inside the pilothouse to take them down into the bowels of the engine room. As he spoke, his Scottish accent was challenging for Karl; however, he felt comfortable that the ship's engine and machinery were in capable hands. "Where is the navigation officer?" asked Karl as he looked around the pilothouse.

"He will arrive later this evening. He got delayed in Portsmouth from what I was told," replied Adams.

"Well then, Scotty, show me your engine room if you please," asked Karl, starting to feel more like the skipper of the *HMT Reese*.

"Follow me, Sir; it's going to be rather warm down there—hope you'll be alright."

"Don't worry about me, Scotty; I've been in hot spots all too many times." Karl was now in an almost jovial mood. The open steel stairwell had two landings that turned back upon itself to reduce the rise in the stairs. This was nothing new to Karl. To the surprise of Adams and Scotty, he placed his hands on the steel handrails and slid down quickly to the first landing, then again to the catwalk that made up the engine room floor, followed by Scotty and Adams.

"I can see you are no stranger to navigating ships' stairs; you and I will get on just fine, Sir," said Scotty as he showed the way for his new commanding officer. "The engine is old but in reasonably good shape considering her age, way too many hours on that boiler, though. She is oil-fired compared to the older coal burners; that's one saving grace. The triple steam turbines are almost completely phased out; I've had too many years working on these old buggers, Skipper."

Karl was smiling to himself, thinking, he just calling me Skipper—this is a good start. "Thank you, Scotty; see you topside for dinner." Adams and Karl climbed back up the steel stairs out onto the deck and into the twilight of May 24th. "I'm assuming we do not have a wardroom," mused Karl as they walked toward the foredeck.

"Not really, Skipper; we have a small galley that is for the officers only at this point. It's almost suppertime anyway, so please follow me, Sir," replied Adams, a little embarrassed knowing his skipper had been a first officer on a large passenger freighter before coming to England.

Karl sensed Adams' uncomfortable tone as he apologized for the lack of a wardroom and answered by saying, "You know, Number One, we must be kind to the old lady if we expect her to keep us safe. I'm sure the galley will serve us just fine." Karl, following behind Adams, felt a whole lot better about how he had answered Adams.

"Thank you, Skipper; you're making me feel so much better about being your number one, and I appreciate your kind words about our old girl, *Reese*." Over dinner, Karl listened intently to their stories of life and careers before being recalled to active duty in the Royal Navy. After they had their say, Karl described what he expected from each of them as they prepared for this hazardous mission.

All in all, it was a productive evening, with Karl focusing on building the bridge of trust between his officers. Excusing himself, Karl asked to be shown to his quarters. Aft of the bridge, a small corridor led to the captain's quarters. Karl's first thought upon entering his cabin was that it's only for a few days, so no problem. The cabin had a narrow bed against the wall with a floor-to-ceiling wardrobe equally narrow. A small folding hand basin that had seen better days was in the corner next to a narrow desk that desperately needed refinishing. The old girl has been in hibernation far too long, thought Karl as he stowed his sea bag in the wardrobe. Removing his jacket, tie, and shoes, Karl laid on the narrow bed, his head spinning with thoughts of what would be waiting for them lying off the crowded beaches of Dunkirk.

0430 hours came all too quickly for Karl as he reached for the light switch in the dim light of the small cabin. Dressing quickly, he headed to the galley, downing a hot mug of tea before proceeding down the gangplank to meet Lieutenant Adams on the dock at 0515. "Morning, Number One, did you sleep well?" asked Karl.

"Finally dropped off about 2300 hours; feeling quite refreshed this morning, thank you, Skipper," replied Adams. On the opposite side of the dock, a single overhead light fixture provided just enough light to illuminate the steel door to the converted warehouse. As they walked toward the entrance, they met up with Lieutenant Armstrong and his first officer, John Wright, many other Royal Navy officers, Merchant Marines officers, and a sizable number of civilian captains, all heading to the same orientation for Operation Dynamo.

Inside, steel folding chairs had been hastily arranged in three columns across the center of the massive interior of the building. At the front of the building, a makeshift platform had been built to accommodate the senior officers. Three large blackboards were lined up behind the long table that faced the expanse of steel chairs.

Commander Alan Mathews stood up, holding his hands high in the air and yelling, "Gentlemen, please find a chair and be seated.

We have much to review this morning. This briefing covers how Operation Dynamo will be conducted by an armada of approximately 850 vessels, all heading for the beaches of Dunkirk. This flotilla, leaving from Lowestoft, will rendezvous later today with other ships off the harbor entrance to Ramsgate, all en route to Dunkirk. Please open your packets of instructions and charts given to you as you entered the building. Do not forget to take them with you at the conclusion of this briefing.

"Now, please open your packets. We will be leaving for Ramsey tomorrow morning at 1030 hours; the distance is 78 plus miles on a straight rum line. Stay together in the column you are assigned and remember to allow for the slowest vessel in the flotilla. We expect to join the main body of ships in about ten to eleven hours. Remember, if you are towing smaller boats, steer clear of the wake coming from larger vessels; we don't need to swamp these smaller vessels before reaching Dunkirk. Upon our arrival, they will play a vital part in evacuating our blokes off those shallow beaches. Our approach to the beaches will be from the southwest in a counterclockwise pattern. Approach the beaches in a line astern formation in two columns. The smaller boats with a very shallow draft will ferry the chaps out to the bigger vessels waiting in the deeper waters.

"Do not attempt to get too shallow. If you go aground, you will be on your own, so remember that we do not have the time or resources to come to your aid. If you are attacked and in danger of sinking, try to get your vessel out of the traffic pattern. Now, once your vessel is loaded, head straight back to Dover, or, if instructed, one of the other arrival ports such as Folkestone to unload. On your return trip to Dunkirk, follow the same approach pattern.

"Now, I will turn this briefing over to Captain John Tillerson, who will update you on defenses from the combined forces of the Royal Navy and the Royal Airforce," concluded Commander Alan Mathews, returning to his seat.

"Thank you, Commander. For those of you that don't know who I am, well, you could say you're lucky. Ask the blokes around you; they will tell you the truth." Loud applause came from many of the Royal Navy attendees. "Now, that's out of the way, let's get serious about this briefing and the operation to save our boys.

The Royal Navy has diverted 39 destroyers along with three French destroyers. We have also brought out of the reserve fleet some Armed Admiralty Trawlers and Armed Merchantmen that can provide additional protective air cover for the flotilla. These vessels will be dispersed on either side of the main body. We are expecting a heavy aerial attack from the Luftwaffe. It goes without saying; our losses are expected to be very high. If your vessel is unarmed, I'm assuming you collected hand weapons and ammunition yesterday from the supply stores. If you have not done so, please see the supply officers before you depart this briefing; they are on either side of the entrance at the back of this warehouse. Those machine guns could well save your life and those around you. Now, let's review the operational details, shall we?

"On the way out, all vessels will monitor channel 168 on your VHF radios. On the return trip to England, switch to channel 180. Using two dedicated channels will reduce the chatter and hopefully eliminate confusion. Now, if you are hit and in danger of sinking, if your vessel is still capable of making headway, try to get out of the shipping lanes. If this is not possible, call the vessel or vessels close to you to aid in your evacuation. Another crucial point, if your vessel is still afloat, drop your anchor, so it will not drift into other vessels. Keeping the traffic lanes clear will add in evacuating more blokes off those beaches.

"Many of the larger merchant ships will be using the Eastern breakwater, which has a 1,400-yard-long dock with a wooden boardwalk, wide enough to traverse troops four abreast. Captain William Tennant has been assigned as the Beachmaster; he has tactical oversight for the entire evacuation. Our flotilla will take directions from him. This briefing will now adjourn to allow preparations to continue. When we depart, have your radio set for channel 69 and wait for instructions on when to get underway. Gentlemen, England is relying on all of you to save the BEF; God be with all of us."

Lieutenant Armstrong approached Karl as they all left the warehouse, "Karl, it looks like you're shoving off ahead of me. It's a big job; hopefully, we will come through it in one piece. Take care and be safe; see you out there." With that, he gave Karl a casual salute and headed toward the *Twain* with his first officer.

"Well, Number One, shall we get back to the *Reese*? There is still work to be done, and we don't have too much time left, do we?" Karl was talking to Adams in a relatively subdued tone.

"Are you alright, Skipper? You seem rather melancholy." Adams was seeing a side of Karl he had not seen before. Even though their time together had been very brief, he felt he knew his skipper reasonably well.

"No, Number One, I'm fine. It's just that I've had a storm following me for so long; I just feel it's about to catch up with me shortly."

CHAPTER 3

DUNKIRK

Back on the *Reese*, Karl looked up to see smoke curling away from the smokestack. "Looks like Scotty is getting her fired and ready for tomorrow; that's a good sign." That night, the work continued until way past 2200 hours. Karl and Adams were hard at work, planning and marking the charts they received at the meeting. Karl rose at 0530 hours and dressed. He headed to the galley for some hot tea and a buttered roll, then undertook an inspection of the ship. Satisfied with the results, he returned to the bridge, saying, "Morning all, I trust you had a good night's sleep and now are ready for this long day."

At 0930, the deck crew was busy getting the tow lines ready for the eight smaller boats they would be towing. These smaller vessels had already left and were now waiting outside the harbor entrance to pick up the tow lines that would be laid off the *Reese's* stern by members of the deck crew. The VHF radio crackled into life, "Command to *Reese*, are you ready to drop your lines and pick up your ducklings outside the harbor? Over," came the request from Captain Tillerson.

"*Reese* to command; ready to depart. Over," Adams replied to the command ship.

"Take her out, Number One," came Karl's first command.

"Aye, aye, Skipper," came the response as Adams picked up the bullhorn and headed out onto the starboard pilothouse wing. "Single up all lines," he said, followed by, "Let go forward spring lines, let go rear spring lines." The deck crew pulled the heavy lines aboard and waited for the next set of commands. "Let go stern lines," followed by a brief pause as Adams leaned over the bridge, watching the lines come aboard. "Let go of the bow lines." Looking back into the pilothouse, he gave the order to the helmsman, "Helm over five degrees, make revolutions ten."

The *Reese* gave a slight tremor as her big single propeller screwed itself through the dirty waters of the harbor. "Helmsman, come left to make the harbor entrance; set revolutions for three knots." The *Reese* was now moving very slowly toward the entrance, passing larger vessels waiting their turn to cast off.

Once through the harbor entrance, Adams barked another command, "Helmsman, put your helm amidships; stop engine."

Adams then picked up the bullhorn once again, giving his next command, "Lay off towlines to the ducklings as they approach our stern." Adams turned to Karl with a big grin on his face, "Sir, will you take it from here, or do you wish me to continue the maneuvering?"

Karl responded by saying, "Nice job, Number One, get the ducklings rafted and secured to our lines, then take her out to the marshaling area. The command ship will give us instructions and positioning in the flotilla once we are there." Karl was enjoying being the captain and more than confident in Adams' ability as a seaman. The *Reese* slowly answered the helm as she turned southerly toward the merchantman in front. With a bullhorn in hand, Adams went out onto the deck, giving instructions for Seaman Wilson to remain at the stern, keeping an eye on the tow lines and the little ducklings.

"Thanks, Number One; I'll take her from here. Why don't you get some rest? You will need to be alert once we close on Ramsgate." Karl now picked up the PA microphone, telling all deck hands to be vigilant in watching the skies for enemy aircraft. "Stand ready at your gun positions. You are clear to check your weapons now; try not to sink any of the flotilla while you do so." Karl smiled as he said that. It brought back memories of several years ago when training in Scotland with an instructor who loved to torment his pupils with sarcastic remarks.

Four Royal Navy destroyers and two smaller Corvettes took up their screening position on either side of the growing flotilla as they headed southwest toward Ramsgate. "Helmsman, keep your distance at three hundred feet. No need to bump that merchantman in front of us, right!"

"Command to Flotilla, please report." A crackling message from the command ship came back.

"Sparky, make to Command, *Reese* underway." Karl listened as Sparky reported back to command: so far, so good. Karl walked out onto the pilothouse wing deck, looking up first then around the ship to see that everyone was paying attention. Satisfied that the *Reese* was ready for any incident, he placed his hands on the railings of the steel steps leading down from the bridge. Like an old salt, he half-walked, half-slid down to the deck below.

Approaching the gang of seamen that would be boarding the troops from the beach, he elevated his voice to make sure all could hear him speak.

"Alright, listen up, chaps, when we give way, we will stay on station long enough to board as many troops as we can. Jones, you and your gang will let go of the ducklings and make sure no lines get fouled in their props. Once that is done, lay off on the starboard side the boarding nets and both boarding ladders. When the ducklings arrive back with troops, help the men up onto the deck. Now, I need you all to pay attention to what I say next; we need to distribute the troops evenly once on board. Lieutenant Adams, you and Jones will direct them first to the stern, say a boat load at a time, then to the bow with the next load; make sure they understand not to congregate on one side only. Balancing the ship as we load will help us get underway back to England that much faster; are you all clear on that? Right now, organize your gang, Jones, so they all know the drill. No need for us to act like blue-arsed flies, is there?" Karl was trying to get them all relaxed and focused on the task ahead, and a little humor would go a long way.

One of the seamen asked, "Sir, when we depart, what will happen to our ducklings?"

"Good question; they will continue ferrying troops out to the other boats and ships waiting behind us. With any luck, they can get a tow when their job is done, assuming they don't get sunk," replied Karl.

The semaphore signalman received a message from command, "Silence radio activities; use signal lamp from here on. Use designated outbound VHF channel for emergency use only. The Ramsgate contingency is already ahead of us. Helmsman, make your course 220 degrees. All vessels acknowledge signal by position," came the final instruction.

"*Reese* to command, acknowledge and understood." Karl could feel the tension building as the armada of mismatched boats and ships headed southwest to their destiny off the beaches of Dunkirk.

The seas were choppy with clear skies, the smaller vessels rolling on and off the wave tops. All eyes were searching the sky, looking for enemy aircraft and the first signs of the French coast. The waiting was playing on everybody's nerves. This was quite disturbing until a loud horn sounded from one of the merchantmen, followed by anti-aircraft fire from one of the flanking destroyers ahead of them.

"Aircraft approaching from the East," a sailor screamed out. Out of the sun, three black dots, diving at high speed, made everyone run to their gun stations.

"Hold your fire; repeat, hold your fire until we can confirm if they are friend or foe. Those nitwits have opened fire before verifying that they are enemy aircraft," yelled Karl.

As they watched a signal lamp from the lead destroyer, command said, "Hold your fire; repeat, do not open fire; incoming aircraft are RAF planes, please acknowledge this signal."

"Signalman, make to command, understood." Karl removed his cap to scratch the top of his head in frustration, then threw his hands in the air, yelling loudly, "We are still an hour away, and those trigger-happy morons are trying to shoot down our own fighter aircraft."

The three aircraft could now be seen quite clearly, "Look like bloody Hurricanes to me, Sir," yelled Charlie from his gun position. "Those blokes on that destroyer should be thrown overboard. It's not like we have hundreds of spare planes right now, do we?" Karl and Adams could not contain themselves as they watched Charlie gyrating around his gun position. The three Hurricanes approached the flotilla almost at mast height, saluting their countrymen by rolling their aircraft from side to side, then peeling off toward Dunkirk. Everyone's attention was now concentrated on the coast of France as it came into view through the columns of black smoke and the sounds of bombs detonating as the screaming Stuka dive bombers released their deadly ordinances on the columns of soldiers and abandoned military vehicles scattered along the beach.

Heavy caliber gunfire added to the continuous music of war. "Number One, let's get the boys ready, shall we?"

Signal from command, "Skipper, close ranks and get your boarding nets ready; watch out for submerged wrecks as we get closer."

The images that were now confronting them as the flotilla arrived within a few miles of the beaches were of horrendous chaos. Men and equipment stained their vision, shocking them to the core. There were thousands of soldiers, their uniforms resembling brown lines of ants rather than soldiers of the BEF. From their location, the columns stretched out over the sand dunes for as far as the eye could see. The ones in the front were shoulder deep in the breaking surf, waiting their turn to board one of the small boats. Half-sunk vessels were all around the approach lanes; others were clinging to sinking boats, some on fire, sending soldiers and sailors into the oily waters around the wreck.

"My God, this is worse than I expected. How can we evacuate all those poor blokes when so many boats and ships are being sunk or damaged?" cried out Adams, tears filling his eyes.

"Thank God we have all these boats coming in behind us," said Charlie as he placed his metal helmet back on his head.

"Boats approaching on the starboard side, man the boarding nets; stand by to assist on the railing," yelled out Jones. Six of the ducklings approached line astern. Two boats at a time banged against the *Reese's* steel hull. "Climb up as many as you can, chaps; we need to load and depart as quickly as we can." Jones was making sure they used as much of the clumsy rope ladder as possible, six to eight men at a time. In less than forty-five minutes, all six ducklings had unloaded and cleared the side of the *Reese*, ready for more small boats to unload.

"This will have to be the last load for this trip," called out Adams. "Pull the boarding nets and boarding ladders up after taking on those last two boats so that we can get underway." He had just finished saying that when the waters close to the starboard side erupted in massive columns of seawater. The ship shook violently as the compression of water slammed the old ship's hull. Two Stuka dive bombers screamed back into the safety of the sky after releasing their deadly bombs on the ship below. Thankfully, both missed the *Reese* but annihilated two of the ducklings that now were no more than splintered pieces of wood with dead bodies floating in the debris field. Every available gun was sending the Stukas a message of lead—you're not safe yet. One of the planes started streaming black smoke from its engine, banking sharply to the north. "Keep your firepower on that engine," yelled out Adams as all the guns made an ear-splitting 'ratatat' sound.

The other Stuka dived down to sea level, making its escape back to its base. Less than two miles away, a loud explosion and massive plume of water could be seen and heard as the critically wounded Stuka hit the water; its tail and part of the cockpit were all that remained above the water. Everyone watched in silence as its crew tried to climb out to no avail; the canopy was jammed.

Through his binoculars, Karl could see both men banging against the plexiglass. Their fate was sealed as the Stuka slid slowly below the waves. "Poor buggers," said Adams as they all watched the drama unfold in front of them.

"They would have cheered if they could have blasted this ship and all these blokes to kingdom come," replied Karl with a stone face and ice in his veins. Karl turned, shouldering his way toward the pilothouse without looking back.

"Gov, your skipper is a hard-nosed bugger, ain't he?" said one of the soldiers.

"If you had lived through what he has lived through, you might think very differently," replied Adams as his eyes followed the skipper pushing his way slowly back toward the pilothouse. Military evacuees occupied every foot of the pilothouse wing deck. "You chaps make a hole for the skipper," yelled Adams to the soldier standing in the path of the skipper. Karl entered the pilothouse with Adams close behind.

"Thank you, Number One; it's getting a little crowded out there," said Karl, trying to remain calm. "Once we're clear of the area, have the six sailors on watch duty report to the pilothouse." Karl restrained himself as he thought through what had just happened. Around them, fully laden vessels were making their way back to English ports to discharge their live and wounded cargo. Ahead of the Reese about a mile, a merchantman was struggling to maintain headway. Its forward cargo hatch was belching smoke from an aerial attach while it lay waiting for its human cargo. Its decks from the superstructure back were overloaded as the troops were pushed back away from the damaged bow area of the ship.

"Signalman, make to the *Hampton*, are you in danger of sinking? Do you need us to stand by? Can you maintain headway?" Karl looked at the laboring merchantman through his binoculars.

The *Hampton* responded pumps are handling the seawater entering from our bow. The fire has been put out; only the smoke is left now. We are steady at six knots. We can't take another hit, though; *Hampton* clear. Karl leaned back against the pilothouse windows, his legs crossed and arms folded across his chest. "Sparky, break silence and make to command; we are escorting a stricken merchantman. Please send a naval escort vessel or at least an ocean-going tug to relieve us, not able to transfer troops should the transport founder, *Reese* out."

"Navigator, give me a plot and estimated time of arrival at our present speed." Karl was formulating a plan in his head should the *Hampton* succumb to her damaged hull. How would they assist in recovery?

"Message back from Command, Sir," called the radio operator. "Command to *Reese*, continue to stand by, have an empty returning freighter being diverted to the *Hampton's* position. Will be with you within the next ninety minutes."

"Signalman, make to *Hampton*; we will continue to standby until the relief merchantman arrives in approximately ninety minutes." Adams entered the pilothouse again, asking Karl if he should now bring in the watch crew. "Yes, Number One, let's get this out of the way."

The pilothouse door opened, and in walked six sailors, the leader asking, "You wanted to see us?"

Karl, with anger in his eyes, looked up and, in a loud authoritative voice, yelled, "It is customary to address the captain of a vessel by referring to him as Sir or Captain and stand at attention when doing so." The sailors, looking at each other, quickly came to attention, apologizing for the lack of discipline. "Earlier today, I specifically gave you an order to remain alert by scanning the skies for enemy aircraft with your binoculars. What did you do as we started loading troops from the beaches? You took your eyes off the skies, and that action allowed two enemy aircraft to take advantage of the lack of antiaircraft fire, making a direct hit on two of our support boats, killing everyone in those boats. Given adequate warning, we may have had a chance to defend those chaps."

"Number One, make an entry in the log that these sailors have been charged with dereliction of their duties. It is the decision of this command that their lack of defensive action or warning brought about the loss of two boats, their crews, and the soldiers they were transporting. This reckless action will be reported to command on our arrival back in Dover." Karl was venting his anger on these sailors, fear written all over their faces. "Now, get off my bridge. Number One, you will take charge of turning them over to the MPs on arrival back in Dover; is that understood?" instructed Karl.

"Yes, Sir," replied Adams, now seeing another side to this kind and caring captain. Once the sailors had left the bridge, Adams turned to Karl, saying, "Don't you think that's a little harsh, Skipper?" Adams was thinking about the available manpower for the next evacuation operation. Losing six sailors would put them at a significant disadvantage.

"Yes, it is, Number One. Let them stew for a while, then tell them you talked me out of reporting them. Their opinion of you will be elevated for defending them in that manner, and their respect for how I address slackers will positively affect how they perform their duties from now on. One other thing, forget that entry in the log." Karl was once again showing his leadership strength.

"Thank you, Skipper. I should have had the common sense to follow your handling of this situation." Adams walked out of the pilothouse with a much higher opinion of the captain of HMT *Reese*.

The navigator turned to Karl, saying, "Should be in line to discharge our troops in less than an hour, Sir. We should notify command that we will lay offshore until called into the harbor." The navigator did not have much to do so far on this mission, so handling this phase of the operation gave him a purpose.

"Thank you, Manning. Send a coded message, laying off Dover." Karl walked out onto the bridge wing as he gave the order. Looking down now at the mass of returning troops below, he allowed his mind to drift back to another time when he was the first officer on his last voyage aboard the *Tristian*, how things had changed in his life. As he looked around, a voice behind him snapped him back.

"Excuse me, Sir, may I speak to you?" asked one of the seaman that he had reprimanded earlier.

"Of course, speak your mind," replied Karl in a terse tone. "Speaking for the watch crew, Sir, we just wanted to thank you for rescinding the order to report us. From here on, you can rely on us. We will not let you down again. Should any Hun come anywhere near the *Reese*, they will regret it." With that, the sailor came to attention, saluting his captain.

Karl responded by saying, "All of us on this ship must act as a single unit, relying on the action of the man next to you, so thank you. Apology accepted, dismissed." Karl was feeling good about how he handled this incident, the results of which would prove to be a tremendous contribution so very soon.

"Incoming communication from command, Sir, we are instructed to rendezvous with the navy tug B-1240, two miles off the arrival port," said Sparky as he read the communication to Karl.

"Excellent, what else did it say?"

"It goes on to instruct us to enter the harbor and raft up alongside the merchantman *Cornish Lady*. The tugs will turn us around once inside the harbor." Slowly, the Reese was turned around, being pushed by the tugs abeam of the much bigger *Cornish Lady*, its boarding gangplanks already swung out to come aboard once they were secure. The tugs held the Reese in position as lines fore and aft were secured. Now, the boarding gangplanks were quickly lowered down to the smaller ship.

"Alright, lads, up those gangplanks at the double. We need to return quickly to Dunkirk," yelled Adams through the bullhorn. Karl stood on the wing deck, watching how fast the troops transferred to the bigger ship and onto the dock.

"Mr. Adams, stand by to cast off," came the command from Karl, speaking through his bullhorn. It's your boat, Mr. Adams; take her out."

"Aye, aye, Skipper," came the reply from Adams. "Helmsman, come left to clear the harbor breakwater, then make your heading 180 degrees. Mr. Arnold, ring up the telegraph for full ahead as we clear the seawall. We need to push her as hard as we can."

"Aye, aye, Sir," answered both bridge seamen.

Karl entered the bridge, saying, "Number One, I am going to get forty winks before it gets crazy back at Dunkirk."

"Sounds like a good move, Skipper. I'll let you know when we're about one hour out," replied Adams as he watched Karl leave the bridge. "Poor chap, he looks like he has the world on his shoulders." In the short time he had served with Karl, Adams had come to trust and respect him very highly. The now-familiar sounds of gunfire and explosions were getting louder as the *Reese* and many other vessels approached the devastation ahead of them on the beaches of Dunkirk. "Mr. Arnold, be so kind as to wake the skipper and request his presence on the bridge." Lieutenant Adams liked his responsibilities as the officer in charge, even if it was an armed trawler and he was only its first officer.

"Yes, Sir, shall I bring you a cuppa as well before it gets too hectic?" Arnold was a real Londoner, older than the rest of the crew, tall and well-built for his age. He had jumped at the chance to volunteer for this temporary assignment, getting back on a ship and on the sea again. It was another chance to serve since his retirement as a Chief Petty Officer in the Royal Navy back in 1928. As a civilian, he had joined the Greater London Ambulance Corp, a job he felt would allow him to continue with the skills he enjoyed as a sailor, providing aid to those less fortunate. In the day ahead, this expertise would prove to be invaluable. Knocking on the captain's cabin door, he entered to find Karl seated at the small desk, poring over charts of Dunkirk. "Sorry to disturb you, Skipper. Mr. Adams sends his compliments to join him on the bridge; we are getting close to Dunkirk."

"Thank you, Mr. Arnold. Tell Lieutenant Adams that I'll be along shortly." Karl stood up, carefully folding his charts, then put on his jacket.

"Shall I get you a cuppa, Skipper, and deliver it to the bridge?" Arnold was another seaman that had very high regard for his Austrian captain.

"Thank you, Mr. Arnold. Please tell Cookie to make it real strong; must stay alert from here on, right?" Karl smiled at the older gentleman.

"Will do, Skip," came the response. On the bridge, the view ahead was one of continued chaos and destruction; billowing smoke and ships half sunk, belching fire and burning oil around the wrecks could be seen off the beach.

"Steady as you go, Helmsman. There are men in those waters, slow ahead one third," said Karl, unable to finish calling his command when screams from all over the deck froze him to his core. Rushing out to the wing deck, Karl just had time to see two enemy planes dive down toward them. Antiaircraft fire and every available seaman that could fire a submachine gun focused their combined firepower toward the menacing incoming aircraft. As Karl spun around to look up, a rain of 20mm cannon fire from the lead Messersmith-109 started to shred a path along the deck and superstructure. Pieces of scalding hot shrapnel were flying in all directions. Sailors were thrown everywhere, blood and body parts painting a picture of horrifying destruction.

Karl dove to save the sailor next to him as he gyrated toward the deck, his left leg at a sickening angle. His death screams of agonizing pain were also coursed by the red stains spreading across his turtleneck jumper. Karl, seeing this, reacted immediately, diving toward the deck to save the sailor's head from crashing into the steel deck. As his hand scooped up the already dead sailor's head, the ship shuddered violently, throwing Karl against the superstructure. Excruciating pain in his neck and upper right thigh consumed all his power to remain conscious. Another massive explosion sent him back across the deck again and very close to being thrown overboard.

The forward twelve pounders would fire no more. It lay on its side, smoke coming from the remains of the muzzle, which was split down the length of the barrel. The four-man gun crew lay dead and disfigured, smoldering from the bomb blast. The Stuka Ju-87 dive bomber had found its mark with precision. It released its deadly bomb on the gun and its crew below.

"The skipper is down," yelled Arnold as he rushed out of the bridge to aid the lifeless body of Captain Vita. "Oh, my God, he has shrapnel sticking out of his neck and right leg. The nasty bang to his head has knocked him out. That gash is deep across the top of his head, and he is bleeding badly. Someone, help me; I've got to stop the bleeding." Arnold's ambulatory experience was taking over.

Adams rushed out, yelling, "My God, Arnold, how bad is he? Will he make it?"

"Not if you just stand there. Get me that first aid kit from inside. I'm staying with the skipper; your job right now is to keep us afloat. You're the acting skipper as of right now; now, go." Arnold's leadership and cool head were taking over.

Back in the pilothouse, Adams sent Seaman Bennett with the first aid kit to assist Arnold with the skipper. Adams picked up the P.A., "Calling all departments to report their damage." Looking through the broken bridge window gave him his answer, "My God, we are sinking by the head." He turned toward the voice tube, yelling into it, "Scotty, how bad are we down there?"

His answer came back quickly. "At this point, the pumps are barely keeping up. We need to get her out of the shipping lane while we can still make headway. Once we are out of the shipping lanes, we can lay the anchor to stop her drifting back into the shipping lanes. Once we finish with the engine, I'll blow the high-pressure steam valves to stop her from blowing up around us." Scotty, talking in a very calm tone, had been in a similar situation some years back and knew exactly what to do.

"Sparky, send a distress signal to command that we are sinking by the head and need immediate assistance. Add that we have wounded, including our captain."

Adams' answer came back almost immediately. "Command to *Reese*, standby we have a frigate returning to England. They can be with you in less than thirty minutes. They are overloaded, but they are also the closest to your location. We need to give them a personnel count. Are you capable of giving us that number? Command standing by."

Adams put the mic down, saying to Sparky, "Once we confirm a rescue plan, you may as well join the others gathering on the port side, alright?"

"Command to *Reese*; they can assist you. How many souls are you?"

"Including the wounded, approximately eighteen," answered Adams.

"Command to *Reese*, do you still have a usable lifeboat?"

"Affirmative, we have two. We will start boarding the lifeboats once we clear the shipping lane and lay out the hook. Reese over and out."

"Helmsman, I will handle the telegraph for you. I'm taking her astern; can't take a chance with that damaged bow, stand by. Scotty, make your revs for slow astern. Once you see the telegraph signal all stop, proceed with releasing the steam valves." Adams now yelled out the broken center window of the bridge to Charlie down below on the main deck, "Can you take two blokes and stand by to release the bow anchor?" Adams was moving very quickly to make everything happen while the *Reese* was still afloat.

"Will do, Skipper. Brown and Hepworth, follow me; we need to lay the anchor when the skipper gives the command."

Charlie's years of seamanship were very evident as he barked out orders, "Chief, will we have enough time? She is settling much faster now," said Brown as the three sailors made their way forward to the anchor equipment, seawater now close to the bow's freeboard. The *Reese* rumbled as she started to move backward, her propeller blades throwing seawater high in the air, protesting as the screw neared the surface. Adams, standing on the bridge wing, studied their progress. When he felt they were clear, he rushed back into the pilothouse, slamming the telegraph into all stop.

With the bullhorn in hand, he yelled to Charlie, "Let go the anchor for two hundred feet, then get the hell off that bow." Returning to the bridge, he dismissed the sailors that were still at their stations. Just as he was about to yell down the voice tube for Scotty and his three other boiler room gang to release the steam valves and get topsides, an ear-splitting scream came from the funnel as a column of steam shot high in the air. *Reese* was no longer able to function as a trawler. She had done her country proud and soon would lay silently on the seabed off the coast of France.

Along with Charlie and Brown, Arnold carefully lifted their captain's limp blood-soaked form onto a stretcher. "Keep his head in the center. We can't take a chance with that shrapnel so close to his jugular vein. Stuff those towels on either side of his head but be careful. When we abandon ship, we can walk the stretcher forward to where the deck railing is almost at sea level. That way, we can move him into the lifeboat without tilting him down, alright?" said Arnold.

Adams, with bullhorn in hand, was the last to leave the bridge. His last act was to place the ship's logbook into an oilskin bag. Taking a last look around, with a lump in his throat, he lifted the bullhorn to his mouth, announcing his last command, "Abandon ship; repeat, abandon ship. Clear the wounded first; Scotty, take a headcount before we cast off."

Adams helped to transfer Karl and the other wounded to the first lifeboat, then helped the other survivors climb into the second boat. Looking around at the wrecked and now silent deck, he came to parade attention, saluting the ship that had served them faithfully. "Goodbye, old girl, not the way I thought we would part. Push off and clear the ship before she goes under."

Adams now turned his attention to coordinating the two lifeboats. Each boat had four rowing stations, two on either side, "All together now, lads, row us out into the shipping lane and away from the *Reese*. About fifteen minutes passed. Adams felt they should remain on station until the rescue frigate arrived. "Alright, lads, ship your oars; we will wait here until the frigate arrives. A loud bubbling, hissing sound made them all turn around to see the *Reese's* stern rise out of the water; then, in slow motion, she slipped without protest to her resting place on the ocean floor. She would, however, leave her funnel and two masts protruding above the waves in the shallow water.

"Mr. Adams, is that a frigate steaming toward us?" asked Brice as he stood up in the bow of the lifeboat.

"I think you're right; who has the portable signal lamp?" asked Adams.

"I do, Sir," said Hepworth, the signalman.

"Send a signal that we will come alongside with the wounded first. Request they lower their boarding ladder. Add that our captain is badly injured and cannot be boarded vertically; please confirm this request."

The frigate's signal lamp flashed back a reply: we are lowering it now; stand by, F64 out.

"Alright, lads, let's get those oars back in the water and start rowing toward the frigate. You blokes over there in the second boat, get closer once we come alongside and upload; you can follow us in, is that clear? We need to board quickly, then cast off. Charlie, it will be your job to blow a clip of ammo into the bottom of our boat to sink it. Is that clear? Thompson, use your Bren gun to do the same to your boat; now, stand by."

Adams had saved many of the crew. His training as a naval officer and now leader had saved all those around him with his quick thinking and a well-executed abandon ship plan. "She is slowing down, Sir. I can see some blokes lowering their starboard boarding ladder. Shall we continue rowing toward them, Skipper?" one of the sailors yelled out.

"Of course, now pull for all you're worth," Adams replied. From their location, they could see and hear the powerful props churn up the water as the frigate slowed in reverse to an almost stop. All along the railings, on every deck, soldiers packed in, looking down to watch the rescue. The first lifeboat banged against the boarding ladder. Helping hands quickly and very carefully lifted Karl out of the lifeboat, carrying him up the boarding ladder so that the stretcher remained level. Arnold stayed right behind, reminding them to be careful with their captain.

A few minutes later, Brice opened fire with his Bren-gun, sinking the lifeboat in a hail of bullets. Next came the second boat with its complement of able-bodied seamen. In a very orderly fashion, they all scrambled up the ladder to the deck above. Thompson shouldered his Bren gun, then, standing on the first rung of the boarding ladder, opened fire with ear-splitting rapid-fire into the bottom of the lifeboat. With that many holes, it sank to the gunwales, wallowed for a moment, then disappeared below the waves.

"Come on, you blokes, get up here and off this bloody ladder," yelled out a sailor waiting with four others to hoist the ladder back on deck. The frigate trembled as all its power was sent to its twin screws churning the seawater at the stern. On the deck, it was standing room only. A warrant officer yelled out, "All you lot from the trawler, follow me; make way for the bloke on that stretcher."

"Hey, you, that's our captain you're calling a 'bloke.' Show some respect, or my right fist will do it for you," called out an irritated Charlie Brice. Every soldier and sailor on the deck broke out in a cheer for Charlie and the tongue lashing he gave the warrant officer.

"Look, I'm sorry. I meant no offense or disrespect for your captain. I am only trying to get you all into our sickbay as quickly as possible, and right now, we are so overloaded, it can get very frustrating trying to make any headway. Again, I'm sorry." The warrant officer was showing a little more humility now that someone had put him in his place. Adams was following, smiling and shaking his head.

Suddenly, he yelled out, "Three cheers for Chief Petty Officer, Charlie Brice." The response that came back from the remnant of the *HMT Reese* crew lightened up the tension for everyone on board.

Inside the frigate sickbay, the surgeon made his way over to where Arnold and Charlie sat next to the unconscious form of Captain Vita. "Let's look at your captain, shall we? How long has he been out?" asked the surgeon.

"More or less about four hours, I'd say," said Arnold as he looked at the concerned face of the surgeon.

"Those cuts on top of his head I can clean up and stitch up right away. That will stop some of the bleeding. The bigger concern right now is the shrapnel in his neck. It's in a very difficult position to remove here on the ship, way too dangerous. If not done correctly, it could sever a main artery. This needs to be done in a surgical suite with the correct instruments. At our current speed, we will be back in Dover; no, I stand corrected—that was our previous load. This time, we are heading for Folkestone—in about fifty minutes or so. Anyway, once ashore, we can move him quickly to one of the temporary triage centers set up to handle the returning wounded. Now, let's get him sewn up and see if I can bring him around. Being out this long has me concerned that his head injuries could be worse than they appear," concluded the surgeon.

Adams by now had joined the ship's captain on the bridge. He was, like himself, a first lieutenant, only a regular career navy officer. "Captain, I'd like to thank you for the quick response to our distress call. With the wounded and the critical condition of our captain, the thought of being in open lifeboats for an extended time surely would have led to more deaths, so, thank you," concluded Adams.

"Sometimes, things have a way of working out. I'm glad we were so close to your location, and may I say how efficiently your crew squared away the boarding and sinking of your lifeboats. They knew exactly what to do. We hardly lost any time rescuing you." The captain's comments made Adams even more proud of how he had handled the whole operation. Pity that the Skipper never got to see it thought Adams as he sipped his mug of hot tea.

Back in sickbay, Arnold and Charlie sat watching the corpsman as he gave Karl medicated oxygen supply through a facemask. "We are getting close to Folkestone—should be pulling in in about twenty minutes," said a sailor to the corpsman as he entered sickbay. "Gentlemen, you have to leave sickbay. We must get all these wounded ready to move ashore," directed the friendly corpsman.

Arnold pleaded to remain with his captain to no avail. He would have to wait on the dock. The dim lights on the dock were focused on the boarding ladders as the troops lined up to disembark. "Keep the gangplank clear until we have moved all the wounded ashore," yelled the first lieutenant in charge of clearing the ship. One by one, the wounded were taken up the gangplank, some helped by corpsmen, and many carried off on stretchers. Back in sickbay, the surgeon worked on Karl, trying to revive him.

The first lieutenant said, "Sir, we must move the captain ashore. Can your men stay with him?" He was looking at Arnold and Brice.

"Once he is loaded into an ambulance, give the attendant this note not to touch or move his head; is that clear?" said the surgeon, concerned that his lack of response and the dangerous piece of shrapnel in his neck could become a problem moving him ashore.

Arnold pleaded with the ship's surgeon to instruct the attending corpsmen to let them stay with the skipper until he was moved in the ambulance.

"Once we are dockside, only one of you can go with the captain to the triage center, so which one of you will that be?" asked the attending corpsman.

"Guess that will be you, Arnold; you have been with him since it happened," replied Brice. Two strong sailors carefully lifted the stretcher and walked toward the door leading to the deck. Arnold and Brice followed behind. At the entrance, Brice turned around to thank the surgeon. "Thank you, Sir, all of us appreciate the attention you gave our captain."

"Only wish I could have done more," came the response.

On the dock, ambulances lined up for the wounded. Another long line of military lorries waited to take the troops to the waiting trains, returning them to the numerous dispersal stations. "So long, Charlie. Take care of yourself; hope our paths cross again under better circumstances," said Arnold as they parted.

"Wait a minute, mate; let me give you my address at home, and you can give me yours. That way, we can make a date to visit the skipper. Hey, there—you in the white, do you have a pencil and some paper we can use?" barked Charlie in that London slang of his.

"Got a medical form you can use. The back of it is blank, and here's a pencil you can use," replied the corpsman. Charlie ripped the form in half, giving one piece to Arnold.

"Once I know my new posting, I'll drop you a line; we can make arrangements to visit the skipper after that." Both men faced each other, first a handshake, then a big hug. Charlie marched off toward a lorry that was loading, and Arnold climbed into the ambulance, seating himself across from Karl on the stretcher.

"Looks like he's in a bad way," said the nurse seated at the side of Karl, attending to the I.V. drip and oxygen mask. "He will need a blood transfusion once we reach the hospital." Fifteen minutes later, the ambulance entered the makeshift triage area.

Two burly soldiers with red cross armbands opened the ambulance door, saying, "We'll take him from here. Please, follow us."

"You will have to be very careful. He must be kept level; there is shrapnel in his neck very close to a major artery," said Arnold, staying very close to Karl's head as they offloaded the stretcher just to make sure. Inside the center, injured soldiers and sailors lay on beds lining both sides of the corridor. Nurses, corpsmen, and military types were half running up and down doing only God knew what.

"Follow us, Chief. We are taking him right into the prep waiting area. Once inside, you can find someplace to wait."

"I think, once you go inside, I'll head back to the processing area at the docks. There's nothing I can do now but pray." Arnold would have preferred to stay, but he needed to find out where he should be going.

A tall surgeon wearing a blood-stained white lab coat came over to where Arnold was standing, saying, "I say, have you been with this officer since he was injured? If so, I would prefer you remain here in case we have questions. By looking at him, I would venture to say he's in bad shape, so we can't waste time getting him into surgery. By the way, I'm Captain Terry Mills, and your name?" asked the surgeon.

"Chief Petty John Arnolds, Sir. Thank you so much for asking me to stay. I would much prefer to stay here with the skipper." Arnold was feeling much better now that he knew he could remain with his captain. "I have a question, Sir. I never registered when we got off the ship. I don't think anyone knows I'm here. Should I go back just to let them know?" asked Arnold.

"Come with me, Chief. See that lieutenant over there? I'll tell him that I need you to remain here." The surgeon walked over to where the young naval lieutenant was seated at his desk. "I say, old chap, I need this chief petty officer to remain here until we get his commanding officer out of trouble. Be a good chap and notify whoever is responsible for registering returning chaps from Dunkirk, will you?" The surgeon looked at Arnold, saying, "Give the lieutenant your information and tag numbers, then follow me."

"Now that's done, get yourself some food and drink from the cafeteria down the hall on the left. Return here after you have eaten. I would say you could do with forty winks. Use the couch in my office right over there. I'll wake you up after his surgery." Captain Mills could see the older gentleman needed some sleep.

"Thank you so very much, Sir; you are so kind," replied Arnold. "It's me and everyone around us that should be thanking you, Chief. I can only imagine the hell conditions you have survived. Now, excuse me; I must scrub up for surgery." With that, the surgeon walked off swiftly, calling out to the operating nurses to get Karl ready. Arnold walked out of the prep-surgery area. Turning left, he walked down the hallway until he saw an overhead sign that said cafeteria. Inside, he cast his sight on rows of long tables, some occupied by soldiers and a few naval chaps. Others sat with field dressings on their heads, arms, and legs. As Arnold stood there, he could not help thinking, poor buggers, most of them look like death warmed over. I must look about the same in this dirty, blood-stained, and ripped uniform. How will England survive? Waiting in line, he picked up a metal tray and slid it down the chow line.

"Got some scrambled eggs and chips for ya, mate, alright? There's plenty of hot tea in those big urns at the end; glad you made it home," said the older gentleman, a civilian volunteer behind the counter.

"Thanks, it hasn't sunk in yet that I'm in one piece with no injuries." Arnold was starting to show signs of fatigue and maybe remorse. The old man just smiled as Arnold took his plate, sliding it toward the tea urn. Arnold devoured the food on his plate, wiping it clean with a slice of bread and butter.

"Cor, you look like you haven't eaten in a week," said a cheerful grenadier guard sitting next to him.

"Well, not since yesterday anyway," replied Arnold.

"You're a sailor, so you must be off one of the rescue ships; is that right?" The kindly soldier was trying to encourage conversation with the older sailor.

"Well, yes, I was on a rescue ship. Unfortunately, my ship was sunk off Dunkirk. I'm here with our commanding officer. He's in real bad shape and only now going into surgery. I've been asked to stay here until he's out of surgery. By the way, my name is Chief Petty Officer John Adams; what's yours?"

"Sergeant Mark Williams, and from your accent, I'd say you're a Londoner as well. Glad we made it, mate. I'm dreading hearing the casualty list. It was a miracle me and my boys got off the bloody beach at all. We had to stand almost to our shoulders in seawater, waves washing over our heads at times, waiting for one of those small boats to take us out to a merchantman. Bloody madhouse, scrabbling up the side of that ship, and once on the deck, we literally had to stand shoulder to shoulder. I'm not going to complain, though. We're sitting here safe and warm now, ain't we?" Mark held out a big hand to shake John's.

"Really nice to meet you, Mark. Now, I must be getting back to the waiting area; stay safe." John stood up, collected his tray, and headed for the used tray bin. Back in the surgical area, he asked a nurse if there was any news on Captain Karl Vita.

"Not yet; still too early. Do you need anything before you take a nap in Captain Mills' office?" replied the nurse.

"Nice of you to offer. I think catching up on some sleep is what I need right now," replied Arnold, heading for that couch.

The time was 0330 hours; a gentle push on Arnold's shoulder woke him up from the deep, sound sleep. "Sorry to wake you, Chief; there is someone very anxious to see you. I've also brought you a nice hot mug of tea, which I'm sure will go down nicely right now." The friendly nurse had a smile on her face that told Arnold the skipper was out of surgery. He followed the nurse and sipped his tea as they went through a door marked authorized personnel only. White cloth partitions hung between the row of beds lined up on either side of the ward. Arnold, walking behind the nurse, could not help noticing the condition of the patients in each bed they passed.

The nurse stopped in front of a partition that had a curtain pulled across its front. Arnold could feel himself tense up, waiting for the sight he would see as the nurse slid the curtain to one side. "Come in, Chief; someone here would like to speak to you—not too long, though. Lieutenant Vita is still quite weak," said a cheerful Captain Mills, now addressing Karl by his rightful rank as an officer in the BIS and not the temporary rank of captain. Karl's head was bandaged across the top and one side; a neck support over the dressing held his head straight, making it hard for him to talk. His injured right leg was not visible; it was covered by a device that kept the bed covers off his leg.

"Arnold, so pleased you are here. How can I ever thank you for saving my life?" said Karl in a very low, strained voice.

"It's a life worth saving, Sir. You would do it for me, I'm sure," replied Arnold.

"Please, tell me what happened. I can only remember trying to save a sailor as he fell to the deck, then nothing until a little while ago. What happened to the Reese? Did they save her? And what about the crew?" Karl was getting anxious to find out all the details.

Captain Mills stopped Karl by saying, "There will be time for all those details at another time, but right now, I need you to rest. Chief, there is a military ambulance going back to the docks in Folkestone. I asked them to wait for you so you can say your goodbyes. I'm sure when you can get back here, the lieutenant will demand to hear the rest of your story," said Captain Mills.

"Goodbye, Sir, get well and be assured we will visit you when we have leave. Before leaving with you in the ambulance, Lieutenant Adams did yell to me that he would try to get Charlie and me assigned to a ferry going back to Dunkirk, so I'll have to find them somehow! Arnold had accidentally let the cat out of the bag.

"Arnold, she's gone; is that right? At least tell me that before you leave." Karl was not about to let him leave until he at least knew that.

"Yes, Sir, she is gone; goodbye again." Arnold regretted making a slip like that. He would have preferred to address that at another time when his skipper was stronger. He took one more look at the injured person lying in bed as he walked out with Captain Mills.

The evacuation of Dunkirk was over. What would have been a crushing defeat was now viewed as the miracle of Dunkirk. An overwhelming victory against a superior enemy force saved over 300,000 English troops of the BEF and an additional 125,000 French, Belgian, and Canadian troops. Although the feeling of jubilation for the evacuation was being heralded across all of England, the tragic loss of equipment would now put a tremendous strain on England's industrial capability to rebuild and reequip its army to be ready for the next confrontation with its enemy, the Germans.

CHAPTER 4

THE LONG ROAD BACK

Ten painfully slow days passed by one by one. For Karl, every hour felt like a lifetime since he arrived at the field hospital. Once out of immediate danger and stable enough after the surgery, they had transported him by ambulance to this facility where he would be nursed back to health. He was still confined to his bed and getting very restless with little to occupy his mind and time other than some old books. The matron for the ward, a charming lady in her twenties, started visiting Karl in the late afternoons after her shift had ended. She would sit by his bedside, trying to make him think of something other than what was happening with the war.

"Come on, Lieutenant Vita; loosen that load and talk to me of something else, will you? This obsession with the war is not helping your recovery in any way. Why don't you start by telling me how you arrived in England?" said Sara, trying very hard to distract him.

In a voice laboring with every breath, Karl reached out, taking Sara's hand and shocking her by saying, "Sister, when I get a little stronger, you can show me more of those beautiful legs and thighs. Is that a deal?" Karl was trying to smile while holding her hand as tightly as he could.

"Lieutenant Vita, I must say; you are rather bold and very forward." She stood up, still holding his hand. Leaning over him, she whispered softly in his ear, "Promise me you will cooperate with the nursing staff and strive to get better with the therapy program, and I will gladly show you more than that. Is that a deal?" Sara was sending Karl a message that she liked him a lot more than she had let on. It would not be too long before the nursing staff also knew her secret.

The days remained quite warm and sunny. The patients were encouraged to take advantage of the weather conditions outside; some could walk out, some needed crutches, and many needed wheelchairs, as did Karl. Nurse Julia would help him out of bed and into his wheelchair, taking him outside. At the lower part of the garden, she would wheel him under the shade of a large old oak tree, then check in on him every thirty minutes to make sure all was alright. On one of these days, Karl was reading a newspaper when a familiar voice behind him announced, "Lieutenant, you have visitors; let me turn you around," said Sara, turning the wheelchair around in front of three uniformed officers.

"You buggers, it's taken you long enough to come and see me," said the now very upbeat Karl. "Thank you, Nurse Wilkinson. I guess I'll have to behave myself now that we have witnesses, won't I?" Karl was happier now than he had been in over a month; seeing his friends was the medicine he needed.

"Lieutenant Vita, I swear to God, you are the most incorrigible patient in the entire hospital," said Sara.

"And, my dear, that's why you love me," replied Karl.

"Please, excuse me. I will be back in about an hour. Can I have some tea and biscuits brought out for you? One of the stewards is on his way with folding chairs." Sara turned toward Karl, fussing over him by adjusting the blanket and fixing his pajama collar.

"What a sight you three are. Hazel, I have not seen you in over a year. I think it was a few months after you returned to England with Bill. Clive, I expected to see you weeks ago; guess I rate low on your priority list." Karl could not be happier. His closest friends had come to see him.

"I say, old man, you really embarrassed that nurse; some things never change," said Clive as he unfolded one of the chairs.

"Sara is a wonderful nurse, and, by the way, she is the matron of my ward. She has spent many, many hours pulling and pushing me through some difficult times, including some rough therapy sessions. Did you bring me the statistics on Dunkirk I wrote you about and the files on my crew that did not make it back? I need to write to their families. I'm not sure how to write those letters, though."

Without realizing it, Karl was now conversing in a much stronger sounding voice, a sign he was on the mend. "Why don't you let me help you with those letters, Karl? My family only lives about thirty minutes from here. These chaps are dropping me off once we leave you today. Our boss here authorized a four-day leave, so I'd be glad to help you with those letters," said Hazel as she poured four cups of tea from the large teapot. Hazel still had feelings for Karl that dated back some years when they were training in Scotland. Bill was the last person to see Kitty alive.

Hazel was the radio operator on that fateful mission, and it was she that sent the Morse coded message about Kitty's demise. "Why don't we start tomorrow? What time should I be here—in the afternoon, would that work?" Hazel was moving in on Karl before that matron beat her to the punch.

"That sounds like a plan, Hazel. I'll have to check with Sara first to see when my next therapy session is scheduled, alright?" Karl answered Hazel, then turned his attention to what plans the BIS had for him when he returned to duty.

"Karl, here are the reports, but can you put them aside while we visit with you?" Clive was not prepared to spoil this time together by allowing Karl to see casualties and equipment losses quite yet.

"Of course, that would be rude of me to start looking at those reports while you are visiting." In the back of Karl's mind, he had already determined the extent of the destruction and deaths those reports would detail. Over the next couple of hours, the four enjoyed talking about the good times shared while in Scotland, training and partying in the cold of winter.

"Hazel, I can remember one night at the officers club; you got me to dance with you. My God, how drunk you were." Karl, by saying that, also reminded them of Kitty cutting in, ending any further advances Hazel could be contemplating.

"Well, if my memory serves me correctly, Kitty put a stop to that night of fun for me. I guess I got the short end of the stick, or should I say, no stick at all." Hazel realized what she had just said with a smirk on her face. She looked straight at the faces of Karl, Clive, and Bill for what seemed like an eternity before Bill broke out laughing, melting the ice to what now could only be viewed as funny.

All four of them continued laughing and adding other instances that made the time go by all too fast for Karl.

Sara returned to find the mood light and very cheerful. "Time to get you back inside, and thank you for making this afternoon so enjoyable for Lieutenant Vita." She could not believe the transformation Karl had made in just a few hours with his fellow officers. His energy was recovering, and he was gaining his old self back, the side of him she had never seen before.

"Sara, Hazel and I are going to be working on some very important letters tomorrow afternoon. I know I have a visit with Doctor Mills first thing, then therapy that pretty well takes up most of the morning, so if she arrives, say at 1350 hours, will that be alright?" asked Karl.

"I'm sure that will be perfectly acceptable. Would you like me to see if I can find you an empty room or maybe an office that is not in use?" asked Sara as she folded the blanket from Karl's lap.

"That would be super. That way, we can spread out," replied Karl.

Clive stood, offering to push Karl back up the inclined pathway that led up to the French doors in front of Karl's ward. "So, Matron, what's the story behind this mansion?" asked Bill, walking beside Sara and following behind Clive pushing Karl with Hazel close by.

"Up until six weeks ago, this magnificent mansion had been the home of a leading industrialist. The army requisitioned it for a field hospital based on its proximity to Dover and Folkestone Harbors. Colonel Benjamin Warren, the owner, retired from the army a year after the First World War that ended in 1918. He made his fortune building a manufacturing company that made farm equipment.

"When the Army approached him, he jumped at the chance to serve his country once again, giving up this magnificent home. He just couldn't do enough to assist. Colonel Warren instructed his management team to clear all the furniture out of the first level and part of the second floor. His purchasing department was instructed to buy as many hospital beds as possible that could be used to set up the wards. That also included other furniture the hospital would need. His factory workers were also eager to contribute by feverishly working to make the transformation happen.

"That whole month, everyone involved worked day and night, including the nursing staff and many of the doctors, to set up the surgical theatres, treatment rooms, and, of course, the six wards. It truly is quite an accomplishment getting this mansion transformed, and may I say, just in time for the large number of casualties we have here right now." Sara was enjoying telling Bill this story, and it showed.

"Well, this is where we must take our leave of you for today anyway. I'll put your file in the top drawer of your bedstand. Remember to lock it up in the matron's file cabinet," said Clive as he parked the wheelchair next to Karl's bed. "Will do, Major Knight; I'll start reviewing it after supper tonight." Karl was enjoying kidding Clive like this. Their friendship had been through some wonderful highs; the lows, however, had been extremely painful. It was this bond that bound Karl, Clive, and Bill together as lasting friends.

"Up yours," said Clive, grasping Karl's hand tightly, laughing about how Karl had addressed him.

"Bill, don't wait for this bugger to bring you here. Come anytime; I really would like the company and updates, alright, you gimpy old bugger." Karl now turned his attention to the striking Hazel standing next to Clive. "Hazel, I guess I'll see you tomorrow afternoon. I hope you will be out of uniform, or should I ask, pretty please?" Karl was rebounding back into his old sarcastic and flirtatious self.

Clive looked at the other two with a smile that said it all; he is going to be all right. As they turned to depart, Clive stopped, and in a jovial tone, said to Sara, now standing next to Karl's wheelchair. "Matron, one word of caution, now that this Vita chap is on the mend, you will have to watch him. He has a reputation with the ladies, especially if they're in nursing uniforms." Clive had got the last word in for the day, so he thought.

"Well, Major, I'm glad you told me that because I'm about to give him a sponge bath once you're gone." Sara had a big smile across her face that had a hidden meaning. If they only knew he could have anything he wants, whenever he wants, thought Sara, still smiling.

"See you tomorrow," said Hazel as they walked down the ward and out the door. Sara helped Karl back into bed, thinking that he was getting stronger. What a difference from this morning; I don't think I've seen anyone bounce back quite this fast.

She left then and returned, pushing a cart that had a big white enamel bowl full of warmish water in it. Two sponges and two towels lay across the side. "Well, let's get you ready for supper, shall we?" said Sara as she pulled the curtain shut for privacy.

"Sara, we can do this, but you made a commitment to me earlier today, and I demand that you live up to it." Karl was only fooling with her, but Sara, on the other hand, was going to take advantage of this challenge. Placing her finger across her mouth for Karl to be quiet, she started to undress him, then carefully sponged him all over with sweet-smelling soap. Karl lay back, enjoying the feel of her touch. He closed his eyes and lay perfectly still when suddenly he felt soft, moist lips on his. Sara, pushing against his lips with her tongue, made him thoroughly aroused for the first time in years.

He moved to wrap his arms around her neck when Sara stopped and stood straight up, saying in a very low voice, "There's more of that, you big tease, when you are much stronger. Now, let's get you into fresh pajamas, shall we?" Karl motioned to Sara to come closer. Almost whispering into her ear, he said quietly, "Matron, I will do as you ask, but for now, I want that private viewing you promised."

Karl held her hand and stopped her from pulling away. He kissed the back of her hand, waiting for a reply. Sara walked to the curtain, opening it just wide enough to look up and down the ward. Once she was comfortable that all was quiet and safe for her, she turned in front of Karl, her eyes burning into his, and quietly said, "This is a deposit on my promise." Slowly and very deliberately, she bent over, taking the hem of her uniform with both hands, and proceeded to raise it slowly up to almost her waist for just a very few seconds, then dropped it back down again. Sara returned to his bedside, smiling that she had wiped that look off his face.

"You realize I could be dismissed for what just happened, don't you? So, I guess you're in the driver's seat right now. I will have to do whatever you ask to keep you quiet, won't I?" Sara bent over to kiss him once again, stroking his face with her left hand. "I'll come by after supper to say goodnight; I hope you enjoyed yourself." With that, Sara opened the curtain wide and rolled the cart out into the center of the ward, thinking that would carry some weight until tomorrow when that Hazel is here. Karl sat staring at the ceiling, processing what had just happened. The picture in his mind was the very attractive Sara in the dark hose and black suspenders, her piercing eyes never leaving his. This vision was quickly crowded, falling back into another time when a very attractive lady in similar hose and black suspenders had done the very same thing. This new vision was Kitty, his deceased fiancée.

Julia and another nurse entered his partition with a wheeled bedstand designed to fit over the bed. On it was his supper with a pot of hot tea. "Eat it while it's hot, Lieutenant; got to get your strength back," said the pretty young Julia. "We will be around later to remove the tray and get you ready for the evening. After the supper things were removed, he laid back, and without realizing it, was reverting into his military mode of thinking. He had been out of contact for too long, and it was making him angry at being so lax in a time of survival for his adopted homeland of England, and even more so now after the evacuation at Dunkirk.

I need to put all this foolishness aside and stop this flirtation with Sara. It's not fair to her that I've started something I know will eventually hurt her when it's time for me to leave. Karl, when will you ever learn? When she comes by tonight, I must be firm and sincere about putting this flirting aside until England is safe once more. Pouring his last cup of tea, he stretched over to retrieve the locked fabric document pouch Clive had given him earlier. From the drawer, he also retrieved a small leather key holder. Karl unlocked the document pouch and removed a folder that had Private and Confidential stamped in big red letters across the outside.

Operation Dynamo
Date: May 26th - June 4th, 1940
(Condensed Statistics)

- The total Flotilla: 900 vessels. This included naval and civilian craft, French and Norwegian units. Reported as of May 26th and 27th
- Reported losses: 235 vessels sunk. Royal Navy, French Navy, and units from Norway, Merchantmen, English, and French. Channel ferries and a fleet of small private craft. The final report is still being compiled by type and registry.
- Approximately 106 RAF aircraft destroyed.
- Estimated deaths during the evacuation: 5,000 BEF soldiers.
- Other allied troops were rescued by mostly British ships from French ports: Cherbourg, Saint-Malo, Brest, and Saint Nazaire.
- Allied troops rescued 558,000 from all locations.
- Reports as of June 5th estimate that over 1,000,000 allied soldiers from England, France, and Belgium had surrendered.
- The main rallying point, the town of Dunkirk, was reduced to rubble by heavy German artillery and aerial bombardment.

Projected Equipment Loss

- 2,472, Artillery pieces (Large Caliber only) and 76,097 tons of ammunition.
- 63,879 vehicles, including battle tanks, armored cars, lorries, staff cars, and 20,548 motorcycles.
- 416,940 tons of assorted stores.

The reports went on to say that units of the BEF, French, and Belgium armies held back the German forces in a rear-guard action during the evacuation. Lord Gort, Commander-in-Chief, arrived back in England June 1st, feted as a hero.

Before departing, Major-General Harold Alexander inspected the shores of Dunkirk from a motorboat before boarding a Royal Navy destroyer. He vowed, we may be forced to leave today, but be assured, we will return, and on that day, Germany will regret her actions. Karl laid there reading five more pages of data before he came to a transcript of Winston Churchill's address to the House of Lords the day after the last of the returning troops arrived back in England. Prime Minister Churchill described the evacuation as:

The Miracle of Dunkirk

We shall not fail or falter. We shall go on to the end. We shall fight in France. We shall fight on the seas and on the oceans. We shall fight with growing confidence and growing strength in the air. We shall defend our island, whatever the cost may be. We shall fight on the beaches; we shall fight on the landing grounds; we shall fight in the fields and in the streets, we shall fight in the hills, we shall never surrender.

Karl reviewed the file several more times, slowly shaking his head in disbelief. He gathered the documents, returned them to the pouch, then made sure it was firmly locked. He could feel the sorrow welling up in his eyes and the realization that, from this moment on, he would be all business. He would try, anyway.

Tomorrow, I must call Mama at the bungalow to see if they received any news about Papa and my brothers. I pray their escape from Wien (Vienna) was successful, but where are they? And are they in a safe place? In this time of melancholy, he allowed himself to catalog what he needed to accomplish before returning to the BIS. He would insist on an assignment back into occupied Europe. Field agents would be vital in assessing how the conquering German forces would be enforcing their will and demands on the people of occupied Europe.

Staring at the ceiling, he was brought back to the present by the sound of the privacy curtain being moved back just wide enough for Sara to walk through. Smiling, she closed it once again. At his bedside, she sat on the side of the bed, quietly reaching for his hand. ara, stop. I must talk to you, and you must listen very carefully to what I have to say. Earlier today, we both got carried away in a heated flirtation. As much as we both may have enjoyed that foreplay, it must now stop. It will not and cannot go any further.

"From this moment on, I need your help to regain my health enough to pass the medical discharge exam. What has happened recently to this country means the BIS will need every available intelligence officer. I need to return to my post as soon as possible. Sara, will you do that for me? Please and again accept my apologies for any notion you may have had that I was suggesting a more meaningful relationship. My actions were simply an escape from the frustration and boredom of having to stay here, immobilized and not doing my part back in the BIS."

Karl stopped talking, waiting for her response. Sara did not move or say a word. She remained still, her emotions controlled by her training. She continued holding his hand, sitting on the side of his bed. Collecting her thoughts, she returned his hand to his side.

"Karl, or should I call you by your rank of Lieutenant? Like you, I have a responsibility to this hospital. Hearing you talk like this makes me also realize that we are in a war for survival. Those girlish actions may not be appropriate at times like these. As much as I would love to make it more, it's just selfish on my part. I have worked hard to become a matron, and it's that responsibility that must now keep me from straying until times are more appropriate. So, my dearest Karl, I understand completely.

"As a nurse, I will do everything in my power to help you get back on your feet. When the time comes for you to leave, I expect a big kiss on the cheek, of course. When this war is over, hopefully, we will come through as the victors; I can assure you I will find you, so get that through your thick Austrian head. Do you understand me?" Sara said with a smile on her face, showing her strong professional side and making it clear he was not off the hook by any means. Sara stood up, looking Karl in the eyes, that tender smile still on her face.

"Sara, would you kindly put this pouch in your locking file for me? I can't take the risk of it being opened," asked Karl, feeling relieved by their brief talk.

"Sure, now give me a last big kiss, no strings attached, of course." Sara needed a lasting memory of what could have been or might be in the future.

"Help me stand up then; I can't appear to be half a man when asked to kiss such a beautiful lady, or should I call you, Matron?" Karl was almost his old self, well, almost.

"Do you realize this is really the first time I have stood up without the use of a walker? Now, let's have that last big kiss, shall we?" Sara gave a hearty laugh; her eyes told a different story, though. Karl placed his hands slowly and softly on Sara's cheeks, his facial expression becoming very serious. Sara made the first move by reaching up to his lips, her mouth partially open, hunger in her eyes. Embracing, they kissed, allowing their mouths to open as Sara thrust her tongue into Karl's mouth. This was more than either one of them expected. Karl stiffened at first, then relaxed, knowing that when they parted, it would be over for now anyway.

"God, Karl, you are a wonderful kisser. You got my juices going, and by the look on your face, I would say it's going to stay with you for a long time." As Sara said that, she knew she would often think of this moment in the months ahead and prayed Karl would return to her when this war came to an end.

The following morning, he was awakened at 0530 hours by Nurse Julia. She helped him dress, then brought his breakfast tray in, noticing how well he was moving and now standing without any help. "I say, Lieutenant, you are making a miraculous recovery. At this rate, you could be out of here by next week. We will be sorry to see you go, though. After I have cleared your breakfast tray, I'll walk you down the hall to Doctor Mills' office," said Julia as she cleared the tray.

Karl tried to walk without the walker but reverted to using it after only a few yards. "You're not ready to walk without that walker yet, Sir; give it time." Julia could see that Karl was pushing too hard, concerned the stitches on his right thigh might open if he continued like this.

"Good morning, Lieutenant; you're looking so much better than a few days ago. How are the neck and thigh doing? Let's get a look, shall we?" Doctor Mills helped Karl onto the end of the examination table, followed by nurse Julia removing the dressings on his upper thigh. "Well, that looks so much better—a slight inflammation at the stitches has me a little concerned, though."

"I reminded the lieutenant earlier that he's not ready yet to put too much pressure on those stitches." Julia was trying to make Karl take heed of the doctor's comment.

"Let that stay open, Nurse, until I have looked at Karl's neck, please." Doctor Mills stood next to Julia as she carefully removed the neck support and then the dressing. "This is the one that worries me the most, Karl. When we operated, we removed nearly all the shrapnel. What we did not remove is a longish sliver lying under a main artery. Your neck was too much of a mess, so at the suggestion of Doctor Burgess, we did not remove it; we secured it instead. There may come a time when we can look at that wound again, but not in a field hospital like this. That will have to be done in London— probably at Saint Mary's by Doctor Burgess himself.

"For the meantime, we are satisfied it should not give you any problems other than an occasional pain for a minute or two." Doctor Mills moved to the sink, washing his hands firmly, saying, "He is all yours now, Nurse." Then he left the room, wishing Karl a good day and continued progress with the therapy.

"Are you ready to see Matron and continue with your therapy? You heard the doctor—don't overdo it, alright?" Nurse Julia was hoping he would take note of the doctor's advice.

In the converted ballroom, Karl met up with Sara and a male therapist named Harry. Julia handed the clipboard with the doctor's notes over to Harry to review, then helped Karl onto the therapy table. "We are going to start with slow leg bends, then work the upper thigh. Matron, would you help the lieutenant to raise and lower his right leg very slowly for a count of twenty," instructed Harry as he moved off to attend to another patient.

Sara, true to her word, carefully helped Karl for the best part of an hour, then worked on his neck wound without that annoying neck brace.

"Alright, Karl, time to get you back and washed up for your visit with Lieutenant Collins after lunch. Is that still on?" asked Sara, now holding Karl's arm as they walked through the ward. Karl tried hard not to show the pain he was enduring as he labored with every step down the ward. "Karl, why don't you take a break and allow me to get a wheelchair? You're in no condition to walk all the way yet." Sara could see the stress on his face, knowing full well he was determined to walk to the bathroom.

"Karl, please listen to me. If that wound opens up again, it will set you back weeks. Now, stop being a thick-headed Austrian and sit down in this wheelchair, and that is an order." Sara knew if she didn't demand it, he would continue to limp down the ward. "Alright, Karl, let's get you into the bathroom for a shower and shave. Will you be alright, or would you like me to help you?" After saying that, Sara looked at Karl, now with a big grin on his face. "Karl, what happened to our promise made earlier this morning, or have you already changed the rules?" smirked Sara as she wheeled him into the bathroom.

"As usual, Sara, you are right. I was merely kidding around," responded Karl.

"As I told you, I take my work very seriously. As much as I would like to sponge you down in the shower stall, it's not going to happen." Sara had a way of coming back at him with a sarcastic remark, and Karl enjoyed her spirit so much. Sara left him in the bathroom, saying she would be back in about thirty minutes to help him get dressed and ready to receive his visitor.

Hazel Collins sat at the small make-up mirror in her bedroom, modestly applying her makeup. Her beautiful features did not need too much makeup to enhance her striking beauty. She had decided to wear a pair of grey pleated wool trousers with a wide turn-up at the bottom that would go nicely with the cream-colored silk blouse she already had on. Her long brown hair was perfectly brushed. Usually, when in uniform, she would wear it up in a French twist, but not today, especially considering who she was driving to meet! Downstairs, she entered the kitchen to have an early lunch with her mother and father, already seated at the table. "My, don't you look spiffy out of your uniform," said her father as she sat down next to him. Hazel took his hand and kissed the back of it. She adored her parents so very much. Any chance to spend time with them was a real treat.

"Thank you, Dad. It feels so nice to be in civvy clothes, even though it's only for a few days. What's for lunch, Mum? Whatever it is smells delicious." Sara was always careful about letting her parents know what she really did in the BIS. When asked years back why she had joined the bloody spy blokes, as her father called them, she had fabricated a cover story that her job was to train recruits how to speak German and French, including reading and writing. She had majored in English Literature at University. She was, however, intrigued with other languages, so it was an easy decision to add German and French to her studies. She had grown up in this thatched cottage on the outskirts of Sandwich in Kent with her parents and older brother, currently stationed with the Royal Airforce in Singapore.

Life in those early days was as perfect as it could be for young Hazel and brother James to grow up in. Her mother, Mary, had been a schoolteacher and married her husband, Bill, when he was still in The Royal Corps of Engineers before retiring into a civilian position with the Dutton Company, Ltd. as a mechanical engineer that manufactured bicycles. This environment was perfect to mold life values into both Bill and Mary's children. "Dad, are you sure about letting me borrow your car? I know how you love that Morris 10. Major Knight gave me a petrol voucher yesterday, so I will not be depleting your precious fuel." Sara knew her father would not object. He would gladly give his children the world and sometimes forgot they both were adults in military service. "I must be off. I'll probably be home about six, alright?"

Her mother could always read her daughter's face as she said, "Behave yourself, young lady; your father and I are not ready to start babysitting just yet." Mary was smiling, almost laughing as her daughter picked up the car keys, heading to the kitchen back door.

"Mother, please! How can you think like that?" Hazel was also thinking how she would do anything to win Karl over, and that was probably showing in her facial expressions.

"My sweet girl, we may be getting older, but I can assure you when we were much, much younger, we probably would have made you blush. As the old saying goes, if you can't be good, then try to be careful. Now, off with you; that young man won't wait forever." Hazel threw a kiss to her parents as she walked out the back door into the driveway. Outside, the air was sweet from the colorful flowerbeds on either side of the doorway and others growing up the side of the house. As she walked over to the car, she was thinking, I am so fortunate to have parents that are very much with it and still young at heart.

My mother must have been quite the lady when she landed good old dad. Hazel was quietly laughing as she unlocked the driver's door to the Morris. Once inside, she looked around, noticing that everything was spotless. Her father took so much pride in his car, purchasing it three years earlier from the Morris dealer in Sandwich. She started the engine, turned around in front of the house, then proceeded to the driveway and turned left into the very narrow lane that led to the main road two miles ahead.

She covered the distance to the hospital in less than twenty minutes. Parking the car, she checked her makeup and hair in the small rearview mirror before stepping out into the bright sunshine. Once inside, she asked the nurse sitting at the information desk how to find Lieutenant Vita, a patient in the hospital. "One moment and your name, please," answered the nurse.

"Lieutenant Collins," replied Hazel.

The nurse picked up the desk phone, dialed the extension number from the book in front of her, and waited for someone to answer. "Hello, Nurse Ambone here; a Lieutenant Collins has arrived to see Lieutenant Vita." The nurse, waited for an answer, then said, "Right, I'll send her down." Nurse Ambone wrote a visitor pass and handed it to Hazel. "Your party is expecting you in meeting room B-2. It's easy to find; just turn right at that big column, then it will be on the right side just a little way down." Hazel thanked the nurse, then proceeded to the meeting room. She could feel the excitement building in her chest as she opened the door.

"Hazel, come on in; so pleased you made it," said Karl as he slowly stood up.

Hazel, closing the door, crossed over to Karl standing at the small table, saying, "Well, look at you, standing there like you're ready to come back to work. Really wonderful to see the old Karl on the mend; you heal really quickly." She put her arms around him, giving him a big hug.

"Well, Hazel, I'm glad you noticed. I seem to be getting stronger with each passing day, and yes, I'm ready to return to work—the sooner, the better," replied Karl. "Well, let's get these letters written, shall we? Then perhaps we can take in the afternoon air; it is so nice outside, does that seem like a good idea?"

Hazel was happy to help Karl with these sensitive letters but equally intent on spending some quiet time along with him outside of this hospital. "How did you get here?" asked Karl as they sat down at the table.

"Borrowed my dad's car. It only took me twenty minutes; it was enjoyable driving here—such a pretty part of England in the summertime," replied Hazel, pouring herself a tall glass of water from the pitcher on the table.

"I must say, Hazel, you look fantastic out of uniform. I never realized your hair was so long; it really transforms you," remarked Karl, taking in this new look on Hazel.

"Glad you noticed. You know it's all for you, don't you?" Hazel's eyes found Karl's as she said that, waiting for his reaction.

"Well, in that case, all I can say is thank you for doing this for me." That voice in the back of his head kept repeating, don't start anything, Karl; remember yesterday.

"Shall we get started?" said Hazel as she opened the list in front of them. "Why don't you tell me what it is you would like to say. Will each letter be the same except for their names and addresses? You take half the names, and I'll take the rest, alright?" Hazel quickly drafted a form letter, then passed it to Karl for his input.

"Very well-written, Hazel; I think that says exactly how I feel. Make sure you sign it, Lieutenant Karl Vita, acting Captain *HMT Reese*."

"Alright then, let's get to work," answered Hazel. With two of them writing the letters, they were finished in less than two hours. "Ready to venture outside, Karl?" asked Hazel as she collected all the envelopes from the table, then stood, ready to help Karl stand up. "Do you want that wheelchair, or would you prefer to walk? I'll hold your arm if that's what you prefer." Hazel could not do enough for Karl, and he knew it.

"I would much prefer to walk if you're alright with going really slowly," said Karl as she helped him to his feet. Leaving the meeting room, she held his arm firmly, keeping him close to her side. This added support enabled Karl to walk with less of a limp than earlier in the day. At the reception desk, Karl explained that the box of letters had to go out that afternoon and that somebody needed to stamp them.

"I'll make sure that is taken care of, Sir," replied Nurse Ambone. Outside, the bright sunshine made them squint momentarily. Hazel reached for her handbag and removed a pair of sunglasses. "Karl, you don't have any sunglasses with you. Would you like me to go back inside and get yours for you?" asked Hazel.

"Could you, please? I never thought it would be this bright this late in the afternoon. Let me sit right here on this bench and wait for you." Karl sat down with the assistance of Hazel. As she bent over to help him, Karl caught himself looking down the front of her blouse at perfectly formed breasts in a very lacy white bra. This vision aroused him and stayed in front of him as she stood up again.

"I'll ask one of the nurses in your ward to find them for me. Where would they find them?" asked Hazel.

"They should be in the top dresser drawer." Karl watched her walk back toward the main entrance, thinking she is a very striking woman. I don't think I ever looked at her like I'm looking now. Then again, I only had eyes for Kitty back then.

About five minutes passed before Hazel walked back, waving his glasses. "Found them. Here, put them on before we go walking. I spoke to the matron and Nurse Julia. They told me to tell you not to overdo it and be back no later than 1750 hours. Ready for that stroll, you good-looking hunk?" Hazel looped her arm under his and helped him to his feet, then started walking around the end of the building toward the beautifully landscaped garden. At the end of the hedgerow, they turned toward the lake, surrounded by large oak trees and beds of colorful flowers. "Looks like we are all alone back here. Let's not overdo it. Why don't we sit awhile on that bench in the shade, if that sounds good to you," came the suggestion from Hazel as she guided them toward the bench.

Carefully, she lowered Karl down, then sat next to him, saying, "Karl, there is something I need to tell you, and I've wanted to for a very long time. Sitting here alone and together is the perfect time for me to get it off my chest, and I want you to listen without responding until I have finished. Will you do this for me?" asked Hazel, turning in toward Karl, taking his hand and cradling in between hers.

"You have my undivided attention. What's on your mind? You have a different look on your face that tells me this is way overdue, is it?" Karl had a feeling he knew what was coming. Is this the right time to continue, or was he letting another opportunity for happiness pass him by? Best to wait until she has finished, he thought.

"Karl, we have known each other for a few years now, although most of that time has been work-related. When I was on assignment with Kitty and Bill in Germany, she confided in me one night that she had a bad feeling that she would not be returning to England after the mission. Her biggest fear was how you would react to hearing this devastating news. She continued, saying that your temper may get the better of you against any German you come across. Karl, I know how in love you two were and that torch you still carry for her, but as I said, she did not want you to go on without another love or lady in your life. You must know this?"

Hazel hesitated before continuing, "Karl, I know you know I have always had a special place for you in my heart. Kitty knew that also, so it came as no surprise when she asked me to make her a promise that if she fell in the course of her duty, I would try to replace her. Of course, that's assuming you would come around to accepting me. Karl, I would never try to replace the love you had for Kitty. She was a wonderful, remarkable lady, but when she asked me to do that for her, I also knew she trusted me to make that happen. You may be thinking, why have I never approached you before? It's been several years, after all. Well, needless to say, was too scared to make that move. I did not want to face rejection from you either." Hazel stopped talking, turning away from Karl, ready for his response—whatever that may be.

"Hazel, I can only imagine how difficult it was for you to tell me this. Kitty and I found something extraordinary before these times we live in shattered any chance of a life together happening. My heart is almost permanently damaged. The thought of enduring that again is too much to consider. The only thing I'm capable of is a casual relationship. I'm not sure that's enough for you. Hazel, would you consider such a friendship? Let's see how that plays out, simply enjoying each other's company. And if something happens during those times, well, let's just say war is war, and hormones because of war tend to erupt without notice. I think you have an idea where this is going. I have built a wall around myself, and by doing so, have lived, other than work, a lonely existence without the tenderness of a lady to turn to. Our jobs are such that looking too far ahead is dangerous, here today and sometimes gone tomorrow." Karl stopped rambling on and now put his arm around Hazel, hoping what he was suggesting would be enough for her.

"Karl, I feel like a big load has been lifted from my shoulders, and, of course, I understand where you are right now. If we can be special friends with needs such as making love, enjoying being out together, basically having each other in our lives is all we can really expect with jobs in the bloody BIS. It doesn't leave much time for much else. One thing I must add and caution you on: if I find myself unable to continue because I need more from you, you will seriously consider making this relationship more than casual, or just walk away with no hard feelings, alright?"

Hazel had to add this because she could not tell Karl that she had been in love with him for a very long time. Making love and spending time together would have to do, but she knew, deep down, she would be going down the same road as Kitty did. Karl pulled her toward him tenderly, lifted her head toward his, and kissed her softly. Hazel's head was spinning. She was being kissed by someone she had dreamed about for such a long time. Her left arm went behind his head, pulling him into her, mindful of his neck wound. This was going to be an end to a perfect day.

Back in the ward, Sara looked at her watch, realizing it was now past 1800 hours. "Julia, let's go find Karl and his friend Hazel, shall we? They probably have not been keeping an eye on the time, and we need him back in the ward." Sara was also concerned Hazel had got what she really came for, and that was Karl. As they rounded the corner of the building, they could see down to the lake, and there on the bench, they saw Karl and Hazel locked in an embrace.

"Well, there's your answer to why they are late returning," said Julia with a big grin on her face.

"Julia, that's what I was thinking also. Now, let's remind them it's time for Hazel to go home, shall we?" Sara was obviously put out, even though she suspected Hazel was in a far better position than she was. "I hate to break up the party, you two, but our patient needs to return to his ward." Sara turned quickly to avoid Karl seeing the expression on her face, and with Julia by her side, walked back toward the building.

"Karl, I think the matron is a little put out by me being here with you so long. We better walk back to the entrance and get you into the ward; then, I must be off. Karl, when can I see you again? Let me ask Clive if I can return next weekend. That's, of course, if you would like me to." Hazel stood facing Karl as she said this, waiting for a positive response.

"That, Hazel, would be very nice. What would be even better is for me to request a weekend pass. I think I'm well enough for that to happen. I'll look into available inns close by. Does that make sense to you, darling?" For the first time in a long time, Karl had just called Hazel darling without even giving it another thought.

"Oh, by the way, if Clive gives you any trouble, have him call me." At that very moment, Karl could feel sunshine breaking through the black cloud that had been over his head since Kitty was killed. Back at the entrance, Hazel walked him inside, gave him an affectionate kiss, then said she would call him tomorrow at about 1130 hours to confirm her leave, and he should investigate the inns close by.

"I guess I'll be off then. I wish we could stay together tonight, but this will give me something to look forward to during the week." Hazel turned toward the steps, stopped momentarily, then looked back at Karl, saying with a glow to her face, "There are nice looking nurses in there, lover boy; remember, I've got first dibs on you." With that, Hazel walked quickly to her car. She had got what she came for, well, almost.

CHAPTER 5

TIME TO LEAVE

At 1130 hours the following day, Karl waited patiently for Hazel to call, but that did not happen, nor did she call the next week. Something big must have happened back in Slough. There must be a lockdown at the camp with no outgoing calls. Karl was sitting outside and felt the warmth of the midday sun in the cloudless sky, but deep inside, that black cloud was forming once again. *God, please don't put me through that stress again.*

Haven't I paid my dues? And just when I was starting to believe there was a new lady in my life. Once again, Karl was sinking back into that dark state of despair.

Trying to drive those bleak thoughts from his mind, he turned his attention to getting fit again. With each passing day, he worked diligently with Harry and occasionally with the help of Sara in his therapy sessions. Their encouragement to go further was the drive he needed, but he was always mindful of his wounded leg and neck. The visible signs that he was firmly on the mend were encouraging to the staff and the watchful eye of Doctor Mills.

Karl tried to put on a cheerful face, but Sara knew differently. He was not his usual cocky, sarcastic self; he remained primarily on his own in that cloud that had been following him since leaving his ship in Marseilles. It was forming again, and this was not doing anything for his self-esteem. Karl had by now discarded the walker, reverting to only using his cane to help himself. As for the dressing and support around his neck, it still gave him some discomfort when trying to wear a shirt with a collar. However, this seemed a small price to pay considering the alternatives.

On Thursday afternoon, almost three weeks since he said goodbye to Hazel, Nurse Julia found him sitting on the veranda, reading the *Daily Mirror* newspaper. "Sir, you have a telephone call; you can take it in Matron's office. Do you need help, or would you prefer to use your cane to walk there?" asked Julia. Karl thought for a moment, then said, "That can only be Hazel," as he hobbled toward the office. Once inside, he picked up the receiver, hesitantly putting it to his ear, about to ask Hazel what had happened. Before he could utter a word, she cut him off, saying, "Karl, thank God they let me telephone you. I have some bad news, darling. Any plans we made will have to wait as I have been confined to base here in Slough. I can't say too much on an unsecured phone line, but I'm sure you can figure out why.

Gunther and Herbert send you their regards; they are meeting up with me in about fifteen or so minutes. Not too sure when I can contact you again. Please think of me often and those wonderful plans we made only a few weeks ago. I must go now; I think Gunther is at the door. Keep getting stronger; bye, darling."

Karl returned the receiver to its cradle, his mind now in overload. If Gunther and Herbert were joining up with Hazel, it could only mean one thing: they are getting ready to leave on a mission back to the Continent. Hazel had got her message through to him. As he sat there processing her call, he felt a cold chill cross his cheek once again, thinking, I have been down this road before. God, take care of them if it's into harm's way that they are heading. I've got to find out immediately when I can return to Slough. They must be scrabbling for help after the beating we took at Dunkirk.

Karl, in a very loud voice, called Julia back into the office. "Julia, on the double, please find Doctor Mills for me. Don't come back without him; do you hear me? Now, go." How can I convince the doctor that I'm well enough to return to my post?

We are almost at the end of July. If I'm not strong enough to return to fieldwork, I'm at least strong enough to work at a desk in an intelligence position. Karl had started to walk back to his cubicle when he stopped, turned around, and headed back to Sara's office, fully expecting to see Doctor Mills heading toward him.

Reaching the office, he entered to find Doctor Mills, Sara, and Julia talking by the scheduling board. "Karl, come join us and tell me what all this flap is about," said Doctor Mills. Karl sat opposite Doctor Mills, and in a very controlled voice, explained why he needed to return to Slough as quickly as possible. To do that, he would need the doctor's help to give him a conditional release. He looked at the three as they hung on every word he spoke. "Well, Lieutenant, under normal circumstances, I would refuse such a request to return to active duty even on a limited basis.

However, these are not normal times, are they? If I approved this, it must be with your assurance, no with your promise, that you will follow the plan we put together for you. Is that understood?" Doctor Mills knew without saying another word those officers like Karl would be much in demand in the weeks and months ahead.

"Matron, why don't we get a supply of Karl's medication for about a week. That will give me time to contact Major Burns at the base medical center tomorrow morning and explain that one of my patients will be returning to Slough in a couple of days. I'll also give him a list of medications Karl will require during his recuperation. Could you and Harry get together and draw up a therapy exercise routine for Karl to follow? As for you, Lieutenant, you must make me that promise to follow them religiously. Matron, you will also need to contact whoever will be taking care of him in that regiment; get their name, rank, and telephone extension so we can check up on him regularly.

"Now, Karl, our transportation is spread thin. I will not allow you to return on public transportation. You are simply not strong enough for that amount of traveling. Can you call your commanding officer to see if they can lay on a car? I'll be glad to make that call for you if you're not comfortable with making it yourself." Doctor Mills looked at Karl, now displaying a smile of confidence.

"I'll be glad to make that call to Major Knight once we have finished here. He and I have a long-standing relationship. I'm sure there will not be a problem. So, to clarify, I should be ready to leave the day after tomorrow, is that correct?" Reinforced, Karl now looked at Sara for her approval.

"That is correct. I will see you tomorrow afternoon for a checkup. Now, I must return to my other patients—you know, the ones who don't give me problems like you." Doctor Mills patted Karl on the shoulder, chuckling and shaking his head as he departed.

Sara dismissed Julia, then sat down next to Karl, saying, "I'm glad to see the doctor is allowing you to return to your base. We shall all miss you, and I will always think of you as a wonderful excursion away from my hectic daily duties. When I saw you and Hazel sitting embracing on that bench, I knew there was history between you two. Any notion I may have had that we could share more went out the window when I saw you both like that. Karl, I will always think of you fondly. Men like you are very hard to come across. Will you at least stay in touch? I would like that very much."

Karl took her hand firmly, saying, "You will forever be my lady with the lamp that carried me through a very difficult time. Yes, Sara, I will write to you whenever time permits. My sweet Sara, until Hazel came back into my life, I truly believed we would have become so much more." Karl gently kissed her damp cheek, then stood up, saying, "See you before lights out."

As Karl limped away, he could feel Sara watching him, feeling very let down by a romance that never really started. Karl could not sleep. There was just too much going through his brain—like Kitty's first and only visit to Baldock, the wonderful, emotionally charged memory of his mother giving Kitty her engagement ring. Those few days spent with his sister, her husband Ronny, and their son Franchot made them both look forward to a similar life in a town much like Baldock. That vision of living in peace was shattered by Kitty's tragic death, held captive in Germany by the despised Gestapo. To escape these upsetting thoughts, Karl drifted off to sleep, only to be awoken by nurse Julia at 0530 hours. "Time to get up, Lieutenant," said Julia as she handed Karl his bathrobe.

"I must have dropped off again. I've been awake most of the night; there's too much going through my mind about now," said Karl as he struggled to stand.

"You're leaving us tomorrow. I will miss having you in this ward; I kind of got used to having you around, I guess." Julia was just making small talk as she helped him into his bathrobe and slippers.

After getting ready, he ate a quick breakfast, then headed to Sara's office.

"Morning, Sara, can I use your telephone to call Major Knight?" asked Karl.

"Certainly, I've got rounds to do with Doctor Mills, so you will have privacy." Sara was all business this morning. No need to belabor an uncomfortable situation.

Sitting at the desk, Karl dialed nine for the operator, then gave the switchboard operator the phone number. A voice on the other end answered. "Morning, Major Knight's extension," answered a familiar voice.

"Pat, it's me, Karl Vita. It's so good to hear your voice. Is Major Knight in his office? I really need to speak to him right away," said Karl.

"So nice to hear you too, Lieutenant. It's been a rough couple of months for you, I hear. I miss seeing that face of yours. When are you returning to us?" asked Pat.

"If all goes well, probably tomorrow," answered Karl. "Now, that's the best news I've heard all morning. Let me transfer you. See you tomorrow; please hold," said Pat as she dialed the interoffice number.

"Vita, is that you? I'm so pleased to hear from you," said Clive to his friend.

"Clive, I am returning to base tomorrow. However, I need your help to get me back." Karl explained the situation and that Doctor Mills would only conditionally release him if the base would provide a car.

"Well, you know it's not usual to have a sailor picked up from an extended holiday. However, for you, my friend, call it a done deal. What time should the car arrive?" concluded Clive, knowing full well that Karl would be laughing at the other end at hearing his sarcastic remarks like "sailor" and "extended holiday." Their friendship had withstood the test of time and tragedy.

"How about 1300 hours? Will that work?" replied Karl. "Pat, get me the motor pool and then let everyone in the department know the crazy Austrian will be back tomorrow, so plan on a get-together after hours. Everyone will attend, and that's an order." Clive could not be happier. Karl hung up the receiver, chuckling at Clive's wisecrack remarks. The weather was still sunny and warm, so Karl grabbed his walking cane and headed outside for a walk around the beautiful grounds. He so wanted to inhale clean, fresh air. It was good to be alive. Down by the lake, he decided to sit on the bench for a while, watching the ducks as they paddled around without a care in the world. He took out a small notebook and pencil from his inside pocket, turning the pages until he found his to-do list.

One: was done. Next, Two: Call Mama at the bungalow. I need to schedule some time with the family. Three: See Doctor Mills for the last examination and discharge papers. His thoughts now turned to calling Gunther to ask him to pick up his spare uniform from his flat with his spare key, then give it to the driver picking him up. I can't return to the base in borrowed shirt and trousers. Oh, I need to add a shirt, tie, and shoes to that list. Karl could feel the excitement building as he wrote in his notebook. I nearly forgot I need to get Sara's address. I made her a promise, and I intend to keep it. Without realizing the time, Karl had been sitting there for the best part of an hour. A tap on the shoulder made him spin around to see Sara's smiling face.

"My, you made me jump. I did not see you coming," said Karl, not expecting to see her down here by the lake. "I had just made myself a note to get your address when I got back to the ward, and just like that, you turn up. Great minds think alike, I suppose." Karl could see through the smile that she wanted to talk.

"Karl, I am wrestling with the fact that tomorrow you will be gone. Will I ever see you again? Probably not. There always remains the possibility that you'll turn up on a stretcher because you got yourself shot up again, so I decided to find you while you're in one piece—well, kind of. Since you were nowhere to be found in the building, I figured that I would find you down here enjoying the solitude," said Sara.

"You know me so well, Sara. Yes, I love my quiet time to reflect on the times around us and where will I be by year's end." Karl was also wrestling with the right words. He did not want to get her hopes up that there could still be a relationship.

"Shall we walk back to the hospital together, or would you still prefer to be alone?" asked Sara, hoping he would kiss her goodbye while they were still alone down by the lake.

"Sara, I think I know what's on your mind, and quite honestly, it makes me somewhat uncomfortable. As much as I would love to kiss you goodbye, it might send the wrong message, and Sara, I have far too much respect for you to allow that to happen." Karl was now standing, facing Sara, trying to find the appropriate thing to say without upsetting her more than she already was.

"Why don't you let me be the judge of that?" replied Sara as she placed her right arm around his neck, followed by a very moist kiss squarely on his lips. "Did you honestly think I was going to let you run off without this? If you did, you are very naïve, Mr. Vita. I am a big girl. In times like these, we all should grab at any chance for happiness. Karl, stay the night with me, so I'll know what has slipped away from me." Sara moved again to kiss Karl.

"Sara, that's enough. I cannot allow this to go on any further. Let's go back right now." Karl was getting angry, and Sara realized she had crossed the line.

"I'm sorry, Karl, I should not have taken that liberty with you. As I said, I'm a big girl, so no harm done. I hope you're not too offended by my actions. Now, let's walk back. How's that leg feeling? Walking around as much as you do could cause those stitches to bleed. I'll take a look at them once we are back inside." Just like that, Sara had reverted to being the matron she was.

Back in the ward, Sara, along with Julia, cleaned Karl's wounded thigh, then put him to bed, wishing him a good night's sleep. Tomorrow would come quickly, but not fast enough for Karl.

The staff car turned into the circular driveway of the hospital. The army corporal entered the hospital, walked up to the attendant, and said, "Morning, Corporal John Webley. I'm here to drive Lieutenant Vita back to Slough. Could you please let him know I'm here?"

"One moment, I'll let the matron know. Would you like some tea while you wait?" said the nurse. Sara answered the phone, then asked Julia to get Karl from the breakfast room and bring him out to the lobby, as his driver was waiting for him there. She then called Doctor Mills to inform him that Lieutenant Vita was ready to depart.

"Matron, let me take a look at his wounds again before he leaves us." Doctor Mills would only sign the discharge papers once he had examined Karl for the last time. Sara walked briskly to the breakfast room just as Julia was leaving with Karl.

"Hold on, you two. Doctor Mills would like to examine Lieutenant Vita before he leaves us." Sara reached out and took Karl's arm, leading him down the hall, followed by Julia. As they entered the examination room, a cheerful Doctor Mills rose from his desk, extending his hand toward Karl.

"Well, let's give you a last look, shall we? I've set up your medical care with Slough, so everything is arranged. Now, up on the table. Nurse, please remove the dressing on his neck, then we can look at that nasty wound in your leg. You need to lower your trousers, old man, for that." Carefully, new dressings were applied. The doctor was very pleased with how Karl was healing. Karl thanked Doctor Mills for the exceptional care he administered during the weeks he had been there.

"I hope our paths cross again, Doctor. When things are less hectic, maybe we can have dinner when you find yourself in town." Karl stood up, accepting Sara's hand to steady himself from the table.

"Shall we go? I have a bag here with your medication, enough for the first week. Make sure this medication list is given to the attending physician once you arrive at your base. The therapy instructions are in an envelope marked therapy instructions; don't lose them. The nurse from reception asked me to give you this bag with your uniform in it," said Julia. Karl just laughed.

"That bugger Clive forgets nothing. Where can I change?" asked Karl. Julia opened the door to an examination room, hanging up the uniform on a hanger, then putting the accessories on the table.

"There you are, handsome; we'll wait outside." Julia had always taken exceptional care of the handsome Austrian officer. He was not your ordinary officer, for sure. The door opened and out walked a striking Lieutenant Vita minus his forage cap, which had been forgotten in the rush to pick up his spare uniform. "Wow, will you look at the new Lieutenant Vita?" said a cheerful Julia.

Sara stood with her arms crossed, shaking her head slowly and smiling at Karl in his uniform, thinking, almost mine—well, I guess it wasn't meant to be. Sara moved over to take his arm with Julia on the opposite side and Doctor Mills bringing up the rear as they walked toward the lobby. "How can I thank you for the care and attention you all have shown me? From the bottom of my heart, I will always remember my time here." While Karl was talking, he turned, addressing the sizable group that had turned out to see him off. Karl went around shaking hands, then stopped in front of Sara. "Thank you, Matron, my lady with the lamp. I will write you once I'm settled back in Slough; thank you." Karl could see the look in her eyes. He reached over and kissed her on the cheek, saying out loud, "That's the one I promised you when I first arrived, remember?"

Turning around, he raised his hand in a parting gesture. Then, with his walking cane as support, he limped out the front door and down the steps to the waiting Humber staff car. The kindly corporal driving the car helped him into the rear passenger seat. Inside, he rolled down the window and waved once more to those that had walked out to see him off. Karl sat back in the rear seat, feeling tears welling up in the corner of his eyes. At the end of the driveway, the car momentarily stopped while traffic passed in front of them. Something made Karl turn in his seat, looking back toward the entrance. There she was, standing alone, waiting to see the car disappear around the corner. It would be a long time until he saw Sara again, even though they occasionally wrote letters to each other. They had met under trying conditions during his recovery, that attention turning into a brief flirtation. They had started something that would never come to fruition, even though Sara wanted to make it so much more. It was simply not to be, and now it was time to start a new chapter back in the BIS.

CHAPTER 6

RETURN TO THE INTELLIGENCE SERVICE

The ride back to the camp in Slough was slow going—too many military convoys heading God knows where added close to an hour to the trip. Karl drifted in and out of a shallow sleep, which perhaps was a good thing. Finally, the driver said, "Almost there, Sir. Sorry, it took longer than normal. The Army is on the move for sure." Karl could see the familiar signs that led up to the entrance barrier. The military police guard approached the staff car. Karl had already rolled down the window and had his military identification ready. The guard looked at the ID, then saluted, saying, "Welcome back, Sir, proceeding to raise the barrier." The guard stepped back as the big Humber drove through the entrance, Karl feeling like he had returned home.

"Excuse me, Sir, Major Knight instructed me to take you to the main building, then leave your things in his office. You are to meet him in the cafeteria. Do you need me to help you, Sir, or can you manage on your own?" asked Corporal Webley.

"I'll be fine, Corporal; thank you for offering, though," replied Karl, feeling the excitement of being back in familiar surroundings. The car came to a complete stop in front of the entrance. Corporal Webley smartly walked around the car to open the rear door, helping Karl onto the pavement. The front door opened, and out came an ATS private, covering the steps two at a time.

"Welcome back; so pleased to see you back safely in one piece. We have all been very worried about you." Crossing over to where

Karl was standing, she told the corporal, "I will help Lieutenant Vita climb the steps; thank you. I've got him now," said Jean as she handed him his walking cane, then looped his arm with hers. "You look smashing, Sir. After what you've been through, I never expected to see you look this good." Jean always liked seeing him when he came through the door first thing in the morning. He would greet everyone with a big smile. Today was no exception, seeing that smile once again. Climbing the steps one at a time was a painful exercise for Karl. He hid that pain from Jean and relied heavily on his cane.

"I have been asked to help you to the cafeteria to meet up with your pals. Would you like to rest a while or go straight there?" asked Jean, not sure if those steps were a little too much for him.

"No, Jean, I'm fine. Let me lean on you a little if you don't mind. This leg can give me problems if I put too much weight on it." Karl would have much preferred to sit for a few minutes, but that, to him, would be a sign of weakness. The lights that usually shone through the cafeteria door windows looked dark. "Are you sure I'm supposed to meet them here? It looks kind of dark, don't you think?" asked Karl.

"No, Sir. Major Knight was emphatic about where to deliver you. Could it be because you arrived a little late?" Jean was trying to hold back the urge to laugh. She knew precisely what was waiting for them on the opposite side of those doors. "Let me open the door, Sir, and put the lights back on. I'm sure they will be along shortly." Jean quickly opened the door, and at that moment, all the lights came on, followed by a very loud cheer from everyone in the department. Karl was back.

"You bugger, Clive. I should have known you would pull a stunt like this. Thank you; thank you for making this such a wonderful way to welcome me back." For once, the cocky, sarcastic Karl was lost for words. Everybody pushed forward to welcome him back. Jean helped Karl sit down with his old friend, Bill, putting a chair under his wounded leg. Karl was now the center of attention. "Jean, thank you for helping me, you sneaky bugger; give me a big kiss on the cheek." Karl was sliding back into his old self.

"On the cheek? Like buggery, I will. I'm not a schoolgirl, you know. Now, give me a real kiss." Jean and everyone cheered as she bent over, giving Karl a real lip-smacking kiss. She was laughing out loud, obviously enjoying the liberty she had just taken.

"Gunther and Herbert, so pleased to see you chaps. I was under the impression you both were on assignment. Isn't Hazel on your team? If so, is she here?" Karl was trying to downplay his excitement at seeing Hazel before she left on their mission to someplace in Europe.

"Right behind you, lover boy," said Hazel as she worked her way up to Karl. "Well, if young Jean got a lip smacker, I want one even bigger." Hazel had a way about her that reminded Karl of his dead fiancée, Kitty. As much as he enjoyed the attention Hazel showered upon him, it still brought back memories of his only true love. "Well, I'm waiting," said the laughing Hazel as she bent down to kiss Karl squarely on the lips. Hazel, satisfied with her kiss, pulled up a chair next to Karl.

After about an hour, the party started winding down—everyone filed by to bid farewell to their returning hero. Clive stood, saying, "We have made arrangements for you to take one of the duty doctor's quarters in the medical center. He will not be back for quite a while, so that works out well. In your present condition, you aren't going to be able to climb those stairs to your flat. As much as I would love to spend more time with you, there is still a war to attend to. Ready, Bill?" Clive and Bill had to return to planning the upcoming mission, which was only days away.

Hazel looked around the cafeteria, then sat back down next to Karl. "Well, lover boy, guess everyone has left us. Clive has already moved your things to your temporary quarters. Yesterday, Gunther went to your flat and picked up everything you will need, so you're well taken care of. I know where it is in the medical center, so why don't we take a slow walk over there and get you settled in, shall we?" Hazel was still tickled pink that she would have this time alone with Karl. She was trying hard to win him over, and that would not be easy. There was still a tender memory stopping that from happening.

"How much further, Hazel? My leg is starting to hurt me," said Karl as they crossed over the small courtyard that led to the medical center. Hazel opened the side door, then guided Karl into the small hallway.

"The first door on the left, Karl. It should still be locked. I have the key in my purse. Gunther gave it to me earlier, before you arrived. I have about an hour before I need to meet up with my team. Let's get you comfortable on the bed. That way, you can rest up while I'm in my meeting. How does that sound? I should be back in about an hour, but it could be longer if we run into overtime, though.

Before leaving, I will stop down at the nursing station to let them know you are in the room and ask the matron to stop in to see you. She can give you the once-over and make the arrangements for the camp doctor to see you in the morning, alright?" Hazel helped him remove his shoes and uniform tunic, hanging it neatly in the wardrobe. "There, does that feel better? Earlier, I put a pitcher of water on the shelf in the bathroom for you. If you need anything else like coffee or a sandwich, the NAAFI (Navy, Army, and Airforce Institutes) stays open until 2000 hours. Just call ext. 108. You, Lieutenant Vita, are very lucky. These rooms have their own bathrooms; surgeons around here live well. When I get back, we can get dinner. Would you like me to ask Clive, Bill, Gunther, and Herbert to join us? That's if you would enjoy that; it's up to you." Hazel was fussing over him, and Karl was enjoying it.

"Hazel, if everyone is restricted to camp, where are you staying?" asked Karl as he propped up his pillows.

"I'm billeted in the female officer's quarters, two buildings down from here," answered Hazel as she took off her khaki tunic, draping it over the chair in front of the desk. "There, that's better, even if it's only for forty minutes or so. Can I join you on your bed?" Hazel thought again about what she had just asked. "Or would you prefer I sit on the chair next to it?" Hazel was looking straight at Karl, waiting for a reaction to what she had just asked.

"Hazel, you're trying to be coy with me. Come over here and share this pillow with me. Not much can happen in forty minutes, or can it?" With a big smile on her face, Hazel lay down beside Karl, wrapping her right arm over his chest.

"When I heard you were returning before we left on our mission, my heart would not stop pounding. I felt like a skittish, lovesick schoolgirl, well, maybe not a lovesick schoolgirl." Hazel did not mean to use those words, especially knowing how sensitive Karl was about love and commitment. "Well, you know what I mean, don't you?" Hazel said, brushing off what she had just said.

"That's alright, Hazel. I was looking forward to seeing you as well. I'm glad we have established that," concluded Karl, trying not to laugh.

Hazel's face went from smiling to concern. "Karl, my darling, there is so much I want to say to you, but quite honestly, I'm still walking on pins and needles when it comes to you and me." Hazel knew she had to bring that up. Weighing every word was not the way to start a relationship, and Karl had to decide if there would be one.

"Hazel, as I told you only a few weeks ago, since Kitty's tragic death, I closed off my feelings so I would not be hurt again. Look, I have dated other ladies, some in the military, not many civilians, though, which suited me just fine. No commitment, just fun and making love, and that was it—short-term mostly, one or two dates. Then, you came back into my life. Kitty was smart in encouraging you to become part of my life. That is just like her to do that. You two are very much alike. I told you as much back at the field hospital when you said that if a casual relationship was not for you, you would tell me. Are we already at that point? If so, you need to tell me right now," said Karl, trying to read between the lines.

Unbeknownst to Hazel, Karl had already made up his mind that he did not want to go on in his lonely existence without someone special to share his time with. This could well be that right time. "Karl, let me be very open with you. You must realize I'm very much in love with you and have been since Scotland.

Kitty guessed as much, and that's probably why she confided in me the way she did. There, now that you know, are we finished before we've begun?" Hazel had tears in her eyes. She was going on a mission, and this distraction was not helping.

"Hazel, you sweet, sensitive lady, you don't have to worry. I have already made up my mind. An empty life without you is not going to work for me either." Karl stopped short of telling her he was slowly falling for her in a big way, and yes, that meant love. "Now, come here and give me a big kiss. I could use one about now."

They looked at each other in a whole new way, but no wedding bells would chime, not while there was a war going on. Karl would not open that door for a very long time and telling Hazel at this point would not be the right thing to do, not right now, anyway. Hazel kissed him passionately, her tongue thrusting into his mouth to find his waiting for her. With only thirty minutes left, she trembled with excitement. She wanted him so much, but that would have to wait until tonight or even tomorrow. *There is no way I'm going on this mission until I have had my time with Karl. I want him so very much; I can understand now how Kitty felt before she left. At least she had the time for those romantic interludes with him, those private times in a bed, skin to skin. I want that also before I leave.*

"Karl, you know my time is getting really short, but darling, I need this time for us alone in bed, making love. Is that too much to ask before I leave you? If it's to be just one time, that's better than no times, don't you agree? Tomorrow afternoon, I will make sure I have no commitments, nor should you. Thanks to good old Major Knight, we have this private room. It's the closest place to heaven for me right now. Now, let me put my tunic and shoes back on and find that matron. Hopefully, this one is old, fat, and ugly."

They both laughed at Hazel's wisecrack remark. "See you later; don't lock the door as the matron will be around shortly." Karl lay there, his head swimming with excitement and the ever-present fear that he was going down that same road that took Kitty from him back in 1938. With his eyes closed, his cluttered mind running a hundred miles an hour, Karl was about to make a big decision—better to have love in his life than the emptiness of none, even though the risk would be painfully high. Somewhere down the road, the likelihood of being hurt again was a real possibility. With that decision made, he sat up, feeling so much better than an hour before. A knock on the door snapped him out of the twilight he had been in.

"Come in, please," said Karl as he looked toward the door and the new matron. The door opened, and in walked the matron along with the duty nurse. "Well, we finally meet the popular Lieutenant Vita. My name is Elizabeth, and the nurse here is Ann," said the friendly matron. "Nurse, please hand me the clipboard. Let's see what we need to take care of, shall we? Can you turn toward me, Lieutenant? I need to remove that dressing around your neck. The instructions are to clean and replace this dressing every evening, making sure the neck brace is secure. As for your thigh, we are instructed to change that one twice a day. I can see why; it's a very nasty gash, and it's still weeping. Are you comfortable with us calling you Karl? It makes it less formal," said the matron.

"I would prefer that. May I also call you Liz and Ann? I'm assuming, Ann, it will be you that will be taking care of my dressings, is that right?" Karl already liked the middle-aged matron.

Her accent would indicate she came from the Midlands. As for Ann, she was in her early twenties with a noticeable Scottish accent. "If I need your assistance, how do I get ahold of you?" asked Karl.

"There is a two-way control next to your bed and another in the bathroom. They are really for the doctor on duty if we need to contact him. By the way, it goes straight to the nursing station. Nurse, would you please refresh Karl's water pitcher once we finish with changing his dressing?" instructed the matron.

"Liz, I would like to have a shower. Could one of you help me in and out of the shower? I'm still a little wobbly on my own," said Karl as he sat on the edge of the bed.

"I wish you would have asked that question before we changed your dressings," said Liz.

"I'm so sorry, ladies; guess you got me excited." Karl was enjoying these new hospital staff members.

"Well, that shower may be out for today, so let's settle on a sponge bath, shall we?" Liz gave a little chuckle as she said that.

"Oh, yes, please," replied Karl.

"I've heard that about you. Best to be careful with what you say to Lieutenant Vita. He usually has a comeback that has a double meaning," said Liz, laughing along with Ann.

"Oh, ladies, you really don't believe any of that silly stuff, surely." Karl was enjoying himself. After a somewhat limited sponge bath, Ann helped him change into a fresh shirt, uniform trousers, socks, and finally, she helped him tie his shoes.

"There you are, Karl; now you are ready for Lieutenant Collins when she returns." Ann's strong Scottish accent intrigued Karl. It reminded him so much of the friendly staff at the training camp in Scotland years back.

"It's such a nice day. I think I would like to sit outside and freshen my tan until Lieutenant Collins arrives. Could you please be so kind as to find me a deck chair?" asked Karl. Outside in the fresh air, the warm sun was very therapeutic to Karl's condition. Within thirty minutes, he fell into a deep, relaxing sleep, which he needed so much.

A warm kiss on the lips awoke him. Squinting from the sun brought him back to a vision of beautiful Hazel leaning over him. "Welcome back, lover boy; I guess you needed this time sleeping in the sun." Hazel, looking at him, was the perfect picture of a young Englishwoman. "Let's get you ready. Where should I put this deck chair before we go back to your room?" asked Hazel.

"Why don't we stash it in my room so I can use it again? I believe this nice weather will continue tomorrow. In the room, Hazel kissed him passionately, then retrieved his tunic from the wardrobe, saying. "Ready to do some walking, lover boy?"

"Yes, so long as you don't think I'm going to power walk to the club," replied Karl.

Inside the officer's club, Clive, Gunther, and Herbert sat at a corner table, talking and drinking pint-sized glasses of beer. "Well, look what the cat dragged in." Gunther took a jovial shot at Karl.

He responded by saying, "Hazel, do you really want to have drinks with these blokes? They're not the best company to spend time with," Karl said, returning the sarcastic banter at his friends.

"Sit down, you crazy bugger. What can I get you two from the bar?" said Clive, getting up to buy another round.

"We will have a gin and tonic, please," Hazel said, answering for Karl.

When Clive returned, he asked if he could change the subject while they were all together and in a quiet corner of the room. "The day after tomorrow, you three will depart. If all goes according to plan, you will rendezvous with the team embedded with the resistance group early next week. We are not expecting any significant problems with this mission, as it's more of a fact-finding mission than anything else. Still, you need to be very careful, though.

"As for you, Karl, now that you are back, you will be their inside liaison back here in Slough. Your responsibility will be to keep the lines of communication open for incoming encrypted messages. Karl, your knowledge of the local area they will be operating in will be invaluable when we review that data on troop buildup and movements in strategic locations to our planning people. I cannot stress enough, Karl, your team will man the radio twenty-four seven. Starting the day after these three leave, our strategy will be to outthink those bloody Germans, excluding present company, of course. The evacuation of Dunkirk is over. Now, we must brace ourselves for the next major offensive by Herr Hitler. Our intelligence chaps predict a direct assault, probably airborne in conjunction with a seaborne assault somewhere along the south coast. Our readiness will be reliant on where to concentrate troops and artillery to save this country. Our massive losses from the enormous amount of equipment left behind in Dunkirk has left us desperately short of equipment for a sustained campaign. As for the RAF, well, they have been working around the clock training new pilots. Aircraft production is in better shape. They are building parts in every spare garage around the country, then shipping them to the aircraft manufacturers for final assembly; it's quite amazing, really. The Air Ministry believes our reserve of new aircraft should put us in a survivable position, but who knows?

"Karl, I have already cleared your return to duty with the medical chaps. They understand the importance of having you directly involved during this next phase of the expected attack. Just promise your friends and me here that you will not overdo it, alright?" Clive stopped talking, taking a long swig of beer, and silently waited for the response he knew would come from Karl, and it did.

"Clive, thank you for allowing me to be part of the operation. You can rely on me to back them up. The Germans are acutely aware that the RAF pilots and their fighters are an equal match to those of their Luftwaffe. They obviously are concerned that, without dominating the skies over the channel, it could be devastating for any sea assault. If I were Hitler, I would throw every available fighter at the RAF to gain aerial supremacy before launching an amphibious assault. Now, let me ask Gunther and Herbert to do something for me. Hazel will be your radio operator on this mission. She is special to me. As you know, I have been down this path before. Please, keep her safe. Look, I know a promise like this can't really be kept, but please shield her as much as you can; that's all I can hope for."

When Karl said that he reached over for Hazel's hand; he felt they should know that he and Hazel were becoming an item, no wedding bells, though. Clive lightened the conversation by saying, "No throwing kisses on those communications, Hazel. It could confuse the Germans." That line made them all start laughing, breaking the tension that was building around the table.

Clive was eyeballing Karl and Hazel, looking for a telltale expression. That did not happen; they were painfully aware of the danger confronting them only a few days away. At 1700 hours, Hazel stood, saying it was time to get Karl back to the room because they would be coming to change the dressings soon. She knew the longer they stayed in the club, the less time she would have alone with Karl.

"Of course, you must be getting fatigued by now, Karl. Why don't you make your way over to my office tomorrow morning after having therapy and seeing the doctor, alright? As for you, young lady, I'll see you and these two geezers at 0600 sharp. Now, be off with you."

Clive recognized they needed some private time to say their goodbyes. As Karl, with Hazel holding his arm, hobbled away, Clive turned to the other two, saying, "I can't help thinking it's Kitty all over again. You know how Karl has a habit of diving headfirst into most situations. He could well be heading down that same road again. If I had more time to replace Hazel in this operation, someone with equivalent field experience, I would pull her out of this mission, but there is no one to replace her at this late date." Clive remembered the hell Karl went through when Kitty was killed.

"Clive, Hazel has already pleaded with me not to cut her from this mission when I confronted her about this blooming romance with Karl. She is very much like Kitty. We are at war, and she has a duty to perform; nothing will stop her from performing that mission. I have known about her feelings for Karl since we were in Scotland. She has been carrying that heartache over the past several years. Giving them their time together will fortify her commitment to the BIS and this mission. If she holds on tight to the notion that she is returning to someone special waiting for her, it will give her strength," said

Gunther, thinking of his own family back in Hamburg and the daily heartache he also lived with.

Back in Karl's small room, Hazel helped him remove his tunic and shoes, then helped him onto the bed. "Well, lady, now you have me where you want me, what do you propose we do?"

"Well, playing chess is really out of the question, don't you think?" answered Hazel, her hormones in high gear.

"Did you say play chess or was that playing with your chest?" The old Karl was back in action, even though it would only be for two nights, but in his mind, he had blocked out anything beyond that.

"Well, since you asked, I might as well get comfortable, shouldn't I?" Hazel was going to tease him into submission. Well, maybe not submission because she could see he was already ready for her on the bed. "Where is that small radio I brought you? We could do with some romantic music about now. There it is; I'll plug it in on that desk. Now, that's more like it, the Glenn Miller orchestra. What was I going to do next?" Hazel enjoyed this immensely as she crossed over to the bed, leaning over Karl, and gave him a moist kiss. Remaining there, her blouse without a tie gave Karl a commanding view, much like that day by the lake.

"Hazel, this is the second time you've got me going with that marvelous view down your blouse." The beautiful Hazel was teasing Karl, and he loved it.

"Darling, are you so naive you think I did not know that?" replied Hazel as she slowly unbuttoned her blouse, then removed her skirt. She stood there, love beaming across her face. "Well, what do you think, lover boy?" Hazel now had his full attention. When she had dressed that morning, she did not put on the regulation military underwear. Instead, she elected to wear seductive silk and lace, thinking no one would know—only Karl when she removed her uniform. Her seduction was going as planned. Now, it was time to make love to this Austrian she had waited so long for. "Darling, as much as I want to screw your brains out, we must be careful. We don't want to put you back in surgery, now do we? Please, let me take care of you first. I really want to anyway," said Hazel, sitting down on the edge of the bed.

"Hazel, you better lock the door first," said Karl in a controlled voice.

"Already done that when we arrived. I confided in that lovely nurse Ann that we would like to be alone for a couple of hours, so now you can relax and enjoy our time together." Hazel was slowly pulling the bed sheet down. Unfortunately, that revealed the bloody bandage around Karl's upper thigh. "Oh, my God, Karl, I did not realize the wound to your leg was still weeping like that. I was more worried about your neck and the movement of your head. Darling, this might not be a good idea right now."

As much as Hazel wanted to make love, she certainly did not want to jeopardize his recovery by any movement that could be dangerous. I know what Ann meant when she told me to be aware of his condition; one false move could set him back weeks. Hazel now sat upright, holding Karl's hand. "Darling, I'm sorry you have to see my leg like this. It really looks so much worse than it is. My neck, well, that will be a problem until they remove that blasted piece of steel." Karl, trying to comfort her, took his other hand, placing it over the tears on Hazel's cheek. "There is always another way to skin a cat, and I have an idea that will give us what we both need."

Karl felt that he needed to be creative and find a way to make love to this beautiful woman seated before him that would not cause a problem to his wounds. This might be the only time before she left on a very dangerous mission. "Hazel, please help me up from this bed, then get me into the bathroom," said Karl, a plan firmly in his mind.

"Alright, do you need to use the bathroom?" she asked. "Not for that. Take those towels and put one on either side of my neck, now lady, back up to the wall and reach as high as you can, so I will not have to bend too much to enter you." Karl had found a way to make love to Hazel.

"Oh, Karl, I could not follow what you were up to. Now, I know why they always say Karl never does things in the expected manner." As she spoke, his hand found her wet mound, and the last words she spoke changed to a moan as Karl continued to massage her with his thumb and index finger. Hazel stood, shaking as a wave of ecstasy drove her to her first orgasm. "Karl, what you just did put a powerful torque on this body of mine." Hazel, with a noticeable quiver in her voice, was about to say something when she felt a thrust inside of her that stopped her cold. Karl had entered her without her noticing what he was doing in front of her. No wonder he wanted me to stand as high as I could. Oh, God, this is beyond heaven. "Karl, please don't stop; I want all you can give me, darling. I love you so much; you can have anything you want. As she tried to finish that line, she felt that intense feeling coming over her again, and with a loud sigh, she surrendered to another powerful orgasm, which triggered Karl into doing the same.

The two stood there locked together in an embrace for just a few minutes that felt like an hour. "How do you feel, darling? Now that you have gotten rid of all that dirty water." Karl had a grin on his face like a Cheshire cat.

"Karl, honestly, you come up with the most bizarre things to say, especially after giving me a workover like that. Thank God you can only function at half speed. I dread to think what's in store for me when you're all together again. Hazel helped Karl stand back from her as she said that.

In the back of Karl's mind, a voice was telling him he had heard someone say almost the identical thing. That black cloud was trying to move in again, only this time he said, "Stop!"

"Stop what?" asked Hazel as she was putting her blouse on in front of the mirror.

"It's nothing, darling, just some thought that crept into my head," replied Karl, staring at Hazel in a different manner. He hobbled over to her. Turning her around, he pulled her to him and wrapped his strong arms around her, kissing her softly on the lips, not in an animal way, but more in an affectionate, loving manner. Pulling back, he held her face between his big hands, staring into her eyes, saying nothing.

"Karl, is everything alright? You look so sad. What's bothering you like this?"

"For too long, I have felt nothing when making love. It was only a means to escape and relieve my tension. Today, we were not having sex, we were making love, and for the first time in over two and half years, I feel alive again. You, my darling Hazel, gave me that. So, no,

I'm far from sad. Feel like another round?" Karl said, breaking out laughing.

"Are you crazy? They will be doing rounds shortly. Can you imagine the look on their faces, seeing the two of us up against that wall, banging away with hardly anything on? Come on; let's get you dressed, then I'll make the bed before they come in to change your dressing. Over here, lover boy, let me wash you down. We need to get rid of that love scent before Ann gets the wrong idea." After they had made themselves presentable again, Hazel said, "While you wait for the nurse to arrive, I'm going over to command to get an update on the mission status." Hazel kissed him on the forehead and headed for the door. Hearing her last statement about checking in on the mission cast a dark shadow again in Karl's mind. He had been here before!

A knock on the door brought Karl back. "Come in; it's open," Karl called to Ann.

"Alright, Karl, let me get those stained dressing off, shall we? Did you have a nice afternoon? I just saw Lieutenant Collins going down the hall, such a lovely lady; you should be very thankful she is your girlfriend." Ann was just making small talk as she cleaned and replaced his dressings.

Over dinner, Gunther asked Karl once again if he was still up to being their mission contact. "You know I am. I must interject, though, that I will be going up to London shortly for a second operation to remove this chunk of steel in my neck. I'm not sure what it entails. I venture to say, if it goes wrong, you will need another inside contact for the mission." Karl was trying to make light of what could happen in that operating theatre.

"Don't talk like that, Karl; you will have two of the best surgeons working on you, Doctors Burgers and Mills, so stop scaring me," said Hazel, reaching for his hand.

"Now that everyone around here knows you two are an item, will it create a problem for us out there in the middle of God knows where?" asked Helmut, looking at them both.

"Helmut, my dear friend, you should know that neither one of us will let our personal lives interfere with this or any future mission either one of us may be involved with, isn't that correct, Hazel?" said Karl as he squeezed Hazel's hand.

"That is very true. Both of you have worked with me before in Germany, so you know how I conduct myself. There is a time for everything, and as of tomorrow morning, I will be covering your backs as you cover mine, are we clear on that?" replied Hazel with a stern look on her face. When called upon to be all business, she could focus exceptionally well.

Clive came in, pulled up a chair, then flagged the steward to bring him his usual pint of mild and bitter beer. "Anyone else like a drink while I'm buying?" Clive had joined them with some long-awaited news for Karl. "I just got off the phone with Doctor Burgess. It looks like he would like to schedule your neck operation for next Wednesday. Doctor Mills will be returning to London and has agreed to swing by and drive you to St. Mary's Hospital, so that works out nicely. Once I knew the date, I took the liberty of calling your brother-in-law, Ronny, at his base in Duxford to give him an update on when the operation is scheduled. Here's the good news, old boy, Ronny will be driving your mother down from Baldock next Wednesday. This must be fabulous news for you, Karl, considering you have not been the best at staying in touch with her," said Clive as he lifted his pint to celebrate this long-overdue announcement.

"Now, as for you three, I'm assuming all your gear is ready for tomorrow morning. If not, get it done today, and that is an order. I'll be there to see you off at 1850 hours; care to join me, Karl?" asked Clive.

"I would not miss it. Are there any additional instructions I should be aware of before your departure tomorrow?" asked Karl.

"How about joining us after breakfast for a quick refresher," answered Gunther.

"Sounds great to me. Clive, will you be there as well? Don't forget, as of next Wednesday, I'm going to be out of circulation for a while," replied Karl.

"Oh, on that subject, Ronny will be picking you up on the Friday after the operation. Doctor Burgess has approved your medical leave. He notified me that two or maybe three weeks of rest is mandatory in this case, so please convey to your mother that I am keeping my promise to send you home for a while," said Clive, beaming with a smile on his face.

"She asked you that, Clive? When did you talk to her last?" asked Karl.

"Well, I took it upon myself to call her at least once every other week, seeing as you very rarely do, and by the way, Hazel and Gunther, from time to time, have also been keeping her abreast on your recovery." Clive was sending Karl a message to stay in touch more often with his mother.

"Sounds to me like you have everything under control, so thank you very much." Karl felt humbled by the way his friends kept his mother updated.

"Karl, I think we need to get you off your feet. You are starting to look really tired. Let's say goodnight, shall we?" Hazel could see the pain was returning, and as much as he was trying to make light of it, he knew he needed to lay down.

"See you tomorrow morning then, good night, chaps," said Karl as he stood up with the help of Hazel. After they had left, Gunther, making small talk, remarked that he thought they made a good-looking couple and that he and Herbert would do everything within their power to shield her from danger.

"Very commendable of you, Gunther; just remember, she is your radio operator, and we all know the survival rate for an operator these days, don't we?" Clive knew all too well that this mission was safer than most but felt he still had to interject that question.

Back in the small room, Hazel helped Karl out of his uniform, hanging it up in the wardrobe. "I can't stay long, darling. I have a lot of preparations to take care of before tomorrow," said Hazel as she moved back to sit next to him on the bed.

"I can see from your face, you are already in mission mode, am I correct?" Karl was giving her the out to leave.

"You're getting to know me very well, my darling. I guess you know the feeling you get when it gets close to leaving on a mission, so yes, I think I'm going to tuck you in and return to getting my equipment sorted out. I hope you're not too disappointed." Hazel, answering him, could feel the tears welling up in her eyes, and this she did not want him to see. Hazel sat down again next to him on the narrow bed, thinking, I hope I can come back to you, Karl. I have never felt so alone as I do right now, and there is nothing I can do to prevent it.

"Come here, Hazel; let me hold you for a few minutes," said Karl as he looked at her, knowing full well what was going through her head. He had been in this position once before, only a few years back. Lying together with Karl's strong arms around her, he could feel her tension. "Hazel, it's time to put your feelings in a safe place at the back of your mind until you return. No need to worry about me. I am getting better and stronger with each day, and once that hunk of steel is out, I will be able to return to my normal duties after a lengthy recuperation. "When you send a message, add this word occasionally in a sentence, *better*. Never use it in a way it could be construed as a pattern. I'll see it and know you're alright." Karl kept stroking her face and hair as he said this.

"One last kiss, then I'll be off." Hazel was over that brief period of melancholy. Sitting upright once again, she leaned over and kissed him good night. Any devilish thoughts Karl may have had, such as sliding his hand up her skirt, were now gone. He knew she had to focus her mind and concentration back into military mode, and he had no intentions of complicating matters. Hazel opened the door, turned, and blew him a kiss. "See you tomorrow morning for breakfast. Better still, I'll come over early and help you; then we can go together; how's that sound?"

Hazel, while saying that, had a thought go through her head. If I come too early, Karl will surely try something, so I'll get him just before it's time to leave. As she briskly walked to the female quarters, she realized what she was thinking. Change that idea; tomorrow morning will be the last time I get to be alone with Karl for at least four months or maybe longer, so if he's up to fooling around, I'm his girl. With this change in her head, she smiled, then laughed to herself as she entered her building.

Hazel's roommates woke her at 0530 hours. "Come on, lass, up and at 'em—long day ahead for you," said Claire, her Scottish roommate, heading for the bathroom. Hazel lay there for a few minutes, still half asleep; her mind was drifting in and out of consciousness. Claire was correct; this would be a long day with the strong possibility of real danger before it ended. *Why am I getting up so early then?* Now, almost awake, she sat up stretched, then put on her dressing gown and slippers. Picking up her toilet bag, she headed for the door, almost like a programmed zombie. Walking down the hallway, her faculties began slowly returning.

You're getting up early, you idiot, to see Karl, remember? With her vision and focus finally clear, she picked up her stride, covering the remainder of the distance to the bathroom in just a few long steps. Back in their room, Hazel finished dressing and applying her makeup, giving the finishing touches to her hair in its French twist. Finally, she inspected the contents of her suitcase. Satisfied, she locked it, then placed it at the foot of her bed, ready for later in the day. Her footlocker was alongside her bed, packed and locked with everything that would go to the storage room. She was ready. Turning to the three other roommates, she said nervously, "Well, girls, I'm off to see Karl, then on to a mission briefing. I'm not sure I'll get to see you before I leave later today. Wish me luck and a speedy return."

The three roommates closed into hug Hazel, each with tears in their eyes. As field agents, they had all lived that fear which lay ahead for her. In their minds, they saw that hell that lay ahead. "Bye then, see you soon, God willing, I hope," said Hazel, heading for the door. Outside, the air felt clean and fresh as she filled her lungs, allowing the sun to warm her face. The brisk walk felt invigorating, and stretching her long legs helped her condition herself for what lay ahead. Entering the medical center, she walked up to the nursing station, looking for familiar faces. "Morning, Ann. How is he? Are you finished with changing his dressing?" Hazel asked.

"He's all yours, Lieutenant, too much energy, though, first thing in the morning. Maybe you could work on discharging that battery of his?" said Ann, laughing at what she had just said.

Hazel knew exactly what the friendly nurse was implying. She must think I'm a nymphomaniac or something like that, chuckled Hazel. Entering the hallway, she walked down to Karl's room, still thinking about Ann's last remark. Well, this morning, she could be right. In front of the door, she took a moment to ensure her uniform and hair were perfect, then tapped twice on the door.

From the other side came a response, "Come on in, Lieutenant, you're early." Hazel, hearing his voice, could feel her excitement building as she opened the door to see Karl standing, fully dressed in his uniform, minus the tie due to the neck collar.

"Well, look at you. What a handsome devil you make in that uniform." Hazel stood there in the doorway, just absorbing the feelings she could not contain.

"Come over here, you sweet thing, and lock the door behind you," instructed Karl.

Hazel quickly looked at her wristwatch as she moved toward him. "Good morning, darling. Did you manage to sleep well last night? I did not fall asleep until way after midnight. You know the things that race through your head before a mission." Hazel regretted saying that almost immediately, thinking, you idiot; you should know that would hit a nerve with him. "Oh, darling, forgive me for rattling away like that. I was so excited to be here with you this morning; my nervous energy kicked in and has turned me into a babbling idiot." Hazel stood in front of Karl, her hands holding his forearms tightly.

"Darling, that's perfectly alright; no apologies necessary. I remember that feeling before being deployed. I think what may calm you down is a good romp in the hay; how does that sound?"

Hazel, hearing this, let out a big sigh. "Let me remove my tunic and shoes; these heels make me too tall for you," said Hazel as she unbuttoned her tunic. This will have to be a quick one, darling; we only have a little over an hour."

"That's alright, darling; an hour is better than nothing at all, right?" Karl could feel she was trying to rush their time together. Making love to her this morning would be like running on autopilot. "Hazel, you have way too much going on in that head of yours, cramming every thought into this moment. Rushing like this will only frustrate things by trying too hard to please me, so let's just enjoy some quiet time instead, shall we?" Karl said this, knowing it would throw cold water on her advances.

"Karl, forgive me. I'm a mess right now. I don't know what's the matter with me this morning. I was all excited, knowing I would have some time with you. Now, look at this train wreck I've created."

Hazel was becoming unhinged, not uncommon before the start of a covert operation.

"Come lay down next to me, Hazel. You need to relax mentally as well as physically," encouraged Karl, feeling this was not going very well. Hazel curled up next to him, locking her arms around his chest. Karl cradled her head very carefully into the nape of his neck, making sure he kept his head upright. They lay there quietly for a few minutes. Karl could feel her tension subsiding. Slowly, Hazel's right hand caressed his face, then went down to the front of his trousers. Neither one spoke a word.

Hazel's long fingers, with deliberate intent, started unbuttoning them, then without looking at him, she moved her head to his chest, remaining there while she finished opening his trousers. Hazel placed her hand around his erection, and with slow movements, started stroking in long slow motions.

Karl realized Hazel was trying to resurrect the mood she had started earlier. He decided there and then that he would not say a word. To do so would destroy the mood Hazel was desperately trying to rekindle. Hazel was aroused once again, and she also knew that wound on his leg could cause a problem. On the day she would leave, she did not want to have that on her mind. With that thought in her head, she moved over his very erect penis, her mouth sliding down its length. Hazel moved in slow, precise movements, enjoying her conquest by doing this for the first time. Karl was in heaven—well, almost. Two can play that game, he thought as he pulled at her to move her legs toward him so he could slide his hand up under her skirt. With a bit of adjusting, Hazel put herself in a position for Karl to make that happen.

Hazel continued with slow movements until an electrifying feeling sent her into a frenzy with mounting excitement. Karl was giving her the same treatment as yesterday with almost the same results. Hazel lifted her head as she shook with a powerful orgasm. Karl had done it again. "Darling, don't move. I need to feel you in my mouth; please, I really want this," she cried out as she once again started to squeeze him in her mouth. Within seconds, Karl exploded, making her moan even more. "Well, my darling, that did not take long at all, did it?" said Hazel as she swung her legs over the side of the bed. "How did you like that, lover boy? A little extra treatment to keep those voluptuous nurses away from my man. I'm going to fix my hair and straighten myself out. You should think about doing the same."

Karl lay there for a few minutes, thinking about what had just happened. A feeling of extreme guilt started crowding his thoughts with a clear image. He was still in love with Kitty, and that thought would stop any further romance with the beautiful Hazel. *Damn you, Karl, you are doing it again—breaking poor Hazel's heart. I can't let on at this late stage of her deployment. When she returns, you will face the music and tell her you really tried, but there will always be Kitty between us.* Karl started to dress once again. Hazel, now neatly dressed, came out of the bathroom.

She was about to say something but froze in her tracks as she looked at the facial expression on Karl. It was giving him away, and she immediately knew what it was. "My darling, Karl, there are more than two of us in this romance, am I right? Your face is giving you away, am I right? Please, talk to me, Karl, please." Hazel was trying very hard not to lose her composure as she reached for his hands.

Karl's disciplined mind jumped into defensive mode as he stood silently for a mere few seconds before answering her. "Hazel, my mind is in turmoil. You know very well I've been in this same situation before. Later today, you will leave on a very dangerous mission, and it's that same feeling of emptiness that is turning me inside out and making me feel the way I do right now. Please, forgive me; I have no right to upset you like this," answered Karl, knowing full well he was deceiving her. I cannot let her go into harm's way with the thought of a broken romance on her mind, so I will play along until she is back. Maybe I will change in the following months; who knows! For a few silent minutes, they embraced. Speaking at this point would serve no purpose.

Hazel spoke first, "We should think about joining the others for breakfast and the pre-mission briefing. Are you ready to go?" Karl could sense the difference in Hazel's tone of voice. Was she feeling there was no future in this relationship, and, like him, was she just going through the motions?

"Where did I leave my cap? Is it in the wardrobe, dear?" asked Karl, trying to salvage something from earlier this morning that she could hang onto. The walk over to the main building was charged with silence. Reaching the main entrance, Hazel helped Karl navigate the few steps to the front door. Karl made small talk about how walking was becoming so much easier than yesterday; even the steps were easier to climb. "I must admit, my damn leg does feel stronger," remarked Karl, holding onto Hazel's arm.

Once inside, Hazel stopped and turned toward Karl, saying, "Karl, I was thinking as we walked over here, after the mission briefing, it may be easier if you did not come to see us off. I now understand what Kitty meant when she told me she did not want you to see her off either. Are you alright with that?" Hazel was uncomfortable standing there when what she really wanted was to hold him and cry her heart out; her world was coming apart.

"Are you sure about this, Hazel? I will do whatever you feel is best." Karl was going through the motions, making him feel even more guilty.

"I really think it's for the best. We are both too emotionally tense right now. When I return, God willing, I will return, I'm hoping you will be there to throw your arms around me and smother me with kisses. Karl, do you think that will happen?" said Hazel, holding back the tears she was feeling from a heart that was being broken.

Karl just stood there momentarily before he wrapped his arms around her, pulling her in tightly before he answered. "I will be there, my darling Hazel. I have hurt you on this, the day you should be leaving with love in your heart. Can you forgive me? I was feeling too sorry for myself, and it was not fair to burden you with that black cloud hanging overhead. Beyond all doubt, you can count on me. As for seeing you off, there is no way or no one that will stop me. Are you listening to me?"

Karl, in a matter of seconds, had pushed that cloud out of his mind. He would be there with open arms when Hazel returned, or would he? Over breakfast, their spirits were high. Karl and Hazel were holding hands under the table. Hazel had that wonderful smile back on her face, knowing they had just gone through a war zone that nearly killed their relationship. The briefing went according to plan, with Karl interfacing with Hazel on when to expect radio transmissions and when Hazel should schedule instructions from Slough. With the briefing over, Hazel, Gunther, and Herbert returned to their quarters to retrieve their luggage, while Clive, Bill, and Karl remained in the meeting room.

"Karl, how do you feel about next Wednesday? You must be anxious to get that dog collar off your neck," said Bill.

"You have no idea how I'm looking forward to putting this behind me. I need to be over there where I can be most effective doing my job," replied Karl.

"We need everyone we can get to man the BIS in the months ahead, so hurry that recovery along, Karl. You're needed back here right after your operation and home leave." Clive knew a lot more about what was expected for the English people and the painful steps needed to save their island. The three returned, luggage in hand, joining the others as they waited in front of the building for the van to arrive.

Karl excused himself, then said, "Major Knight, do you mind awfully if I borrow Lieutenant Collins for a few minutes? There is something I must say that is of a private nature."

Clive looked at Karl, then Hazel, and in a soft tone of voice said, "Of course, go right ahead, you two, but make sure you're back here in fifteen minutes." Clive was thinking, whatever happened this morning between those two looks like it has passed; I'm willing to bet it has something to do with Kitty.

Inside the building, they found an empty office. Hazel was now dressed in wool trousers, a turtleneck pullover, heavy boots, and a field jacket fitted at the waist. Her hair was pulled back in a ponytail, making her look so much different from the officer of this morning. "Hazel, this morning, I was not in control of my thoughts. In fact, I will admit to you that I was feeling pretty sorry for myself, and by doing so, allowed old memories to flood my mind. Am I making any sense to you?" asked Karl as he held Hazel very tightly.

"Karl, I asked you were there three of us in this relationship. Is that still the case?" Hazel felt she would rather know now than have her hopes shattered when she returned.

"Honestly, I was questioning that myself, but my darling Hazel, as we stand here, I can tell you emphatically that I will be here for you. There may come a time when that cloud brings me down again, but know this if it does, I will be ready for it." Karl was stumbling, trying to find the right words to tell her that he was desperately struggling to bury the past.

"Darling Karl, before I leave, tell me honestly, and please don't lie to save my feelings. Do you love me? If not, can you see a time when that could happen? I need something to hang onto while I'm away."

Karl, holding her face, looked deep into her wet eyes, waiting a moment while he asked himself that same question, then he reached down for her hand and quietly whispered in her ear, "Yes, Hazel, I do. I have not said that in so long; it scares me, so again, yes, Hazel, I have fallen in love with you. Now, you must promise me you will be careful and come home to me." Karl had finally made the commitment that Hazel so needed to hear.

They walked back to the van parked in front of the group, "Well, it looks like this is it; let's get loaded, shall we?" said Gunther. Clive shook hands with each of them, then saluted them as they boarded. As Hazel started to board, she stopped, turned toward Karl standing next to Clive with tears in her eyes but under control, shouted, "Think of me, lover boy, while I'm away!"

CHAPTER 7

TIME TO RECOUP AND FACE THE GERMAN INVASION

The following Wednesday came quickly. However, the communications from the Delta-1 Team did not. Then again, no one expected to hear from them until they reached the safe house in Brittany, France, the first stop on their mission.

Karl sat in Clive's office, drinking coffee and whiling away the time until Doctor Mills arrived to take him to St. Mary's Hospital in London. Clive, however, was engrossed in a pile of documents awaiting his approval. "Sorry if I appear to be ignoring you, old boy. I'm terrible at getting these documents signed, most are duplicates, and some are triplicates, and that simply drives me absolutely crazy. If things could be changed, I would gladly swap this desk job for a field assignment," remarked a frustrated Clive.

"That's alright, Clive; you carry on. I should be leaving shortly anyway," replied Karl as he continued sipping his awful coffee.

A rap on the door was followed by a corporal saluting as he entered. "Sir, Doctor Mills has arrived to pick you up; I'll take your suitcase to the car for you. Do you require any assistance getting down the steps, or can you manage with your cane?" asked the young corporal.

"I'll be fine. Yes, take my suitcase and tell Doctor Mills that I'm on my way, thank you. Well, Clive, wish me luck, and please let me know when Delta-1 makes contact. I will plan on hearing from you daily, using Ronny's secure base phone at the bungalow, say 0900 hours each morning, with an update. I wish you would consider my mother's offer to visit us in Baldock. That would work out perfectly for me to return to camp with you; try to make that happen," said Karl as he opened the office door. The weather outside was perfect, sunny and dry, with a few wispy cumulus clouds drifting by.

"Morning, Doctor, so nice of you to drive me to St. Mary's," said Karl as he approached the passenger door.

"Karl, please drop the formalities and just call me Terry. That will be fine. Are you ready to go?" asked Terry as he slid in behind the steering wheel of the Humber staff car.

"I've spent many an hour in one of these big buggers," said Karl, realizing he was letting those haunting old memories slide back into his mind. Reacting quickly, he blocked them entirely.

"I think they're the most popular car on the road right now. They look more like an oversized pregnant saloon with those enormous tires, don't you think?" Terry chuckled as he said that. "Well, let's get going, shall we? It's about thirty-two miles, so with moderate traffic, we should be there in about ninety minutes.

Once I get you checked in, I would like to look at that neck before tomorrow's surgery, alright?" asked Terry.

"You're in charge. Whatever you think is best. How long will the surgery take, and will I be able to get rid of this blasted neck collar after it's over?" inquired Karl, hoping the answer would be yes.

"Once we have opened the incision and cleaned around the artery, we will know what we are dealing with. It's not a big surgical procedure, but it could be very dangerous for you if we run into problems removing that chunk of steel. However, once that shrapnel is removed, the rest is straightforward, stitching you up and replacing the bandages around your neck. With all going well, you should be able to take it off permanently in about a week. That does not mean you can return to duty. Does that answer your question? When you eventually return to Slough, you can return to your regular quarters if the leg wound has healed sufficiently enough to climb the stairs to your flat. If not, you'll have to stay in the officer's quarters at the camp for a while," concluded Terry.

The drive was very pleasant except for the continuous convoys of military vehicles going in the opposite direction. "I would venture to say the army is fortifying the coastal approaches; what do you think? Sorry, I suspect you are under some gag order regarding what is going on, is that right?" Terry realized his question was not the most appropriate thing to ask an intelligence officer at a time like this.

Terry turned the car into the main entrance of St. Mary's Hospital, parking in front of the door, then walked around to the passenger side to help Karl out of the car, handing him over to an orderly who would help him into the lobby. Once inside the lobby, Karl's heart skipped a beat. There, seated on a bench in the hallway, were his mother and brother-in-law, Ronny. "Mama, God, it's so wonderful to see you! And Ronny, thank you for driving Mama here. Come here, Mama; give me a hug. You need to watch my neck, though. I have not had surgery yet, alright?"

With his arm around his mother, Karl reached out with his other arm to shake hands with Ronny. "I suppose Freida could not make it because she has to take care of Franchot. Not to worry; after this, I will be home, and we will have plenty of time to catch up." Karl's spirits could not have been higher. Doctor Mills parked the car in the reserved physicians' parking area and then proceeded to the rear entrance to meet up with Doctor Burgess. While the doctors prepped, Nurse Rachel was instructed to fetch Karl from the main waiting area.

"You must be Lieutenant Vita, is that correct?" asked Rachel. "Yes, Nurse, that's me. I suppose you are here to collect me, is that right?" asked Karl as he released himself from his mother's hold. "My mother and brother-in-law are going to wait here while I'm in surgery. How long before they can come to see me?" asked Karl.

"I'm not really sure. The procedure itself will not take long, but recovery, well, that's not for me to say. Be assured, I will keep them informed of your progress," said Rachel, leading Karl by the arm down the hall to the surgical prep room. Once inside, two nurses in surgical gowns helped Karl remove his clothes and put on a hospital gown, open at the back. This got a chuckle from Karl. One of the nurses now lowered the bed so that Karl could climb onto it.

"Sir, I will be rolling you onto your side after I have shaved you. The next part, I don't think you will like. Because of the surgical area, I will need to cut your hair on that side of your head, followed by a close shave up to the parting line. With thick hair like yours, Sir, I'm sure it will grow back in quickly."

Two nurses entered the pre-op area, introducing themselves. "I'm Sister Julie, and this is Sister Ann. We will be with you through the procedure and recovery."

"Another Ann," said Karl in a jovial mood. He was so relieved at finally getting that piece of steel out of his neck.

"I'm leaving now to go change for surgery. Sister Julie will stay with you while the anesthesiologist administers the pre-surgical medication," said Ann. "See you shortly, Sir."

Karl lay there on the bed for less than ten minutes before the anesthesiologist, Doctor Mitchell, pulled back the curtain, saying, "Lieutenant Vita, very nice to meet you. I see the sisters have gotten you ready. I'm going to give you a couple of injections that will make you very sleepy. Once inside the operating theatre, I'll be administering medication to put you to sleep. Do you have any questions for me before I start?" asked Doctor Mitchell.

"No, Sir, I am about as ready as I will ever be," replied Karl. Inside the operating theatre, both surgeons welcomed Karl, already in the twilight zone. "Karl, we are going to roll you over on your side, then strap you in place, followed by another strap over the top of your head to ensure you don't make any sudden movements while we operate to remove that shrapnel in your neck," explained Doctor Burgess as he stood back to let the sisters position Karl on the operating table. "Are we all ready?" said Doctor Burgess as he looked to Doctor Mitchell for that nod that Karl was under.

Back in the waiting room, Mama sat quietly on one of the couches, having been there a little over two hours; time was dragging. "Ronny, do you mind getting me a hot cup of coffee if they have it? Tea will do if not," said Mama, a bundle of nerves worrying over her youngest son.

"Mama, you have not eaten since early this morning. Let me get you a sandwich. You really must try to eat something. I know it's the furthest thing from your mind right now but try anyway." Ronny was standing over his mother-in-law, his heart heavy seeing her like this, stressing until some news came that her son was out of danger.

Ronny came back with two mugs of coffee and two ham and cheese sandwiches; then, he sat down next to Mama.

Turning her attention toward Ronny, she said, "Ronny, you are such a good man. We are fortunate to have you in our family." Mama reached for his hand as she said this. The coffee and sandwiches were wolfed down very quickly. "I did not realize I was that hungry. I'm not sure I can eat both halves, though. Ronny, would you like to finish the remainder? We must always be thankful for having food available. Thousands are going without in this evil world," said Mama as she handed Ronny the remainder of her sandwich.

Mama, resting her head on the armrest of the couch, slipped into a shallow slumber to while away the waiting. About an hour later, the surgeon came walking down the hall toward them. Ronny woke Mama just in time to get an update from the surgeon. "Mrs. Vita, I'm Doctor Burgess. First, let me apologize for the surgery taking longer than we originally anticipated. The good news, however, is we managed to remove all the shrapnel from Karl's neck. It was a very nerve-racking procedure; that sharp piece of metal was lodged in an area that made removing it very difficult. Karl is in the recovery room.

He will be out for about another forty or so minutes. I will have Sister Julie come and get you once he comes to. We will be keeping him overnight for observation. If all goes well, we should be able to release him tomorrow afternoon. Doctor Mills will be driving himself to Cambridge tomorrow afternoon. Seeing as he will be driving right through Baldock, he has offered to drive Karl right to your doorstep. Now, I must caution you to be very careful with his neck. Any sudden movement could open those sutures, so just remember that. When his leave is up, he should be fit enough to travel back to Slough," concluded Doctor Burgess as he turned to walk back down the hall.

"There you are, Mama. Karl is out of danger now. Try and relax until Sister Julie comes to take us to his room," said Ronny, thinking forty minutes seemed like an eternity. Watching the clock, Mama was very fidgety. She was anxious to be with Karl, and Ronny was doing his very best to keep her calm. The doors at the end of the hall swung open, and through them came Julie, now back in her regular uniform.

"Mrs. Vita, ready to see your son? Please, follow me." Julie had a big smile on her face, thinking, when a procedure goes well, it makes the day for the staff so much brighter, and today was no exception. Julie held the door open to the recovery area, allowing Mama and Ronny to pass through. Karl was lying flat on his bed, his eyes open, but the bandages stopping his head from moving to the side to look at his mother.

Speaking in a semiconscious voice, he said, "Mama, Ronny, you're still here. How long has it been?"

Mama sat down carefully on the corner of the bed, looking at her son, tears in her eyes, saying, "Son, it was a wait well worth waiting for. That nice Dr. Burgess told us you would be kept here overnight and that Dr. Mills will be dropping you off tomorrow afternoon in Baldock. Karl, it's going to be wonderful having you home, even though it's only eight days." Holding her son's arm, Mama was secretly praying he would not be going on those mysterious operations to places they never could talk about. Wishful thinking will not stop that from happening, I suppose.

Karl's eyes were becoming heavy. He was falling asleep and trying to speak, "Sorry, I'm having a hard time staying awake. I'll see you tomorrow afternoon." With those last slurred words, Karl went into a deep, relaxing sleep.

"Mama, I think we can go now. He will be out for the rest of the night, and that's something he needs right now. Tomorrow will come quickly for all of us." Ronny helped his mother-in-law to her feet and guided her toward the door. Back in Ronny's little Austin car, driving the ninety minutes back to Baldock, they had time to talk about Karl and Kitty's tragic demise.

"Ronny, I wonder what this crazy life has in store for all of us. It's been almost ten months since I received a letter from Papa. I'm trying to keep that from Karl. He was his father's favorite son, probably because they were so much alike." Mama was making small talk to pass the time on the drive home.

At 0530 hours, the low blue lights were replaced by the soft white overhead lights as the nursing staff started their morning ritual of getting their charges ready for the new day. "Well, Lieutenant, how are you feeling this morning after that really long sleep? We decided not to wake you last night for dinner. Dr. Burgess told us it would be better to let you sleep." Sister Ann helped him sit up, propping his pillows behind him. "After you have had your breakfast, Dr. Burgess or Dr. Mills will be along to examine your incision. After that, you're free to use the bathroom and get dressed. I'll help you dress. I understand you will be going home today, so we will get you a package of medication and bandages to cover you for the rest of the week." Ann was talking to Karl, watching his movements as she applied the new smaller bandage around his neck, replacing the large uncomfortable type he had been wearing since being injured.

"Feeling bloody marvelous, Sister. That constant pain in the side of my neck is almost gone. It's still a little sore, though. I feel like a new man." Although Karl still had restricted movement from side to side, this added range of motion made him feel more like his old self. When the time came to return to Slough, he would be able to move around much easier, and that thought was driving him forward.

After breakfast, Dr. Mills stopped by to examine Karl's neck and make the final decision to discharge him. "Morning, old boy, you're looking one hundred percent better. Now, let's get those bandages off, shall we, Nurse?" Ann carefully removed the dressing to reveal a long line of heavy sutures running from Karl's shoulder to just below his ear. "You will have a great war story with that scar, old boy. Sorry, we couldn't hide it better; however, your collar will conceal quite a bit of it. Now, Karl, I want you to turn slowly from right to left, then repeat it. It's going to feel very stiff at first, so don't expect too much at this point." Slowly, Karl followed the instructions. He could feel the pulling from the sutures. However, that constant pain was almost gone. "Well done," said Doctor Mills. "You can buy me a pint one of these days; is that a deal? Guess I'll sign the discharge papers now, Nurse Ann. As for you, Lieutenant, plan on being ready after lunch. I'll pick you up at the front of the main entrance where I dropped you off yesterday, alright? Say 1230 hours."

With a cheerful wave, Doctor Mills proceeded down the ward to his next patient. Karl, without any assistance, headed for the bathroom and a nice hot bath. Doctor Mills had cautioned him to keep the neck dressing dry. Karl relaxed, feeling the hot water penetrate his entire body. After a careful, close shave, noticing the side of his head had been shaved clean made him feel like a circus clown. Oh, well, he thought, it's a small price to pay for being alive. Walking back to his cubicle, he realized the limp from the thigh wound was also feeling much better. The hot water did not affect it whatsoever. It was amazing how fast a gash like that could heal, he thought as he entered the cubicle. Sister Ann arrived at his bedside to find Karl dressed and packed, ready to leave. "Well, Karl, you look very smart in your uniform.

"Thank you, Ann; we are blessed with another beautiful morning. I think I will sit outside until it's time to leave. Could you be a sweetheart and get me today's *Daily Mail*? I might as well get caught up on what's happening with this bloody war!"

Sitting outside, Karl tried hard to read the newspaper dated July 7th. His eyes kept crossing in the combination of warm sun and soft scented breezes, and the feeling of relief lulled him into a deep, relaxing sleep. "Wake up, Karl, it's time to go," said Ann as she gently shook him.

"My goodness, I guess I needed that. How long have I been out?" asked Karl.

"About sixty or so minutes. I decided to leave you out here; you really needed the rest. The hospital requires me to walk you to the entrance, so if you're ready, we can go," said Ann, standing back while Karl stood up. She was watching to see how he would stand, followed by a walk down the length of the long hallway.

"Wait up a minute, Ann. Will you hold this for me?" Karl had made up his mind that he would not rely on that walking cane anymore.

"Karl, should you be doing this so soon? Why don't you wait a few days before walking without that cane?" Ann was concerned that he was taking unnecessary chances by putting too much strain on that leg. Karl walked all the way down the hall, carrying on a conversation with the very young, nervous sister.

"I feel wonderful. I think that leg of mine is well and truly on the mend. As for this neck, well, let's say it's so nice to be able to look around, and especially when a beautiful young nurse is walking by my side." Karl's flirtatious old self was almost back. Ann blushed at the attention Karl was bestowing on her.

"Karl, really, you are such a big flirt. I really don't know how to react to your comments but thank you anyway." Ann could not be more pleased to see Karl walking without his cane. In her mind, she imagined being out on a date with someone like Karl. Oh, well, one can always dream, I guess, she concluded as she sat down next to him on the bench. Looking at her watch, she said, "Doctor Mills should be along momentarily. Karl, you must be getting excited about spending time with your family," said Ann, trying to fill the silence.

"Tell me, Ann, do you have a young man? Is he in the military?" asked Karl.

"Yes, I do. He is two years older than me. Before the war, he was studying to be a civil engineer, but that had to be put on hold when war broke out. David is in the Royal Navy as a gunnery officer. His new orders just came through two weeks ago; he is so thrilled. He is to report to *HMS Hood* in ten days. I'm sad to see him go but excited for him. He wanted this posting so very much. Here he is, Karl. So very nice to have met you. Stay safe, and who knows? Our paths may cross again when we are both out of uniform."

Karl stood up, turning toward Ann. "Would you mind if I give you a big hug and a kiss on the cheek for all your help?" asked Karl as he looked down at Ann.

"It's against the hospital policy, but heck, there is a war going on, so why not? Don't squeeze too hard, though; I bruise easily."

Karl put one arm around her neck and the other around her waist. As promised, he kissed her softly on the cheek; her soft skin and perfume against his cheek were awaking the images of loves that would forever hold a special place in his heart. "Karl, are you getting sentimental on me?" asked Ann as she returned the kiss.

"Yes, Ann, it's times like this that remind me why we put ourselves in harm's way. We do it to give our future generations a chance to live in happiness in a world where war has no place." He didn't want to tell her what was really going through his mind. "Now, young lady, let me be off. I can't wait to return to my post and join all the men and women that are fighting to make peace a reality."

Karl released Ann, picked up his small suitcase, and walked toward the Humber staff car waiting at the curb. Karl opened the passenger door, and as he slid into the cabin, one last gesture was to throw a kiss to Ann, who was standing and waiting to see him off.

"Are you ready to be home, Karl?" asked Doctor Mills, as he put the Humber into gear and pulled away from the hospital entrance.

"Yes, I am. It will be wonderful to recharge my battery, but I must admit, I can't wait to return to my post in the BIS. There is so much hate and death spreading across Europe, and this must be stopped!" Karl was once again reverting to his military training.

The drive to Baldock was uneventful. Neither of them really spoke; they had their own agendas. After passing through Stevenage, Karl started giving directions to get to the bungalow in Baldock. "Well, old boy, here you are. Remember to follow the instructions we gave you. Only take those pain tablets if you really need them, alright? Let me also add, what you free Europeans are contributing to this war effort inspires all of us here in England; thank you, Lieutenant."

Karl opened the car door and reached over the bench seat for his overnight case, then slid out to the open arms of his mother and sister, Freida. "Goodbye, Sir, thanks to you for saving my life; I promise to use it wisely." Karl saluted Doctor Mills as he backed out of the driveway. Their paths would cross again when life and death would once again hang in the balance.

On Karl's first day home, he relaxed outside, continuing his recovery. Ronny called the following morning, tension in the sound of his voice. "Karl, I'm heading home to drop off the Austin and pack a bag. As of 1600 hours today, everyone will be restricted to the base. Something big is expected to start within days; need I say more?" Ronny arrived home quickly, packed a bag, then asked to talk to Karl alone in the garden. "Karl, our intelligence is reporting an unusual buildup of aircraft along the coast of France. We now believe the attack we have been bracing for is about to start. It will be up to you to take care of Mama, Freida, and Franchot if it looks like bombing could be in this direction. Get them into a shelter right away." Ronny kissed and hugged the family, then jumped into the waiting staff car, a quick wave, and he was gone.

"Mama and Freida, Ronny asked me to explain what is going on; as you saw, he was very much in a hurry." Over coffee, Karl explained what could happen and what precautions they would start immediately. "Mama, you and Freida go to the shops. Use up all your ration books; we must be ready if Baldock gets hit, even though it's highly unlikely. We are close to military airbases, so a stray bomber might drop one in our general vicinity, so let's not take any chances. I am going to call my base in Slough to see if they can provide me with more current information." Karl now was thanking his lucky stars that he would be home in Baldock to take care of the family.

"Clive, it's Karl. What is going on? Can you share any information with me?" asked Karl, hoping for a better understanding of what was expected to commence.

"Karl, we have been expecting a raid on our airfields. The Germans are going to try and soften us up before launching a land-based attack. We believe our new radar system along the southern coast will give us an advantage to where those raids are coming from and an estimate of how large their formations could be. The Hun has no idea what those towers are for. We believe nothing will happen for a few more days, so don't go crazy just yet. I'll call you in the morning with an update. Try to act normal; no need just yet to upset your mother. Bye for now." Clive hung up the phone, thinking this is going to be very difficult for Karl.

The following morning, Karl went for a walk through the old streets of Baldock. He decided to stop at the George and Dragon for a pint. Sitting in the lounge, he imaged the beautiful Kitty seated beside him, staring at her engagement ring. Remembering those times would continue to hold his heart until he could stand in front of her grave and return her letter to him containing the pressed petal. This farewell letter would remain in his safety deposit box at Lloyds Bank here in Baldock until that time came. Karl also spent some solitary time thinking about Hazel and the roller coaster relationship they found themselves on and the final day before she left on that dangerous mission back into occupied Europe. He thought deeply about how he had committed to loving her. Did he really mean that, or was it a good intention to ease her pain? Hazel, in a heated moment, had insinuated that there were three in their relationship. Was that still true?

On the way home, he stopped to sit on a bench near the park. He milled over all these thoughts as they collided in his mind. Yes, he did believe that he, in a peculiar manner, could love the sweet Hazel, but not the way he loved Kitty. Yet, something else in his head kept repeating, Karl, you are happiest when you are out at sea. Life always seemed uncomplicated out there. When this crazy war is finally over, I would like to return to my first love as an officer in the merchant service. With that course firmly established in his brain, he stood up, adjusted his cap to one side, and set off back to the bungalow about three miles away. His walking cane was now a thing of the past, so he simply deposited it in the collection box at the church of St. Mary the Virgin. From here on, he would walk tall, the limp becoming less of a problem with every step.

On July 9th, Ronny called from his base at Duxford, "Karl, although we are on a secure line, what I'm going to tell you is still highly confidential. Yesterday, we intercepted a communique from the western command of the Luftwaffe. We are now confident the Germans will attack within the next several days. Karl, you must prepare; have a bag ready to go to the air-raid shelter up the road and keep the radio tuned to the BBC for the latest updates. Must go now, and remember, if you hear the air raid siren, go immediately to the shelter. Unfortunately, I am confined to the base, so Karl, I am relying on you to take care of the family."

On July 11th, Karl was listening to the BBC radio when an announcement came on. "We interrupt this program to bring the following news. Less than an hour ago, a large aircraft formation has been detected crossing over the French coast. Their direction has been plotted to cross the South Coast of England. You are instructed to seek shelter immediately. Karl sat up. This was no surprise to him; he and everyone in the BIS had been bracing for this day. The phony war had come to an end. Later in the morning, a sizable formation of Stuka 87 dive bombers crossed the coast, the first wave to attack. Their targets were to bomb the radar installations along the coast. From that day on, all the newspapers and the BBC would provide the latest casualty reports on aircraft shot down or damaged on both sides. The numbers were staggering; how long can we defend ourselves like this, thought Karl.

By the beginning of August, the concern was, could the RAF continue to hold the Luftwaffe at bay, their numbers growing to as many as 750 bombers on each raid. The bombers were mainly Heinkel 111 and the Dornier 17 in smaller formations protected by Messerschmitt 109 and Messerschmitt 110 fighters.

Day after day, the RAF scrambled their Hurricanes and Spitfires, their young pilots continuously throwing themselves at a sky black with hostile aircraft. Throughout the aerial attacks, the RAF relied on the advanced guidance of the radar to locate the formations. Each wave of attacking aircraft was always intercepted by the deadly fighters, spitting hot lead into their formation. By early August, most RAF squadrons had no reserve aircraft to replace damaged or lost ones; England was almost on its knees. Then, a blunder by the German high command gave England the opportunity it so desperately needed to recover and rebuild. The aerial bombardment of English airfields was abandoned in favor of revised night operations by the relentless bombing of London and other major cities throughout England. This change in tactics would cost Germany the invasion of England, known as Operation Sea Lion. Now, the RAF could rebuild its decimated air force and once again rebuild its reserve of aircraft.

On August 20th, the BBC aired a recorded public message from Prime Minister Winston Churchill to the people of England.

"For many days and weeks, the German Luftwaffe has thrown the might of its air force against our island to no avail. The seabed of the English Channel and the fields of England are littered with crashed German aircraft. Without the vital air superiority over the channel and England, there can be no way a successful invasion can take place. It is the belief by the war department and this government that Operation Sea Lion has been postponed until further notice.

Churchill finished the broadcast by saying, *"Never in the field of human conflict was so much owed by so many to so few. The Battle of*

Britain is over. The battle to protect London and other major cities has just begun. God save the King."

Every person in England sighed with relief and sorrow for the cities in England that continued to be bombed nightly.

CHAPTER 8

RETURN TO DUTY

On his last day in Baldock, the family had lunch together before Karl got picked up by a returning staff car, heading back from Cambridge to the camp in Slough. "Mama, I would feel so much better knowing the fate of my Father and three brothers. It's this constant worrying about them that is bothering me. I can only imagine how the two of you are handling this."

Karl could always tell when Mama or Freida was hiding something with no intention of sharing. "Karl, they are in Italy. The problem is that the same craziness that overran Austria is now spreading through Italy. Your father has relatives in the mountains who are hiding them. So, right now, they are safe. Those mountains are of no interest to the Fascists. They are more intent on taking over the factories and major cities. The downside is receiving mail from those remote locations is almost impossible. Karl, pray they remain safe in their mountain hideout until this terrible war comes to an end." Mama sat back in her chair; the look on her face painted a grimmer picture that Karl could see through.

The sound of a car door closing in the driveway told Karl his ride had arrived. "Well, Mama and Freida, it's time for me to return to work. My driver is at the front door. Promise me you will not worry unnecessarily. You have bigger problems than worrying about me. I will write as often as I can; I'll probably call you on the phone, though. But there will be times when sending letters or calling could be difficult. You have enough spies at my camp who are keeping you updated, so I don't see that changing any time soon." Karl laughed loudly when saying this. Putting his tunic and cap on, he kissed them both, then picked up Franchot, kissing him on the forehead and hugging him before heading to the door. As he got into the car, he wound down the window, yelling, "Goodbye, stay safe, and remember not to worry." This would be the last time Karl would see them and Baldock for many long months.

Karl was getting used to this drive back to Slough. The convoys congesting the roads around Watford were the only delay they experienced. Approaching the main gate, the driver rolled down his window to show his ID, then Karl did the same. The guard recognized the driver as well as Karl saying, "Welcome back, Sir. Did everything go as planned?" The guard was making small talk as he examined their passes, then waved them through.

"Drop me off at building B-3, will you?" asked Karl as he buttoned his tunic and reached for his suitcase. "Thanks, Charlie, that was not a bad drive at all." Karl liked this driver, a real Scotsman who had driven Karl on many occasions. Smartly getting out of the car, Charlie walked around to the passenger side to open the door.

"Have a great rest of the day, Sir; I hope to see you again soon," said Charlie, saluting as Karl got out, taking in the all too familiar surroundings. Then, looking up at the main door and those dreaded steps, Karl thought, well, let me tackle them one at a time. Surprising himself, he walked up the steps with no difficulty and entered the lobby".

Well, will you look who has arrived back here," said Julie from behind her reception desk. "I can see you are on the mend; wonderful to see you, Sir." Julie had worked for Karl before being assigned to the clerical staff that also operated the reception desk.

"I'll announce myself, Julie; thanks for the warm welcome," remarked Karl as he started down the hallway that led to his cubicle.

"Chaps, look what the wind just blew in. It's Karl Vita. Welcome home, old man," yelled his good friend, Bill Lowes. Karl felt at home with the people in the room; he had worked with them for over two years now. Hearing Bill announce Karl, Clive stood up from his desk, opened the half-closed door to his office, and entered the operations room, a beaming smile across his face, so pleased to see his friend almost back to normal.

"You old bugger, I thought I told you to call before leaving Baldock. You crazy bloody Austrian, we have all been worried about you. It looks like the surgery went well; otherwise, we would be sending flowers about now," said Clive. He could not be happier to have Karl back in operations.

"What's the news from Delta-1? Where are they? Have they uncovered anything worthwhile yet?"

"Typical Vita, he's been back less than five minutes, and he's already going a hundred miles an hour. Slow down, you maniac. The latest communication from Delta-1 came late last night. It said they had made their way down to Saint-Nazaire. There appears to be a substantial amount of German construction equipment on the road south. They advised that once they know that heavy equipment has reached its destination, would we send a marine architect or someone who can assess what the intent is for such heavy equipment. The last part of the communication said the weather tomorrow looks '*better*' for getting a closer look." Clive stopped talking, looking at Karl smiling. He was thinking, there's that word again, "*better*." Thank God she is safe.

"I should plan on getting over there maybe after the Christmas holidays, or maybe before if it looks like they are moving faster with their final plan. Clive, do you agree?" asked Karl.

"Not in your present condition, you're not. I have already asked the Navy for a marine architect to rendezvous with them in about four or five weeks. Your job, starting tomorrow, is to analyze all the communications coming in from all the Delta teams. Something is going on down the entire Atlantic seaboard of France, and we need to know what the hell those buggers are up to. Right now, you're the best man for this job, and stop looking at me like a scolded schoolboy. Your turn will come soon enough." Clive always had a problem with keeping Karl working behind a desk. Once he regained his strength, there would be no way he could keep him tied to that desk, but for now, his ability to understand these communiques was just as important as the work of field agents.

"I'm buying," came a voice from the back of the office. Bill was putting his tunic on, ready to blow off steam in the officer's lounge.

"Sounds good to me," said Karl. "I've got to check into the officer's quarters first. Doc Mills wants me to stay there for a while. I'll catch up with you in a little while, alright?" Before leaving, Karl walked over to the radio operators' station, saying, "When are you next scheduled for a communication from Delta-1?"

"Will have a receiving band open at 2130 hours tonight," answered the operator.

"When you acknowledge that transmission, add this somewhere in the message," Karl wrote a message down on a pad. *All good with Mother.*

"Sir, I'm not sure I'm authorized to do that," said the confused operator.

"As of tomorrow morning, you will be reporting to me, so just do it." Karl was throwing his weight around in front of the operator.

"You're the boss. Can you just initial that note you handed me so that I can put it in the outgoing file?" asked the operator.

Entering the lounge, the laughter and saucy jokes were in full swing. "Come over here, you old bugger," said Bill, pulling a spare chair toward the table. "Did you blokes welcome back Vita yet? As of tomorrow morning, our good Austrian friend here will be directing the communication support for all the Delta teams, so wish him luck. He will be putting in long hours in that job. Karl, what did you do with your walking cane?" concluded Bill, knowing full well that Karl was already pushing for another field assignment.

"Thanks, Bill, you're always so generous with those back-handed compliments. With any luck, it won't be for too long. I never did like pushing papers around a desk." Karl was throwing it back at his good friend. "And as for the walking cane, well, I deposited into the church donation box back in Baldock." Karl immediately regretted saying that, as Bill still needed his walking cane to support his deformed leg, wounded years back while escaping the Gestapo in Germany.

After about forty-five minutes, Clive entered the lounge with someone Karl did not recognize in a French uniform. It must be a visitor, thought Karl. "Hey, you noisy bunch, I would like you all to welcome our newest member, Captain Jean Yves Jerva of the French 1st Light Cavalry Division. Jean Yves will be our liaison officer on assignment from the Free French Forces stationed here in England. His primary function will be to support the Delta Teams operating in Southern France. Karl, you two will be working together later," said Clive, his eyes firmly fixed on Karl as he said this. Clive always had a way of finding the best people for his beloved BIS. "Bill, Karl, please join us for dinner tonight. It will be a good time to get to know our new member. How do you feel about that, Jean Yves?"

As usual, Clive was getting the introductions squared away before proceeding. He then steered the small group to a quiet table, tucked away from the rest of the officers in the lounge. Karl sat across from Jean Yves, not speaking until the drink orders had been taken, then he asked in his fluent French, "Tell me, Jean Yves, were you one of the Dunkirk evacuees?"

Speaking English with a strong accent, the French officer replied, "Yes, I was. The major here tells me you were injured in that operation. Too many good men were lost, and so many are now prisoners of war. It breaks my heart to see what happened. I never ever expected to see my beloved France fall to the Germans. Major Knight told me about your ship. I am so sorry to hear it was a casualty of Dunkirk. On the positive side, now that I have met you, I am enthusiastic about working together. When the time comes for you and me to return to France, I can assure you I will do my best to be the operative you will come to rely on. Major, will it be tomorrow I join Karl or do you have other plans for me?" asked the French captain.

"Jean Yves, I'm afraid It will be quite a while before you start working in the Delta support group. The BIS requires all agents to go through a condensed orientation program before being phased into any operating unit. Poor Karl here went through many months of training just before the outbreak of the war. I can assure you; I will do my best to keep that as short as possible. However, we really need you up and running as soon as possible," replied Clive, recognizing that both these Europeans were anxious to get involved in planning to disrupt the German expansion into French ports and supply lines.

"Jean Yves, would you mind if I just call you Jean? It will make things much easier," said Karl.

"Of course, that will be fine," replied Jean Yves. "From your rank, I'm assuming you're a good learner, so please get back here fast. You haven't even started yet, but I'm already missing you!" By saying that, Karl got everybody laughing, and by the look on Jean's face, he had a new friend who would watch his back when they ventured into harm's way.

Karl threw himself into the new job, even finding out he liked the constant intrigue that was a daily occurrence—the months zoomed by into late autumn. The Christmas season was now upon them; however, staffing the support group had to continue. Along with John and Peggy, Karl volunteered to remain behind to man the support for the Delta Teams. Without most of the personnel in camp, it felt more like a morgue than the busy military camp of only yesterday. Most of its personnel were now with their families and loved ones, spending the Christmas holiday together, the thought of war being the furthest thing from their minds. On most evenings, Karl would sit alone in the lounge, sipping his mild and bitter pint of beer, not a good time to be remembering a Christmas only a few years ago in the cold of a Scottish winter. Those were the times when he and Kitty would take Clive's big Humber to a remote location for an evening of passion, escaping the threats of a war yet to start. These images would forever burn in his mind. Kitty would never celebrate or share the joys of Christmas again. It was that image that blocked him from freely committing to a lasting romance with Hazel.

The New Year came and went with a grand party in the lounge. Karl attended, but unlike his usual, boisterous self, he was very withdrawn, saddened by those haunting memories. Looking at each other, Clive and Bill knew the reason for his sadness. Clive reached over to him, putting his hand on Karl's shoulder, "My dear friend, we know what's going through your mind about now. You must try to let go of those memories, or they will continue to eat you alive." Clive was speaking in a very concerned tone of voice.

"You are right, as usual," replied Karl, fighting again with that following storm cloud in his mind. "I feel like another beer. You blokes care to join me?" Karl was trying to make this a good start to 1941. Excusing himself, Karl wandered over to the operations center to see if any new communiques had been received.

"Only one tonight, Sir. I got this only a few minutes ago. Not sure what it means, though. Take a look, Sir? See if you can make head or tails of it," said the confused operator. The message read, *This next year, it will be the "best."* A smile came across Karl's face.

"Send this reply, will you? *All good with Mother.*" Once again, Karl could feel those clouds of despair rolling away. 1941 would be full of changes and danger for Karl and those around him.

By now, the Delta-1 Team had the naval marine architect working on analyzing the reports and photographs taken of activities in the early stages of construction in Saint-Nazaire. "Sir, this communication arrived late last night from Delta-1. They are pretty convinced those new structures could well be fortified docks for U-Boats," said John, the wireless operator. "It looks like the Huns are going to group their bigger Mark-VII U-Boats along the Atlantic seaboard. Operating from those new bases, the U-Boats will dramatically reduce the time it takes to get out into the Atlantic shipping lanes, extending their range by using less fuel."

The time was now 0900 hours. Karl was leaning against his desk, the communication still in his hand, mulling around in his head the Delta-1 communique. His brain was in overload, thinking, but why so much material for building concrete docks? Could it be those structures are not just reinforced docks? Then, like a lightning bolt, the answer came to him. Karl stood upright, a light going off in his head. He knew exactly what the Germans were up to. "My God, they are building bunkers to protect the boats from air attack. Those buggers are masters at building massive structures like this. Find Major Knight for me straight away," said Karl as he looked at the big wall map, studying the many harbors along the coast with deep water access to support the needs of such submarine bases.

Clive entered the room with Bill hobbling along beside him. "What's the big flap about, Lieutenant?" Clive knew, if Karl had sent for him, there must be something very wrong.

"Come over here to the wall map. See these French ports?" he asked, pointing to the ports of Brest, Bordeaux, La Rochelle, and Saint-Nazaire. "Now, let me read to you a communique that came in last night from Delta-1." Karl pointed to each of the ports as he read the communique. "At first, I thought all that material being taken to those ports would be used to build new docks. However, there was something fundamentally wrong with that thought. The more I studied the wall chart, the more I realized what they were up to. They are going to construct reinforced submarine pens. When finished, they will protect the U-Boats from aerial bombardment by the RAF. When operational in the North Atlantic, these subs will deliver untold havoc to our conveys crossing to England from America and Canada. Gentlemen, our main supply lines are in danger of being severed. Germany is planning to starve this Island into submission; need I say more?" Karl watched the expressions of Clive's and Bill's faces and others that had gathered in the operations office to listen to Karl's assessment of what was happening. They all studied the wall map intently as Karl circled each port with a red grease pencil.

"Lieutenant Vita, we have long suspected that once the Germans had control of France, they would reposition many of their Atlantic U-Boats to these western ports of France, but this soon? God almighty, it's only been a little over six months since Dunkirk!" said Clive loudly, obviously shaken by what Karl had discovered.

After a few minutes, Karl spoke, "Sir, we must get the RAF to start daily reconnaissance flights over these ports, then follow them up with bombing raids. Our strategy should be to disrupt the construction at every phase; creating as many delays in delivering construction materials as possible. Whatever it takes, we must throw roadblocks up to slow down the completion of the submarine pens. I can assure you; I have seen firsthand how effective German civil engineers can be in building structures such as these. When they are operational, there is not a bomber currently available in the RAF that could deliver a big enough bomb to penetrate those fortifications. As I just said, and to repeat, the Germans are masters at projects like this. Gentlemen, time is not on our side." Karl stopped talking while the gravity of what was happening sunk into the small group gathered around the big map of Europe.

In silence, they stood waiting for Major Knight to respond. "Lieutenant, can you be ready tomorrow morning to accompany me to the minister of defense for a meeting with all the heads of each branch of the services? Captain Lowes, even though Captain Jerva is still in orientation and training, get ahold of the base commander and have Jerva brought here today. He must be available to accompany us tomorrow morning. Better still, have the RAF boys fly him down; that's the quickest way. I am calling the French minister in London to have him available for that meeting as well. Lieutenant, your understanding of engineering has identified what those Huns are up to; well done."

Clive, the ever-professional soldier, turned and headed for the door, saying, "Captain Lowes, accompany me; we have work to do."

Karl sat on the corner of his desk, pondering what steps he would recommend to all the ministers and top brass tomorrow in London. "Excuse me, Sir, did I do something wrong?" asked John.

"On the contrary, you did an excellent job by bringing this to my attention." Karl looked back at John, asking. "John, do we have another big map like this one that I can take with me tomorrow? Could you also make a file for me with the last six intelligence reports from Delta-1?"

John hurried off to the supply room to find the wall map then collect the field communications Karl asked for. "You are in luck, Gov," said John, waving a rolled-up map in front of Karl. "Oops, sorry, Sir, for a minute, I thought I was back in my civvy job," said John, trying not to blush at his remark.

"That's alright, John; you can call me that if you prefer." Karl walked over to the big plotting table, then spread out the large map. "John, get some weights to hold the corners down, then bring over some of those grease pencils." Karl marked up the areas of interest, then created a legend with approximate distances to each target. Next, he marked the present locations for Delta-1, 2, and 3 Teams and their proximity to each port. "John, could you find one of those tubes we use for storing maps? Then, you better call over to the typing pool for an assistant.

Make sure they send someone who knows how to type very quickly." Karl spent the rest of the day working feverishly until about 1730 hours with the assistance of the young corporal from the typing pool, compiling multiple copies of various documents that would go into each package.

A loud rap on the door made them look up to see Bill and Jean standing in the doorway. "Mind if we join you, old boy?" asked Bill.

"Please do; we're almost done. Peggy here has been a tremendous help; she stayed on when John left to go home. Thanks again, Peggy, for staying late. I could not have done this without your assistance," said Karl as he finished the last package.

"Jean told me walking down the hallway that he is in the mood for some English fish and chips, so we are heading into Slough. Please join us, Peggy. This boss of yours has been working you too hard," said Bill, looking for approval from Karl and Jean.

"Personally, I would enjoy some female company this evening, so please come with us, Corporal, or may I also call you Peggy?" asked the tall Frenchman.

"Well, Sirs, I was going to go back to my quarters and probably do something with the other girls, but how often does a girl get to go out with three handsome officers? Count me in." Peggy was a young, bubbly, fair-skinned redhead from Bradford in the Midlands. Since joining the ATS, she had worked in the typing pool, always with an eye on working her way up to a permanent position as an assistant in one of the BIS groups.

"All ready?" asked Bill. "Let's get going, shall we? The Bull will still be serving, so if we hurry, we'll be alright," yelled Bill as he hurried the other three out the door and into the waiting staff car.

The drive took all of fifteen minutes. Bill sat in the front passenger seat, Peggy sandwiched between Jean and Karl in the back seat. "Well, I did not expect to be the lady in the middle tonight," said Peggy, loving every minute of being squeezed tightly between two warm-blooded foreigners. The Bull was busy but still had tables available.

"Charlie, are we still in time for fish and chips?" yelled Bill as they trooped into the lounge.

"Be with ya in half a mo', gaffer. Shall I put an order in for four fish and chips then?" he said as he wheeled two big mugs of frothy beer toward two air force privates sitting at the bar.

Once they sat down, Karl asked if he could buy the first round. "What would you like, Peggy?"

"Could I have a pink gin, Sir?"

"Of course, you can, and please call me Karl; we're off duty now and amongst friends in this wonderful old inn. Bill and Jean, will you join me in a pint of mild and bitter?" asked Karl, remembering another time several years back when a beautiful lady by the name of Kitty asked him the same question. Would he like a pint of mild and bitter, a term he had never heard before. That dark cloud was trying to move in and spoil this nice evening.

"Hey, Karl, did you hear me? We said yes to that beer order. It looks like you're drifting away; still thinking about that problem we have, are you?" Bill, saying that, found himself thinking along the same lines. He was the last person to see Kitty alive.

This break away from the office was what they all needed, a brief escape from the dangers lying in wait only a few months into the future. So, with dinner and drinks over, the four headed for the door. "Night, Charlie, see ya soon," yelled Bill as they walked out into the evening air. "Karl, I have to sign Jean into the officer's quarters. Do you mind awfully taking Peggy back to the camp in a taxi? I did not realize the late hour. There's a taxi rank at the next corner, really sorry for doing this; hope you will forgive me, Peggy," said Bill as they waited for the staff car to turn around in front of the Bull.

"No problem, I love the idea of being alone in the back seat of a taxi with Peggy. What do you think, Peggy?" Karl was trying to be his old self, even if it was said in jest.

"I must say, you blokes are showering me with all sorts of compliments tonight," replied a tipsy Peggy. The staff car drove off, and Karl and Peggy walked slowly to the next corner to find a taxi. "The air tonight makes me think of my home in Bradford, although right now, it feels like a million miles away. I can only imagine how you feel, Sir; sorry, I meant Karl." In the dim light of the moon, Peggy reminded Karl so much of Hazel and maybe a little of Kitty. It must be the uniform, he thought.

"We live in troubled times. Our todays may never be repeated; all our tomorrows are a gift. Living for today maybe is all we have," replied Karl as he opened the taxi for Peggy.

"Thank you, kind sir," said Peggy as she slid into the taxi, giving Karl a wonderful view of her nicely shaped legs as she did so. Not tonight, you're not, thought Karl as he slid in beside her. They made small talk driving back, each playing a what-if scenario in their heads as they talked.

"Karl, I'm much younger than you and far less worldly. In fact, Slough is the farthest I've ever been away from Bradford. I guess you could say I'm somewhat naïve about so many things. Over dinner, I listened to you three talking about the many places you all have seen and things you have done. It makes me feel quite sheltered. As you just said, this war makes all of us, and especially me, realize there may be no tomorrow. It would sadden me to think of all I have missed, should something happen that might end it for me." The alcohol was making Peggy a little more open and melancholy than she usually would be in the company of a senior officer, and Karl knew exactly where her mind was taking her.

"Peggy, you should not be talking like this. You have a lifetime ahead of you; there will be time for good and not-so-good adventures. There will be time for new romances, and one day, a lucky someone will be your lasting love." Karl was trying to give her advice about the ups and downs of surviving in this war. Unfortunately, the lecture he was giving Peggy was resonating in his own head. Practice what you preach, he concluded, was not working for himself. The taxi came to a stop in front of the base guardhouse. Karl got out first, noticing Peggy's shapely legs once again as she slid across the seat to get out. Karl paid the driver, then the two walked up to the guardhouse, producing their identification cards for the guard.

Karl, the gentleman, walked Peggy to the entrance of the female quarters. "Well, young lady, here you are, safe and sound; I hope you had a nice time this evening, and again, thanks for staying late to help me. Peggy, your work ethic has really impressed me. You would make someone the perfect assistant." Karl stopped short, letting an idea process in his brain. "Peggy, would you consider coming to work for me if I can swing it? Today was my first day in the department. All that work has made me realize I can't do it all without help, so what do you say, Corporal Townsend?"

In the dim light, Karl studied her face for a sign that she would consider his offer. "Would I consider it? God, you are making a perfect end to this day, Sir. Damn it, I did it again, calling you sir. Karl, I promise you, this will be the best decision you have made on your first day as head of the communication department. You're out tomorrow; can I expect your request for my transfer by week's end?" asked a very excited Peggy.

"By week's end, hell no. You will start the day after tomorrow," answered Karl, enjoying the excitement Peggy was displaying. "Thank you so much; see you soon, good night." Peggy had been given her wish; opening the door, she smiled and cheekily blew Karl a kiss.

CHAPTER 9

OPERATION FREE LAND

The sky was still dark as Karl walked from the officer's quarters to his department in the main building. He enjoyed the cool morning air, thinking *it's so quiet this early in the morning. Even my limp is getting better; there's hardly any pain—not like last week, anyway.* His first stop was to the cafeteria for a big cup of coffee, then on to his office to gather the materials he would need for today's meeting.

He sat down at his desk with time to spare to write an interservice transfer request to his department for Corporal Peggy Townsend. He elaborated on her efficiency the evening before in helping him prepare documentation for a very important meeting. He concluded by asking that this request be expedited with a start day for the following day. Folding the proposal, he sealed it into an inter-department envelope. Karl walked down to the reception desk, manned during the off-duty hours by a guard from the military police. "Morning, would you make sure this gets to the supervisor in charge of clerical staffing first thing this morning? Thank you."

Walking back to his office, Karl decided to stop for a coffee refill before returning to his desk. As he sat, sipping the hot coffee, he started to formulate a convincing proposal he would present to Clive and his operations advisory staff. His proposal would be to authorize a mission for Jean Vyes and himself to be dropped into Southern France to observe firsthand the extent of construction. Furthermore, and if possible, to gain access to German plans for the type and number of submarines to be based along the Atlantic seaboard. *I can't for the life of me see how they would deny this request.* It's probably the most aggressive fact-finding mission proposed to date.

Yes, Clive will make excuses about my injuries. He will argue they should utilize the Delta teams already operating in that region. I need to be ready for that question with a compelling answer. I need to give that more thought driving up to London. Without realizing it, Karl had been back in his office for the best part of an hour.

"Morning, Sir," said John as he removed his tunic and beret, hanging them on the hook by the door. "What did I miss after I left last night?" asked John, sitting down across from Karl with his hot mug of tea.

"Well, it worked out really well; see that stack of folders over there? Thanks to Peggy, we managed to finish what you and I started earlier in the day. As for Peggy, I offered her a permanent position working with us. What do you think of that, John? I hope you approve because you will interface with her more than me," inquired Karl, looking for approval.

"Well, if my opinion matters, I think she will be a welcome addition to the team and very easy on the eyes, I must say." John was grinning at the last part of that statement.

Karl simply smiled, then chuckled in agreement. Karl looked at his watch and guessed he should get going as he entered his office to put on his tunic, then carefully buttoned the top button of his blouse and straightened his tie, not too tightly, though, because of the dressing around his neck. The last thing he did was put on his Sam leather belt with its diagonal shoulder strap. Walking over to the file cabinet, he retrieved his forage cap, placing it on his head to one side; old marine habits don't fade away!

I'm now ready for those boffins in London, he thought as he walked out into the office. The small staff was happy to see their new boss ready to take on the big brass. "Sir, you have a call from the clerical department," said one of the office staff.

"Thank you, Sergeant. Lieutenant Vita here," replied Karl as he put the receiver to his ear.

"Morning, Lieutenant, your request for Corporal Townsend to be transferred has been approved. She is on her way right now. Is there anything else I can help you with?" said Susan McCabe, the senior officer at the other end.

"Thank you so much. I did not expect to see her until tomorrow; no problem, though, we are overloaded with work." Karl hung up the phone and turned toward John with a big beaming smile, saying, "John, Peggy is heading over here; she is starting right away. I'm leaving for that meeting in London. Could you please give her the rundown on how things work around here? That should keep her busy until I return tomorrow morning." Karl was feeling good about how this day was starting. "John, you will have to help me carry all those packages to the car."

As Karl was asking John, a reply came from behind him, "Let me help you, Sir, with those packages! Where do I put my things in the meantime?" asked Peggy, carrying a cardboard box.

"That will be your desk over there, Corporal," said John with a look of approval across his face.

"Right, I'll carry this pile if you can carry the remainder, Sir. Be right back, Sarg! Care for more tea on my way back? Anyone else need some?" asked Peggy, walking confidently toward the door which Karl was holding open.

Three others in the department responded, "Yes, please, milk and sugar if you don't mind."

Walking down the hall, Karl spoke first, "Well, Peggy, you just jump right in, don't you? I like that; I did not expect to see you this morning, though," remarked Karl.

"Well, Sir, my supervisor told me that opportunities like this are few and far between, and if I liked the idea, I should go right away just in case someone else beat me to it. She also said that the new department head is a smashing-looking bloke." Peggy was cheeky with her answer, and Karl, being Karl, loved her boldness.

"See you tomorrow," said Karl, climbing into the back seat of the staff car, giving a cheerful wave to Corporal Townsend.

"It looks like you have brought along everything except the kitchen sink," laughed Clive, sitting in the rear-facing seat. The big staff car had room for five in its double-row interior. Seated next to Clive was Bill, and across from them sat Jean Vyes, the stack of folders placed between Karl and Jean. "Well, chaps, I hope you're ready for today. Everyone attending has voiced concern about the latest findings. I talked last night to a couple of chaps who were in the Kriegsmarine before the war broke out, and they concur with your findings. In fact, they both felt that the best opportunity for the German Navy would be an offensive from U-Boats stationed on the Atlantic seaboard. Moving those boats would also mean increased exposure to aerial attack, so concrete reinforced bunkers would make absolute sense. I did not expect them to move this fast, though."

Clive was watching the eye play between Karl and Jean; how well he knew his friend. "There is something on your mind, Karl; I can tell you want to discuss something, is that correct?" Clive saying that now left the door open for Karl to speak.

"Well, seeing as you know me so well, I might as well share my thoughts with you three before we arrive at the defense department. For the record, Jean here has not heard this before. Sorry about that, Jean; this plan I have was only conceived yesterday. Major, would you make sure that the privacy window is closed before I outline my plan?"

Over the next forty-plus minutes, Karl explained the main points of his plan and how Jean and himself would go undercover. Karl would pose as an officer in the Kriegsmarine, and Jean would pose as a Vichy French Naval Officer assigned to assist in the occupation of French port facilities. Their cover assignment would be to coordinate munitions and spare parts for the four submarine bases being built. Karl finished his proposal, then sat back, waiting for the backlash he knew would follow.

"First, let me say this plan is brilliant. It's very ambitious but also very dangerous. I would, however, ask you why one of the Delta teams could not do this? They are already embedded in France and very familiar with German activities in and around those ports. Why not use them instead of the two of you?"

As Karl was about to speak, Jean butted in, saying, "Sorry, Karl, may I add to this discussion? Karl's plan is aggressive, yes, but let's face it, who better to go undercover than two officers who know their way around ships and ports in Southern France than the two of us working together? If this plan gets approved, we should be given the opportunity to participate. Our countries are the ones that have been overrun when all is said and done, isn't that right, Karl?" Jean had made up his mind that he and Karl should be the ones on this mission.

"Well, it looks like you two have already made up your minds. Karl, remember you are still recovering from those Dunkirk injuries, and have you considered the very high risk of not coming back from a mission such as this?" Clive could see the determination in both their faces. Clive looking up at the roof of the car, thinking, they will never give this up or have someone else do it. It's their lives that are in danger. "Have you given any thought to, if you're captured, what then?" Clive was throwing another roadblock at them. "Remember, Bill here has already seen and felt the cruelty of the Gestapo. Why don't you ask him what that's like? You need to understand that being a tough guy doesn't matter much in the hands of the Gestapo." Clive was now asking Bill to interject.

"Clive is correct; the Gestapo doesn't give a dam about the Geneva Convention or, in fact, any form of humanitarian rights. They have one objective, which is to break you and drain every last piece of information from you, after which, they more than likely will shoot you." Bill remembered his time with the dreaded Gestapo and the daring escape planned by local freedom fighters, ramming the van transporting Kitty and himself to Gestapo headquarters a few years back. His leg was severely injured in that crash, but poor Kitty was killed instantly. Karl sat without saying a word.

"Well, Karl, any more thoughts on this plan of yours?" asked Clive.

"Yes, Sir, I do. Jean and I have a lot of training and research to do when we arrive back tonight, isn't that right, Jean?" With that defiant smile, Karl put out his hand to Jean, who grabbed it, saying, "*Viva la France.*"

Arriving at the very impressive Ministry of Defense Offices in London, they got out of the car. Clive told the driver it could be a long meeting, so he should get something to eat but stay in the building in case he was needed. Karl and Jean, with the help of Bill, carried the packages down a long hallway. At the end, they were asked for their identification cards. The elevator stopped at the third floor, and once again, an MP looked at their IDs, after which he asked them to follow him to the meeting room. The room was large, with a long conference table running down the length of the room. The left wall was all windows; the other three were clad in dark walnut paneling with impressive large pictures to enhance the look of the room. At the head of the room, to one side of the presentation board, hung the biggest picture in the room. King George VI was prominently displayed in his Royal Naval uniform.

"Gentlemen, please come in and have a seat at the front, if you please," said the Right Honorable Winston Churchill. The Prime Minister of England had appointed himself Minister of Defense on May 10th, 1940 and would remain so throughout the war. Present at the meeting were ten high-ranking officers from each of the British services and eight cabinet ministers. Also in attendance were French government officials with staff members from the Free French Army and another from the French Navy.

"Would you take your seats? Coffee and tea are available at the rear of the room, but please refrain from moving about or talking while these gentlemen present their report," requested a high-ranking English Naval attaché.

Clive approached the front of the room, thanking the prime minister and each of the services for making themselves available this morning. "Yesterday, Lieutenant Karl Vita received information that he immediately brought to my attention, and that is the purpose for this meeting this morning. Since the fall of France, we have speculated that the Germans would move quickly to utilize the Atlantic ports for their U-Boat fleet. However, we did not consider they would immediately start constructing heavily reinforced pens for those boats.

Lieutenant Vita is a former Maritime Officer and Structural Engineer; he has extensive knowledge of German Civil Engineering capabilities. During the evacuation of Dunkirk, he volunteered to command an armed trawler, and during that operation, Lieutenant Vita was severely injured. His command was sunk by an aerial attack during their second return trip. We are fortunate to have him here today, not fully recovered yet, but very determined to present his findings at this meeting. Lieutenant, please take it from here," concluded Clive as he returned to his seat.

Karl stood up, approaching the presentation board, which now had the wall map attached to it. He was about to speak when the prime minister rose and started clapping, followed by everyone else. "Young man, we commend your actions. Austria can be proud of its son, and we in England bless our good fortune that you are on our side; now, please proceed." Everyone sat down, turning their attention to Karl and his big map. Jean and Bill passed out the packages to everyone, thanking God that Karl had made more than they anticipated would be needed.

Over the next two-plus hours, Karl made the presentation, making sure that everyone was in total agreement about the severity of what the Germans were doing.

Clive leaned over to Bill and whispered, "He always makes a compelling presentation, every point clearly discussed, never leaves a stone uncovered. We better hope this bunch doesn't try to steal him away from us!"

Karl concluded by adding, "I propose that Captain Jean Vyes Jerva and myself investigate further by going undercover in Southern France." Karl had once again usurped Major Knight from assigning the mission to others in the BIS. Karl now detailed how the mission could be undertaken and what resources would be needed to prepare for such a complicated endeavor. The prime minister turned to the French minister, asking him if he approved of one of his officers taking part in a mission such as this.

"Of course, the captain is an excellent officer. I'm sure that if he can disrupt the German advancements, he will be doing it for Mother France. How can we assist?" concluded the minister, making a saluting gesture to Jean Yves.

"Well, that's settled. Major Knight, you will spearhead this operation through the BIS, and any resources you need will receive the full backing of this office. As for you, Lieutenant Vita, thank you again for an excellent presentation. If I were Major Knight, I would be putting your name in for a well-deserved promotion. Once again, we thank you for your brave contribution to bringing our boys home." The prime minister rose, and once he did that, everyone else did the same, filing out into the hallway.

"Well, let's gather our stuff and head home, shall we? It's been a hell of a day so far," concluded Bill with a smile.

The drive back was a little busy with work traffic and the convoys heading in and out of London. Clive broke the ice by saying, "Nice job, Karl; I think you got across the gravity of what is happening over there very nicely. As for you buggers heading over to the Continent, well, I can assure you, I will not challenge my boss Winny! Tomorrow morning, we will meet to start laying out this plan, shall we, if that's alright with you, Jean? Say, 0830 hours, is that good for everyone? Now, let's get a pint in the lounge, shall we? I believe the new Captain Vita is buying. I'm only following orders from the top, so don't thank me; thank Churchill. A nice follow-up letter would be nice also." Clive could not be more pleased to make this commendation. Their friendship had been through so much, and Karl never stopped impressing him with his planning abilities and a driving commitment to set Europe free once more.

Arriving back at the camp, they all filed into Karl's work area to find that everyone had left except for John and Peggy. They were rearranging the filing system, which had been overdue for some time. "Well, I did not expect to see you two here at this time of the day. I can see some house cleaning going on, is that right?" remarked Karl, putting the map tube down on the planning table. "John, I need this file to be stored in the safe; can you do that for me," asked Karl. "Peggy, I'm assuming you have met these officers already, haven't you?" Karl was engaging Peggy to strike up some dialogue.

"Yes, I have, Sir, but thanks for asking me." Peggy was standing at attention with very senior officers present.

"At ease, Corporal; it's after hours, and your boss is not a big one for strict enforcement of military protocol, so relax, will you? Now, tell me how you like working for Lieutenant Vita? He will be working you very hard; he's known for that," said Clive, thinking too much saluting gets me tired.

"Well, Sir, this is my first full day on the job. I think it will be challenging, and that, I like. If you're done with me, I will head out. I promised to meet up with my roommates for a pint." Peggy was still a little uncomfortable around such senior officers.

"Please remember, young lady; in the BIS, mum's always the word." Clive was making sure whatever happens in this office stays in this office. Peggy and John headed for the coat rack at the back of the room, putting on their tunics, caps, and shoulder bags containing the mandatory gas mask and steel helmet.

"Goodnight, Sirs, see you tomorrow."

"Is that the new girl you hired earlier today?" asked Clive, obviously taken by her looks.

"Way too young for you, you randy old bugger. She would probably kill you if you ever got that far," said Karl, laughing and very pleased to see his friend taken by the new corporal.

"Alright, enough of this standing around. Let's wander down to the lounge, shall we? Karl, you did agree to buy the first round, did you not?" said Clive, walking ahead of the others.

"Why don't you chaps go on ahead and get a table? I'll be along shortly," said Karl as he walked over to the night wireless operator's station. "Any important messages that I need to be aware of, Corporal?" Karl really wanted to see if Hazel had sent news.

"Nothing of real importance. This one came in earlier today from Delta-3," said the operator. After reading the communication, Karl gave it back to be filed in the daily log. Walking down the hall to the lounge, he started thinking about agents he would recommend for consideration for the upcoming mission and their cover stories. I wonder if we can meet up with the Delta-1 team? Jean would like to work with those agents; that's a given. The advantage is, they are already in Southern France. Hazel is part of that team; that could create difficulties. Gunther would agree with me on this logic. Karl stopped his planning as he entered the lounge.

"Over here, Karl," yelled Bill over the noisy bar crowd.

"My God, this is a very noisy place tonight. I guess we will put aside any business-related talk for tonight anyway," said Karl loudly, so everyone could hear him.

The following morning, the team gathered in meeting room #3, along with Sheryl and Peggy taking the meeting notes. "Gentlemen, this first meeting is to organize the strategy and assets for Operation Free Land. Captain William Lowes will be the operation director once the plan has been cast in stone. Along with the support team yet to be assigned, they will back up Captain Jerva and Captain Vita while they are in Southern France. Now, let's begin by having Captain Vita bring us up to date on the plan, shall we?" Clive now turned the floor over to Karl and the stack of support documents they would all study repeatedly until there was no chance of a slip-up or mistake that could derail the operation.

This intense training and coordination continued daily for five days, heavily charged with role-playing and rehearsing the parts Karl and Jean would play. Their stories had to be exact and traceable, should their identities be questioned or challenged. That part yet had to be formulated. A timetable of sequences was also to be documented. They discussed who would join them in the field, timing events, and a list of French Resistance Fighters who could be trusted with the plan. Jean and several fellow French officers also present at the meeting would take charge of organizing these contacts and exploring suitable parts that he and Karl would play in the operation. The final detail would be the date and place for their extraction, assuming they would be coming home at the completion of the mission.

At the end of each day, all the support plans, charts, photographs, and mountains of other vital documentation would be stored in a very large safe that had been installed in M-3. The room itself had military police inside as well as outside the entrance, securing it until the following morning, then taking stations at the entrance throughout the day. Karl and Jean got fitted for their uniforms; then photographs were taken, ready to be inserted into their forged documents. Their uniforms were altered from the original issue; they had to be very convincing. Even their watches, cigarette lighters, cigarettes, and sidearms had to be fool-proof; nothing was left to chance.

The drop was changed from parachuting into France to being flown in by a Royal Airforce Lysander aircraft further North.

Then they would make their way by road into Southern France. A German driver loyal to the Free French had disclosed that two officers would be traveling to port facilities down the Atlantic coast, compiling information on the construction planning. Jean, seeing this report, said, "Here is our perfect cover story. We will take their places and modify their documents that can be forged, ready for new photographs by the partisans. Once this is done, no one will suspect us." By taking their places, Jean and Karl had the perfect cover story.

Two officers would have to lose their lives making this happen, and the partisan group had no problem sending these unlucky chaps to their maker. Once in Southern France, they would commence their new roles as inspectors for the German Supply Corp. A Vichy French Naval Officer would accompany the German officer. The same German driver would now be driving Karl and Jean along the same route in the same Kubelwagen. Their story was close to being ironclad.

Wednesday morning, the day was drizzling rain but perfect for the evening drop into occupied France. "I guess this is where I say thank you for all the hard work you have done; *au revoir* as we French say," said Jean, putting his raincoat and cap on, then picking up his canvas carry bag and heading for the door.

"I'll be along in a minute, Captain. I need just a few minutes with my people before we head out, alright?" Karl wanted to speak privately to his hard-working staff. "I can't believe it's time for us to head out. But, God willing, we will be back amongst you once our work is completed. Please think of us and look for those communications on our progress. Thank you all again." Karl reached for his raincoat that hid the German uniform until they were on board the aircraft. In the lobby, Clive and Bill waited to say their goodbyes, neither one wishing to say more. This mission was very dangerous, and with that came the high probability this would be the last time one or both would be in Slough.

The drive to RAF Tangmere was uneventful; neither one of them really wanted to talk. Their thoughts were of family and loved ones and that this could well be the last operation they would participate in. It was dark when they finally arrived at the base and home for the 161 Squadron. The lorry rumbled out over the grass to the waiting Lysander aircraft, stopping at its tail. Three uniformed RAF privates approached the lorry, saluted, then took the luggage. The only acknowledgment they made was, "Evening, gents, your pilot this evening will be Lieutenant Ronald Cooke. The aircraft is warmed up and ready to depart."

Cooke yelled from the cockpit, "Evening, chaps, climb aboard. Then, I need to review what you need to know about this night flight and especially the speedy turnaround once we land. Now, climb up that ladder behind me; mind those boxes and bags. We are also delivering tonight. Once we land, it will be your job to hand down those bags and boxes to the blokes waiting below on the field. The time on the ground will be less than three minutes, so move smartly. Once we are in the air, I will be wave-hopping over the channel at approximately 50 or so feet until we reach the French coast. Then, I'll tree hop until we get to the designated landing field, a little over an hour away. When we reach the landing area, I will circle the field, flashing a coded recognition signal, using a signal light on the underside of the fuselage, which I operate with my left foot. If we get a return signal, they will put out fire buckets to illuminate the landing strip. Try to get comfortable; strap in, and let's be off."

Captain Cooke fired up the big Bristol Mercury radial engine, its nine-cylinder engine producing a cloud of exhaust smoke as it thundered into life, sending vibrations throughout the aircraft and its crew. Releasing the brakes, the Lysander moved forward; then, it turned toward the grass runway with the right brake squealing. Captain Cooke, standing on the brakes, brought the engine up to full power. As he released the brakes, the big single-engine aircraft leaped forward; in less than nine-hundred feet, it left the grass runway, climbing into the velvet blackness of the night sky.

The time to the coast was short, followed by a quick drop down to fifty feet as they headed toward the French coast. Captain Cooke called back, "I will be flying at this height until I have the French coast in sight. Then, I'll climb only enough to clear the cliffs and the line of trees; enjoy this wild ride, gents." In the very noisy rear cockpit, talking was almost out of the question.

Karl moved close to Jean's ear, yelling, "This flight is quite nerve-racking—a little exciting, though. But, these pilots have nerves of steel, don't you agree?" Jean simply nodded his head in agreement before turning toward the plexiglass canopy, watching the whitecaps of the channel fly by. Karl's legs were wedged between two big sacks and a long wooden crate. This flight was not about passenger comfort; he too was watching the breaking whitecaps that seemed to be reaching up to capture the Lysander as it flew by at over two hundred miles per hour.

Through the half-moon and clouds, Captain Cooke could see the coast rapidly approaching. "Chaps, we are almost over the French coast. It won't be long now." From here on, the pilot would be watching for higher trees, telegraph poles, wires, towers, and other tall structures, such as the occasional church steeple. After about twenty minutes, the pilot climbed, then throttled back, banking to the left in a big circle.

A flashing signal lamp tapped out a Morse code recognition signal from the ground as the plane flew overhead. On the next pass, Captain Cooke responded with the aircraft's signal lamp on the underside of the fuselage. "That's it, chaps; get ready. We need to be moving very quickly once our wheels touch down." Captain Cooke looked at his watch; it was 2212 hours. He was thinking, I need to airborne no later than 2220 hours. The field, completely black only a minute ago, now blazed a path for the Lysander to touch down safely. The big wheels shook the aircraft as they bounded through the uneven grass to a stop in less than three hundred and fifty feet. Turning the plane around, Captain Cooke taxied back down the field to where the signal lamp was flashing. Applying the brakes, he came to a full stop, throwing the plexiglass canopy up against its stop.

"Alright, you two, out you go. Hand those bags and boxes down first. Please, be safe out there; I look forward to maybe seeing you on your return trip." Captain Cooke kept the big radial engine idling, ready to depart within minutes. Karl climbed down behind Jean, jumping the last two rungs of the ladder—not a wise thing to do considering his right leg. Two men moved quickly up the boarding ladder, past Karl and Jean, making a silent gesture of good luck. Once inside, the new passengers knew the drill, pulling down and locking the canopy. With a wave from his cockpit, Captain Cooke gunned the engine, speeding off down the makeshift grass runway. The French partisans doused the fire buckets as the aircraft went by, then carried them off to the waiting lorry. Any evidence that a plane had been there only minutes before was now gone.

Karl and Jean remained beside the bags and boxes until a man approached them, whispering in French, "We must get away from here; please, move quickly. You never know if the Bosh is close by. My name is Albert; we can talk in the lorry. Now, let's get going, shall we? The other men will carry these supplies you brought with you to the lorry." Walking fast, half-running, they reached the old Citroen parked between a clump of trees and bushes. Two men helped them climb up the tailgate into the canvas-covered cargo bed, the supplies being handed up behind them. "Good, now we can leave. Welcome home, Captain, and to you also, Sir. Your mission code names we already have. Which one of you is the Vichy French officer?" asked Albert.

"That would be me. In this light, it's hard to see our faces and uniforms, so yes, that's me, Lieutenant Claude Marceau. This is the Kriegsmarine officer, Lieutenant Herbert Krause, very pleased to meet you all," replied Claude, speaking once again in his native French and using his assigned mission name.

"The identities for the two officers you are masquerading as were shot only yesterday. We are not merciless killers. They could have given you away if they were to escape, knowing our plans. We could not take that chance. These are not the kindest of times; I'm sure you will agree. Now, you know why we told your people in Slough to use those names." Albert stopped talking momentarily, allowing the two intelligence officers to process the cover story. "Once we arrive at the safe house, you will meet your driver, Sergeant Rudy Muller, a loyal German to the Allies; he is the one that drove those two officers down yesterday from Rennes in their Kubelwagen. Starting tomorrow, this will be your transport for the time you are here in Southern France.

"A little over a week ago, we discovered we had found our perfect cover for you two. Those unsuspecting officers were heading to Saint-Nazaire on a fact-finding mission. We were fortunate to intersect that communique for this particular trip, swapping their driver for Muller before they set off from Rennes. This could not have worked out better," concluded Albert, now passing around a bottle of French wine with some bread and cheese, saying, "This should keep you going until we reach the safe house. Wine is easier to come by these days than water." Albert and the others in the lorry started laughing; it was a good introduction for the two weary travelers.

The lorry turned into a narrow lane, slowed to cross a stream, then turned again into a long driveway. It stopped to flash its headlights as it approached the old barn and waited for a return signal before it proceeded into the farmyard, momentarily waiting for doors to swing open. Inside, the partisans moved quickly to hide the supplies unloaded from the lorry in a room hidden by a haystack, its door ingeniously concealed with hay. Inside the old farmhouse kitchen, the partisans gathered around to greet the new arrivals. Albert once again passed around several bottles of wine before they all sat down at the table, waiting for the rabbit stew still steaming on the blackened wood stove.

"Gentlemen, tomorrow morning, you will start your mission. The first stop will be the docks, where construction is moving very quickly. Many of the French civilian dock workers are loyal to our cause; however, with that said, some will report you for a reward. Hunger for their families makes them turn to stool pigeons for the Bosh. Our people on the docks will do their best to shield you from these traitors; however, you yourselves must be acutely aware of those around you." Albert stopped talking as the hot stew was passed around the table.

The following two hours were spent refining the plan to gather information and get copies of blueprints if the opportunity presented itself with the miniature camera brought by Claude. "Gentlemen, we should adjourn for today. Try to rest tonight as tomorrow will be very taxing."

In the upstairs room, Herbert laid on top of the squeaky old bed, tossing and turning; sleep would not come easy this night. In his mind, he kept asking himself the same question: if my cover is blown, will I be strong enough to withstand the brutal methods used by the Gestapo? If it becomes too much that I cannot maintain my silence, I am prepared to use the cyanide capsule wedged at the back of my mouth between my molars. These thoughts weighed heavily on his mind; however, sleep eventually overcame him in the early hours' past midnight.

Albert's voice quietly awoke him, saying, "You need to get up and get ready, Herbert; it's almost 0600 hours."

"Thanks, Albert; I will be right down." Herbert felt the chill in the air. He opened the bedroom door and walked down to the small closet, where the commode was kept. As he opened the door, the intense smell made him gag. He thought, I better get used to that perfumed aroma, I guess. Back in his room, he crossed over to the table that had a jug of water and a basin on it for him to have a painfully cold shave. Next, he made sure his uniform was properly adorned with its insignias in the correct locations. Feeling much warmer now that he was dressed, he stood in front of the cracked wall mirror to make sure one more time he would pass any scrutiny by Germans at the base. He thought, I must admit, these Kriegsmarine uniforms are very smart. It's a pity the wrong side wears them.

Downstairs, Claude was drinking hot coffee, standing against the sink, his brown knee-high boots shining in the morning light. Other familiar faces in the kitchen were doing the same, drinking strong hot coffee, with the addition of one new face dressed in a German Wehrmacht uniform. "You must be Muller, is that correct?" asked Herbert, speaking German.

"Yes, I am, Sir; glad to make your acquaintance."

"And a fine good morning to the rest of you," said Herbert in a cheerful French voice, "I hope you all slept well last night. Let me get some coffee; then we can coordinate today's plan."

Convinced their plan was watertight, the partisans retrieved their weapons from the hiding place behind the stove, then filed out the door to the waiting lorry. "Muller, are you ready, my friend?" said Herbert, speaking in German to the driver.

"I am, Sir." Standing up and straightening his uniform, he was a tall figure of a proud German soldier. The three walked over to the barn, where the doors were already open with the Kubelwagen facing out in front of the Citroën lorry. "Shall I leave the canvas top down, Sir, or would you rather I put it up?" asked Muller.

"No, leave it down. Let's look the part, shall we?" said Claude, climbing into the back seat ahead of Herbert.

"The drive will take about fifty minutes. I will stay to the main roads just in case other partisan squads see us and decide we should be killed," said Muller, laughing. The roads were jam-packed with convoys of heavy equipment heading toward Saint-Nazaire and the other French ports.

"When the Germans decide to undertake a new construction project, they are a force to be reckoned with," said Herbert. "Muller, before you drive us to the port, swing by the Hotel Lutetia so that we can check-in. I'm assuming you know the directions to the Boulevard Raspail. After that, you can drive us right into the dock area. Naturally, we must act the arrogant German part. At the port entrance, they stopped at the guardhouse to show their credentials, asking directions to the headquarters for the construction offices. Muller pulled up in front of the building, ran around to the passenger door, and saluted the two officers as they stood to exit the vehicle, saluting as they did so.

"Park close by; I'm not sure what will happen in there. If you suspect something is going south, leave and return to the safe house. Don't attempt to find us. Is that clear, Muller?" said Herbert. Inside the building, they looked for the construction or engineering office, finding a sign hanging over an office marked project engineering about halfway down the hall.

"Here we go; are you ready?" said Claude.

Opening the door, they entered to find rows of desks and drafting tables lining both sides of the sizable area. An officer, wearing the regular gray uniform of a captain in the Wehrmacht approached them, saying, "State your business," as he raised his arm in a Sieg Heil salute.

"We are here to inspect the progress being made on the new submarine pens. Here are our orders," said Herbert in an arrogant-sounding voice. The officer inspected their identification cards and then reviewed the orders issued by the office of Admiral Donitz.

"This document instructs this office to give you full access to all areas. What would you like to review first?" asked Captain Max Meyer, now showing a friendlier side to his personality. "Gentlemen, before we continue, would you excuse me while I verify you being here? It's just a formality; I'm sure you understand." Meyer picked up a desk phone, instructing the operator to put him through to Headquarters. "Major Schneider, Meyer here; the two officers you sent down have arrived. I'm just confirming the orders they presented, Sir." Meyer stood up and, with a scared tone, answered, "Of course, I will show them every courtesy, Major, thank you." Meyer's attitude had done an about-face after getting an earful from his superior officer. Turning, he approached Herbert and Claude, saying, "Gentlemen, thank you for your understanding; I think we should start by reviewing the routing schedule and corresponding time schedules, followed by a review of the current construction blueprints. I'm sure there will be many changes before the project is completed. The construction has not really started. We are still clearing the site of old buildings and equipment," explained Captain Meyer.

"So, I'm assuming there has not been any progress such as cement slurries or steel forms and footings forms, is that correct?" asked Herbert, not taking his gaze off Meyer. "Captain Meyer, if the schedule I handed you is acceptable, we can proceed." Herbert seized the opportunity to get the upper hand. "Captain Marceau would like a tour of the port facilities, so while I do my due diligence here in the office, you can escort the captain on that tour. This way, we will be out of your hair that much sooner." Herbert was pushing the envelope, but then again, this was the nature of being an agent in the BIS.

"I will leave Sergeant Grucker to assist you in your review and for the security of all documents," said Captain Meyer, giving Herbert a questioning look. "Captain Marceau, shall we get started?" said Captain Meyer, directing the Vichy French officer to the door.

"Grucker, let's start by reviewing the layout schematic, followed by the material requirements, shall we?" commanded Herbert. The documentation was extensive, like most German military documentation. The files are extremely well prepared, thought Herbert as he started his review. How can I take pictures of these prints with that Grucker breathing over my shoulder? The other two will be back in an hour or two, so whatever I need to do must be very soon. Herbert's mind raced for an answer.

Over the next thirty minutes, Herbert reviewed the files, making mental notes of which ones needed copying. Once he was ready, Herbert broke out into a coughing fit, attempting to clear his throat as part of the act.

"Grucker, can you find me some pain tablets and some water? I have been fighting a sore throat for most of the week. Also, a mug of hot coffee would be appreciated." Herbert was silently praying the corporal would oblige his request.

"Would you like milk and sugar with that coffee, Sir?" Once Grucker had left, Herbert sprang into action. He reached inside his uniform for the miniature camera. Time was against him.

Would he be able to copy all the documents in such a short time? As Herbert got to the last blueprint, he heard the door at the far end of the office opening. Slamming the camera shut, he quickly returned the camera to the concealed pocket inside his tunic, then resumed his masquerade of pondering the document in front of him, continuing the cover story by coughing.

"That does not sound good, Sir. Maybe you should continue this tomorrow. Here are the tablets and water. I also brought you a pot of coffee in case you would like more than one cup. Grucker was showing concern for the captain. He really is a nice, considerate chap; pity he is on the wrong side, thought Herbert as he downed the pain medication with the glass of water.

"I thought the medication I took earlier this morning would last for most of the day. I guess I misjudged. I should have brought more with me. Hopefully, these tablets you just gave me will carry me for the rest of the day," concluded Herbert. Herbert continued his construction review for the next forty-five minutes when suddenly he stumbled onto a file labeled structural specifications update. The document inside clearly described how thick the roof of the bunkers would be, along with the extent of the steel rod reinforcements to be used. Herbert looked around to see where Grucker was. Luckily, he was returning the blueprints to a flat storage drawer where they were kept. Herbert reached inside his briefcase and removed a small pad and a pencil. He started to scribble down the most pertinent information. The reinforced roof would be a minimum thickness of over eight meters (twenty-six feet). The total number of sub pens was fourteen, eight of which were dry docks. Each pen could accommodate two U-Boats. Other details included sixty-two workshops, one hundred and fifty offices, ninety-two dormitories for sub crews, four kitchens, two bakeries, two power stations, a hospital, and a restaurant. As he took down this information, he kept looking over his shoulder to see what Grucker was doing.

Returning the pad and pencil to his case, he returned to reviewing additional files for the build schedule. The actual construction would not commence until February 1941—only a week away. The file had a routing schedule with a projected completion date of June 1942. One last document had the overall dimensions, approximately three hundred meters (nine hundred and eighty-five feet long) by one hundred thirty meters wide (four hundred and twenty-six feet). This is a very ambitious construction plan, thought Herbert. Considering the other ports involved in this project, I think the Germans will use forced labor from other European countries and those here in France.

The office door opened, and in walked Captain Meyer with Claude behind him. "Well, are you satisfied with the extent of the documentation we have on file?" asked Meyer as he pointed toward a small table at the side of the room.

"Yes, I am very impressed with the extent of detail and the preciseness of the routing sheets; well done, Captain. I must also compliment you on how accommodating Corporal Grucker has been. I had a coughing episode earlier. Thanks to the corporal, he found me some tablets, water, and a pot of coffee. I took two tablets this morning and thought they would last all day; that was a mistake. I'm feeling much better now, thank God." Herbert was eyeballing Claude as he explained the incident to Meyer. He was also sending him a signal that he had successfully photographed most of the files they needed. He also removed any doubt Meyer might have at finding out he was alone for a while when Grucker left the office.

"Well, do you need anything else while you have my attention?" asked Meyer, really wanting to get rid of these two empire builders.

"Only one request, and you may have already covered this on your tour earlier. I would like to observe the actual construction site if that's not too much trouble."

"Not at all. Will you both be accompanying me?" asked Meyer, standing up to get ready to leave.

"Captain Marceau, I would like you to accompany us as well," said Herbert, again looking at his partner in this deception. The three walked outside to Meyer's Mercedes staff car. "One moment, please.

Let me tell our driver we won't be much longer. The poor fellow has been standing around all morning. Muller, why don't you get yourself some coffee? We'll be back shortly."

Herbert was acting very much like a considerate Austrian, but then again, he was. Arriving at the construction site, Herbert walked confidently around the area. Stopping at the bulkhead, he looked over to the narrow entrance and the lock gates that led to the outer harbor. He thought, I wonder if these arrogant Huns have considered that lock to be a potential choke point if it is bombed. "Captain, there is one observation I have. That lock, if bombed, could stop any coming or going of submarines. What contingencies are there in place if this lock was indeed blown up?" asked Herbert, using the same tactic he used back in 1938 in Kiel when he gave the shipbuilders an observation about adding extra shielding on the incomplete aircraft carrier *Graf Zeppelin*. Giving useful advice can sometimes work if it makes a real contribution to the project. This tactic generated a higher level of confidence, and this time was no different as Herbert confidently pointed to the locks.

"Excellent observation, Captain. I can see you are already looking at the downfall of this harbor, and you are absolutely correct. When we first considered this location, that entrance nearly made us reconsider its viability. The newly revised blueprints, which unfortunately I do not have here, detail the construction of a reinforced roof like the submarine pens. This addition will prevent any aerial attack from happening." Meyer had a big smile on his face, pleased to see these visitors were volunteering constructive criticism to this monumental project. "Gentlemen, what are your plans for tomorrow? Your orders said to give you the time you needed before you move on to your next location at La Rochelle, is that correct?" asked Meyer.

"No, that's being handled by another group. Our next stop will be in Bordeaux," replied Herbert, thinking this bloke is trying to trick me.

"Oh, that's correct; sorry, I got my ports mixed up," replied Meyer, his smile more like a smirk as he acknowledged his mistake.

"I believe we have most of what we need. We can always return if we need more clarity; wouldn't you agree, Captain Marceau?" asked Herbert in perfect French, just to irritate Meyer. "Oh, I'm sorry, Captain. I forgot you don't speak any French." Herbert was deliberately intimidating the German officer by speaking in French. Back at the main building, they thanked Captain Meyer for his time and help. Before climbing back into the Kubelwagen, they turned, raising their arms with a Heil Hitler Salute, then were seated. "Drive on, Muller," said Herbert in a loud voice.

"Well, that went well, don't you think?" said Claude.

"Yes, and maybe no. However, I'm willing to bet that bloody Meyer will be calling around about our visit," replied Herbert.

"Why did he not do that while we were there?" asked Claude.

"Those types are sneaky. They will not do that in front of you.

They are concerned about reprisals should they say something wrong or put themselves into a compromising position, gutless swine," answered Herbert. They drove out of the harbor, out of harm's way for a while anyway. "Let's go to the hotel, shall we? It's time for a cocktail; what do you say, chaps? Muller, why don't you change into civilian clothes and join us in the lounge? No need for you to be alone tonight. Before you do that, take this film and give it to Albert's men waiting at the hotel. Pull over while I take a picture of my handwritten notes, then you can pass it on." Herbert was feeling so much better than he did this morning.

Upstairs, Herbert opened the door to his room and placed his bag on the bed. He was thinking, tonight, I will sleep well. Herbert returned to the lobby. Not finding Claude, he strolled over to the lounge and found him waiting at a secluded table in an alcove off the restaurant. "This will do just fine. Let's sit here and wait for Muller, shall we?" said Claude, pleased with this very secure table.

"I think we obtained some really meaningful information today. Don't you agree? That Meyer fellow is typical of the arrogant representation and attitude of the German officer corps." Herbert was displaying his continued dislike for the new German military.

"Not all Germans are evil. Look at Muller. He wore the uniform until he saw what the Nazi Party was doing to his country. He was one of the few who decided to do something about it by joining the resistance fighters. From the top down, there are thousands of Germans who are secretly scared to speak up or act against the Brown Shirts, the Gestapo, and S.S. officers. They refrain from making their opinions public in fear of painful reprisal. Their families' safety comes first, and it's that fear that makes them subservient. It simply amazes me that just a few power-hungry evil bastards can control the masses using brutality and the control it generates," remarked Claude, a Frenchman who refused to surrender to the victorious Germans or the traitorous Vichy French puppet government.

Muller entered the lounge, looked around, then crossed over to their table. "Sorry for taking so long. My quarters are all the way at the back of the hotel. I also took care of that matter you asked me to do for you, Captain." Muller was confirming the transfer of the roll of film to one of Albert's men.

"Let's get our drink orders, shall we? Then we'll decide if we have enough information from this first day or if we need to return tomorrow morning," said Herbert, putting the question out to the other two for their input.

"Well, while you two were with that pig, Meyer, I managed to strike up a conversation with some of the lower-ranking military fellows. It's quite amazing what you can gather with useless gossip. One of the drivers was from Hamburg. He told me that before the war started, he had a woodworking shop. He really had no choice; he was required to enlist. He also said quietly to me that most of his neighbors were deeply concerned that Germany was taking on more than it could handle and asked what I thought. I, of course, evaded giving him a response in case he was a plant. He went on to tell me that most of the present labor used in the port was rounded up from French towns and villages surrounding Saint-Nazaire. Still, due to the extent of the project, they were shipping additional labor down from Poland and other countries that were now under German occupation. This included prisoners from the POW camps. The fear some Germans have with this is how much sabotage will there be from those workers?"

Muller had found out a critical piece of information. Could the BIS and Free French recruit from this new labor pool? "Nice work, Muller; that can help us down the road," said Claude, thinking these POWs could also be a good source for new recruits for Albert's partisan group.

"Claude, how did your tour of the docks and work areas go?" asked Herbert.

"What I expected, most of the docks and piers are in bad shape. Some you can see were deliberately smashed in a hurry with whatever means the dock workers could find once they knew France was lost. I also gathered that many of these workers were here before the war, and from the way they looked at my uniform, I would say they would willingly strike a blow for Mother France, given the opportunity. There are others I gathered would sell you out for a few francs; you could see the hate in their eyes. As for the dock equipment, the larger derricks and rail mules, for the most part, are operable but in desperate need of servicing. If you look at one of those schedules, there is a substantial amount of documentation on the condition of existing equipment."

The discussion went on for about an hour longer before Herbert said, "I'm calling it quits for tonight. We can decide in the morning if we are moving on to the next location or remaining here in Saint-Nazaire. Good night, chaps, and thank you for a job well done." Herbert stood up and left the table. Tomorrow would be another hectic day of deception.

Herbert rose at 0530 hours, put his trousers and shirt on, picked up his toilet pouch, not forgetting his briefcase, then headed down the hall to the bathroom. At that time of the morning, there was no one around—another reason to claim the bathroom before anyone else could beat him to it. Back in his room, he packed the small suitcase, then headed down to the lobby. He gave a waitress a coffee order, then settled in on the couch to wait for Claude. This hotel must be one the Germans have a contract with—too many military uniforms not to, thought Herbert as he sat drinking his coffee, watching the traffic in the lobby.

After about twenty minutes, Claude entered the lobby. "Fancy breakfast or are you fine with just coffee?" asked Herbert.

"Coffee will be fine for me," answered Claude. "Herbert, I think we should move on. I have a funny feeling about going back down to those docks. It's almost like a voice in the back of my head is telling me that someone down there could recognize one of us and turn us in for a reward, and that thought concerns me. I may be overreacting, but my sixth sense is telling me we should leave this morning." Claude was showing Herbert a side of himself he did not expect to see.

"Claude, we really don't have a reason to stay. We have almost everything we came for, so you're right. Best not to push our luck. Drink up, and let's check out. Do you have your voucher for last night?" After listening to Claude, Herbert was starting to feel relieved that they were leaving Saint-Nazaire.

At the reception desk, Herbert asked to use a telephone, "Please, connect me to the operator at the port." Herbert waited for the call to go through, then asked for Captain Meyer's extension.

A voice at the other end replied, "Captain Meyer's office."

"Morning, Captain Krause here. Could you locate Captain Meyer for me?" asked Herbert.

Meyer picked up the phone, and in a friendly voice, said, "Captain, I was just wondering what time I would see you this morning."

"Well, we have decided to move on to our next stop. Last night, we reviewed what you showed us and felt there is really no reason to return this morning. We would be wasting your time. Thank you so very much for the assistance you gave us; it was appreciated. We will be in touch very soon. Again, thank you." Herbert hung up the phone, feeling so much better about their decision.

Meyer said goodbye, then sat thinking about his visitors from yesterday. *There is something that doesn't feel right. I just might call the base commander in Bordeaux and convey my thoughts—that I'm suspecting they may not be who they say they are. I need to think about that carefully, though.*

After checking out, they walked out of the hotel, looking for Muller. They found him talking to several other drivers waiting by their vehicles. "Good morning, Sirs. Did you sleep well? Will we be returning to the port this morning?" Muller could sense from the expressions on their faces that the answer would be no.

"No, Muller, we are heading to our next stop in Bordeaux instead. So, let's get going, shall we?" replied Claude, stepping into the rear passenger seat of the Kubelwagen, followed by Herbert.

"When I spoke to Meyer a little while ago, he sounded almost relieved to hear we would not be returning this morning. However, I also got the feeling he was not totally convinced our visit was above board, just a feeling I was having," said Herbert, now having doubts about the next port inspection.

CHAPTER 10

Prisoner of the Gestapo

The drive to Bordeaux took over four hours. Little was said as they had their own reasons to question what they were doing. It was war, and this was their job. Herbert broke the silence, saying, "The forged documents we are using are the same in every respect as the originals, other than the ID picture and country of origin; is that correct, Muller?" asked Herbert.

"Yes, Sir, they have been printed on the same paper, using the same ink, the same typeset, and page size; the seals are copied from Donitz's own stamp. Everything is exactly the same; why do you ask?" replied Muller.

"I was just contemplating… if Meyer decided to investigate further into our visit, could he uncover anything or trace that these documents are forged?" Herbert speaking like this was starting to concern the other two.

"Are you suggesting we should call this mission off? I thought we were doing very well in our role-playing yesterday," said Claude, now questioning Herbert's statement.

"As an intelligence officer, it is always best to proceed with extreme caution. Sometimes, when you think you have the perfect cover is when someone will try to trick you. So, if I am sending caution signals to you both, it's because, yesterday, Meyer tried a couple of times to test me. Luckily, I was onto him. He realized I was not playing his game. I believe that, by now, he has called the base commander in Bordeaux to give a head's up and perhaps even the Headquarters of Admiral Donitz. Think more about this. When we decided not to return, it probably triggered Meyer's instinct that we could well be foreign agents," concluded Herbert.

"So, what are your thoughts right now? Are we in harm's way? Should we continue? Perhaps we could consider modifying our cover story. Herbert, you're the leader on this mission. Tell us what is going on in your head at this point?" concluded Claude.

"When we get to our hotel, I am going to call Meyer's office. I will tell him that once we have completed our inspection of the progress in Bordeaux, we intend to return to Saint-Nazaire to make one last inspection before we conclude our findings and return to our headquarters." Herbert had a new plan that would create fear in Meyer's head. "Chaps, we must plant in Meyer's thick head that, as part of our inspection tour, we will be submitting a progress comparison on both commands at each facility. Making this call could well put Meyer on the defensive and perhaps make him think twice about pursuing any further investigation into who we could be. That, gentlemen, is our story; let's pray it works. How long to the hotel, Muller?" concluded Herbert.

"Should be there in about thirty minutes, Sir," replied Muller. Arriving at the hotel, Herbert immediately called Meyer's office. "Captain Meyer, I'm so glad I got through to you this afternoon. After we have completed our inspection tomorrow, we will be returning to Saint-Nazaire for one more visit. Please make yourself available. Sorry for such short notice; we just received additional instructions only an hour ago. Have a nice evening." Herbert hung up the phone, thinking, I hope that worked.

The following morning, they met early to rehearse their cover story, then proceeded to the dining room for a light breakfast. Muller drove them to the main entrance and presented his ID card to the gate guards. The guards then moved to the rear of the Kubelwagen, saying, "Your papers, Captains, and your purpose for being here." The guards were businesslike with no intent of being polite to the occupants of the Kubelwagen. One of the guards took all three sets of documents into the guardhouse. From their seats, they watched him as he made a telephone call. As the guard listened, he kept nodding his head, agreeing with whoever was on the opposite end of that telephone. Finally, the guard returned, saying, "Corporal, once

I open the barrier, pass through and park over there next to that black Mercedes. Stay in your car until your escort arrives." The guard stepped back, snapping his arm upward in a Heil Hitler salute.

"Not a friendly sort, is he?" said Claude as they waited patiently for their escort to arrive. Herbert was becoming nervous; that sixth sense was telling him that something was not right.

"Muller, turn the car around and exit the gate. I will tell the guards we will be back very soon. I have forgotten some very important documents in the hotel safe; do it now." Muller turned the Kubelwagen around, then approached the gate.

Herbert leaned forward to tell the guards why they were leaving. "Remain here," said the guard as a gray Mercedes car screeched to a halt, blocking the exit. As this was happening, a black Mercedes did the same behind them. They were completely blocked in. Four armed guards from the front car and three more from the rear car sprinted over to them with their weapons at the ready.

"Hands up and get out of the car. Do not attempt to reach for your sidearms. We are ordered to shoot if you attempt that."

The lieutenant in charge walked up to them, saying, "You are all under arrest for spying and impersonating German military personnel. Guards, take them to Major Siegler's office."

Herbert looked at Claude and Muller, then slapped each of them on the shoulder, saying, "Be brave, you two. God willing, we will see each other soon."

Unbeknownst to Herbert and Claude, a dock worker who was a plant for the local resistance group witnessed the incident. When he finished his shift, he would report what happened to his leader.

Inside a large office, a German major sat at his desk, signing some documents. The lieutenant led the three captives into the office; snapping his boots and saluting, he yelled, "Remain standing until the major is ready for you."

The minutes ticked by slowly, the eerie silence only broken by the sound of paper being turned. "Relax, gentlemen, my young lieutenant gets carried away with events like this. Sit, please; would you care for coffee?" Major Siegler was an older officer, in his late fifties or early sixties, wearing a regular German Army uniform. Herbert was thinking this chap was probably some bank manager or businessman before the war; he is just doing his job and not interested in interrogating English spies. "So, you are wondering why you are under arrest. Are you not? This morning, we received a call from Captain Meyer at the Saint-Nazaire facilities. He said we should investigate two officers that had toured his base yesterday. He strongly suggested you could be imposters masquerading as an Austrian Naval officer and a Vichy French army officer, so we investigated and were convinced his observations were wrong until we heard from a dockhand that the Austrian Naval officer was in fact an officer for the Langstaff shipping company, who disappeared from his ship when it was docked in Marseille back in 1936.

"Finding this out, we immediately contacted the Vichy French authorities to find out about the captain here. According to the description they gave us, you have either grown very quickly in the last year, or you must be an impersonator, so which one are you?" The mild-mannered Major Siegler was very deliberate. He was trying to manipulate the interrogation, being nice to see who would fold first.

"Corporal Muller, am I on track with this line of questioning? Are you a conspirator to this deception? As it turns out, you have a clean record with the army, so explain to me why you are driving two impersonators around France. Could it be that you are also spying for the English?" Yelling, he walked over to Muller. Face-to-face, he slapped him hard across the face. "Look at me when I'm talking to you. Do you all take me for a fool? Did you really think you could get away with this? Guards, take them away; let them ponder this in their cells until tomorrow when the Gestapo will arrive to interrogate them further. I want no part of this," yelled Siegler as he sat back down, waving his hand to the guards to take them away.

Three guards pushed them down the dimly lit hallway. Another guard unlocked the prison-style door to the overnight holding cell, pushing them in before locking the cell door again. Muller went to speak, but Herbert put his finger across his lips, and with his left hand, pointed to his ear. Herbert moved in close to Muller and beckoned Claude to do the same. In a whisper, he said, "This cell is probably bugged with microphones, so only speak up when there is something you want them to hear. I think we are in for a rough time with the

Gestapo. Only tell them useless information like we were instructed to see what was going on with the new docks and how big of a force would man the facilities once it is finished. Under no circumstances mention or imply that we took pictures. If that comes up, simply state that we were always with guards or military personnel." Herbert was avoiding the question that would be next.

"We will be tortured for certain, but do you think we will be shot as spies? Going to a prison of war camp does not look like it's in our future, does it?" whispered Claude, reaching out for the hands of his companions.

Lying down on the wooden cot, Herbert could not conceive of sleep. His mind was racing, thinking of the torture training they had received years ago in Scotland. The Gestapo had a reputation for torture methods that most governments would never endorse, but here they were, only hours away from experiencing such atrocities. Muller would be slapped around, but more than likely, because he was merely the driver, would be sent to a hard labor prison camp. On the other hand, Claude faced torture before being turned over to the Vichy French for prosecution. As for me, I will not go through all of that. I will break that cyanide capsule and free myself once and forever of this black cloud that has followed me for so many years. Sweet Hazel, I have let you down. I hope when you return to England—if you make it back, that is—you'll find a nice young man who will give you a good life. You and I never really had a chance to start a long-term relationship, did we? Whatever time I have left, I will be thinking of you. I love you, Hazel. Karl let all these memories and thoughts run through his mind while he still had one to use. Sleep eventually overtook the fatigue he was trying to avoid.

Before dawn, Herbert was awakened by a guard carrying some old clothes. "Remove your uniform now and put these on." The stale smell on the old wool trousers and a shirt that at one time was white, now a stained beige, gave Herbert an insight into what would be coming. His polished shoes were replaced with wooden clogs. Standing up, he looked through the barred window. The dawn was changing from a dark gray sky to a fiery shade of blue and orange. The wind had not picked up yet. All was peaceful as he stood there thinking, this could be a perfect day to leave this troubled world behind. A rattling noise from down below made him strain to look down at what was happening. Three armed guards, along with a shackled Muller, walked slowly across the forecourt to the very same Kubelwagen they had been using. Karl watched as Muller was pushed into the back seat by one of the guards. Turning around the Kubelwagen, they headed for the main entrance. Muller turned around in his seat, and with both hands shackled, tried to wave toward the holding cells on the second floor. God, keep him safe, thought Karl. Will we ever meet again? I don't believe so. He continued watching until the car was out of sight, then sat down again on his cot.

The sound of a key being put into the lock made him stand up to face the guards as they entered, telling him to put his arms out, so the shackles could be put on his wrists. Shuffling down the hallway, he could see Jean and two guards ahead of him; Jean was wearing the same shabby clothes and shackles. The big steel door was unlocked for both prisoners with their guards to pass through into the main building. The first door on the right opened into the same office they were in the day before. Major Siegler leaned against his desk, one leg hanging across its corner, arms crossed across his chest.

"Gentlemen, sit down and have some coffee with me. Last night, I hope you took the time to consider your limited options because, if you haven't decided to cooperate with us, I will have no alternative but to call Gestapo headquarters to pick up both of you. Realize that if I make that call, they will arrive here in less than an hour. Help me keep you out of their hands. I'm told their methods are extremely painful. You can be assured you will be praying for death sooner than later. Again, once the call is made, there will be no turning back. That van will arrive to take you both to the Gestapo interrogation center. I deplore such violence; war is not the answer. But the English must realize we cannot be stopped. Europe, once united, will be a better place; believe me. Now, why don't you tell me why you were sent to spy on our facilities? Let's stop this foolishness right now and save you both from unnecessary pain and suffering." Major Siegler stopped talking, walked around his desk, and sat down, looking at both the men in front of him. The silence between them and the lack of any body movement convinced the major he was wasting his time.

Slowly shaking his head, he thought, that did not work; let me make that call. "Lieutenant Gerber, please get me Gestapo Headquarters, will you?"

The phone rang, and the Major lifted the receiver, putting his hand over the voice-piece in a last-ditch attempt to get the prisoners in front of him to talk. Those ten or so seconds felt like hours as Karl and Jean waited in silence, not moving a muscle. "Major Siegler here, the two prisoners we discussed yesterday are ready for you. I'll have them brought down to you. Their driver was picked up early this morning. By now, he is on a train back to Munich. I am told he will be sent to a hard labor camp, Heil Hitler." Major Siegler hung up the phone and stood up, saying. "Well, now you know that I was sincerely trying to keep you out of Gestapo hands. I apologize for deceiving you. The Gestapo is already downstairs; the call was made to a Gestapo captain waiting in the lobby. I suggest you drink that coffee; it may be the last you will have for a very long time. Guards, take the prisoners down to that waiting van."

Karl stood, then spoke, controlling his tone, "You have played your little game on us, Major, and may I say, well-acted. You are right. If we told you a story, whatever that story may be, it would be the easiest way out for us. However, that would be the cowardly way out, and may I remind you, we did not start this war. Before we part, let me conclude by saying, Herr Hitler cannot dictate or enforce his Nazi criminal ways on the good people of Europe. There will come a day when all of you will be forced to pay for the atrocities you are committing against others. No war can go on forever, and like the dictators before Hitler, this regime will also crumble and fail. Freedom cannot be chained forever. Germans will pay the price one day." Karl turned to Jean, saying, "I believe we have an appointment. No need to keep these guards waiting; shall we go?"

From the upstairs landing, they could look down on the two Gestapo officers and the four guards waiting to escort them to the interrogation center. Negotiating the stairs was difficult and clumsy due to the leg shackles. "Are you alright?" Jean asked Karl as they reached the final steps.

"One more step," said Karl. Major Siegler following them down to the lobby.

"Captain, please sign for the two prisoners; then you can take them away." Siegler turned to address Karl and Jean. "You are very foolish. You should have cooperated with me because whatever you're concealing will now be forcibly taken from you by this officer." The major turned away and climbed the stairs, turning his back on the fate of these two perpetrators.

"Get into the van," yelled the younger lieutenant, slapping Jean on the back of the head. The four guards climbed in behind them, their black uniforms and helmets making them look so menacing. In silence, they drove approximately an hour to the Gestapo Headquarters. The van stopped briefly at the guardhouse to show documents, then proceeded to the main entrance. As the van turned in front of the entrance, Karl and Jean could see on either side two enormous red banners with equally large black swastikas on white circles slowly waving in the breeze. The doors swung open, followed by the guards jumping out, ready to escort their new interns inside.

"Move, you treacherous pigs," one of them said, hitting Jean on the back of the head with the butt of his submachine gun. Then, pushing and almost dragging the two prisoners into the building, he said, "You go into this interrogation room, and you go into that one. Split them up," yelled the guard.

"Jean, you must stay strong," Karl yelled out to his friend as they parted. Inside the dimly lit room, Karl was pushed into a wooden chair. Other than the chair he was seated in, there appeared to be only a makeshift desk and an array of devices against the wall on a stand. The guards stationed themselves on either side of the door, remaining perfectly still. Karl could hear loud voices from the room right next door. Whoever was yelling was doing so in French, not German.

Karl could just make out what was being screamed at Jean, "You are a traitor, an English collaborator; tell me right now, what was the primary objective in spying on our facilities or suffer the consequences. I don't have time to waste on traitors like you." A brief period of silence came from next door, then a spine-chilling scream of pain erupted as the interrogator slammed his fist into Jean's face repeatedly, followed by more demands.

As Karl sat in his chair, imagining the horror taking place just a few feet away on the opposite side of the wall, the door opened, and in walked two muscular Gestapo henchmen, who, by their appearance, took great delight in administering pain to defenseless prisoners. Behind them, a major entered the room, saying, "Your French accomplice has passed out. That's alright; the electro-shock treatment to his testicles will bring him round very quickly. I don't think he will be much good to the ladies after that. Now, let's you and I get to know each other, shall we? My name is Major Becker, and your name is Captain Karl Vita of the British Intelligence Service. I must say, you have had a colorful history so far. It's a pity to spoil it starting right now. Tell me why I should not order these two animals to turn your beautiful face into a bloody pulp. Then again, we could introduce you to some water games, seeing as you were a maritime officer before the war. Yes, Vita, we know all about you, so why don't you start telling me what your orders were?"

The major, from his accent, is probably from upper Bavaria, thought Karl. I would not expect a Bavarian to be associated with a torture squad like this one, though.

"You're not talking, Vita. You're from Wien (Vienna), is that correct? It's such a nice city; I attended university there for a brief period back in thirty-five. Pity we are not on the same side right now; we could exchange wonderful stories about that charming city.

Karl remained very quiet, staring right at the pompous officer in front of him. Still, no response from Karl. The major, silently waiting, realized that would not be forthcoming. He assessed his next move; this strong-willed Austrian will not break that easy. It's time to let these animals loose on him, pity. Becker stood up and addressed the two soldiers, saying, "Call me when he's ready to talk."

Karl braced himself, getting ready for the punishment that would start within minutes. One of the soldiers moved forward, putting on a pair of black leather gloves, then stood less than a foot from Karl. Again, Karl braced his teeth together, waiting for the facial blows to commence. That did not happen; instead, a powerful smashing blow to his abdomen took his breath away, and in doing so, made him scream out in pain, releasing his clenched teeth. Before he could catch his breath, that gloved fist slammed into his face, sending his jaw to one side. Again, the same treatment was administered: left to the abdomen, right to the jaw. Karl was in total agony. His mind, however, was processing how the punishment would proceed.

After about thirty minutes, the agent was tiring, so the next agent took over. At this point, Karl could barely open his left eye, which was severely swollen, and the right one was close to becoming the same. Karl's top lip was split open, blood freely flowing down his face. Somewhere in between this merciless punishment, Karl somehow continued to think about what they would try next. He did not have to wait long. The straps that bound his arms and legs to the chair were removed, allowing Karl to fall to the floor. One of the guards moved forward to throw a bucket of cold water on his face. The two soldiers moved to the desk, sitting on top, freely swinging their legs as they enjoyed a cigarette break, laughing at the workout they were getting using this prisoner as a punching bag.

Karl, trying to handle the pain, just lay there, thinking, I've gotten this far; that water sport Becker mentioned may be too much for me to handle. Perhaps I should consider cracking that cyanide capsule lodged in the back of my mouth. I'm kind of surprised that the beating did not dislodge it already—in which case, I would already be dead. A crooked smile crossed his broken lips. Hazel would be looking for another boyfriend if she could see me right now. Karl forced his brain to take him to other places where the pain could be tolerated easier. The two sadistic muscle men returned, looking down at the disfigured face lying against the cold floor.

"Shall we call the major back in, or are you having too much fun to talk to him yet? Why don't you take a few more minutes to consider your answer?" The guards walked out of the room. Karl took this time to listen for signs of activity from next door, but all was quiet. His eyesight was now severely impaired as the left eye was completely closed and caked in dried blood. The two animals returned, stopping in front of Karl's body on the floor, and once again asked him if he was ready to talk.

Karl did not make a sound or move a muscle, defying his captors. "Right, let's get you ready for a bath, shall we?" said one of the animals with a big grin on his face.

From across the room, Karl could hear running water and the movement of what looked like a big wooden water barrel being positioned by a low long bench. "You two pick him up and bring him over here," ordered one of the soldiers. "So, you were a sailor, is that right? Well, you are not going to like this too much. Put him face down on that board, then strap him tightly onto it. One last time, are you ready to talk to the major?" asked the soldier again. Not one word left Karl's shattered lips.

The two guards lifted the board, so Karl's head could be pushed into the barrel up to his shoulders. "Ready?" asked the senior soldier, "Give me two and a half minutes on the first dunking. Alright, push him in, and I will hold his head down."

Karl once again braced himself for this water torture. As his head entered the icy cold water, it was hard for him to keep his mouth shut and hold his breath—the water was that cold, but he did. All those years swimming with his sister as a boy in the Danube and jumping into the Donakanal from the bridges that circled Wien would now help him hold his breath. It would be so much easier just to let the water end all this pain and torture, but that would never be the case with Karl Vita! The only way they have left is to shoot me. If I could get my hands on a gun, I would gladly shoot these barbarians. They are less than humans. His mind kept him from gagging or choking, but his lungs were saying something else.

"Pull him out," yelled one of the agents. "What is it with this pig? First, we beat him to within inches of his life with no reaction, and now with water torture, still nothing? Dunk him again. This time for three minutes. If we can't break him with that, I'm telling the major we're getting nowhere, so he can decide to make the next move." The second dunking would take Karl within inches of losing his life, and that would have been fine with him at that point.

Once again, the ice-cold water was taking all his concentration to resist opening his mouth. His lungs were screaming out for fresh air. The pain of holding whatever air he had not released was about to give in to the cold water.

"Pull him out," said the same soldier. "The major has made it clear we cannot use electro-torture on this one, so let's call it a day. You two guards, drag him to a cell. Tomorrow's another day; that's if he doesn't die on us during the night." The two animals walked out of the room, leaving Karl close to death on the floor.

The youngest of the two guards finally spoke up, "I can't believe what they have just done to this poor fellow. I did not sign on for this kind of inhumane treatment. Yes, we are at war, but there is certain conduct that we all should be abiding by, don't you agree?"

The other guard was bending down, carefully lifting Karl, trying to give him a glass of water.

Barely able to speak, Karl managed to say, "Thank you; don't you think I've had enough water for one day?" The words were hard to form as he said that, vehemently holding onto his sense of humor. The two guards took one arm each and walked him, half dragged him, through the door down the hall to his cell, placing him on a cot for the night.

Karl lay there in the dim light. The pain was all over his body. *I think I have a cracked rib or two and maybe a broken nose as well; best not to dwell on it.* Karl now willed his mind into a more pleasant place. As a younger man, he would call on his girlfriend, Annie Lourie, at her parents' house in Wien (Vienna). Those long walks through the Stadtpark and afternoons at the Spanish Riding School watching the Lipizzaner Stallions rehearsing were amongst his fondest memories. *I always believed Annie and I would eventually get married. I wonder if she still lives with her family in Switzerland? The last time I heard from her, she had a new love in her life, and so did I—my sweet Kitty. Stay safe, Annie; I will always think of you fondly.*

Karl continued to drive his thoughts to events, people, and places that would forever remain part of his memories. *Poor Kitty also became a prisoner of the Gestapo. Thank God, that was before the declartion of war in 1939.* She died on her way to a Gestapo interrogation center, a blessing in disguise. Sleep was overcoming him, even though he tried to resist, but to no avail. He simply did not have the energy to fight sleep.

Loud sounds from a door opening, then slamming minutes later, woke him up just as dawn was breaking. The pain immediately returned as he lifted himself up on the cot. Voices in the hall made him wonder if Jean was being returned to the interrogation room. Please, God, no more, he thought out loud. Down in the courtyard, armed soldiers were forming in a line facing the wall. Karl dragged himself to the windows, holding onto the bars to support himself. Looking down, it took milliseconds to realize what was about to happen. Two guards were dragging Jean's blood-spattered body toward the wall. God, please, not after all he has been through. Where is your mercy? Karl could feel himself shaking and crying simultaneously, his head in a spin as he continued to watch. He was almost at that point, about to give up and crack that cyanide capsule in the back of his mouth.

Suddenly, a tremendous explosion, followed by another, seconds later, rocked the building. Taken by complete surprise, the execution squad were falling in all directions as a hail of machine-gun bullets shredded their uniforms, sending blood and body fragments in all directions. The Gestapo captain was running for cover but not sure where to find it, shooting blindly in the direction of the gunfire. Another hail of gunfire sent him into a sickening spin as the bullets kept coming; he was dead before he hit the ground. The two guards holding Jean had put their hands in the air a little too late as three partisans took them down with knives. Jean, having no strength left, fell to the ground. The partisans lifted him by his arms, half running out of the courtyard to the waiting vehicles at the front of the building. Karl's attention was now directed to the loud gunfire in the hall outside his cell door. He could hear the bullets ricocheting off the walls and his cell door.

The shooting finally stopped. French voices were yelling to get all the cell doors open and help the prisoners who could not walk out of the building. "Get them all down to the vans quickly," yelled the leader.

Karl's energy, miraculously returning from God knows where, spurred him to the door and the friendly face of a partisan. "Quickly, we must go. The Germans will be sending more troops very shortly." At the end of the hall, four partisans had the two animals that had tortured Karl, standing with their arms behind their heads.

"Wait," yelled Karl. "Someone, give me a pistol; we cannot leave until I give these barbarians a taste of their own medicine." Karl's anger was consuming him, giving him a surge of energy. He would rather die than leave without his revenge on the two barbarians.

Someone gave Karl a revolver, saying, "Whatever you're going to do, make it quick. We are out of time."

Speaking German, Karl pushed them against the wall. One started to cry; the other pleaded for forgiveness. Karl pointed his gun directly at the animal who was crying, lowering the weapon in line with his crotch, saying, "Death is too quick for you. I want you to remember this to your dying day. A loud bang, followed by a sickening scream, sent that soldier to the floor, blood spreading over his trousers. The second agent, now in hysterics as he watched, pleaded for Karl to show some mercy. Karl laughed at him as he triggered the gun and watched as this coward fell, screaming, to the floor.

"We must go right now, Sir, please." Karl half-ran down the stairs, assisted by the strong arm of a resistance fighter, out the main entrance and into the waiting van.

"Karl, thank God you're alive," came a feeble voice from the front of the van. There in the corner, supported by two men, was Jean. "Thought I was almost to the pearly gates back there, everything happened so fast. Somebody must like us up there," said Jean, barely able to finish the sentence.

"You could be right, Jean; however, it took him long enough to come to that conclusion, though." Karl felt the release of freedom; pain or no pain, he would enjoy this moment as he looked out the rear window at the Gestapo Headquarters burning, with one side already collapsing into the courtyard, hopefully never again to operate as a torture center.

CHAPTER 11

Returning Home to England

The three vehicles bounced through the farm lanes at high speed. They needed to put as much distance between themselves and Bordeaux as possible. By now, the Gestapo headquarters would be swarming with storm troopers. In the dim light, one of the partisans spoke up saying, "Remember me?"

Karl strained through his one good eye to see who was talking to him. "Albert, oh, my God, so good to see you again. Was it you who organized this breakout? Jean and I will be forever in your debt and to all of you that took on this extremely dangerous rescue. Thank you will never be enough." The small talk continued until the van slowed to cross the forge over the lane and into the farmyard.

"By the sound of it, we have arrived back at the safe house. Good luck is on your side this day, as the brigade commander sent us a doctor and nurse to take care of our wounded. They arrived yesterday, just in time for their first patients," said Albert as he climbed over legs to the rear of the van.

The doors of the van opened, strong arms helping Jean and Karl out and into the farmhouse. The other two vans had their injured men helped by their friends into the safety of the farmhouse. "Bring those two in here. My nurse will start dressing their wounds while I care for these chaps with bullet wounds first," said Doctor Bernard Dubois.

Karl's energy was almost depleted. Jean was about the same, lying on an old couch, his legs hanging over the arm. As Karl lay on the makeshift examination table, his left eye was becoming infected. His vision from it was barely a blurred image at best. The pressure from that eye was giving him a severe headache. After taking care of Jean's wounds including the burn marks from the electro torture, the nurse came over to Karl's battered face.

"Oh, my God, it's you. I can't believe this. It's been over four years since I said goodbye to you in the café parking lot. You can't remember, or have I changed that much? Please, lay back and let me start dressing your wounds. The doctor will be in soon to examine that left eye. I'm sure, when you're feeling better, you may remember me," whispered the nurse, moving closer to Karl's left ear. Lying there while she tended to his wounds, he started processing the information she had given him. Four years ago in a French café… I must have still been in my maritime uniform… in a parking lot… which means I was driving my Opel Kadet. His brain may have been fuzzy, but his memory was able to link the events together, and the memory of that night on the road to Austria came back clear as a bell. He remembered!

"My God, Monica, can this be you? From a waitress to a nurse, I can't believe this. How fortunate am I today." Karl was trying to smile, but his face hurt too much for that.

"Karl, please, don't move too much. I believe you have two fractured ribs; your nose is a mess but does not appear to be broken. The doctor can make that assessment shortly. I would know you anywhere. I often wondered what became of you after you left me hanging that night. I must have appeared to be a lovesick schoolgirl, making a real fool of myself like that. If you would have stayed that night, I can assure you that you would not have forgotten it that quickly." Monica now had a huge smile on her face as she continued cleaning the blood off Karl's face.

Karl being Karl, simply answered, "Well, it's never too late." It was now completely dark when the doctor entered the kitchen. Karl was snoozing, so he moved over to where Jean was lying on the couch. "Let's take a closer look at those wounds, shall we? It looks like you have a badly bruised rib cage but no apparent fractured bones. Your nose appears to be broken. Jean reacted as the doctor gently applied pressure to the sides of his nostrils.

"Monica, I am going to strap his rib cage. Come and give me a hand, will you? I need to reset his nose, so I will give him a local anesthetic to reduce the pain. Would you prepare a syringe for me?" asked Doctor Dubois. "While that anesthetic numbs around your nose, let's get you sitting upright. Monica, cut away his shirt, then wash his upper body. Once you have dried him off, you can strap his ribcage. While you are doing that, I'm going to look at Karl's eye," said the doctor as he moved over to the limp form of Karl.

"Sorry to wake you, young man, but I need to look at that eye of yours. Can you try opening it for me?" Karl tried to open the left eye, but dried blood had caked it closed again. "Alright, let me wash it out with this eye cup, then clean and medicate it with a swab. You should be able to roll it open after that. If it becomes too painful, just squeeze my arm or tell me to stop. I'm sorry to put you through this, but I must examine your eye wide open. I realize this is painful for you. There, it's almost open." Dr. Dubois covered all around Karl's eye, then, with a small penlight, looked at the eyeball, which was completely bloodshot. "Monica, get me that vial from over there. I'll put some ointment into his eye to ease the pain as well as lubricate it, but this is really bad, Monica. Fetch Albert for me right away. This man needs a hospital and an eye surgeon as soon as we can airlift him back to England. The right eye is bruised but should heal fine. I'll put ointment in that one as well."

Next, he addressed Karl's ribs and nose, after which the doctor said to Karl, "I think we should also remove that cyanide capsule. Can you open your mouth wide for me so that I can pry it out?" The doctor helped Karl lie down again, then returned to administer the same ointment to Jean's eyes. Although badly bruised, with time, they would recover nicely. He would, however, be left with a permanent scar over the right eye.

Monica sat holding Karl's hand while the medication took hold. "So, you're a nurse now, Monica?" asked Karl, trying to remain perfectly still as instructed by the doctor.

"Well, I did not quite make it to getting my nursing diploma. Herr Hitler spoiled that for me. Nevertheless, I am totally qualified to perform all nursing duties." Monica kept a close watch on Karl's left eye, which the doctor did not want to cover until he was certain the medication was working. Karl, holding still with a firm grip on

Monica's hand, started to drift off into a deep sleep. All the tension and excitement were catching up to him.

Once she was sure he was sleeping, Monica carefully released the grip he had on her hand. Standing, she went into another room, coming back with a blanket to cover up the battered form of Karl Vita. Satisfied he was as comfortable as she could make him, she walked out into the large room where many of the partisans were sitting and talking quietly so as not to disturb the nine injured sleeping in the other rooms on makeshift cots.

"Jean looks to be in better shape than Karl does. Those two took a hell of a beating. The two that tortured poor old Karl will probably bleed to death unless they are given immediate medical attention, and that seems highly unlikely," said Monica, repeating the story she was given by Karl—a just ending to those bastards in the Gestapo.

"Albert, did you manage to get off that wireless message concerning the urgency of airlifting Karl back to England?" asked Doctor Dubois.

"Yes, we did. They are requesting… if he is in such a bad way, we should consider sending a medic to escort him back to England. No telling what could happen from pressure differences once airborne," explained Albert.

The doctor sat, pondering what he should do next. "When will that plane be arriving to pick him up, and where will that pickup be?" asked the doctor.

"All going well, it will be close to here; they never tell us exactly until the last minute as a precaution—probably tomorrow night if the weather holds up. They will also be delivering another shipment of arms at the same time," replied Albert, wondering where this line of questioning was going.

Turning his attention to Monica, the doctor asked her, "Ever been to England in a plane?"

With a look of surprise, Monica simply answered, "No to England, and no to ever flying in a plane, Doctor." Monica was now feeling somewhat excited at this line of questioning.

"In that case, you will accompany Karl back to England. Once you have turned him over to the medical people at the airdrome, I need you to meet with their medical supply people and deliver this list of medical supplies we are so desperately in need of. Whenever the next supply drop is planned, you will return with those supplies. You're the only one we can spare, even though it's only a few days. I need you back here as quickly as possible. Monica, are you alright doing this for me?" asked the doctor.

"If that's what you want me to do, Sir, the answer is yes," she replied. Monica returned to the sleeping patients in the other room, quietly checking each one to ensure all was well before she climbed the stairs to her small area in the attic.

The morning was already sunny, waking Jean with its brightness. Feeling so much better than the day before, Jean moved to stand up, but those deep bruises reminded him that he would be in recovery for a long time. Those sharp pains stopped him from standing upright. Bent over, he quietly moved toward the old kitchen door. "Morning," said Albert, standing up from the table to make room for Jean at the table.

"What's the prognosis on Karl's eye? Can it be treated here, or will he need surgery? It looked really swollen as I walked by a few minutes ago," said Jean, his own appearance looking pretty beaten up as well. He would recover with time, unlike Karl.

"We are sending him back to England tonight. Monica will accompany him on the flight, then return on the next available flight with desperately needed medical supplies," answered the doctor. "As for you, Jean, I'm holding you back here until you are fit enough to travel back to your command in England." Dr. Dubois noticed a look on Jean's face that indicated he would not accept the doctor's explanation.

"I am relieved to hear you are sending Karl back to England. It's best not to take a chance with that eye of his. As for myself, I am going to request from my brigade commander that I remain here, where I can best serve the needs of France. Albert, can you arrange that wire for me? I'll write down what to send if you give me some paper and a pencil."

Albert looked at the doctor before answering Jean. "Are you sure about this request? Joining the partisans is extremely dangerous with a very good chance you will land right back in the hands of the

Gestapo; have you thought about that?" asked Albert as he slid the writing pad over to Jean.

"I came within minutes of being shot, so facing death has given me a completely different perspective on combatting oppression. I'm staying, and that's that."

For most of the day, Karl was out of it, sleeping deeply; he so desperately needed to regain his energy. Monica would tiptoe into the room regularly to check on his eye, which remained very red and swollen. "Doctor, what instructions do you have for me tonight, and what should I be prepared for in case that eye becomes a problem?" Monica would be alone in that plane if things went wrong with Karl's eye. This concerned her greatly. Would her nursing skills be enough during that dark night flight?

About two in the afternoon, the doctor asked her to wake Karl, so he could determine whether to proceed with lancing the corner of his eyelid to relieve the pressure. He really did not want to do it, but battlefield medicine was not always a perfect science. Entering the room, Monica found Karl awake, his head still lying straight on the pillow. Speaking in an almost whisper, Monica asked Karl how he was feeling and informed him that Doctor Dubois would be in momentarily to relieve some of the pressure on his eye.

The doctor entered the room, carrying a bowl of warm water and medical instruments on a tray covered with a towel. "Good afternoon, Karl, glad you slept. You were near total exhaustion yesterday. First, let me examine that eye of yours, then we can decide whether to relieve some of that pressure. Let me also bring you up to date with what we have planned for you later today. Albert and some of the partisans will be transporting you, along with Monica, to a location about forty minutes from here. Karl, I have come to a decision; that eye of yours needs expert surgical attention sooner rather than later. So, tonight, you will be flying back to England.

"I have decided to send Monica with you just in case a problem arises from altitude and pressure. Albert will instruct the pilot to fly as low as possible to reduce the possibility of this happening. Once you're on the ground, Monica will leave you to meet up with our medical supply contacts, returning with much-needed supplies on the next available Lysander." The doctor could see that Karl was about to protest but quickly stumped him by adding, "Captain, there is no negotiating on this matter. My decision is final. Now, let me attend to that eye. Monica, please thoroughly clean around his eye for me."

The doctor laid clean cloths over Karl's face, then injected his cheek to deaden the area. With precision, he lanced the eyelid, splattering congealed blood onto his gloved hand. "There, that should make you a little more comfortable for that flight home. Monica, your help, please. I need to suture that incision. Keep his head very still and apply very light pressure to the opposite side of the lid." With a very steady hand, he inserted two sutures into his eyelid. The final thing Doctor Dubois did was to bandage Karl's eye with a gauze pad, placing a bandage around his head to hold it in place. Now, let's get you sitting upright, shall we? I'll help you if you need me to. A big bowl of hot soup will help you regain some of that lost energy."

Karl, being Karl, stood up on his own, thanking the doctor and Monica for the excellent attention they had administered. He also mentioned he was feeling much better now that the pressure had been reduced. In the kitchen, Karl sat next to Jean, the friends obviously pleased to see each other. Several other partisans sat, devouring their soup and fresh-baked bread at the long farm-style table. "That is the best meal I have had in a long time," said Karl, wiping the bowl clean with bread. In the meantime, Jean did not say too much, allowing Karl to dominate the conversion. "Jean, you have not said anything about returning to England. I know Monica and I will be going tonight, but when will you return?" Karl did not expect the answer that came back at him from Jean.

"Karl, I have requested that I be allowed to remain in France. I believe I can serve my country so much more effectively by doing so. I will very much miss working with you. God willing, we will meet again." Jean looked straight at his friend's face, waiting for an argument that did not happen.

"In the time we have worked together, I have grown to trust the decisions we have made together, and this one is no different. Of course, I'm disappointed you're not returning with us, but your love of country is one I will never challenge. There is never a day when I do not think about my homeland of Austria and the family members

I left behind." Karl was showing Jean his support for this decision he had made.

The daylight was fading; it was almost time to depart for the landing field. Dr. Dubois took another look at Karl's eye, applying additional ointment to the corners one more time. Satisfied he had done the best with the limited resources available to him, he carefully replaced the dressing over Karl's eye, securing it with a bandage around his head. "Time to go, you two. This fresh application and dressing should get you back to England. Karl, you need to tell Monica if that severe pain returns to your eye. Don't try to be a martyr; tell her, alright?" Dr. Dubois was showing his concern about sending them off on this flight to England.

"I guess this is where we part company, old friend; please, take care of yourself. Remember, Rome was not built in a day, and this war will last a lot longer than that, so please be careful until we meet again." Jean stepped forward, giving Karl a big French hug with a kiss on either cheek. "Tell Peggy I look forward one day to buying her fish and chips along with a pint of mild and bitter." As the two friends parted, Karl walked over to the doctor, standing next to the lorry, and thanked him again for the excellent care he exhibited with his eye. Jean followed, walking over to Monica and embracing her with a kiss on the cheek, then asking her to take good care of his friend. Then, speaking out loud so everyone could hear, Jean said, "Monica, you know those rear cockpits in the Lysanders are really tight. They also bounce quite a lot during flight. If I were you, I would not sit on Karl's lap. You never know what could happen." Everyone started laughing, and the tension was broken for the departing comrades in arms.

"Really, you men are such pigs. If there's not much room in that plane, well, it's not the worst thing that could happen, isn't that right, Captain Vita?" replied Monica in a very jovial voice. Albert helped Monica and Karl climb into the covered lorry, along with six other armed partisans. Once everyone was aboard, the lorry rumbled down the lane, leaving Jean and the doctor standing silently, watching until they were out of sight. The drive through the backroads was uneventful, and Karl was thinking about the many dangers Jean would face in the months ahead, showing such strength and conviction to free his country. It makes me wonder how a large military force like the French collapsed so quickly to a smaller military like the Germans—arrogance probably!

The lorry slowed as it approached the landing field. Turning its lights off, it moved very slowly to the edge of the clearing. Ahead of them, they could see images of other men running stealthily to take up defensive positions around the field. The quiet was deafening as they waited patiently for the sound of an aircraft. Finally, after about fifteen minutes, an overhead sound announced the aircraft's arrival, everyone looking skyward, straining to see the Morse code recognition signal. The black shape of an aircraft made a second pass, this time flashing the code for that night's operation. The return signal from Albert put the team of men into motion, running out of the bushes with their pots of flammable material to illuminate the landing strip.

"Alright, let's make this fast," whispered Albert as he led the two passengers out to the edge of the strip. At the far end, they could hear the Lysander's big radial engine throttling back as it made its approach, bouncing just once as it contacted the rough terrain of the field, stopping almost immediately. Moving quickly, the group approached the left side of the aircraft and the permanently attached boarding ladder to the rear cockpit. One of the partisans jumped onto the ladder, opening the canopy, then climbed inside to remove the boxes of supplies and munitions, handing them down to the others waiting below.

"I say down there; just want to confirm Captain Vita is one of the two returning with me tonight, is that correct?" whispered Captain Cooke from the cockpit.

Karl turned to Albert, thanking him again for putting their lives on the line and rescuing them from certain death. "One day, I hope our paths will cross again when Europe is again free." Karl, saying this, turned to Monica, saying, "Let me go first as I know the cockpit arrangement."

As a parting gesture, Albert replied, "You know he means let him get in first, so you have no alternative but to sit on his lap."

The group quietly chuckled as Karl climbed up the ladder, saying, "Nice to see you, Cooke; will this be a champagne flight?"

Karl was showing signs of relief, knowing he was heading home. "Up you come, Nurse; let me help you settle in. I told you it would be tight, did I not?" remarked Karl as the canopy closed. The whole operation—landing, unloading, and reloading took less than six minutes. By the time the Lysander left the ground, the firepots were doused, returning the field once more to darkness.

"Captain Vita, when we land, there will be an ambulance waiting for you. As for you, Miss, a car will take you straight to the Free French Headquarters. This flight will be quite bumpy as I have been instructed to fly as low as possible because of your injury. Sorry for this, but orders are orders," yelled the pilot over the noise of the engine. Monica looked at Karl as they both broke out laughing.

Thirty or so minutes into the flight, Monica took out a penlight from her pocket, saying, "I need to look at that left eye, Karl. Are you in any pain right now?" Slowly, she unwound the bandage holding the dressing in place over his eye, saying, "The light from this penlight may cause some discomfort; just try to remain as still as possible. I guess that might be difficult the way this plane is moving around; sorry for that," said Monica as she removed the dressing.

"In that case, stop bouncing on my lap like that. I can't do two things simultaneously. Although I must say, I prefer the bouncing," laughed Karl, trying to make light of the pain.

A quick response came back at him, "As I said earlier, men are such pigs, but I will not squeal if you bounce me again." Monica was acutely aware he was fighting tremendous pain, so whatever she could do to take his mind off the splitting pain in his head was alright with her. Apart from this, when she looked at Karl, she still saw the dashing maritime officer she had served dinner to at the roadside café back in 1936. If only he would look at her in the same way, but that will never happen, will it? As difficult as it was, Monica managed to apply ointment to both sides of his eye before replacing a fresh pad and bandage. Monica felt quite fatigued after holding onto the side of the cockpit as she replaced the dressing. "There, it's done. What a struggle; it's taken most of my energy. I feel like all my strength has been drained," said Monica, looking for a way to stretch out and get some sleep.

"Lean back against my chest and put your head on my shoulder. I think you will find it to be much more comfortable." Karl was thinking, this brave lady has not stopped since we returned from our mission. Now, it's my turn to take care of her as he placed his hand on the side of her face to stop her head from rolling off his shoulder. Karl was also starting to feel the strain of the day's excitement. He could feel the waves of sleep rolling over him. Within minutes, he surrendered, also falling asleep.

"I say; you two back there, time to rise and shine. We are over the English coast and only minutes from landing. Make sure you wedge in tight for touchdown, will you please?" instructed Captain Cooke. The Lysander touched down in a remarkably short amount of runway, then taxied to the dispersal area and spun around by revving up the engine and applying the right brake. Once in place, the pilot shut down the engine, and silence returned to the evening—what was left of it, that is.

An R.A.F. private jumped up onto the ladder and swung open the canopy, latching it securely to the top. "Welcome home," said the smiling private as he helped Monica climb down the ladder backward. "You're next, Sir. Are you carrying any luggage tonight?"

"No, Private, we are it for this trip anyway," replied Karl as he proceeded to navigate down the ladder backward. On the ground, Karl looked toward the front of the aircraft to finally face the pilot, "Captain Cooke, I presume," laughed Karl, using a line from English maritime history.

"You are correct. Sorry for a turbulent flight, old man; flying that low can be hair-raising," he said as he wiped salt off the aircraft's wheel spat with his finger in a sign of, believe it or not, we were that low tonight! "Glad it was me, old boy, that they selected to pick you up tonight. We were told you have a badly injured eye, and altitude could be a problem. I have a reputation for wave-hopping, so that's how you got to fly with me twice. I hope all goes well for you in surgery. I must be off now." Captain Cooke made a casual salute, picked up his bag, and walked off toward the hangar. Although the area in front of the hangar was dimly lit, Karl could make out the form of Major Knight.

"Karl, over here. Thank God you made it home. I can only imagine what you have been through," said Clive, shaking Karl's hand.

"Major Knight, may I introduce you to Monica, my French nurse. Believe it or not, we first met one night in a French café back in '36. Oh, my goodness, Monica, after all these years, forgive me. I don't know your surname," Karl said, feeling somewhat embarrassed.

"It's Thompson, Sir. My grandfather was in the First World War. Although he was in the British Flying Corps, he returned to France after the war to reunite with my grandmother and never returned to England." Monica looked at Karl, seeing his jaw drop in disbelief. "See, Captain Vita, you're not the only one with a good story." Monica had a smug look on her face and was loving every minute of it.

"No wonder your English is so good. Some intelligence officer I turned out to be." Karl was still dumbfounded as they all walked toward the waiting vehicles. "Major, would you mind awfully if I take a few minutes with Monica? She has done so much for me; I really would like to thank her privately." Karl's brain was racing to find the correct words to say, knowing that when they parted, it could be the last time, but then again, he thought that once before. Karl took Monica's hand and led her back toward the aircraft. Stopping, he reached out for her hands, then started speaking, "Monica, words cannot express my thanks for what you have done for me. This is the second time we have said goodbye, and quite honestly, I find myself asking why. Would you consider coming to see me before you depart back to France? Suddenly, I want to say so much. I suppose in a way we are back in front of that café, only the roles have been reversed, haven't they?"

The flood of emotions was consuming Karl's head, making him very confused and vulnerable. He sensed by the look on her face that she was looking for that kiss never given so many years ago. "Oh, to hell with it. Monica, come here; let's make this a memorable farewell," said Karl as he swooped her into his waiting arms.

Monica's reply said it all. "Took you long enough, didn't it?" she said as she eagerly responded, thinking, make it last; it probably will be the first and last time I get to kiss him. Over by the vehicles, Clive stood smiling, slowly shaking his head, thinking, here we go again.

The attending doctor walked over to Clive, saying, "We must get Captain Vita to the hospital, Sir. I don't want to break up the goodbyes, but his injury needs immediate attention."

"Give them a few more minutes. They've been through a lot together; five more minutes will not make a big difference." Clive knew his friend so well, and when a situation like this occurs, it's best to let it play out.

Monica slowly pulled away from Karl, placing both hands on his cheeks. "Karl, you dear man, how I have imagined kissing you like that. We will never have the time to make it more than this once, will we?" Tears welled up in her beautiful dark brown eyes before she spoke again. "Karl, when we leave here, I will be going to the Free French Headquarters, and you will go on to the hospital. You will need this medication pile box to give to your commanding officer over there, or had you forgotten about the film it contains?"

Karl's head snapped back at hearing this. "I thought that film had already been sent. You have had it all along. But why you?" Karl was dumbfounded once again.

"Because Albert thought it would be safer returning with you, so he instructed me only to give it to you as we parted here in England." Monica opened her medical bag, withdrawing the medication pile box, then pressing it into Karl's hand, saying, "You nearly gave your life for this, Karl; make it pave the way for a free France." Monica held his hand for a moment. Lifting it, she pressed it against her cheek, then kissed the back of it. Turning, she walked over toward the waiting French officer standing by the vehicle. Speaking out loud as she walked away, she said, "Karl, don't forget me. I will always have a place in my heart for you, but I'm sure you already knew that, didn't you? And please, make sure they send me the results of your surgery." Monica refrained from looking back as she walked that short distance to the car, tears slowly rolling down her face.

The French officer kissed her on both cheeks, then opened the rear door, saying, "I hope those tears are tears of joy, young lady."

Monica simply replied, "They are tears of goodbye, Sir." As she entered the back seat, she turned once more, throwing Karl a kiss before the officer closed the door, also waving goodbye. The car's engine started, the driver making a wide turn away from them as they sped off toward the main gate out onto the road leading to London.

"Karl, we must get going right now." Clive was out of time, waiting around for Karl.

"Clive, one quick question, did you ever get the microfilm I took?" asked Karl, thinking, here is that BIS secret stuff again.

"No, Karl, we received another film from another group. We were told it would be better to send it with the agent who took it, so do you want to give it to me now? Clive waited for Karl's response.

"The bloody BIS secrets at it again. You knew all along that it would be on that plane, didn't you?"

"Yes," was the only response he got from Clive. "Karl, I'll stop by tomorrow if I can to check up on your progress." Shaking hands, Karl looked at Clive with a concerned expression on his face. Clive's parting words were, "Captain Vita, this has been a dangerous year for you so far. If cats have nine lives, you probably only have four or five left. Now, go and get that eye taken care of, will you?" Clive was smiling, knowing that within a week or two, this strong-willed Austrian with his driving convictions would be hounding him for a new assignment anywhere on the Continent. Thank God he is not on Hitler's side, thought Clive as he broke out into a chuckle.

Dr. Phillips climbed into the ambulance and introduced himself to Karl. "It's going to take the best part of an hour to reach Saint Vincent's Hospital. Once we arrive, I'll accompany you into the surgical suite. I need to take a closer look at that eye before we can determine any type of procedure. Hopefully, it's going to be something we can take care of relatively easily. So, while we are en route, let me look at that left eye to make sure we don't have an emergency on our hands, alright?" Doctor Phillips carefully removed the head dressing, then, with a very steady hand, he removed the gauze pad covering his eye. The male nurse in the ambulance held a diffused light, shining it directly into Karl's eye.

"Sorry if this light gives you some discomfort. I need to see as much of your eye as I can. I am going to roll your eyelid up with this wooden pin so that I can see the upper eye clearer. I say that French doctor and that nurse traveling with you did a splendid job of containing the problem. From what I can see, I would say there may be blood vessels that have ruptured. There may be more once we remove your eyeball." Doctor Phillips lowered the eyelid, applying a new dressing with tape instead of a bandage.

"Remove my eyeball?" asked Karl, not sure what would be involved with this procedure.

"Don't get alarmed, Captain. It sounds a lot worse than it really is. You would be amazed at how quickly I can remove an eyeball. The reason they asked me to meet your plane is I'm the resident ophthalmologist at the hospital. The wireless message received at the BIS was vague, to say the least. I'm told, Captain Vita, you're a very important member of that service, is that correct? Let me put your concerns to rest. This eye problem can be taken care of rather quickly. That French doctor made the right call. If it was left for another three or four days, you might have run the risk of permanent damage. My suggestion is, if you ever get to see him again, you need to thank him for making the right decision. Now, lay back and relax; we are almost there." Dr. Phillips moved to the opposite side of the ambulance so that Karl could spread out.

"Here we are; let's get you taken care of, shall we?" said the doctor, standing up to help Karl out the back. A hospital attendant pushed a wheelchair up to the back of the ambulance for Karl.

"We won't need that thing, but thanks for assuming I'm not capable of walking. It's my eye that's the problem, not my bloody legs. Alright, Doctor, lead the way." Karl felt a little guilty about how he had spoken to the old-timer who was trying to help. Karl stopped by the main door, turning to face the attendant. "That was a bloody stupid thing to say. I'm really sorry for saying that. You must think I'm an arrogant sod, sorry." The old-timer merely smiled and waved a signal that no harm was done.

Inside the surgical area, a male nurse handed Karl a hospital gown to put on, with instructions to climb into the bed once he had undressed. "I'm going to give you a close shave, then shave the left side of your head. Don't worry; I'm not going to scalp you. I just need to make sure there is no hair close to the surgical area. First, I will need you to have a shower in that shower stall over there. Make sure you wash your hair thoroughly with this medicated shampoo," instructed the nurse.

Karl, complying with the instructions, added jovially, "I've not had a real hot shower in quite a while; guess you sensed that, right?" They both chuckled at that remark as Karl entered the shower stall, the hot water cascading down his body. Feeling so much better, he returned to the bed, waiting patiently for the nurse to return with a tray containing a straight razor, shaving brush, and shaving cream for that close shave and partial scalping. Lying there in that bed, he drifted back to another surgery earlier in the year. That one was much more intense than this one, he thought.

The surgical nurse entered the room, saying, "Hello, I'm Helen, your nurse. I'm here to get you ready. First, I'm going to cover around your eye, followed by medication to make you feel sleepy. Once we enter the surgical suite, the anesthesiologist will be administering the medication to put you under. Any questions?" asked Helen. About ten minutes later, Karl started to feel drowsy. The feeling of being calm for the first time in so many weeks was almost therapeutic, so he let it take him into the twilight.

Inside the theatre, Dr. Phillips, along with his assistant, gave him a brief overview of what he would do, followed by the anesthesiologist placing the face mask over his mouth and instructing him to breathe deeply. Ninety minutes later, he was in the recovery area, a nurse hovering over him, saying, "Welcome back, Captain. That didn't take long, did it? Let me prop you up; then I'll get you some tea and biscuits. I'll be back in a minute."

As she turned to leave, a drowsy Karl asked, "Nurse, could you make that coffee instead? I'm not ready for tea just yet."

"Of course, you can; no problem—back in a jiffy." As the nurse hurried off down the ward, Dr. Phillips and his assistant entered, both with big smiles on their faces.

"Well, my good man, you are a very lucky individual. The surgery was not only successful but nowhere near what we were expecting after we removed your eyeball." Karl could see from their faces that they were pleased.

"What exactly was the problem, Doctor? Can you describe it for me?" asked Karl anxiously.

"Well, as I said, once we removed your eyeball, we found an accumulation of dried blood in the anterior chamber. That's the space between the cornea and the iris. You also had numerous ruptured blood vessels, which caused the leakage into the white part of the eye that resulted in a subconjunctival hemorrhage. Under normal circumstances, this would have taken care of itself, but seeing as we already had your eyeball out, we cleaned that out also. Because the injury was severe, the supporting muscles and ligaments to the eyelid were damaged quite badly; however, they will recover with time. Now, the good news, we are only keeping you overnight, so Major Knight will be here to pick you up in the morning at 1000 hours. Now, there is an inconvenience you will have to live with for about two months that could be less or more, depending on how well you obey instructions, something, according to Major Knight, you are not good at following. The patch over your eye must be kept on during the daytime and only removed when you go to bed. The eye drops I have prescribed for you must be applied first thing in the morning and last thing at night. Do not forget to do this, alright? Now, can I rely on you to keep up this regimen?" asked Dr. Phillips.

"Your directions will be followed as instructed," laughed Karl, delighted at the outcome. Karl ate a hearty supper, feeling truly happy for the first time in weeks. Tomorrow, I can return to running my department. I'm looking forward to seeing John and Peggy again and the rest of the gang. I wonder how many wires were received from the Delta-1 team? It's been so long since I've heard or seen Hazel. I hope she is safe. For the first time in months, Karl slept soundly throughout the night. There were no bad dreams or storm clouds to wake him up in the middle of the night in that cold sweat, which had been the case for so long. A gentle touch on his shoulder made him jump with visions of the two Gestapo interrogators about to start beating him mercilessly.

"Sorry, Sir, I did not mean to startle you like that, but it's 0630 hours. Time for you to shower and get yourself dressed. Once you have done that, I'll clean and replace that dressing for you. The doctor will be along about 0800 hours to take another look at your eye. How does it feel this morning? I understand you'll be leaving us this morning at 1000 hours, is that correct?" asked Helen as she handed him a hospital dressing gown.

Karl, as he stood up, thought about what she had just asked him. "Helen, I don't have a headache or any pain—just a little twinge of soreness when I move my eyes. You chaps are the best, thank you, thank you." Karl was enjoying the feeling of freedom from relying on others. "I'll be back soon. It won't take me long in the bathroom. I hope you have breakfast ready for me; I'm famished."

The time flew by. The doctor met with Karl for an examination. Pleased with the condition of the eye, he parted by saying, "Well, old chap, I would say you're on the way back to having normal eyesight. I will need to see you back here in a week. Other than that, just follow the instructions I gave you. Bye for now." With that, Dr. Phillips walked out into the hall.

Good old Clive arrived punctually at 0950 hours to find Karl waiting in the hospital lobby. His smile needed no further explanation. "Morning, Clive, I am so ready to be back at the camp. I hope you're ready to put up with me again?" The old Karl was showing through, and Clive simply gave Karl's arm a two-handed shake, indicating that all was well. "Clive, when we reach the camp, I would first like to retrieve my stuff from long-term storage, then head over to my apartment to change and unpack before returning to camp. Would that be alright with you?" Karl's mind was already going a hundred miles an hour—almost his old self again.

In his apartment, Karl got himself squared away. Instead of calling for a staff car to pick him up, he elected to get back into his old habit of taking the bus to work. Walking to the corner of the street, he queued up, waiting for the #5 bus that would make a stop at the main gate in front of the camp. Other than a few soldiers saluting him as they got off the bus, traffic was relatively light. He enjoyed the bus ride immensely. Who would ever think riding a bus could be so enjoyable looking at all those faces, each with a different story to tell?

The conductor announced the next stop as Hammond Circle. Karl stood up and moved to the open platform at the rear of the bus. The squealing brakes and sudden slowing down announced they were stopping. Approaching the main gate, the MP saluted him, looked at his ID card, then said, "Pass through, Sir, nice to see you." The tall MP had passed Karl through this gate so many times before. However, he would never say "welcome back," just in case someone was listening.

Karl walked up to the main entrance; the patch on his eye made him look more like a pirate than a captain in the British Intelligence Service. He was home.

CHAPTER 12

ESPIONAGE OPERATION

Karl entered the lobby of the BIS headquarters and was about to say, glad to see you to the attendant when he was usurped by a group of army and air force personnel from the secretarial pool. "Welcome back, Captain Vita; we are so pleased to see you back amongst us. With that patch eye over your left eye, it makes you look more like a rusty old pirate—very appropriate. If you don't mind our humor, we will address you as Captain Cooke, the famous pirate!" said First Lieutenant Susan McCabe, the department director, as she laughingly made the welcome back speech, clapping along with the other ladies.

Karl smiled at the welcome back reception he was given. "You can call me anything you like, but never call me late for a big hug from each and every one of you." Karl was always the favorite amongst the ladies in that department. "We aim to please. Now, ladies, remember he is recovering from combat wounds, so be gentle." One by one, each of the twelve girls walked up to Karl and kissed him on the cheek before returning to their department. Two of the junior clerks cheekily preferred to take advantage of the welcome back event by planting a big kiss right on his lips, even though they were still a little sore from the beating.

Karl was thinking, I am so fortunate to work with these wonderful ladies; if they only knew how close I was to never seeing them again! "Lieutenant, how on earth did you know I was about to enter the lobby?" asked Karl.

"Well, old Harry down at the gate called us as soon as he passed you through. We had heard from Major Knight that you would be here later in the day, so I asked Harry to call as soon as you arrived. We are so thankful to know you're home safe and sound, Sir. By the look of that patch over your eye, you had a rough time wherever you were. No need to say where; it's none of my business. All of us have been praying for you, Sir; again, welcome back." Susan stood back, saluted, then, like a flash, gave Karl a big kiss, saying, "I have wanted to do that for a long time; apologies for taking advantage like that."

Susan was blushing as she looked at the lipstick on both of Karl's cheeks. "Well, Lieutenant, I could put you on report unless you have a good enough reason for me not to?" asked Karl, trying to keep a straight face.

"Well, Sir, if you let me buy you a pint tonight, I could try to persuade you not to do that. So, what do you say? How does the Ship's Knees sound after work, say at 1730 hours?"

Karl's response was what Susan wanted to hear. "Well, if I may call you Susan, I think that would be a wonderful way to spend my first evening back in Slough. I will meet you there. Are we in or out of uniform? If we are out, make it 1830 hours, so I can change at my flat before meeting up with you. Question, do you live here on base, or do you have your own digs off base?" asked Karl.

"I live close to the pub, so that time will be great; see you later." She saluted again, then turned to return to her department, her face beaming with a wonderful smile. Karl remained standing in the lobby, thinking, what the hell are you doing? Only home two days, and you are already accepting a date for tonight. Oh, to Hell with it; I've looked death in the eye twice so far this year, so I'm not going to get a guilty conscience over a pint of beer, especially when a very charming lady is buying it. Laughing out loud, he thought, I have a thing for ladies in uniforms as he turned to leave.

Karl walked down the hall to his department and opened the door. Once again, he was mobbed by members of his small staff, so thrilled to have their boss back safe and sound. Peggy was the first to speak. "Sir, when we heard about your eye from Major Knight, we decided to buy you an appropriate gift. We hope you like it," she said as she brought her hand from behind her back, holding a brightly colored gift-wrapped box, then continued speaking. "John let me take off for a few hours earlier today, and Major Knight kindly allowed me to borrow his staff car to go and find this gift."

Peggy handed Karl the box just as Clive entered the department, barking, "And who gave you all permission to stop working just because this bloke arrived back here today? Even though it's against regulations, I think we all need to welcome him back properly. Don't you all agree?" Clive opened the door, and in came his sergeant, pushing a cart with rows of glasses and two champagne bottles in ice buckets, along with a welcome home frosted cake. It made it feel more like a birthday party than a welcome back party. "Now, we can welcome this old bugger back properly."

Clive, as usual, had thought of everything. While two of the office clerks poured the Champagne, Karl ripped off the paper from the box, then, with a look of total surprise, started laughing out loud. "How appropriate. You people are the best." Inside the box were two beautifully stitched leather eye patches, one in brown and one in black. Clive had mentioned that Karl would be wearing an ugly hospital patch for at least two or more months. Hearing that gave Peggy the idea to visit the leather accessories shop in Slough, confident they could provide such an item for her.

"Allow me to put the brown one on for you, Sir," said Peggy as she carefully placed it over the gauze patch and tied it at the back of his head. "Now, that looks so sexy; you will have all the ladies around here following you." Peggy had not intended to say that, but she did, and everyone got a big laugh from it.

"Not if I can help it, young lady; this chap gives me enough problems without all the females in this building going giddy over his patch." Clive was enjoying this small gathering, finding something good to celebrate during these strenuous times in a war that was forced upon them. This was the medicine they all could enjoy. As he stood watching the merrymaking, he thought more about how he knew his friend so very well and the painful reality that they came close to losing him, so let him enjoy this attention.

The welcome back gathering finally came to an end. Karl thanked everyone, then proceed to his small office, saying, "John, would you bring me all the latest wires from all the Delta groups and any correspondence that needs my attention. One other thing, make sure I leave by 1600 hours. I need to go over to my flat and change out of this uniform. I have a dinner engagement that I don't want to be late for," said Karl as he dove into the pile of communiques on his desk.

"Will do, Sir; so good to see you back behind that desk." John was showing his admiration for his commanding officer. Karl separated all the Delta teams, then started reading the ones from the Delta-1 team. He skimmed through each communication, carefully looking for that word "better" that would tell him Hazel was safe. There it was in many of the wires until he got to the last two that simply stated, we are moving to a new location, stop. Getting too hot to stay in present location, stop. Could be several weeks until we transmit again. Out. Karl sat behind his desk, not moving, with the last communication still in his hand. I hope they are going to be alright. It sounds so much like what happened to Kitty's group back in 1937. John walked in and advised him it was time to leave.

"Thanks, John, see you tomorrow; have a nice evening," replied Karl as he closed the door to his office. He walked out into the hallway, wishing everyone still at their stations the same good evening. At the bus stop, he waited patiently in a short queue for the #5 bus to arrive. Around the corner came the familiar green double-decker bus, leaning to the right as the driver wheeled it around the left-handed corner. The queue moved quickly once the passengers getting off had done so. On-board, Karl found an empty seat toward the rear, near the open platform. Looking out the window, he thought how drab all the buildings looked, most having tape across their windows in an X pattern. An announcement brought him back to the surroundings of the bus, "White Chapel Lane, next stop," said the bus conductor in a very loud voice. Karl stood up and stepped down onto the platform, waiting for the familiar squeaky brakes to announce the arrival at his stop. With a lurch, the bus came to a complete stop. Karl got off and started walking down the road until he arrived at his apartment building.

As he opened the gate to the small garden, he started to tremble, those feelings and painful memories flooding back into his subconscious mind. His left hand started shaking on the doorknob while the other fumbled uncontrollably for the key slot. Karl, get a hold of yourself; you are far away from that Gestapo Headquarters now. Start thinking about your date for this evening; block those ugly thoughts that will unglue you. Do it right now, or you will not be able to cope. What seemed a long time was only seconds as Karl stood there with his hand on the doorknob, allowing his brain to take control of his emotional being. Feeling the waves of anguish subsiding, he opened the door and carefully climbed the stairs to his flat. Feeling so much better now, he opened the door, entering the small efficiency unit.

Inside, he undressed, hanging his uniform up in the wardrobe. He put on his bathrobe and went down the hall to the bathroom for a bath and shave. Due to wartime regulations, the use of hot water was limited. However, he did not care what water he had in the bathtub; it was refreshing. Back in his room, he took out a white shirt, grey trousers, and a double-breasted dark blue blazer from the wardrobe. Hanging them on the open door, he crossed over to a chest of drawers and chose a pair of grey socks and a black leather belt. Smiling, he changed the brown eye patch for the black one. Standing there, he pondered whether to wear a tie. It's a pub I'm meeting Susan at; I guess we will have a drink, then have dinner, so maybe I will wear that tie after all.

Thinking again about what had just happened by the front door, he willed himself to take charge of future emotions. I will have to start being aware of when an attack could flare up and what brings it on. I don't want to take the risk of being sent to a sanitarium for therapy. If that were to happen at the office, I would be in trouble. Now that I'm aware of the symptoms, I should be able to control them. Well, I pray to God I can.

Karl walked down the stairs, stopping momentarily to glance into the hallway mirror when a voice behind him made him jump. "Mrs. Mann, you made me jump," Karl said as he turned to address his landlady.

"Sorry to startle ya, Captain; cor' don't ya look smashing. I haven't seen ya in months." Mrs. Mann was a typical Londoner, short and stocky, rollers in her hair most of the time, but tough as nails with a big heart. Her facial expressions gave her away; she was so pleased to see Karl back home. It was war, and he was in the intelligence service, which meant he would be in harm's way most of the time. She never asked him where he had been because she also knew he would not tell her or take the easy way out by lying.

"Well, it is so good to see you too. It's been quite a while, so glad to be back here. I did a stint in hospital, months back, after Dunkirk, then I did a very stupid thing a couple of weeks ago in a training accident. I ended up bashing my eye, which needed surgery. All's well, though; the patch should be off in a couple of months."

Karl was feeling good about his cover story. Mrs. Mann, however, was not sure which part of his story she would believe—maybe the part about Dunkirk. Karl wished his landlady a good evening and promised to have tea with her in a couple of days, then walked out into the deserted street. At the corner bus stop, he waited for the bus to take him to the town center in Slough. Susan's directions to the Ship's Knees would take him about ten plus minutes to walk. The evening was quiet with clear skies. Karl was walking reasonably fast, and he kept thinking, it's amazing how good my leg feels. Now, if I can get my eyesight back in the left eye, I'll be as good as new.

Fourteen minutes later, he saw the sign for the Ship's Knees dimly lit due to the blackout regulations. Opening the door, he was surprised at how large the lounge was. It was charming with its low-beamed ceiling and heavy dark oak furniture. Very nice, he thought as his one good eye focused on the patrons sitting at the bar and a few more sitting in booths. Susan does not appear to be here yet. I guess I'll sit in that booth at the back of the lounge until she arrives. The proprietor came over, asking if he would like to order a drink and if there would be anyone else joining him.

"Yes, I'm expecting a young lady shortly. In the meantime, I'll have a mild and bitter, if you please," replied Karl. The beer arrived, and Karl took a long first sip, enjoying the taste as it went down his throat. He started to relax, enjoying this time alone with his beer.

A voice behind him said softly, "So sorry to keep you waiting, Sir. I got delayed leaving the base earlier. How long have you been waiting?" Susan looked a little flustered as she slid into the bench seat opposite Karl.

"Please, no apologies. I have been enjoying this quiet time alone with my beer. What can I get you to drink?" Karl waved his arm to get the proprietor's attention.

"Miss Susan, so nice to see you in civilian attire. You look really smashing, don't you think, Sir?" said Ben, the proprietor.

"I would totally agree with you. She also looks really smart in a uniform." Karl was looking at Susan in a whole different way. Even with his one eye, he could see the dark blue fitted suit made her look completely different. I'm such a lucky chap when it comes to meeting and dating the ladies, he thought. "So, tonight, we will not talk shop, nor will you keep calling me sir, agreed?" Karl was looking to have a nice evening alone with a brand-new lady friend. There would be no guilty feelings this evening. In his mind, having looked death in the face more than once, he reconfirmed there may not be a tomorrow. War had a way of changing your perspective on life. "Well, Susan, what's our game plan for this evening? Shall we stay here in this nice lounge for dinner, or did you have some other plan?" asked Karl as he watched her fidget in her seat, moving her sherry glass from side to side, no longer the cocky, overconfident army officer hiding behind that uniform anymore.

"Susan, you surprise me. You have always impressed me as being a very confident young lady. However, take you out of that uniform, and you become a very shy, and may I say, very attractive lady." Karl was smiling, enjoying how he was affecting the lady opposite him.

"Karl, you have no idea how the girls in my department talk about you and the relationship you have with Lieutenant Collings. It's a little intimidating, sitting here, knowing you could be out with any one of the single girls at the base. I also realize you're only here this evening because I was goading you on to have a drink with me. Lieutenant Collings has been on assignment for many months; am I to assume when she returns…"

"If she returns," interjected Karl as he listened to her speak. "That you will become a couple once again?" concluded Susan, looking so much calmer now she had got that off her chest.

"Susan, I have had this discussion a few times before, and now I'm finding myself doing it once again. So, let me clarify this right now for you. We are at war; there could be no tomorrow, especially for chaps like me who find themselves in harm's way all too often. My forward vision for next week, month, and year is, I probably won't see another year, so no matter what the scuttlebutt is about Lieutenant Collings and myself, I intend to live for today and nothing beyond that. Does that answer your questions?" Karl could feel his temper trying to overcome him. Taking a large swig of his beer, he quickly regained his composure. "Sorry for that outburst, Susan. I had no right to unload on you like that, again my apologies," said Karl, not really feeling good about his actions.

"It's me who should be apologizing; I started this. So, can we start again, Karl?" asked Susan, trying to reset the mood. Over dinner, they both shared stories, laughing about things they both did growing up and the path that brought them together this evening.

"Well, that was an excellent dinner; thank you for recommending it," said Karl as he drank the last of his beer.

Looking at her watch, Susan calmly asked, "What time is your last bus? It's still early yet. Then again, we could go back together in the morning?" Susan was exploring to see if there was an opportunity for romance when they left the Ship's Knees.

"Well, we could do that, but I'm in civilian attire; that may be a little too much first thing in the morning." Karl was being diplomatic to get out of Susan's invitation. "Tonight was wonderful; maybe we can do it again when I have two good eyes, shall we?" Karl could see by her facial expression the disappointment of the evening coming to an end.

Ben brought over the bill, placing it between them on the table. Susan went to pick it up, but a firm hand on her arm stopped her. "Tonight is my treat, young lady. I have had a wonderful time, so please; it's my pleasure to do this," said Karl as he retrieved some cash from his wallet.

"You do realize I was trying my best to seduce you into staying with me tonight, don't you?" said Susan as she reached over to grasp Karl's hand.

"Susan, I am flattered to think you would like to make love to me, but right now is not the time for such thoughts, as much as I will regret it in the morning. Let's see how things go in a few days. Maybe we can take a weekend out in the country; what do you think of that?" Karl had already made up his mind; if no news came from Hazel, then he would pursue a romantic weekend away with this charming lady.

"Can I at least walk you to the bus stop?" asked Susan as Karl paid the bill.

"Of course, you can. Maybe we can find a quiet spot to have a good night kiss. I would like that; what do you think?" Karl stood first, reaching out for her hand as she slid across the seat. The material on the cushion made it difficult to slide while holding her skirt in place, providing Karl with a view of her thighs. Hmm, I'm willing to bet she did that intentionally! The air seemed a little cooler outside, so Susan looped her arms tightly around Karl's left arm as they started walking toward the bus stop. The blackout created a challenge for pedestrians with no streetlights to show the way, just the occasional torch in someone's hand as they passed them by.

"This is ridiculous, Susan. Let me walk you home; then I'll catch the bus. It would concern me, allowing you to walk home on your own. It's not the gentlemanly thing to do." Karl was also thinking it was his way out of an impossible situation.

"Karl, you are such a gentleman; no wonder I have a crush on you." Susan was once again fortifying how she felt about this charismatic Austrian, sending him another message that she was trying to persuade him to stay overnight. "Karl, my house is over there, and the park is here on the left. Let's sit for a while on the bench before you leave, shall we?" Susan would give it one more chance to convince Karl to change his mind about spending the night. The benches were not entirely in the dark. Dim lights gave just enough light to show the path. They sat in the middle of one of the benches, Susan making sure she was right next to him.

"Now, handsome, how about that good night kiss you promised me earlier?" She was wasting no time as she turned in toward Karl, putting her arm around his neck. Karl reciprocated by putting his arm around her waist and pulling her in closer. In the dim light, Karl could see and feel her tensing in anticipation of that contact. She did not waste any more time; with moist lips, she found his mouth and kissed him deeply. Momentarily, they parted, looking at each other without uttering a sound. Karl placed his hand on her cheek.

She responded by leaning her head to one side, trapping his hand between her shoulder and cheek. Once again, they kissed. This time, Susan opened her mouth, her tongue forcing Karl's mouth open and connected with his. That kiss was exciting her to no end; she wanted Karl so desperately.

Susan pulled away, breathing heavily. "Karl, if I can't persuade you to stay with me tonight, would you please touch me? I want you so much." Karl, hearing this, pulled away from her, holding her hands to calm her down. She was totally out of control. The alcohol had removed any inhibitions she may have had up to this point.

"Susan, I can sense you are emotionally aroused—maybe a little too much. I've delivered on that kiss, and now, lady, you need to sleep off that wildness those drinks have put you into. So, up you get, and let's cross the road to your house, shall we?" At the front door, Karl hugged her and gently kissed her cheek, saying, "Thankyou; this was a wonderful evening. See you tomorrow morning; don't be late."

Susan started to turn toward the door, then stopped, saying, "You realize because of you, I'll probably not sleep a wink tonight. If that happens, you will owe me big time, and I will collect on that next time. See you tomorrow, you sexy man." Giggling at what she had just said, Karl simply laughed out loud, walking away into the night. Walking the ten minutes back to the bus stop gave him time to digest the evening and the events that kept him laughing as he walked. I think this one is wild out of uniform, not to be handled lightly. I can't believe what a few drinks could turn her into. Of all the women I have known or dated, she is, without a doubt, the wildest. God help the chap she eventually ends up with. I must admit, I prefer women who have strong convictions and go after whatever it is they want.

Thinking this made him laugh again as he arrived at the bus stop. The following morning, Karl got an early start had a quick cup of tea with his landlady. "Don't be late tonight, Karl; remember, you are still recovering from that eye wound," said Mrs. Mann, more of a mother to Karl than a landlady.

"Will do, Mum," replied Karl as he got to the front door. Instinctively, he reached for his umbrella customarily kept in the hallway stand, then remembered he had given it to that pretty

Sergeant Gwen Phillips on another rainy morning. "Mrs. Mann, can I borrow one of your umbrellas? I must have left mine in the office." He did not elaborate any further.

"Go right ahead, my boy," replied Mrs. Mann. Walking to the bus stop, Karl started thinking, why do I continue to take the bus? On my salary, I can easily afford a little car. The petrol ration books I will receive will be more than enough for driving locally around here. When I go to Baldock to see Mama and the family, I can still use the train. That way, I'll never run out of petrol stamps. With a new objective in his head, Karl started to think about all the freedom a car would give him.

On the crowded bus, a businessman sitting next to Karl said, "I'm getting off at the next stop, old man. Care to take a gander at the *Daily Mail?*" Then, as he stood ready to exit at the next stop, he said, "I'm all done with it, so be my guest."

Karl thanked him and immediately started scanning the classifieds. After four more stops, the conductor announced, "Next stop, Hampton Lane." Karl, hearing this announcement, folded the paper and made his way to the rear platform. Like so many times before, the bus squealed and shuddered as it slowed to the next stop. Karl stepped off the platform before the bus came to a complete halt, tucking the newspaper into his briefcase, then walked briskly toward the camp entrance. At the gatehouse, the guards took a quick look at his ID, then waved him through.

Entering his department, Peggy smiled, handing him a pile of folders for his review, saying, "Good morning, Sir. Last night's communications are in the sealed pouch on your desk. Why don't you start reviewing them while I get your morning coffee?"

Karl smiled back, his immediate thoughts turning to the contents of that pouch. "Thanks, Peggy, be a dear and include a buttered roll with that coffee. I'm feeling a little peckish this morning. Take some money from my cash box in the top drawer and buy yourself something as well." Peggy opened the drawer and took four shillings from the box, then walked out. That girl is becoming my right arm. She is so efficient at everything she does, thought Karl. Taking the keychain from his pocket, he opened the dispatch pouch, removing its contents onto the desk. The dispatches were separated by elastic bands. He opened the Delta-1 batch first to see if Hazel had included their code word. Out of the four communiques, the very last one contained that particular word; it read, "En route to meet up with southern partisan's cell, stop. They will guide us over the Pyrenees Mountains into Spain; better for us right now, stop. Hun has been one step behind us for last twenty days, stop. Getting too dangerous to stay, stop. Believe we have a mole operating amongst us, stop. Better not to use radio until we are secure again, stop. Karl sat back in his chair, the communique in his hand, thinking, thank God they are safe but for how long?

He turned his attention back to reading the remaining communiques; however, he found it hard not to continue thinking about the Delta-1 team. The more he thought about that communique, the more he realized they needed to act on this information right away. Karl stood up from his desk and headed for the door, saying, "John, when Peggy returns, tell her I've gone to see Major Knight. Have her bring the Delta-1 personnel file as quickly as she can."

Walking down the hall, he noticed Susan coming in the opposite direction. "Captain Vita, may I have a moment of your time, please?" asked Susan with a timid tone in her voice.

"I would love to talk to you, Lieutenant, but right now, we have a code red condition. Let me take care of this; then I'll come to find you. I had a very nice time last night; bye for now." Karl was not wasting precious time talking to Susan. Telling her that he had a nice time would settle her frayed nerves for a while anyway.

Karl arrived at Major Knight's office and asked his secretary if he was in his office. "Yes, Captain Vita, he's on the phone with London right now. Please, take a seat, and I'll let him know you're waiting," said Mrs. Mary Evans, expecting Karl to take a seat.

"No time for that," said Karl as he knocked loudly on Clive's office door, then walked right in.

"Captain Vita, you can't do that. Please, close the door and take a seat," pleaded Mrs. Evans. Karl closed the door alright, once he was inside.

"General, can you hold one minute, please? One of my officers has just entered, and by the look on his face, there is trouble afoot. May I call you back in about an hour? Thank you, Sir, and sorry for ending this call so abruptly," concluded Clive. "Alright, Karl, you have that look of anger on your face. What the bloody hell is it now?" Clive was rattled as well. He was concerned, as he knew Karl would not do this unless something were drastically wrong.

"Read this latest wire from the Delta-1 team we received this morning." Karl placed the wire down on Clive's desk, then sat quietly, facing his commanding officer as he read the wire.

"Karl, you did the right thing bringing this immediately to my attention. A little less theatrics next time, please. If this is correct, their locations and radio traffic has been compromised, but who could that mole be? They are in severe danger, and there is nothing the BIS can do to help them, from here anyway."

Karl sat back in his chair, saying, "Is there anyone over there that could join them and help identify the whistle-blower?" Karl was racking his brains. Who in that handpicked team would betray their movements?

There was a knock on the door, and Peggy entered, carrying personnel folders for the Delta-1 team. "Here are the files you asked for, Sir. I have also taken the liberty of bringing you your coffee and roll as well. We all know how you get when you're on a mission!" Peggy placed the files in front of them and put the roll and coffee to one side of the desk, saying, "Is there anything else I can do for you, Sir, before I return to the office?" Clive looked at Karl with a frown on his face.

"Thank you, Peggy. That will be all. Tell John, if any more communiques come in, especially from the Delta-1 team, bring them straight to me. Find me if you have to." Karl and Clive started spreading the files out to review, beginning with the team leader, Gunther.

"Is there anything that would sway Gunther to provide information to the Germans?" asked Clive, studying his file.

"Don't be ridicules, Clive; I would trust Gunther with my life," replied Karl.

Clive folded his arms behind his head as he ran through all the scenarios that would force a man like Gunther to turn on his team members. "Gunther has family in Hamburg, is that correct?" asked Clive.

"Yes, but they may have been evacuated to another part of Germany by now. Why do you ask?" Karl answered with a concerned expression on his face and anger in his voice.

"Let's create a scenario as an exercise. Let's say the Gestapo or S.S. got word to him by some means that they knew he had returned to the Continent, then threatened to torture and perhaps kill his family members if he did not cooperate with them. That's one avenue we should be investigating further, don't you agree?" asked Clive, knowing full well he was hitting a nerve when it came to the trust and loyalty of Gunther.

"He would never betray his team, nor would he cooperate with the Germans in any way, even if it meant putting his family in harm's way. Let's not forget, that is a big concern to us when screening new agents who still have relatives on the Continent, correct? In the unlikely event that they discovered he had returned as an English agent, a capture or kill order would become a high priority. As much as this line of investigation angers me, we must pursue it further for everyone in that team and every other team, Delta or otherwise, currently deployed. This could well be the weak link in our security screening. I'll get Peggy back here to help us further with each of the agents who have family on the Continent."

Clive stood up and proceeded to the office door, saying, "Karl, be a good chap; gather those files and follow me to meeting room A-1. We need to spread out, and tell Peggy that she and John should plan on going home very late tonight. Let's go." Clive and Karl walked down the hall toward the meeting room. As they approached it, they noticed all the lights were on, and a meeting was in progress. Clive, pulling rank, instructed those in the room to hold their meeting someplace else as he was taking this room for the foreseeable future.

"Yes, Sir," said one of the junior officers with a hint of sarcasm in his voice.

Karl picked up the wall phone and dialed his department extension. "Who's this?" asked Karl.

"It's Private Ann Watts, Sir; what can I do for you?"

Karl responded, "tell John and Peggy to pull up the Delta team files.

"Yes, Sir."

"Ann, would you also tell them they should plan on being here very late tonight and hurry up with those files? Thank you." Karl hung up, then returned to the conference room table.

"When the other two get here, we can start by identifying each group by nationality. Then we can start background checks and current locations of family members," said Clive as he removed his tunic and unbuttoned the top button of his shirt. "Might as well get comfortable; it's going to be a long night. Karl, call my office and tell them to bring down some hot coffee in thermoses; include some biscuits with that request as well," said Clive as he started into the first folder.

Shortly thereafter, John and Peggy arrived, pushing a trolley piled high with personnel files. "Blimey, it's going to take a long time to weed through all these files," said Clive as he stared at the pile of files on the conference table, John arranging the files by Delta team numbers. Karl explained the plan to John and Peggy, then told them to get comfortable by removing their tunics and loosening their ties. Peggy started spreading the files out down the length of the table. With so many files to review, they took up its entire length. To make things easier, John moved all the chairs away from the table, other than the four being used.

"Alright, we're ready. Karl, you and Peggy start isolating the foreign members of each team, placing each folder to one side. John and I will do the same on the opposite side of the table. Once we have separated them, we can start the real work of reviewing and taking notes on what we find out about their families. Are their parents still alive? Is their husband or wife still over there, or are they in a safe place like here in England? Have we missed any updates? That sort of stuff, alright? Do they have siblings still alive; if so, where are they residing? If that information is not available in the folder, make a note to have one of our agents investigate to confirm. We must not leave any stone unturned. Children? Don't forget to note how old they are. Who do they live with? Maybe it's a wife, husband, brother, sister, grandparent? People, we are looking for a needle in a haystack, so don't assume anything. If there's a question, flag it in your notes."

With those instructions, Clive started to take apart his first folder. The only sound in the room was the shuffling of papers and quiet discussions between them. After an hour, the coffee arrived with biscuits and a large plate of assorted sandwiches.

"I took the liberty of ordering sandwiches for you all; the tea is labeled just in case one of you doesn't drink coffee. The cafeteria said they would check in with you before they close at 2000 hours, just in case you need refills," said Nancy as she removed everything from the trolley.

The hours clicked by with no real concrete information until Peggy found a link between the Delta-1 and Delta-3 teams. "Sirs, I think this may be worth investigating further. These two teams have been operating together for over three months. For the most part, they are traveling together—only hours apart. Now, here is the interesting part; in the D-3, there is a Polish agent by the name of Jakub Czeslaw. He was living and working in Berlin before the war. His wife and daughter are still there, according to this file. His wife's brother is in the German Army stationed in Southern France. The initial BIS interrogation report does not mention the German brother-in-law anywhere. This could be our first big break." Peggy was feeling really pleased with herself over her discovery.

"Well done, Peggy, but we still have to go through all of the other files. Great start, though; now, let's take that coffee break, shall we?" said Clive as he stood, stretching his back. The four of them sat drinking coffee and devouring the sandwiches. Clive looked at his watch, then, with a look that suggested he had a question, he asked John, "Are we in a transmit mode right now?"

John also looked at his watch, saying, "Got another twenty minutes left, Sir; what are you thinking?"

Clive stood, pacing back and forth as he spoke. "Karl, why don't we have John wire Gunther to contact us. John, the message should read, 'Mole close by, stop. Get to secure location with H' wireless, stop. Will wait for your call signal, confirm, out.' Go over to your wireless station and send that right now. I will join you once they confirm they are ready to transmit/receive.

"I always thought our background checks were very thorough. How could something so obvious slip through like this? I remember so very well my interrogation and the lengths you people put me through to make sure I wasn't a German spy." As Karl spoke, he started to formulate a new procedure for the BIS to follow for all existing agents and all new prospects entering the BIS.

The wall phone started ringing, "That must be John; Peggy, you continue to review those folders. Karl, you come with me to the radio room," commanded Clive as he picked up a pad of paper as he walked toward the door. Entering the radio room, they found John taping out a signal with his Morse Code key.

"Sir, we are going to make this call an audio transmission in about fifteen minutes. They are setting the equipment up as we speak." John was showing signs of excitement, knowing they could talk instead of Morse Coding. "Remember, three minutes or less; we can't take a chance on the Germans getting a radio fix," reminded John.

The three sat around, jotting down talking points. Time was of the essence when using audio communications. "Our code name for this call is 'Overlook,' and theirs is 'Willow,' said John as he arranged the microphone in front of all three.

"Let's go over how to address this call. Karl, let me see your notes and compare them to mine. Damn it, Karl; they're in German. Couldn't you have written your questions in English?"

"Sorry, Sir, I have a habit of doing that when it's for my own use."

"Too late now, good thing I read German, I suppose." Clive settled down again.

A crackling sound came over the speaker with a female voice quietly saying, "Overlook, this is Willow, over."

"Overlook receiving you loud and clear; stand by. Go ahead, Sir; the line is ready," said John to Clive.

"Willow, we suspect you are being compromised by a leak from your Polish agent, giving the Hun your ongoing activities. Take whatever action is necessary to neutralize agent immediately. Send wire when it's done, over."

An intense brief silence made the seconds of waiting more like minutes until the answer came back. "Overlook, drastic measure, but if this is a command, it will be done as instructed immediately. Are there any other instructions before signing off?" the female voice came back on saying.

"We have one last message to pass along. Tell Grandmother she is the best, over and out!"

The line went dead, and Clive turned to look at John, saying, "What the hell was that last statement meant to imply?" John lowered his head, trying to hide a smile. Karl was quietly doing the same. Clive watched the eye play, then sternly replied, "Alright, I got what's going on. Can we all remember that every second those people are over there, their voice transmissions are in extreme danger? Now, let's go back to work." As Clive stood to walk out the door, Karl and John saw him chuckling to himself. All was forgiven.

Back in the conference room, they returned to the job of screening each agent operating in the Delta teams. Peggy identified three more that could become a problem in the future, a result of the leak from the Polish agent. At 2300 hours, the last folder was closed. All four sat back with relief at completing their purge of the BIS foreign agents.

"John, when you transmit to D-4 and D-2, send the same transmission as we used earlier, using the code names for these three. Add this at the end: Make arrangements to recover agent immediately. You might as well fire up the receiver. Isn't it about time to make contact?" asked Clive.

"Will do, Sir; maybe there is an answer from D-1. I will tell the night wireless operator to get himself some tea while I do that," replied John as he walked toward the door.

"Alright, young lady, Karl and I can return all these files. You look really tired, so thank you for staying this evening, and a real big thank you for being so astute at identifying the leak. Now, off you go," said Clive, looking at Peggy.

"Nonsense, Sir. I always finish what I start. Now, let me get the cart over here, and we can start loading the files." Peggy was not about to bail out just yet.

"Well, in that case, let's get started. After that, if you're so inclined, we can all have a whiskey chaser in my office before heading home. By the way, Peggy, your boss here will not expect you until at least 1000 hours tomorrow morning, isn't that right, Captain?" said Clive, looking at Karl for approval.

"Could not have put it better myself, Major," replied Karl as he walked in the vanguard behind Clive and Peggy. In Clive's office, they sat enjoying some vintage single malt whiskey as they waited for John to return with an update.

"Peggy, while we wait for John to join us, tell me about yourself and how Captain Vita managed to have you join his department, thinking he pulled one over on me. Ever thought of becoming an analyst here in the BIS?" Clive was not making small talk; he meant every word.

"Girls like me rarely get those opportunities, Sir," replied Peggy, her heart pounding as the commander in chief of BIS Operations asked her if she would consider this opportunity.

"I can make that happen, Peggy. You would have to go through extensive training—not an easy task, may I add. It will be your call. Sleep on it, and let me know in a day or so, any objections, Captain?"

Clive turned to Karl, looking for his approval, "None whatsoever; glad you see what I saw in Peggy's abilities. I think you should jump at this, Peggy, while there's an offer on the table," responded Karl, swigging down the last of his whiskey.

The office door swung open, and in walked John, a solemn look on his face. "Got a wire back from D-1, Sir. It reads, 'Have eliminated problem. Did not like doing it, though, stop.' I also dispatched to the other groups your directive about those other agents."

"Thanks, John; now, how about that glass of whiskey?" asked Clive as John pulled up a chair. Clive went around, refilling everyone's glass, then toasted them by saying, "Today, we eliminated a problem. As painful as that may be, we have safeguarded our agents out there in harm's way. Thank you for making that happen." Clive gulped down his whiskey, then said, "Alright, you two, let's head for home. Karl, do you need a ride, or are you planning on staying here at the camp tonight? How about you, Peggy? Are your quarters here on the base? John, how about you? It's late; how will you get home?"

John answered, "I have my motorbike, so I'm fine, Sir." Peggy answered next, "I'm only two buildings over in the female quarters, so don't worry about me."

Peggy went to stand up when Karl spoke up, "Well, young lady, I will not allow you to go unescorted, so allow me to do that." Karl had decided to get a spare shirt and toilet bag from his office and stay at the officer's quarters for tonight. "Well, shall we adjourn? Again, thank you for an outstanding job; well done." Karl stopped at his office, picked up his shirt, underwear, socks, and a travel toilet bag, and headed for the lobby to wait for Peggy to join him. He did not have to wait long; the door swung open, and out walked Peggy, looking like she had stopped at the powder room to freshen her makeup. "Ready?" said Karl as he opened the main door for Peggy. The evening was a little chilly. English weather tended to be damp this time of year, and tonight was no different.

"You must be feeling quite weary about now, Sir," said Peggy as she walked out the door.

"Got my second wind. How about you?" answered Karl.

"I'm feeling really good about now. We worked hard as a team and managed to plug the leak in our intelligence, so today was a success." Peggy was feeling proud that she was the one who found the culprit. Karl agreed but felt sorry that a husband and father had panicked, acting recklessly in defense of his family. Unfortunately, that decision cost him his life not that many hours ago.

"Peggy, we lost a good man tonight; our training let him down. An agent should never believe they can make a deal for the safety of family members by leaking information to the enemy. We are trained to always confide in our own leaders. If there's a way to extract them, they will find a way. Betraying your team members will never be the right way. It will cost you your life, which was the case this evening." Karl was trying to justify why a man had lost his life while trying to save his family without pouring cold water on Peggy's achievement.

Reaching the female quarters, they stopped in front of the entrance. Peggy's parting words were, "I think we have done this before! Thank you for escorting me to my quarters. I think your explanation is well-taken. Good night, Karl. See you after 1000 hours tomorrow."

Walking over to the officer's quarters, he made a decision. I'm going home to Baldock this weekend. I have a family that has not seen me in a long time. God, tomorrow is Friday; better asked Clive first thing for a pass. Checking into the room reserved for officers in Clive's division, Karl felt the wave of fatigue taking over as he stripped and climbed into bed, falling asleep almost immediately.

CHAPTER 13

HIS FINAL LOVE

The following morning, Karl made his way to his building while it was still dark. His first stop was to buy a large container of coffee before proceeding to the office. At his desk, he sat, feet up, mulling over the tragic events of yesterday. He did not like himself, or the others involved, taking another agent's life; right or wrong, it would be insensitive not to show some remorse for this action. Changing his thoughts, he lightly touched the leather patch over his left eye, thinking it's feeling so much better. Having only one eye makes it harder to focus on things, but I still have a month and a half to go before I can remove it altogether. Better stick my head into Clive's office, then wander over to the medical building to have the dressing changed.

I think I will call Mama and tell her to start cooking the Goulash. She will be ecstatic to hear I will be there tomorrow. I will also talk to Ronny about buying a car once this patch comes off. Walking toward Clive's office, he remembered the brief meeting in the hall with Susan and how nervous and embarrassed she was. I better stop over there as well. "Morning, Clive. I hope you slept well after that long day yesterday?" asked Karl as he plonked himself down on the couch.

"Not really. I kept thinking about having to eliminate poor old Jakub. He must have been really desperate to fall into that trap. Surely, he realized it would end badly," said Clive.

"Clive, I have an idea on how we can address that moving forward. With so many agents involved, it will be no easy task, but let me ask you this first. Would you mind awfully if I went home to Baldock this weekend?" Karl already knew Clive would not object.

"Of course not; you deserve some time off. Report back on Tuesday morning, alright?" replied Clive as he filled out the travel pass. "Now, tell me about your thoughts on how we can add another layer of screening to the field agents' security, or would you like to work on that plan in Baldock?" asked Clive, knowing full well what the answer would be.

"I'll have it on your desk on Tuesday, alright?" Karl stood up and headed for the door, a spring in his step.

"Don't do anything crazy," yelled Clive as he watched his friend leave the office.

Entering his department, he could see everyone was hard at work, heads down with only the sounds of typewriters and shuffling papers. "Peggy, John, could you join me in my office, please?" Karl wanted to bounce his idea off them on improving security when it came to their foreign agents with families still on the Continent. Seated around Karl's small conference table, he started by saying, "Yesterday, Major Knight was faced with the horrible decision of condemning Jakub to death, a trusted agent that, in his mind, had no choice by put family first. Moving forward, we need to consider whether we can continue using foreign agents who have similar situations. If we cannot deploy them for security reasons, we could be severely handicapping our intelligence operations. Therefore, we need to overhaul the existing requirement, changing it to protect these agents if a similar situation happens again, and we must assume this may already be happening. I have been racking my brains with what we can come up with to address this in a revised training program to combat the blackmail tactic being used by the bloody Gestapo and S.S. bastards. What I would like to do is propose to Major Knight, when I return from seeing my mother this weekend, that we have the counterintelligence boys join us in exploring an effective plan to counter blackmail incidents in the field. Don't be surprised if they suggest recalling all our foreign agents immediately. Can you see Clive going along with that idea?" Karl stopped talking, waiting for a response.

John spoke first, saying, "Sir, that type of planning and recommendation is way above Peggy and my pay grade. If it were my decision to make, I would recall all of them."

Peggy, holding her hands together on the table, simply nodded with her agreement. Karl realized that there was no easy way around this problem, and maybe this disruptive move was the only way to go. "Well, I'm starting to think you two are right. Let's address this on Tuesday. Peggy, while I'm away, draft a memo to Major Knight with a copy to Colonel Jacks saying that I would like to schedule a meeting next week to discuss this glaring weak link.

"Another thing you can assemble for me while I'm away, can you compile all the agents in the field with families on the Continent? Then list all the single ones. Finally, purge the trainees in the same way. I think they're way too close to that weak link. Now, I must be off, or I will miss my train. I'll see you on Tuesday; you know how to reach me if it's important. Peggy, be a dear, and call my mother, and tell her I shall arrive by 1650 hours."

Karl walked out into the fresh air, walking quickly to catch the #5 bus back to his apartment. He had laid out what he was taking with him, which was little as most of his civilian clothes and accessories were already at the bungalow. His case packed, he headed back to catch the bus that would let him off at the train station.

This was the same as the times before he changed trains in London, catching the Baldock train from Kings Cross. When the train pulled out of the Letchworth station, Karl took his case from the overhead rack and watched the countryside go by for the fifteen minutes it took to arrive in Baldock. Karl could feel the excitement building. It was always so good to unwind back here. After all he had been through recently, this would be the medicine he needed. The train slowed to a complete stop.

Opening the carriage door, he stepped down into the smoke and steam drifting down the length of the platform, creating a familiar sight in Karl's mind. Something made him look back, hoping in his mind to see the lovely Kitty walking to meet him. That image was as clear today as it was years back when she arrived to meet the family and consent to becoming his wife.

Instead of shaking off that vision, he embraced it for a few extra moments, thinking how close we came to having that perfect life together. Could he ever really open his heart to Hazel? In the depths of his heart, he knew that probably would not come to pass. Standing there, he also started to realize that if this was what he really thought, he was not being fair to lovely Hazel.

She would always feel that a ghost existed between them, condemning any future to failure. Shaking his head, he headed to the familiar tunnel that ran under the tracks to the small entrance at the front of the station. The evening temperature was not too bad, so he decided to walk the two miles to the bungalow. Walking through the town center, he passed the George and Dragon, thinking, I will go there tomorrow—maybe with Freida and Ronny for a pint; that would be nice.

Arriving at the bungalow, he walked up the driveway. The curtains parted, and the image of his mother looked out, excited to see her youngest son approaching the front door. The door swung open, and out came Mama, followed by Freida, holding Franchot in her arms, with the windup car Karl had bought for him last Christmas. "I'm home, and you are the medicine I need right now. Come and give me a big hug; mind my eye, though," said Karl, feeling so much happier to be back with family. Mama had supper ready, and the wonderful aroma coming from the kitchen made him quite hungry.

"Karl, how is your eye doing?" asked Freida as he took off his coat and cap.

"It really feels good; I can't wait to remove this patch, though. The people in my department had two leather patches made for me—very thoughtful on their part." Then, Karl changed the subject away from his injury. Over a wonderful dinner, Karl devoured everything on his plate, then asked for seconds, saying, "Mama, you have no idea how I miss your cooking. Now, you know why I lost so much weight."

After dinner, Mama made hot coffee, and the three sat talking about Papa and his brothers, still in hiding in the Italian mountains. Karl could see the look on their faces. They wanted to know more about where he had been and what or who had hurt his eye, but they knew he couldn't say too much. "Mama, Freida, what I'm about to tell you is highly classified, so I need your promise to respect its secrecy. If you mention it to anyone, and that's including Ronny, I could face a court-martial or worse. The reason I'm doing this is to put your minds at ease for a little while anyway.

"The injury to my eye is the outcome of a severe beating by thugs in the Gestapo, and yes, I was on the Continent. The countries and places, I will not tell you; however, I feel you should know what it is I am doing currently in the BIS. As of this last deployment, I was a field operative, and I'm now the department director for field agent support. At this point, my days of going back to being a field agent are over. The injuries I have sustained over this past year have eliminated me from doing what I do best: field operations.

"Mama, let me put your mind to rest. From here on, I will be in Slough, operating my department. Other than a stray bomb landing on the camp, I will be out of direct danger. The upside to all this is that I will try and schedule most of my weekends to be here with you all. Having been that close to leaving this earth on several occasions has made me aware I need to be with my family more frequently—something that I have not been too good at doing." Karl stopped talking, waiting for a response.

"My darling brother, I have suspected your lack of writing and calling could be associated with the work you have been doing. This year has been terrible for us here, not knowing if you were hurt or somewhere you could be in jeopardy has kept us on a mental roller coaster. Each time you came home, you always looked worn out, underweight, and those black shadows under your eyes are a dead giveaway. Are we surprised at what you have just told us? Not really. When we landed that first time in Dover, Mama said that with your background, you would be in high demand, and from what you have just told us, she was right. This news you have just given us is wonderful, knowing that from here on, you will be stuck behind a desk, even though, my wonderful brother, you will hate being tied down in an office like that." Freida had spoken something she had wanted to say for several years.

"Now, for some good news!" That perked up Karl, needing to change the subject. "When Ronny comes home, I want him to help me buy a car. I'm getting tired of taking the bus to work every day. I can afford it, so why not?" Karl reached over to grasp his mother's and sister's hands, knowing they would rest easier with the information he had just given them.

The sun was shining through Karl's bedroom window, with wispy clouds floating by. Karl put on his dressing gown and walked into the kitchen. Mama was already cooking for the day, the smell of strong coffee filling the air. Karl walked up behind her and put his arms around her waist. Speaking in German, he wished her good morning, kissing her cheeks as he did so. "Today's a wonderful day, Frau Vita; let's you and I have coffee together in the living room, shall we?" said Karl, feeling comfortable about being home.

Ronny was next to enter the living room, wearing a shirt, trousers, and in bare feet. "Karl, so good to have you home. I'm sorry I didn't get to see you last night; it was really early morning by the time I arrived home. You can't imagine how worried we've been about you and that patched-up eye of yours. How you got it is none of my business. I can only imagine, though," remarked a concerned Ronny, sitting down next to Mama.

"Ronny, I have been given an office assignment, in charge of a communications department. From now on, I will be home more often." In his mind, he thought my spying days could well be over, well for now anyway. "Ronny, I have a favor to ask. I need your help finding a car to buy," said Karl.

"Glad to help; when do you want to start looking?" Hearing Karl talk like this was a welcome relief. Seeing the strained looks on his wife's and mother-in-law's faces each day was hard to live with day after day. Then again, they were also worried about the rest of the family hiding in the mountains somewhere in Italy.

Ronny never said much about his own family. He had lived and grown up in the North of England. His two older brothers were both in the Navy, stationed in Portsmouth, secure in maintenance positions. Both his parents had passed on before the war, hard-working people that lived long enough to see their three lads grow up with the same work ethic as they had.

"Good question, Ronny. I'm in no rush until this left eye is better, and I can see normally again. I thought, over this weekend, I could start looking. I need to get an idea of how much I need to spend for something decent. Does that garage on the high street still have used cars for sale? Quimby's, I believe is their name?" asked Karl.

"The problem right now is used cars are mostly available from people who have lost a loved one in the war. Other people have stored their cars until this war is over, whenever that is. New cars are not being manufactured for private use, so that's out. We can start at Quimby's and go from there. Here are the classifieds from our local newspaper. While I'm in the bathroom, why don't you start scanning the classified for private sales?" Ronny stood up and headed to the kitchen for his second cup of coffee, taking it with him to the bathroom.

Karl eagerly looked at the limited offerings from garages in Baldock and Letchworth. Finding nothing of interest, he started circling cars of interest in the classifieds. I'm a single chap; why am I looking at family cars? He thought, not sure how long I'll be around, so let's look at something sporty that's more my style. He did not have to look too much further. A new listing in Hitchin described a 1935 MG-PB for sale. The reason it was for sale was that the husband died flying during the Battle of Britain. Will not negotiate price 185.00 pounds. Please call Hitchin 4569. Karl sat back, thinking how tragic to lose your husband and now be faced with having to sell his car.

Ronny came back in, dressed in casual attire, saying, "Find anything of interest?"

Karl gave him the paper and said, "How about an open MG sports car? Perfect for a chap like me, what do you think?"

Ronny, taking the paper, let out a very loud belly laugh, "Karl, it is definitely you. God help the ladies at your camp when they see you drive up in a spiffy little gem like that. Let's call and find out if we can go and see it this morning." Ronny was still laughing when he went back into the kitchen to get a cup of coffee for Freida, who was still sleeping. After bathing and shaving, Karl dressed in gray trousers, a dark blue V-neck pullover, and black socks and shoes.

Ronny was already on the telephone, getting details. "Got it; thank you, Claire. We should be there in about an hour." Ronny, beaming, turned to Karl, saying, "Let's head to Lloyds and get some money out of your account. We need to move fast, though. Claire, the owner, told me she has had three calls on the car so far this morning. By the sound of it, we are the closest to her, so let's get going."

Ronny was moving fast, grabbing a light jacket as he headed for the front door with Karl right behind him. At the front door, they both yelled, "Be back later; wish us luck." The first stop was at Lloyds Bank, where Karl withdrew 220 pounds. Then, driving quickly, Ronny headed for Hitchen. Claire's directions said to look for St. Michaels College on the right, then take the very next street on the left, which will be Hemmings Way. Her house number was #46.

"Almost there," said Ronny, excited to be out looking at cars. Number 46 was a detached home with a single garage at the end of the driveway. The brass door knocker was very unusual. It represented a Hawker Hurricane fighter in flight. "Poor devil, hope he did not suffer too much," remarked Ronny as he used the Hurricane to knock three times. The door opened, and there was the smiling face of Claire, dressed in a tweed skirt and a sky-blue jumper set, with shiny brown brogue shoes. She was how Ronny expected a true fair-skinned English rose to look.

"You must be Ronny, and you must be his brother-in-law, Karl, is that correct? Gentlemen, please come in. May I offer you some refreshments before we go out to the garage?"

With a smile on his face, Karl answered, "That's very kind of you, but would you mind awfully if we look at the car first?"

Claire reached for the keys, hanging on a peg by the front door, smiling at seeing the schoolboy smile on Karl's face. It reminded her how her husband looked when they visited the MG dealership in Luton before the war. As Claire unlocked the garage door, Karl asked, "Excuse me for asking, but have you thought about keeping and using the car yourself?"

Claire shook her head, the tears freely rolling down her face. Karl instantly knew he should not have asked that of a woman who had lost her husband. "Forgive me, Claire; that was not appropriate. I was not thinking straight. I should know better." Karl was now feeling angry with himself, his mind thinking rapidly about how to correct that stupid statement.

Claire pulled the two garage doors open, and there sat the beautiful low-slung MG-PB in flawless British Racing Green. Standing back with her arms crossed across her chest, Claire had recovered from her moment of sadness and now was enjoying watching Karl fall in love with his soon-to-be new car. Claire handed Karl the ignition key, saying, "Well, why don't you start it up and see how you like it?" Claire was thinking Patrick would be pleased to see this, knowing his baby would be going to someone who really enjoys this type of sports car.

"Can we give it a quick run up and down the road?" asked Karl. "Of course, we can, but I will have to go with you, alright?" Claire was starting to enjoy this transaction very much, and riding in the MG again with a man beside her after a very long time was healthy medicine for her frame of mind. Ronny went back out into the driveway, backing his Austin into the street. Karl and Claire waited while he did that. "Karl, forgive me for asking, but what is that accent I'm hearing?"

Claire was hoping it was not German because if it was the deal would be off immediately if that were the case. "I was wondering how long it would be before you asked me that, and quite honestly, I should have brought that to your attention right up front, in case you would have preferred to slam the door in my face. I'm Austrian, from Vienna, now serving as a captain in the British Intelligence Service. Before escaping to England in 1936, I was the first officer on a German registered merchant ship. Would you like me to shut off the engine now and leave?"

Karl waited to see Claire's reaction; he didn't have to wait long. "You will not, Captain; you're taking me for a drive." Claire was thrilled that whatever apprehensions she had a few minutes ago were gone, thinking, this bloke is one of those spy people you hear about. God, I'm stupid.

"Claire, before we leave, can we settle the bill of sale? You know I'm going to take it, don't you? Your asking price is extremely fair, so what I'd like to do is pay you in full, and I'm hoping you will allow me to add another 50 pounds for you to donate to the RAF benevolent lost airman's fund. Will this be alright with you?"

Claire turned to face Karl, those tears back in her eyes, saying, "Karl, you are so thoughtful, but don't you think that's a little too generous?"

Karl quietly answered her, "Your husband gave his life for this country. Fifty pounds is the least I can do." Karl sat motionless, watching her.

Claire sat, pondering, then opened the door, saying, "I have an idea. Wait here while I get the logbook and the bill of sale.

Walking briskly down the driveway, Claire approached Ronny's car. Then, leaning into the open window, she started telling him something. Karl was becoming confused, thinking, what is she up to? Claire stepped back, waving as Ronny drove off, also waving goodbye. Karl was now thinking, alright, I'm really mixed up now; what just happened? Claire returned after going back into the house. She came back with a scarf in her hand, wearing a tweed three-quarter-length jacket. Opening the door again, she slid into the cockpit beside Karl.

"Could you tell me what just happened and where Ronny is going?" asked Karl.

"Ronny is heading home. We will drive there later. Then, Ronny can take me home later today. Right, Captain, I am going to buy you lunch at the Fox Pub in the village of William." Claire had a strange smile on her face when saying that. "Over lunch, we can finalize the sale, alright?" Claire, for the first time in a very long time, was feeling alive again. She had mourned too long.

The last time she saw Patrick, he made her promise if he did not make it that she would not become an old maid. He had said, "You're too young and full of life; please, don't let that flame die out—live life. Please, promise me that, so I can go off to fight, knowing I need not worry about you."

"Claire, you realize I'm only using one eye right now, don't you," said Karl as he started up the car.

"I won't tell anyone if you don't," replied Claire. "Turn right, then left; we will take the back roads. You will enjoy them more, as they are made for a sports car like this." The drive to the Fox was delightful, full of winding country lanes that made them both enjoy the wind blowing through their hair and over their faces, and the exhilarating sounds coming from the exhaust pipe made for a perfect day. "Here we are, Karl. I think you will enjoy this. I haven't been here in a while; let's say, far too long." Karl could see in her eyes she was remembering another time when Patrick was driving the little MG.

"Shall we eat outside? It's such a beautiful day." Claire was coming alive. In just a few hours, she had transformed herself from a grieving widow to a young lady full of life, even though that could change in a moment. Over lunch, she turned over the logbook and bill of sale to Karl, who then gave her an envelope containing the cash. Claire thanked him, placing the unopened envelope into her handbag.

"Don't you think you should count it first?" asked Karl as he put his paperwork into his inside pocket.

Claire simply smiled, saying, "I trust you, Captain. Now, tell me all about yourself, excluding the classified parts. Looking at that eye patch, I'm assuming you will not be able to tell me how you got it, is that correct?"

Karl smiled back at her, then started from that fateful day in Marseilles, holding nothing back about his dangerous drive across Europe, including the wonderful ladies he has met and the one that died, taking his heart with her. "Claire, I have tried to bury that lost love. The relationship I'm in right now will not go any further. That lady is far away right now. I must be man enough to end it when she returns; it's really not fair to her, trying to put a round peg into a square hole. Believe me, I have tried so hard to convince myself I love her, but that has been nothing but wishful thinking. That ghost is still between us. I'm not sure how to move forward, Claire, other than becoming a monk maybe." They both laughed at his last statement. Now, tell me all about Claire, leaving out none of the juicy parts."

Karl felt comfortable with Claire. She was not like anyone he had met before, but then again, he had said that before, hadn't he. That isn't true. A bell sounded loudly in his head. She is so much like Kitty. Why did I not see that right away? In the back of his mind, a quiet voice was saying, thank you, Lord; thank you.

"Well, let me see; I have a professional position in a law firm in Hitchen, which has been my saving grace through the dark time after Patrick's death. Karl, I have lost a very special man. From what you have told me, we have so much in common, and I can see Kitty is still very much a part of you. Life sometimes has a way of dashing your chances for a rewarding future, and when all looks lost, someone else enters your life to change that. I have known you just a few short hours, but I will not lie to you, Karl. I hope this is the start of a new chapter for both of us. I think I have just overstepped my boundary, though; sorry about that." Claire sat, eyes fixed on Karl, waiting for his response.

"Claire, I'm lost for words. We are definitely thinking along the same lines. I can't believe we are talking like this. I should have thought about buying your MG sooner." Karl's humor was kicking in at just the right time.

"How long is your leave, Karl?" asked Claire.

"I have to report back on Tuesday, so I only have three days left. Why do you ask?" Karl could feel Claire was about to propose spending time together until then, and he was right.

"Have you ever toured Cambridge?" asked Claire as she slowly reached over to take his hand.

"Only on work-related visits. Why do you ask?" answered Karl. "I was just thinking; it's been a long time since I have been on a field trip. Going on my own is not for me. Going together could be so much fun." Claire was a little nervous, asking this stranger to accompany her.

"Count me in. You will have to drive, though; is that alright with you?" asked Karl, wondering what would come next.

"Not a problem. I love driving that car, but I never wanted to do that on my own, though," replied Claire.

"Let me get the bill, and we can go meet my family. I can't believe I went out this morning looking for a car, found one, and now I'm driving it home with a brand new girlfriend." Karl started shaking his head, quietly chuckling to himself as he stood up to pay the bill.

"I said this was going to be my treat. Put your money away, and that's an order, Captain." Karl loved the way she started giving orders. Those memories were flooding back, only this time, there were no clouds to spoil the feeling of happiness.

"Claire, maybe it's best you drive to my mother's. She will go through the roof if she sees me driving with this one eye," remarked Karl as they walked back to the car.

"Alright, where am I going?" answered Claire.

"Go right and head toward Baldock. We will be there in about fifteen minutes." Karl's head was in a spin. Could it really be true that he found a loving soulmate at a time when he least expected it to happen? Karl, with his one eye, stared at Claire as she shifted gears. "Claire, you are making this such a wonderful day for me, even though it scares me somewhat."

Claire smiled at him, taking her eye off the road momentarily, and answered him, her hand reaching for his. "I feel the same, Karl." Turning into the driveway, Karl could feel himself tensing up. Claire sensed this as she reached over again to take his hand, saying, "We are going be fine. Stop worrying, darling." Karl sat there, thinking, she just called me darling. I still can't believe this is going so incredibly fast, but it feels so right. Can this really be happening? Karl got out and walked around the car to open Claire's door. By then, Ronny, Freida, and Mama had come out to see the car.

"Wow, will you look at this baby?" said Freida, running her hand down its side.

"Mama, Freida, let me introduce you to Claire McGivern. She is the lady I just bought the car from." Karl wanted to say so much more but felt he should not rush this first meeting.

"So very nice to make your acquaintance, young lady. I see you are married," said Mama, looking at her left hand.

"Was," came the cold response from Claire. "My late husband was a pilot in the RAF and gave his life during the Battle of Britain. Before leaving on his last patrol, his parting words were for me to live life to the fullest, and that I have not done until now. Does that answer your question, Mrs. Vita?" Claire was a strong woman, and Mama loved that.

"I did not intend to hit a nerve; forgive me if I gave you that impression. Welcome to our home. I can tell there is a bond already starting between you and my Karl. If it's meant to be, I will be thankful that Karl has found what he has been missing for so long." Karl was still in a strange place, and his mother and Claire were already comfortable with each other. "Let's go inside and find out more about each other, shall we?" said Mama, thinking that, by accident, Karl may just have found his life mate.

Ronny approached Karl, saying, "That is an incredible woman, Karl. When she approached me at her house, she simply said, "Ronny, go home; I need to spend time with Karl. He will give me directions to your house." Ronny could not believe what had just happened. It was like the first time Kitty had visited them. For the next three hours, they all shared stories—some funny, some so very sad.

Ronny looked at his watch, then said, "Claire, I think I should be getting you home."

Claire looked at Karl, then said in response, "Thank you, Ronny, but Karl and I are having a day out in Cambridge tomorrow, so maybe the best thing is for him to return home with me unless any of you object to that? Karl, why don't you get some things together for tonight and tomorrow?" Claire had taken complete control, and no one had any objection.

Karl packed a small bag, along with a garment bag, then returned to the living room, where Mama and Claire were sitting on the couch, laughing and holding hands. Freida and Ronny were seated on the opposite couch, enjoying the small talk that was going on.

"Karl, let's think about leaving. We should put the top up on the car. It could be quite chilly driving home in the dark." Karl, the calculating intelligence officer, was lost for words. Claire had moved in and staked her claim. War has a way of making relationships happen that much faster, Karl always had a habit of saying. There may not be a tomorrow!

"Good night, Mama. We will stop by after we leave Cambridge tomorrow afternoon to see you. That little MG has brought us all together. Don't worry about Karl. I intend to take care of him, and that you can be sure of." Claire hugged Mama, then Freida, and finally Ronny, concluding, "Well, Ronny, it has been an interesting day, has it not? I never thought when you called me this morning, we would be saying good night like this. I guess you could say fate played a big part in this. I'm so very thankful, Ronny, that you made that call this morning. War is strange; it brings people together so much quicker, don't you think?" Claire slid in behind the wheel. Karl, getting into the passenger seat, was still not sure what was happening. "Ready, darling? It won't take too long," said Claire, still controlling everything.

CHAPTER 14

New Beings

Turning into the driveway, Claire asked Karl to open the garage doors for her. Karl was feeling very strange as she led him through the back door into the kitchen. Everything inside was completely tidy, nothing out of place. "Would you like a drink before we go to bed?" asked Claire, realizing Karl had not processed that they would be sleeping together.

"Claire, this affair is spinning me off my feet. I can't believe this is happening so fast, and my mother appears to be alright with this. Please, excuse me, but is this really happening?" Karl felt out of his comfort zone with a woman that was still a virtual stranger to him but totally committed to making this a lifetime commitment.

"Let's take it nice and easy tonight. We need to feel comfortable with each other before becoming intimate, don't you agree?" Claire knew she had come on fast and strong and decided she needed to take one step at a time. Karl swigged down the whiskey Claire had poured for him, then accepting her hand, she led him upstairs to her bedroom. Karl undressed, putting pajama bottoms on, then pulling back the bedcovers and lying there, excited at being in bed with a woman that had every intention of being the last love of his life. This thought was still consuming him with anxiety. The bathroom door opened, and there was Claire, standing in a pink nightdress that simply took Karl's breath away.

"Darling, forgive me if I'm nervous, but I have not been with another man since Patrick. I want this to be perfect for both of us. I know we are meant to be together, so for as long it takes, I want this to work." Claire climbed into bed, reaching for Karl's arm and pulling it around her. Feeling the warmth of her body, Karl responded, lifting her head toward his. Their first kiss was so much more than Karl expected; it felt so natural. Could this be happening just like this? As he kissed her softly, he surrendered to the beautiful Claire.

"Karl, tonight I know I will sleep so much better, probably for the first time in I can't remember when. Hold me tightly until I fall asleep, will you?" Claire was looking at him again, asking, "Am I disappointing you? Were you expecting to make love tonight? As much as I really want to commit to you completely, I can't bring myself to being intimate just yet. Karl, it may take a while to reach that point. I am so afraid I could lose you; please, forgive me. This morning was just another gloomy day for me, feeling lost and alone; it's being alone that depresses me so. Now, here I am, not many hours later, lying next to a man that could make my life whole again. Is any of this making sense to you, Karl?" Claire said as she snuggled even closer. Maturity could have something to do with this, she thought. I hope we can have a life together based on love, truth, understanding, and lasting devotion to one another's needs. Would Karl be alright with all of this? Right now, I'm feeling I'm risking too much. Maybe I'm better off acting out the part of a lover with few feelings for the act itself.

While she lay there, pondering these thoughts, she was brought back by Karl saying, "Claire, please don't beat yourself up over this. It just may be a better way to start this new relationship. You are like nothing I've ever experienced before. I won't lie to you, I have always had my way with the ladies, but something is changing within me. I find myself embracing a different feeling, one that is changing me completely. Maybe I'm finally growing up and need more than just making love to make it feel real. Claire, take whatever time you need. I'm not going anywhere other than back to work on Tuesday. Now, there is one thing you must promise me, and I do mean promise." Karl was about to add a little humor to this otherwise serious conversation.

"And what is that, darling?" asked Claire wrapping herself around her new love.

"Well, I'm sure you did not really give much thought about coming out of the bathroom in that very sheer nightgown with the light shining through it. It has left little to my imagination. That act could have well reverted me to the old Karl Vita."

First, there was a brief silence; then, Claire pulled the bedcovers up to her neck. This made them both start laughing. "Oh, I'm so sorry. I should have thought about that first.

However, one day in the future, I will repeat that, and you, kind sir, will take appropriate action; is that clear?" Claire was now becoming comfortable with her new beau. Karl simply laughed, still holding her tightly. "Good night, handsome," was the last thing Claire said before falling asleep, still holding his arm tightly.

Claire woke up about 7:30 a.m. Rolling over, she momentarily panicked, patting Karl's side of the bed only to find he was not there. Jumping out of bed, she grabbed a bathrobe and took a quick look into the other two bedrooms before heading downstairs. Stopping at the bottom, her look of fear turned to relief and a big smile. In the kitchen, there he was in one of her old housecoats he found in the bathroom. Sitting with his feet up on the counter, Karl was reading yesterday's newspaper, a steaming hot mug of coffee in his hand.

"I could strangle you, Karl, you bugger!" Her beaming face gave her away, though. You scared the life out of me. I rolled over to kiss you good morning, only to find you gone. For a moment, I thought my frankness last night had made you bolt." After saying that, Claire thought it feels like we have been together for years; this feels so right.

"I'm sorry, dear. I am a very light sleeper, so about 0500 hours, I found one of your housecoats to put on. It's way undersized for me, so that's why I can't close the front," said Karl in a very jovial voice.

"Wait right there. I'll be right back. Claire ran back upstairs, returning with a box. "This will work, lover boy." From the box, she removed a navy-blue man's bathrobe. "Here, try this on." Claire had bought it several years back for her departed husband but never had a chance to give it to him. Karl stood up and tried it on. It fit perfectly; however, there was a strange look on his face, and Claire recognized a nerve had been hit, so what did I do?

"Claire, are you sure about this?" asked Karl.

"Of course, it's yours now and will always be hanging up next to mine in the bathroom. Karl, did I do or say something wrong a few minutes ago that hit a nerve from your past?" Claire wanted no secrets between them ever.

"Claire, it's nothing, really; thank you so much for making me feel right at home with this beautiful bathrobe." Karl had a telltale look on his face that gave him away, and Claire picked up on it right away.

"Karl, don't give me that look. I thought we agreed, good or bad, we would not have secrets between us. Now, what did I bloody well say or do?" Claire, the strong-willed woman, would not let this go that easily.

"Alright, seeing as you will not let this go, Kitty had several pet nicknames for me. Lover boy was one of those names. There, I told you it was no big thing." Karl just wanted to move on.

"And what are the other ones, so I can be aware of what not to call you?" Claire was showing a little anger saying that.

"Sailor was the other one. Now, can we move on?" "I like that, Karl. Do you think Kitty would mind if I also called you Sailor as well?" Karl looked at her adding, "for the record Hazel also used those nicknames."

Claire was so much like Kitty in so many ways, and Karl could relate to those headstrong ways because of that. "You can call me that and anything else you like, but never call me late for a good morning kiss." Karl put his arms around her waist, pulled her into him, and then bent down to kiss her softly. This time, she responded by opening her mouth; her tongue met his in an electrifying moment. In Karl's mind, he was thinking, this beautiful lady, when she finally decides the time is right to make love, will be amazing, but as my father once told me, everything comes to those who wait, and I am prepared to wait for as long as it takes!

"Alright, how long do you need to get yourself ready?" asked Karl.

"Give me forty minutes or so," replied Claire. Karl had brought brown trousers, a white shirt, and a light brown tweed jacket. Brown shoes and a beige striped tie made for a well-dressed gentleman. Karl walked down the driveway to retrieve the morning paper. The news was bleak, to say the least. Tragedy was a daily occurrence these days.

Back in the kitchen, Karl made himself another cup of coffee. He was sitting down to read more of the paper when Claire entered.

"Alright, I'm ready; how do I look, Sailor?" asked Claire, entering the kitchen.

Karl suppressed an emotional feeling, hearing Claire calling him Sailor, but that was quickly becoming a thing of the past. There she stood—everything Karl could expect. Claire was beaming with life, happy in her newfound relationship. "You are truly a classy lady, making it harder by the minute to keep my hands off you," said Karl, feeling like he would like to take her right there in the kitchen, which, of course, he would not do.

Claire had dressed comfortably for their day of exploring the ancient city of Cambridge.

"We will have that time real soon, my darling Karl; today, I feel wonderful about exploring as a couple. It's something I have not done in so long. Summer is going by too quickly, and the war seems far away, don't you think?" asked Claire, her arms around her new beau.

"Today, the war will not spoil our day. But, two days from now, it will again consume all my available time." In the back of his mind, Karl was thinking about all the horrors that had transpired since the start of 1941 and his own near-death experience at the hands of the Gestapo in one of their prison cells. Despair had made him contemplate ending his life that morning. Thank God he never followed it through.

"Come on; we are getting too serious. Nothing and no one will spoil our day," said Claire as she put on her jacket and reached for her handbag. Karl backed the MG out of the garage, deciding to leave the top up as it would be chilly driving this early in the morning.

"Don't forget; you're driving. Where are the side curtains kept?" asked Karl.

"They're hanging on a peg at the back of the garage; I'll be right out," called Claire as she locked the back door to the house. Karl installed the curtains after figuring out how they attached. Claire slid behind the steering wheel and started the engine. "We need to stop for some petrol. I have been hoarding ration coupons, so we don't have to worry," called Claire over the sound of the engine.

The drive to Cambridge was enjoyable. Karl was thinking, with the top and side curtains installed, it made the cabin feel smaller. It was a sports car, after all. Arriving in Cambridge, finding a parking place was not a problem. They found one on the main square in the center of town. People these days were refraining from using their vehicles, conserving their precious petrol coupons. "Feel like some tea and toast before we start exploring? I don't believe getting eggs will be possible," said Claire, reaching for Karl's arm as they started walking toward the small café on the square. "Darling, this is the way I like it. I have never been a good solo; how about you?" Claire was ready to start venturing out again, now that she could share special times with her man.

Inside the café, they both ordered tea and shared a plate of piping hot toast with strawberry jam. Sitting there, drinking tea, they took the time to find out more about each other and past loves that had left an impression on each of them. "Karl, I am really enjoying hearing all of this, but what I would really love to hear more about is Kitty. Your mother told me I remind her of Kitty." Claire had listened intently to Karl's colorful past and the ladies that had left an impression on him. However, she also recognized it was Kitty that took his heart with her to the grave. Karl poured his heart out, telling everything right up to two days ago.

"Well, do you want to leave without me now, after hearing all that?" asked Karl, a smirk across his face. "Now, young lady, I want all the details of your past, including the sordid boyfriend parts. I need to feel jealous of them all." Karl was teasing her by saying that, and Claire loved how his self-confidence allowed her to tell him everything.

"Well, it's by far nowhere close to your past, but here goes. I'm born and bred in Hitchin, Hertfordshire, and so were my parents and sister. I attended a Catholic school, also in Hitchen; this my mother insisted on for both her girls. My father was a founding partner in the law firm of McGivern, Tilbey & Morrison. I had a relatively sheltered life before going to university, then on to law school. There, I met my first boyfriend, Daniel Bell, also studying to be a solicitor. We were together for about four years. He was the one that I lost my virginity to, a very stupid thing to do on my part because I became pregnant. We had talked about getting married; however, I could tell he would only do that to save face. Two and a half months into that pregnancy, I lost the baby.

Daniel bolted right after that, emigrating to Australia with another law student. He left me with a broken heart but so much the wiser.

"After that, I dated a few fellows but never anyone I wanted to stay with. Then, in 1937, I went to a dance with two other girlfriends in Bedford. There, I was swept off my feet by an RAF pilot, who turned out incidentally to be my father's partner's son. What a strange coincidence. I had not seen Patrick since he went off to the RAF College at Cranwell. Patrick and I were married right after I graduated from Cambridge Law College. We honeymooned in Looe Cornwall. Right after that, Patrick went off to train on Hurricane fighters, and I joined my father's firm as an intern, working up to a fully-fledged solicitor; I still work there to this day.

Only one of the partners is still alive. He retired last year, so right now, I'm the senior partner with two junior partners to help me. The families decided to retain the original shingle out of respect for the founders. Our life was wonderful, although Patrick only came home on weekends. We both accepted that is how it had to be. My life took a turn for the worse on May 28th, 1940, when I received a telegram from the War Department informing me that Patrick's plane was missing. Two days later, two RAF officers came to the house to notify me that his body had been found, still wearing his parachute and life vest in the English Channel.

"After he was given a military funeral, I thought my world had come to an end. My work has been my only salvation until about a week ago, when I open the garage door, looked at the MG, and decided it was time to sell it. I needed to move on. I had mourned enough, and that is not the way Patrick would like me to continue living. Two days ago, I started to live again, and it's all because of that little MG. Oh, about the house—that was my parent's house. My mother continued to live there after Father passed in April 1939. I moved in to keep her company. Mother only passed away five months ago, so I bought my sister out. She lives with her husband and children in Oxford; we both agreed we did not want to sell the house where we were raised. If you're wondering about my surname, I kept McGivern for business purposes, adding Patrick's surname of Bennett when we married. After he died, I had it reversed, so now you know. There you have the complete Claire story up to date." Claire ordered another cup of tea, then waited for Karl's questions that she knew would follow.

"Wow! I can't believe I've fallen for a brainchild who's also a solicitor. Claire, I also noticed a beautiful upright piano in your living room. Who plays that beauty?" asked Karl.

"My mother, my sister, and I love classical music. I have not been near it in years, though." Again, Karl was somewhat surprised by how Claire detailed everything. "Well, if we don't get going, it will be too late to see the historic sites," said Claire.

"Right," replied Karl as he stood to pay the bill, then helped Claire with her coat before they headed out into the town square. The first stop they made was to visit the historic Trinity Church to see the famous and amazing pipe organ, built and completed by Metzlerin in 1735. Karl had seen many such organs in Europe, but when they started rehearsing, he just sat there, mesmerized by the clarity of those tones coming out of the big pipes. The next stop they made was down by the river. Karl had always wanted to go punting down the River Cam after seeing pictures of it before the war. Claire looked at Karl, and she could see that twinkle in his eye.

"You want to go boating, don't you? It warms my heart to watch your facial expressions. Let's go!" Karl bought two tickets.

The guide smiled and said, "Not much business lately, so I'm going to give you the deluxe tour." Karl stepped into the boat first, then turned to help Claire step down into the boat. Karl looked up at Claire as she held his hand. Stepping down into the boat, their eyes locked onto each other's as her skirt slid up her thighs, revealing what Karl knew was a vision of times yet to come. Claire shook her head, smiling as she realized what Karl was looking at. She sat down, thinking, it's going to be a long night tonight. I know it, and I can't wait. Punting down the river, the guide gave them an excellent description of buildings and events that shaped English history; however, these two people were thinking of something more important and their own history yet to come. After the boat ride, they visited the places Claire had spent time in her younger years as a student in this magnificent town.

Several hours later, while walking through the small shops and narrow streets, Claire, out of the blue, said, "Karl, what say we head back to see Mama and Freida before we head home? Tuesday, you will be leaving to return to your camp in Slough, and I would like some private time with you before you leave. Lieutenant Vita, you are not leaving without making love to me, even though I told you it would be a while before that happened. Darling, can't you see I've fallen completely in love with you!" There, she had said it. Claire had surrendered to a decision that was BEYOND ALL DOUBT, evaporating any barriers that might remain between them. Those memories of her past life were now locked in a compartment in her mind. Karl, the intelligence spy, had noticed she was wrestling with mixed feelings all day, and now he knew why. Claire had just openly made her intentions perfectly clear; she was in love with the stranger from only two days ago. He was quickly becoming her life companion; could that really happen? she continued to think.

Karl replied to her distant look, "Of course, darling, let's head out. It's been a wonderful day so far, and from what you're telling me, the best is yet to come?" Karl pulled her in close, his arm around her waist as they walked back to the car. There was no reason to say more; they both knew their future was starting from this moment. Driving back, Karl suggested they make a stop before seeing the family and returning to Claire's house.

"If that's what you would like to do, Sailor. Where is it that you would like to take me?" replied Claire, more interested in returning to her home.

"Why don't we have a cocktail at the George and Dragon before making that stop to see my mother. Claire, I need you to see and feel the emotional ties that have shackled me each time I have come close to committing to someone. Claire, you can help me close that chapter. Will you do this for me? Because when I leave tomorrow, I want to feel my return will be to you and you alone. The George is where I spent my last Boxing Day Holiday with Kitty. It would mean so much to me, knowing you understand that I'm trying to say goodbye, and strangely, I want to feel her approval for the woman that I will share the rest of my life with." Karl, saying that, realized he was asking for Claire's help to make that final goodbye to Kitty happen. If their magic had strength, it would happen.

"Karl, I really don't know what to say. You could say I'm speechless. Most girls would probably take offense at such a request. I'm not most girls, though, am I? If we are always to be open with each other, I will do whatever is needed to help you make that closure happen. Don't forget; I also am wrestling with my own demons and will lean on you to help me through them as well. Karl, we could say we are both physical and emotional wrecks. Now, let's get that bloody drink. I need one about now. We might as well order one for Kitty and Patrick as well. If they can't drink them, we can do it for them." They looked at each other, a smile of agreement crossing between them that led to laughter; another barrier had just crashed and burned!

The George had not changed at all. The same decor and staff had made time stand still. Karl and Claire felt very comfortable in this old-world charm. Claire sat next to him by the big dark fireplace, without those burning embers throwing a warm glow in its large opening. Watching and listening to him, she sensed he was living out a vision of that last time he sat here with Kitty. "Darling, tell me what you're feeling, so I can become part of it as well." Claire was starting to read his expressions very well. It must be that professional training that gave her this ability.

"These are the very same chairs Kitty and I spent time in together when she visited Baldock. The only difference is there is no fire in the fireplace today. You are sitting in the very same armchair she sat in on that last night." A cold chill crossed over Claire's face. The more she embraced the feeling, the more she felt Kitty's presence. It was as if Kitty was sending her a message: he's yours now. Love him the same way I did; convince him to let me go. The more she concentrated on that feeling, the more she could feel the strong will and personality of someone she would never meet, not in this lifetime anyway.

"Karl, are you ready to let those feelings go, or are those demons still with us?"

He turned to her, then replied with a wicked smile across his face. "If I were sitting here with Hazel or any other lady, I would be throwing a shield around myself and making all kinds of excuses about now. However, with you, I can honestly say there are no shadows, demons, or dark clouds; they simply are not there, nor will they ever be again. Claire, back there, you came right out and told me you were in love with me after only a couple of days. Well, my sweet lady, when do you want to make that permanent? I have no more skeletons in my closet. For whatever it's worth, I'm yours. From here on, I want us to plan a life together after this inhumane war is finally over."

Karl had come full circle. The womanizing and running from the truth were over; from here on, Claire would be his life. The biggest problem he faced now was how and when to confront Hazel when she finally returned to England.

"Karl, you have drifted off someplace; let's settle up and stop by to see Mama before heading home, shall we?"

"Claire, something happened a few minutes ago back there. It's like you were someplace else. What a beautiful smile you had on your face, and your eyes had tears in them. I decided you were making your goodbyes to Patrick, so I left you alone, was that the case?" asked Karl cautiously.

The look on Claire's face said something completely different. "It's alright, Karl; it's just girl talk." Karl looked around, thinking, what girl talk? There is no one else here. Claire paid the bill.

Standing up, she reached for Karl, saying, "Everything is going to be just fine from here on. Promise me this, when the war is finally over, we will find Kitty's grave in Germany and give her a new headstone with her correct name on it, Lieutenant Kitty Johnson. That's the least we can do, correct?"

With tears welling up in his eyes and moisture seeping out below his eye patch, Karl felt a sense of relief. Had Kitty, in this place, connected with Claire? If she did, she had never done that with anyone else, and yes, that includes her friend, Hazel. I think Kitty somehow gave Claire her blessing. That would explain this feeling of relief I have right now. Looking up, he only saw sunshine and blue skies. That Following Storm had faded away. It was all thanks to this complicated, loving lady in front of him; she had made it happen.

Life is starting to have real meaning for me now. There was no need for words as they walked arm in arm back to the car.

"Claire, what do you think about my surname? Do you like the way it sounds?" asked Karl, setting Claire up for the next question.

"Yes, it's a fine name; why do you ask?" Claire started to tense up. She was a trained professional who knew the power of suggested words.

"Then, you will have no trouble with having your surname changed from Claire McGivern to Claire Vita, will you? Stopping in the middle of Church Street, Karl reached for her hand. "Claire, will you consent to becoming my wife?" In his mind, as he said that, he was also thinking, this will be the last time I'll ever say this.

"Karl, I was praying and willing you to propose. Yes, I'm going to love being Mrs. Karl Vita. Do you believe in love at first sight? Well, I do because when I first laid eyes on you, a strange feeling inside me told me: one day, he will become your husband, and here we are, standing on Church Street, making that very commitment. Kiss me, you crazy Austrian." Claire was changing her life away from all the sadness she had been living through.

With a frown on his face, Karl was thinking, why does everyone keep calling me a crazy Austrian? Maybe I am. When we reach the bungalow, I must ask Mama privately if she will consent to me giving her ring to Claire. At least she is not a field agent in the Intelligence Service. That's a blessing, and the fact that she lives and works close by will be a comfort to my mother.

Claire was floating on a cloud. Her life from this moment on would become full of joy, excluding those times when Karl would be called upon to undertake other missions, disappearing for extended periods. That would always be hanging over them. "Let's head back to the car, shall we?" said Karl.

"I'm still in a state of shock. I don't know what to say. I'm lost for words; you have made me a very happy woman. I still can't believe all this is happening to me. War is hell, but at times like this, it makes things move that much faster." Claire, from now on, would enjoy life, waiting patiently for each weekend to reunite with her fiancé. Their next stop was back at the bungalow. Mama and Freida were thrilled to hear about their announcement—maybe a little scared as well that something could happen to Karl, breaking yet another heart. But, at least, this time, Claire would not be going off to war as Kitty did.

After the congratulations, Mama guided Claire to the couch, saying, "He's a good boy so much like his father. Instinctively, I knew when we met that you were the one. So, my new daughter, when will we see you next? Living so close will be nice; we can see each other whenever you can make time."

"Mama, how about you and Freida joining me for lunch at the George and Dragon this Thursday? I'll pick you up at about 11:30 a.m. How does that sound?"

Karl came back into the living room with his luggage, "Here I go again. See you next weekend. I don't believe I'll have a problem getting a weekend pass. Goodbye, you two; love you both, and give little Franchot a big hug when he wakes up."

Mama was thrilled as she listened to Karl; her instincts were correct that he would marry this charming lady. In her mind, she thought, time does not play a part in how long it takes. Falling in love does not happen with a clock; it happens with feelings and chemistry. Earlier, Mama had told Karl she would collect her engagement ring from his safety deposit box at the bank, so when he arrived home the following weekend, they could all join in as Karl slid the ring onto Claire's finger.

"Time to leave. Are you ready, Claire?" asked Karl as he pushed his case into the small space behind the front seats. "Thank God I'm traveling light. Goodbye, I'll call you tomorrow from Slough. I have lots to do, so be patient; it may be later.

Claire will be calling you anyway; love you both," said Karl. Claire backed the MG out of the driveway, turning right onto the Letchworth Road as they drove back.

Claire looked over at Karl, asking, "Guess you could say we've had a very full day. What shall we do about supper tonight? Are you very hungry, darling?" asked Claire.

Karl smiled, answering back, "Fish and chips will do me just fine. I have other ideas about dessert, though!" Hearing his last remark, Claire simply smiled, thinking, I know what's coming. Life will always be interesting, that's for sure. "Claire, will you help me medicate my eye? I completely forgot to do that this morning. My doctor will be giving me hell when I get back to Slough."

Karl enjoyed being the passenger, something he rarely did. "Karl, what were you and your mother talking about back at the bungalow?" asked Claire, sensing there was something afoot.

Stop acting like a solicitor; he is allowed some privacy with his mother, is he not? Claire was scolding herself, thinking like that. They parked the car in front of the fish and chip shop, "Do you want to eat it here or take it home with us?" asked Claire.

"I think we should eat here, then head home for that dessert. How does that sound?" replied Karl, getting an immediate response.

"Karl, I've got a feeling you are going to be a handful. Now, behave yourself."

They sat around the corner in a dimly lit booth, side by side. Before digging in to eat, Karl turned toward Claire, teasing her by saying, "Did I tell you dessert comes first?"

"What on earth are you talking about, Karl? You are making no sense, saying silly statements like that." Claire, a little nervous, could tell from the look on his face that the gears in his head were scheming something mischievous. "Karl, you're up to something, and you're making me nervous doing it." Claire was becoming unhinged as she felt his one good eye burning through her.

"Close your eyes for me, Claire, just for a minute. Don't say a word; just relax and take in the feeling. You are in my hands, and you are very safe." Claire complied, trying very hard to control her breathing. She felt a slow, soft touch on her skirt. She remained very still, even though she wanted to react to the sensation. Slowly, with deliberate control, Karl slid his hand under that skirt and moved with skill up her thigh.

"Karl, please; we are in a fish and chip shop, and I work in this town, now behave." As Claire was speaking, her voice had a quiver to it. Karl looked into her eyes with a soft smile that calmed her fears. Continuing the movement up her thigh, this time Claire was surrendering to this inappropriate behavior, and just like that, all her fear and inhibitions faded as she closed her eyes again, waiting for that touch from a man's hand she had not felt in so long. Karl looked around to make sure there was no one close by. The coast was clear.

Karl continued to slide his hand slowly and deliberately to the top of her thigh, then without stopping, under her panties, feeling her very wet and swollen.

She is more than ready, he thought. With very light, slow movements, Karl massaged her until he felt her tense her thighs and put her hand over her mouth, suppressing any sound she could make as she experienced her first orgasm from her dashing beau. Karl held her softly as she trembled in his arms, followed by warm tears as her tension melted away, loving every touch Karl made. "God, Karl, you could have warned me of your intent to explode my senses." Claire was recovering, pulling her skirt down again and straightening her hair.

"I did give you warning about dessert, did I not?" replied Karl. "Well, if you wanted to shock me, you have succeeded. Now, let's eat up and head home, shall we? I'm famished because of your shenanigans," said Claire. Her face gave her away; she was totally in love and feeling good about it. Karl was thinking how he liked finding the mischievous old fellow he had once been. Sweet Claire was that catalyst in making him feel like that again. "What time is your train tomorrow morning, darling?" asked Claire as they walked back to the car.

"I'm catching the 1130 hours train into Kings Cross, then on to Slough from Paddington. Once I arrive, I will phone for a staff car to pick me up," replied Karl, a part of him already returning to the Intelligence Officer he would return to on Tuesday.

"Darling, we need to make a quick car change at my office. It's close by, so it won't take long," said Claire as she drove the MG toward her office building on Bandcroft Street.

"Car change? We're not going home in this car?" asked Karl. "No, darling, I only brought the MG over after Ronny called me Saturday. I drove my Wolsey to the office garage to make the exchange. The MG is going back into storage until its new owner drives it out, maybe next weekend. Then again, it may be when he has two eyes to drive with."

"You never told me you owned another car, Claire?"

"Well, Karl, it was my mother's car. I just kept it because it's a roomy four-door saloon, so practical in my line of business. The

MG is a fun car but not for everyday use. You can imagine that pulling up in front of the courthouse in a car that low could be very embarrassing with all those barristers gawking up my skirt when I go to get out. You took a few pictures of your own over the last several days, didn't you? You must think I didn't notice. Then again, how could you be sure it wasn't deliberate on my part? Here we are. I'll back out the Wolsey, and you drive the MG in. We must baby her; she is what brought us together—always remember that."

Karl walked around, getting behind the steering wheel and backing the MG out of the way of Claire as she maneuvered the Wolsey around him. Karl was thinking, it's in great shape; she is right. It does look very business-like, though. Karl turned the MG around, backing it into the garage. He retrieved his luggage from behind the front seat and closed and locked the garage doors, giving the key to Claire.

"Ready, Sailor? Let's go home. We've already had dessert. But, by the look on your face, that's not really true, is that correct?" Claire was playing with him, thinking, we have so much to learn about each other. I'm pretty sure, though, Karl likes his sport of teasing and turning me into a babbling wreck. I'm going to love being married to him. He's full of surprises, she thought. Turning into the driveway, Karl took his garment bag and the small case as Claire put the Wolsey into the garage. In the kitchen, Claire made coffee. As they sat at the table, Claire asked, "Karl, when I take your mother out on Thursday, do you want me to bring your clothes and other things back here afterward?" Claire was thinking she might as well get him used to calling this home. "Karl, is there anything else I should be doing for you during the week? Those clothes you've been wearing, I'll have them cleaned before you return home." Claire was making conversation to cover her nervousness, thinking about the bedroom and having to see Karl off tomorrow morning.

The thought of being alone again was not so bad; he would be returning on Friday evening, so she had a lot to look forward to. "Why don't we retire to bed? It's going to be a strenuously long day tomorrow." Karl could see she was feeling a little uncomfortable. Why, he could not understand; maybe it was just sexual jitters. "Don't forget, darling; we have to medicate your eye before we go to bed, or you will be in trouble with the doc. Karl had a quick bath, then climbed into bed, waiting for Claire to join him. After what seemed like a very long time in the bathroom, the door opened, and out came Claire in that same pink nightgown. In the doorway, she stood, teasing Karl with the way she postured herself against the door frame.

"Claire, you are deliberately trying to arouse me. If you are, well, it's working extremely well." Claire pulled back the bedsheet and slid into bed, cuddling up to Karl. She wanted him with every ounce of her being, but that nervousness still gripped her, and Karl could feel it. "Claire, we have all the time in the world. Relax, we can take it slowly." Karl wanted her to need him, but only when she was ready.

"I'm alright, Karl, just a little nervous at being with you tonight." Claire reached over, taking his cheek in her hand. As her mouth found his tongue, Karl reacted to the sensation.

Slowly, he traced the shape of her body. Going over her breast, he placed his index finger on her nipple, making slow circles, feeling you. It was beyond my expectations. From now on, Sailor, you will be on notice to perform as soon as you come through that door at the end of the week. God, I love you, Karl. Let's have a repeat performance, shall we?" Their lovemaking became more intense and more comfortable as they tumbled deeper into their lovemaking.

Spent, they embraced each other closely as they drifted toward sleep. The alarm clock went off at 7:00 a.m., waking Claire immediately. Reaching over, she felt the emptiness on the opposite side of the bed. That bugger, she thought; he gets up so early. I guess I will have to adjust my sleeping habits from here on. She got up and made the bed, thinking, I should be washing the sheets, but not today. When I go to bed tonight alone, I want to smell his presence. I'll do that washing tomorrow. She put on her bathrobe and headed downstairs, expecting to see Karl in his new bathrobe. There, at the kitchen table, what she saw was the figure of a British Intelligence Officer in a very striking military uniform, drinking coffee and reading the morning paper.

"Morning, Claire, I have a bad habit of rising early. Sorry, I tried to remain really quiet, allowing you to continue sleeping. You looked so peaceful and so beautiful just lying there. I nearly changed my mind by ravaging you before you woke up." Karl was all smiles, a happy soldier in a new relationship.

Claire answered him by saying, "I wish you would have. My God, Karl, this is the first time I've seen you in uniform. You are gorgeous. I could devour you, right on that table." Claire was taking in the transformation of her man, sad at his leaving but so happy he would be returning Friday evening. As for her week, well, it would start by announcing to her partners and employees that yesterday she had gotten engaged and consented to become Mrs. Karl Vita, the date to be announced.

"Darling, I'm going upstairs to get ready, then we can have breakfast together before I take you to the station, alright?" Claire wanted Karl to have a hearty English breakfast. She knew eating would be the furthest thing from his mind once he boarded that train back to Slough. She was also thinking, *I've been down this road before.* Karl was still reading an account of the German battleship *Bismarck*, sunk in Denmark Straits earlier that year on May 26 and 27, approximately 350 miles west of *Brest, Franc*e.

Although it was a decisive action for the Royal Navy, there was sadness seeing another ship and its brave crew succumb to its wounds, ablaze and sinking by the stern. This action was not one-sided. It cost the Royal Navy the loss and pride of its Navy, the battleship proudly known as the Mighty *Hood*. Several direct hits to her forward ammunition locker created a massive explosion, breaking her in two, sending her to the bottom in less than three minutes. All but three of the 1,415 crew members went down with the ship. At her commissioning on May 15th, 1920, she was the largest battleship in the world. Karl briefly thought about the sailors on that vessel who would forever remain young at the bottom of the Denmark Straits.

The article questioned whether these gigantic ships were quickly becoming dinosaurs and ineffective, as well as very costly to operate in a modern war, where aircraft and the new aircraft carriers were becoming the new capital ships. Karl, reading this, remembered a report he wrote back in 1937 about this very topic after a covert mission into Germany to assess their shipbuilding program. He also thought back to when he and Ronny had met three young sailors from the *Hood* having a pint in the Red Lion in Baldock. They were nice lads who had their future lives stolen from them in less than a few minutes by those shells fired from the *Bismarck*. He closed the paper when he heard Claire coming down the stairs very quickly.

"Well, let's have that breakfast," said Claire, all businesslike. "Wait one minute, lady; let me take a real hard look at this solicitor in front of me. What a transformation. My goodness, Claire, you are such a classy lady in that business attire." Claire had changed into a bottle-green suit and matching high-heeled shoes, and a single strand of pearls tastefully adorned her neck. That beautiful auburn hair, tied back into a bun, completed the look.

"That's right; we have never seen each other in business attire. We look good together, Sailor. Before we have breakfast, can I please take a few photographs of you, Karl? I really would like a few for here and my desk. Oh, and here is a relatively recent one for your desk. Make sure it's in a position that all those women around you can see it." The framed picture had a message diagonally across the right side; it read: To my loving Karl. Hurry home to your fiancée, who loves you so very much. Love always, Claire. The picture was taken sitting behind the wheel of their MG-PB.

"Claire, this really is beautiful. It's almost like you're saying I'm waiting for you."

Claire took her camera out from the sideboard drawer, then, pushing Karl to the right place, said, "Big smile, Sailor. This one is for me to brag about once it's printed and framed and prominently displayed on my office desk. You can sign it when you return Friday." Karl was enjoying the high-spirited Claire; then he remembered he had a print taken several weeks ago at the camp. He had brought it with him to give to Mama.

"Claire, wait one minute. Can you find an 8" x 10" picture frame?" asked Karl as he ran upstairs to retrieve his case. Claire was thinking, don't tell me he has pictures stashed away in his case. Then again, you never know with Karl, do you?

Karl came back down the stairs, two at a time, beaming a big smile. "I just remembered; I have had this picture inside my case for weeks to give to Mama. I completely forgot to give it to her, so don't tell her I gave it to you when you see her on Thursday. We can give her one of the pictures you just took next weekend," said Karl as he handed over the photograph.

"My, you look good with that wonderful smile of yours; even that devilish look is there. Perfect, now take my pen and write something really nice for me. Don't you write something saucy, Karl." Claire didn't really care what he wrote, so long as it said Love on it. Karl thought for a moment, then wrote across the bottom: *To Claire, the Lady who stole my heart and turned my dark clouds into sunshine. Love always, Karl.* "Now, where is that picture frame?" asked Karl, not letting Claire see it until the picture was mounted into the frame. "Now, you can look at it," said Karl, proud as a peacock.

Claire, eager to see the final product, snapped up the frame, then read what Karl had written. Karl stood, waiting for her to react. She just stood there, then, brushing the tears from her eyes, she finally said, "Karl, my sweet, loving, sensitive man. What did I do right to find you? I have been praying so long for this, and now here I am with a man who is so much more than I hoped for. Karl, you alone will always be the keeper of my heart. Thank you, darling."

Over breakfast, they talked about all the things they should be doing and planning for in the next few months. "Tomorrow, I will have the logbook for the MG changed, as well as having my secretary notarize the bill of sale. It sounds kind of silly, really, because the car will still be here," said Claire, making a to-do list. Time was marching on, and so were Karl's final few hours. He was far from ready to face the music on his return to the camp.

"Claire, before we leave, I need you to apply my medication to my eye. I'm going to catch hell if the doc sees it dried up in the corners like this." Karl flipped his leather patch up, away from the bright sunshine coming through the window.

"When do you have to return to London to see the surgeon?" asked Claire.

"I'm not sure. I think it's the beginning of the following week?" replied Karl. "Why do you ask?"

"Because St. Luke's Hospital is only about fifty minutes from here. If you can use that slick tongue of yours to convince your superiors to change the appointment to a Monday, I can drive you up there for that appointment; then you can arrange for a car to return you to Slough. How about that for a plan?" said Claire, pleased that it could buy her more time with Karl.

"I've got a better plan that you may like. You drive down to Slough and stay overnight. That way, I can show you off to everyone in my department. Later, we can have dinner with my commanding officer and his wife and other members of the general staff who are also my friends. Claire, they will love you. Shall I mention that to Clive later today?"

Karl, always the planner, was also thinking, if everyone finds out that my fiancée is visiting, it will stop any further advances from women like Susan and a few others. The biggest problem is how to handle Hazel when she returns; not too excited about that meeting, he thought. One thing is for certain, someone up there is giving me another chance, and from now on, unless it's concerning Claire, I'm not interested.

Claire responded by saying, "That could work also. I would really enjoy meeting some other spy people from Slough and getting to meet some of those young ladies in uniform who think fishing is a big sport." Claire took his hand, brushing it against her cheek. With tears welling up in her eyes, she quietly said, "Time for us to head out to the station. Now, check your wallet again to make sure you have this telephone number and my private one at the office. Darling, please call me at home once you are back in the camp." Claire was putting on a brave face, well, until his train departed.

Claire drove to the train station, all of six minutes away. Parking the car, she got out and waited for Karl as he took his small case from the back seat. "Here we are. Time for us to part, my darling; have a good week, and don't forget to put that picture on your desk."

"I will call you once I'm back. I don't think it will be the same from here on. Before, it was all about hitting back at the enemy and nothing else other than getting drunk and womanizing away the empty moments. I will do my job and anything else the BIS requires of me, but know this, my sweet, beautiful Claire, my heart will remain here with you." Karl could feel those emotional words were bringing home that empty feeling. He was saying goodbye with the comfort of knowing she would be going to work, far away from the horrors of the war he was forced to deal with. She would remain safe until he returned to her. Claire was holding this moment back as they walked hand in hand to the ticket counter. "One return ticket to Slough, please. Is it on time today?" asked Karl.

The conductor punched out the ticket, clipping the Victory Station stop, saying, "Should be arriving in about five or six minutes, Gov. Just time for one more smooch." They walked up to the platform, buying just a few more minutes. Claire had both her arms around Karl's left arm, her head resting against his shoulder. They didn't say much; all of that was done earlier. Off in the distance, they could hear the train approaching, a large column of smoke trailing behind it.

"Claire, why don't you leave? There's no sense getting yourself upset for only a few more minutes." Karl was feeling the tension of separation.

Claire looked up at him with a smirk on her face, "Not a chance, Sailor, I'm standing right here until that bloody train is no more than a distant smoke stream." That remark broke the tension by this toughie standing next to him. With only a minute or two left, Karl turned to her, put his strong arms around her, and kissed her tenderly until the train pulled into the station.

Karl separated himself from Claire, then shouted for all to hear, "Claire, I love you; miss me until next Friday." With that, he moved quickly to the first open compartment. Placing his case on the overhead rack, he returned to the compartment door, lowering the glass window using the leather strap that held it closed. As he leaned out, Claire rushed over to grab his hand, kissing the back of it with tears flowing from her cheeks; she yelled, "Karl, please be extra careful. No more dangerous assignments, please, now that I've found you. Please, do that for me, or I'll wring Churchill's bloody neck."

Claire walked alongside as the train slowly pulled away from the platform, finally releasing Karl's hand. His last sight was seeing her standing and waving on the platform. As her image got smaller, he yelled on impulse, "Mrs. Vita, I love you." Claire watched until the train was no more than a small image with smoke marking its location.

"I love you too, Sailor," she said under her breath. Claire returned to her car. Inside, she took a moment to regain her composure, fixing her hair and makeup. Satisfied with the results, she started the car, put it into gear, then headed down the driveway toward Bandcroft Street and her office.

Within minutes, she was parking the car in the company's courtyard. Claire stopped at the entrance, thinking, I should make an announcement right away; it's better that way. She opened the door and walked into the busy office. Inside, people were already at work and genuinely happy to see their boss. "Good morning, everyone; nice to see your smiling faces." Claire entered her office and immediately took Karl's picture from her briefcase. She stood there, reading what Karl had written only a few hours ago, then lifted the photo to her lips, thinking, I love you, Karl. Beverly, her secretary, entered, carrying a mug of hot tea for her. "Have a pleasant extended weekend? Did you manage to sell the MG on Saturday?" asked Beverly.

"Yes, I did, for a much better deal than you could ever imagine. Have a seat, and let me tell you what has just happened because of that MG. Over the next twenty minutes or so, Claire gave Beverly a condensed version of what transpired right up to one hour ago when she saw Karl off.

"Is that a picture of your young man, Claire? May I take a look?" asked Beverly.

"Yes, it is isn't he handsome?" Claire was smiling as her secretary continued to stare at the picture.

"Claire, you are going to make an announcement. I'll cover the switchboard while you do so. You owe it to all of us. They will all be elated, knowing the grief you have been carrying for so long is behind you. I'm so happy for you, and what an amazing story to tell your kids when you start a family that is." Beverly went out into the main office, and in a commanding voice, said, "May I have your attention, please! Claire has an announcement she wishes to share with everyone. I will cover the switchboard during this announcement." Beverly walked off to the switchboard.

"Thank you, Bev. Yesterday, I became engaged to Captain Karl Vita, an Austrian in the British Intelligence Service. I know what you must be thinking. How come I didn't mention this last week or even before that? Well, before Saturday, I did not know Karl. In fact,

I only met him when he came to look at my MG. You know the car I keep in the garage." Claire was making light of selling the MG. "There is a long story attached to this, but now, we have work to do. Thank you for your attention." After hearing this news, the buzz in the office was amazing, with everyone crowding around her to give their congratulations and best wishes for a long and happy future. Returning to her office, she dove into her workload, sipping her tea and waiting for the two junior partners to join her.

Arriving at Kings Cross station, Karl made his way to the underground that would take him to Paddington Station, and from there, the train back to Slough. Sitting by the window, he watched the city streets fly by, thinking, I will have to confront Clive first thing, then my staff. This is going to be very interesting. Of course, Clive's first reaction will be, here we go again. It's going to be difficult to convince everybody this is really happening. Back in 1936, Gunther warned me, you alone must correct the mess you have created with your lady friends. And now it's happening again; I think I cried wolf too many times. The train started to slow as it approached the station. Karl reached up to remove his case from the overhead rack, then waited by the carriage door. Outside the station, Karl decided the bus would take too long, so he elected to splurge by taking a taxi instead.

Paying the taxi driver, he presented his ID to the guard, "Good morning, Sir. You are clear to pass. Approaching the steps that led up to the entrance, Karl smiled, thinking it doesn't seem that long ago, these steps would be a big challenge. However, taking them now two at a time was proof that his leg was almost completely recovered.

"Good morning, Captain Vita. Did you have an enjoyable extended weekend?" said Janis as she spun the registry around for him to sign in.

"Very much so, Corporal. You could say it's probably one I will always remember," replied Karl as he headed down the hall toward his department. Stopping before making an entrance, he took a deep breath, thinking, well, here I go. I think I'll wait until later to announce the engagement. I'm pretty sure I already know what the answer will be: here he goes again. I have developed somewhat of a reputation around here. Entering the office, he made himself heard by saying, "Good morning all. Nice to see your smiling faces. John, have you put the communication pouch on my desk yet? Sally, where is Peggy this morning? Have you seen her yet?" Karl was firing question to the staff, covering up his apprehension about making the bombshell announcement about the engagement.

"She is with Major Knight in a meeting until 1100 hours, Sir," replied Sally.

It looks like Clive acted on his offer to move her into operation analysis. Good for you, Peggy, he thought. I will miss having you working for me, but I will keep that promise to not stand in your way.

"Sally, please, could you get me a big mug of strong coffee?" asked Karl. Walking around to the opposite side of his desk, he sat down, removing Claire's picture from his case and placing it at an angle facing him, running his finger over the caption at the bottom. Time to go to work was his next thought as he removed the communication files, noticing on the routing sheet that Clive had already signed each one that he had reviewed. You can always rely on Clive to stay on top of things like this, he thought, proceeding to the Delta-1 file first. Sally entered, placing the steaming mug of coffee on the desk mat. From the corner of her eye, she noticed the new picture on the desk.

"I say, is that a new picture? And what a striking lady at the wheel of that sports car."

Yes, Sally, that's the MG-PB I just purchased Saturday. Pretty snazzy, don't you think?" said Karl, hoping her next question would open the door to, who is the lady? "As for the lady, well, she is the lady I bought it from, and as of yesterday, she's now my fiancée."

Karl did not elaborate, expecting additional questions to come, and they did. "Is this someone you have known a while, Sir?" Sally was discreetly reading the caption at the bottom of the picture.

Karl, the Intelligence Officer, was keeping his eye on her as she did so. "No, Sally; I never laid eyes on her before last Saturday morning."

"Cor blimey, Sir! Talk about a whirlwind romance. You only get to see these in the moving pictures, and here in our office, we have one going on right in front of us. Sir, do you mind if I share this with the other girls? You know, this sort of thing gets everyone excited and feeling good. Congratulations, Captain Vita! She is a very lucky girl." Sally was enjoying this.

"Why don't you gather everyone together, and I will make an announcement." That's a good way of making this announcement, I suppose, smiled Karl.

In a loud voice, Sally said, "Ladies and gents, can I get your attention for a minute? Captain Vita would like to make an announcement. Please, gather around."

"Thank you, Sally, for that. I had planned on making this announcement later today, but this is as good a time as any to tell you all about my extended weekend. As of yesterday, I became engaged to a wonderful lady from Hitchin. When I left here last week, I had no prior knowledge of Claire McGivern. In fact, all I was going to do was buy a sports car, which I did, and I got the owner to boot. My reputation has never been that lily-white, but I can assure you that you will see a big difference in how I conduct myself from now on. Sometimes, events like this happen. I am fortunate enough that it happened to me.

Claire more than likely will pay us a visit within the next few weeks. I told her what a great bunch of people I work with; thank you for your attention." After saying that, Karl felt a sense of relief.

Like a cannon going off, one of the girls yelled, "Three cheers for our Captain Vita." Their loud applause could be heard all the way down the hall.

Captain Lowes came out of his office halfway down the hall, swearing, "What the bloody hell is all that hullabaloo about? This is not a public house. I'm on the bloody telephone with the War Department. I can only imagine what they are thinking. Mary, hold down the fort; I'll be right back."

Bill was fuming as he hobbled down toward the communication center. Entering, he said in an angry tone, "Who the hell is responsible for this outbreak?"

Standing with his hand on his hip came a reply, "I am," said Karl as he approached his friend.

"Karl, for God's sake, control your staff, will you? I was on the telephone with the bloody War Department. What do you think old

Campbell was thinking, hearing that hullabaloo in the background?" Bill was cooling off, now that he knew it was Karl that they were cheering for.

"Bill, got a few minutes to spare? There is something and someone I need to share with you." Karl guided Bill into his office, then closed the door behind them, saying, "Sally, hold all calls for a while unless you get a call from Claire McGivern or maybe the bloody prime minister," said Karl, also adding a little sarcasm to that request.

Inside, Bill sat down and immediately shifted his gaze to the picture prominently positioned on the desk. Karl sat quietly while Bill read the caption. "Karl, don't tell me you have another one. What happened to Hazel, or is she last year's flavor? God, I can't keep up with your romances. Is that what the noise was all about? Now that you have my undivided attention, why don't you tell me all about this one? I think there is still some room left on your page for one more." Bill's sarcasm was coming through. Over the next forty minutes, Karl told the story to his now tentative friend, who sat there listening and occasionally shaking his head.

"Well, Bill, there you have it. I hope I can rely on your support. You have always been a trusted friend, and over the next few months, I will call on that friendship," said Karl as he stood up to walk Bill out into the office. Everyone was hard at work, keeping their heads down in case Captain Lowes exploded again.

At the door, Bill turned around and said calmly, "Sorry for the outbreak. Do me a favor next time. Wait until after hours, then invite me. I can make more noise than all of you put together." Bill left, returning to his own office, saying, "See you at six, Captain Vita—usual table at the lounge." Karl returned to his office and the stack of paperwork still to be reviewed. The communication from Delta-1 indicated that eliminating the mole appeared to have cured the problem of the Germans being one step behind them. They would remain in the present safe house for maybe the next several months.

Before heading down to the lounge, Karl picked up the telephone, got an outside line, and then dialed Hitchin 4567. The phone at the other end rang four or five times before he heard the sweet sound of her voice, "Hitchin 4567." Claire's heart skipped a beat; it was Karl.

"Claire, my gorgeous woman, do you miss me as much as I miss you?" asked Karl.

Claire's tone suddenly changed to that of a woman totally in love, replying, "Do I ever. How's it going? Getting a lot of flak over that picture on your desk? My bunch is over the top with excitement. I promised to have them all over to the house very soon. Mary asked if I throw you away, can she please have you?" Claire was laughing when saying this.

"My situation is a lot more difficult. Old habits and past girlfriends are making it difficult. I guess you could call it payback. My friend, Captain Bill Lowes, is an understanding sort but still a little skeptical. Major Clive Knight, you know the one I told you about, will join Bill and me in the officer's lounge after I hang up with you. These two are like brothers to me. They are the ones that met me on the ship when I first arrived in England, and we have been close friends ever since. I was thinking on the train about asking Bill to be my best man when that time comes.

Darling, are you still having lunch with Mama and Freida on Thursday? I hope you have a nice time with them. This will be a real treat as they are stuck in that house way too much," said Karl, feeling saddened at being apart from Claire. In his mind, he was already thinking, I'm a field agent. I can't put Claire through another loss if I fall in action. This feeling will hang over me until this bloody war comes to an end. "Well, darling, have a nice evening. I will call you tomorrow with an update on how it goes tonight. I love you, sweetheart, bye for now."

Claire could sense that Karl was struggling, so she simply closed by saying, "No matter what happens, what obstacles we may have to face, darling, we will lean on each other and face those times together. I think our love can weather any storm, even the one that constantly follows you around. Good night, darling; remember, you have a lady who loves you so very much." With that, she hung up the phone and headed upstairs to that empty bed.

Karl entered the lounge. Looking around, he saw Bill and Clive at their favorite table. "Karl, you're the bad boy, so beers are on you," said Clive. Karl waved off the sarcastic remark, bringing back three mugs of beer, then he sat down next to Clive, slapping him on the back. "So, what's this Bill is telling me—you are on to another lady? Tell me that's not so." Clive was clearing the way for Karl to tell him about this new lady.

Over the next hour, Karl told Clive all about buying the MG and how Claire had entered his life because of that car, the uncanny likeness she had to Kitty, and how his mother and sister took to Claire immediately. "Clive, I know you think I'm a complete lunatic when it comes to relationships but think back to another time not so long ago when I was totally committed to marrying Kitty and would have been the model husband. We all know that was dashed by her sudden death. Since then, I have been on so many dates. I even went as far as trying to make a go of it with Hazel. Clive, I would run from any relationship and nearly did before Hazel left on that mission. Claire is the woman I want to share my life with; no more trying to make it fit. This war is far from over. Claire and I are willing to take the chance that I make it through to the end. The commitment I made to the BIS will never change; you can bank on that. Do I have your support? When you meet Claire, you will understand." Karl had said his piece. In silence, they drank their beers.

"Alright, you say she is meeting you here a week from today and staying the weekend before driving you to your eye appointment on the following Monday, correct? Well, then, let's plan on a special evening at the Charter Arms in Slough. You know, Julie has not seen you in over eight months. I will tell her to arrange for a babysitter for the girls; it shouldn't be a problem. Bill, that Saturday all right with you?" Clive, saying that, changed it to an order.

"One week from this Saturday, you and Dorothy will be our guests to celebrate Karl and Claire's engagement. That, my friend, is a direct order." Clive had a way with him when it came to an event like this.

"You want this to be your treat? That's not right. Don't you think we should split the bill?" replied Bill.

"Okay, you can buy the cocktails and wine. Gentlemen, we have a dinner plan. Now, let's talk shop, shall we? Karl, has Bill shared with you that I intend to recall the Delta-1 team next month? They are overdue for some rest and recuperation. You will need to have your story straight about how you are going to handle the Hazel situation. It's not going to be easy; she is expecting you to greet her with open arms. On arriving back, the team will be debriefed at the Hammersley Barracks in Aldershot before returning back here." Clive was rattled by the messy Hazel affair, but something inside him was willing to stand by Karl once again. Hopefully, this would be the last time.

Before returning to his flat, Karl made another stop at his office to check the incoming wires for that evening. Seeing nothing of interest, he headed out, catching the #5 bus back to his flat. The week was going by so very quickly. Karl was buried in paperwork, which he hated more with each passing day, but he did promise Clive to run this department efficiently and that he would do. Sally entered his office, happily announcing, "Your fiancée is holding on line two, Sir."

Karl thanked Sally, marking the page he was reviewing. "Claire, so nice to get a midday call from you; is everything alright?" he asked. "Yes and no. I'm sitting here with Mama and Freida, about to leave for the George and Dragon. We want to know, did you put your eye drops in this morning? Don't lie to me, Karl. You forgot again, didn't you?" In the background, he could hear Mama and Freida laughing, enjoying how Claire pushed him around just like an old married couple. "When I hang up, you will go and put them in. The doctor warned you what could happen if you kept forgetting, did he not? Oh, did you confirm if the eye appointment is this coming Monday, or is it the following week? Don't forget to confirm it's a Monday," Claire said, laughing.

"I have already confirmed that it's going to be a week Monday," answered Karl, glad she had jogged his memory.

"In that case, before you leave tomorrow, call me, so I know what time to pick you up at the Hitchin Station. On Saturday, I told Mama we would be over in the afternoon. She is going to give me my first Austrian cooking lesson. I'm really looking forward to that. She mentioned you are also a pretty good cook yourself, my man of many talents. Well, we're off to lunch. Hurry home to me, darling; this lady is missing her man; love you." Claire hung up the phone. On the other hand, Karl was processing some ideas in his mind, still on the telephone, without realizing the line at the other end had gone dead.

His little flat had been his sanctuary away from everyone and, at times, everything. As much as I have enjoyed that flat, it really doesn't make sense to keep it up anymore. I think I will check with housing about availability in the new wing of the officer's quarters sometime next week. Apart from that, when I work late, it's a pain getting home, and even worse when it's raining. So much for buying a car to eliminate doing that. Thinking this, he smiled, laughing on the inside.

Picking up several files, he headed down the hall to Clive's office. "Major, I have the files I need to review with you. I think we need to decide how to handle those German submarine blokes before they are carted off to a POW camp. Over lunch, let me map out a plan of action for you." The files Karl was carrying pertained to recently captured German naval officers being held in Bedford for interrogation. The more Karl examined the files, the more he felt they could have valuable information about the submarine pens that nearly cost him his life not that long ago.

The German Submarine Service was not about to part with any information unless they get tricked into sharing. Finding a private corner table, Karl mapped out a plan to put an agent into their holding area, disguised as a survivor from a German surface naval vessel—someone they would not be aware of. The mission could only be a week at best to gather information; any longer would be taking a chance of that agent being found out. We know what the outcome of that could be, another dead agent.

"As usual, Karl, this is when your mind is razor-sharp. Great plan, but who do we have that is German with a Naval background?" asked Clive, already thinking, here he goes again, but this time, I'm putting my foot down. The plan can work, but not with Karl Vita as the plant anyway.

"We have a few agents who fit the bill, but they're not as knowledgeable about submarine pens as me," said Karl, aware he could be devastating a future with Claire.

"No, Karl. I'm putting my foot down. We have only recently got you back, and that was almost in a body bag. You have gone above and beyond the call of duty. That's an order; do you understand me?" said Clive, still admiring this officer who always put duty first, no matter what the consequences could be.

"Clive, if you won't let me take on this operation, then at least let me train whoever it is we send in. I will need to give him firsthand knowledge of the designs and construction details and what we are trying to learn. At least, let me do that." Although Karl was at first was disappointed at not being the agent, he was, on the other hand, relieved by Clive's decision. It was as if Clive was protecting Claire's future. *How well my boss knows me. Claire is going to love my friends.*

"Karl, you and Bill will be on-site in Bedford throughout this mission. Is that understood, you crazy Austrian?" Clive always enjoyed calling Karl a crazy Austrian.

"Yes, boss! When can I start recruiting? Are you going to bring Bill up to speed, or would you like me to do it?" asked Karl.

"No, get on the interoffice phone and tell Bill we need him to join us over here and on the double." Clive was already putting his own contribution to this plan together in his mind. The biggest hurdle could be justification. Over the next two hours, they tried to formulate a plan, spending much of that time discussing what qualifications their pick of agents should have.

Bill suddenly threw up his arm, saying, "Why are we only thinking of one agent. Why don't we consider two? It would look more believable to our German chaps. What do you think, Karl?" Bill asked, believing he had come up with a safer, more believable plan of action.

Clive stroked his chin, followed by "Brilliant idea, Bill. Now, what's the cover story, Karl?"

Karl finally said, "The submarine arm of the Kriegsmarine is a very close-knit group, so we can't use that approach, but what if our agents were from a surface ship, say based in Norway, that got attacked and sunk, then rescued by an RAF air-sea rescue craft. That could work. We need to find out if any German surface crafts have been lost in the last six weeks or so." Karl's brain was in overdrive as he formulated this web of deception.

"Gentlemen, we have an outline of a plan. Karl, your part is to interview agents for this plot. Bill, you research what ships were sunk recently, and I will write the request documentation needed for the operation. Karl, what time is your train tomorrow? You may want to leave a little earlier. There's a lady in Hitchin who would love to see you earlier rather than later."

"Well, I was planning on taking the 1645 train. Changing in London would get me into Hitchin around 2130 or maybe a little later." Karl was hoping to hear Clive throw him out by lunchtime, and he did.

"Chaps, no need to tell you mum's the word on this operation, alright?" Clive, saying that, thought, *that's a stupid thing to say; these two are front-line spoofs*.

"As much as I would love to stay here with you two, I have a lot of work to do before leaving tomorrow. By the way, from the bottom of my heart, thank you for believing in me even though you still think I'm a 'Crazy Austrian.' Good night, chaps." Karl stood up, gathering the files he would return to the office. Tonight would be a long one for sure.

"As much as Karl may be off the wall when it comes to women, he is a wizard when it comes to intelligence and field operations. The least we can do right now is support him. He relies on us two to always be there to prop him up. Bill, I don't know about you, but I have a gut feeling this time may really be different." Clive was starting to believe Karl had found his soulmate.

"I think you're absolutely right, Clive," answered Bill. Karl walked into his office, then called the motor pool to order a staff car for 1130 hours to take him back to the flat. Next, he placed the call to Claire's house, the phone ringing until he heard her voice. "Karl, how are you, darling? Did you have a productive day?" Claire was stepping lightly, as she knew what he did for a living was very hush-hush.

"Yes, sweetheart, I did. I can't tell you much, but what I did was very productive; it's really fun driving a lorry." Karl laughed out loud when he said that.

"Karl, I swear to God, your humor is sometimes hard to follow. What time should I plan on picking you up at the station tomorrow night?" she asked.

"Want some good news? Clive is taking pity on me. He is throwing me out at lunchtime, so plan on picking me up at 1600 hours. Sorry, that's 4:00 p.m. to you civilians. Saturday morning, when we pick up the MG, why don't you show me around? I want to ravish the boss at her desk. Karl was in a wonderful mood, enjoying his work and loving his new lease on life—no cloud anywhere to be felt or seen.

"Karl, really, you come out with the most idiotic things to say. No, you will not use my office as your own love parlor, and that's that." Claire was trying to control him on the phone, thinking he's capable of turning this phone call into a long-distance love fest. Then again, life with Karl would always be a combination of tenderness, caring, and, yes, off-the-wall moments. "Night darling, see you tomorrow. Don't stay all night at the office. Use your lorry to take you back to the flat, and Karl, put those eye drops in tonight, you hear me?" She deliberately said flat, not home because home was now with her in Hitchin.

Karl hung up the phone, thinking, it feels so good to have Claire bossing me around. It's like we are old married people, and just think, it's only about a week since we met. God does move in mysterious ways, I suppose. Karl returned to the stack of documents on his desk. Time would not stand still tonight. A knock at his office door brought him back from planning that mission.

"Excuse me, Sir. Your car has arrived. Shall I tell the driver you will be along shortly?" asked the night MP.

"Yes, please do. I need to secure these folders in the overnight safe first," replied Karl. The car ride back to the flat was reasonably short at this time of night. Karl thanked the driver and entered the front door. In his little room, Karl could not surrender to sleep. He kept tossing and turning. He had too much going on in his head. To force his mind away from intelligence matters, he started to think of what things had to be done this weekend. Those thoughts calmed him down, and he fell asleep after 0200 hours. At 0630 hours, he hit the bathroom, put some items in his small carry case, made the bed, and quietly slipped out the front door into the cool morning air. At the bus stop, he waited for the #5 bus to arrive. The day was cloudy, not that uncommon in England this time of year. Like a programmed robot, Karl stopped at the cafeteria for his large coffee and a powdered scrambled egg sandwich.

Back in his office, he could hear staffers arriving, cheerfully cracking jokes and telling tales. "Morning, you noisy bunch, is that happiness contagious? If so, spread some my way. Sally, I will be leaving at lunchtime; please inform the motor pool to have a car ready outside at 1200 hours; thank you." Karl smiled and returned to his office, continuing the work from the previous evening. "John, would you and Sally pull all the files we have on German-speaking agents presently here in England? None older than forty-five years old." John brought the first batch of files into Karl's office, overwhelming him with how many they had.

"This is not going to work, John. It's like what we just went through a few weeks ago. Have two of those collapsible tables brought in and set them by the file cabinets. We can work right there." Karl gave instructions about what they were looking for. "We need to weed out any agents that were in the navy or merchant service, men that worked in marine architecture as well, in that order. Next, we want to know where they are presently. I shall be leaving at noon. I can't for the life of me believe this will be done by Monday morning, so have Peggy help you as well. Keep her and John on it until it's done. Major Knight gave me the green light should we need this extra help."

Noon found them all busily separating files with no agents that qualified yet. Sally, seeing Karl engrossed in piles of papers, was reluctant to disturb him. His time was up to catch the train. "Sir, it's time for you to leave. Don't worry about this; we will stay on top of it, and be assured, it will be ready when you return on Monday."

"Have a nice weekend, everybody; see you Monday," said Karl as he retrieved his case and headed for the door. Arriving at Kings Cross, he boarded the train to Cambridge, one of the stops being Hitchin. He found a compartment to stretch out in for the short trip. Leaving Stevenage, Karl put his tunic jacket and cap back on, excitement building at the thought of seeing Claire. The train slowed, entering the Hitchin Station, its bumpers banging at each carriage. Karl looked out the open window; familiar smoke and steam were floating back along the length of the train. Karl, out of habit, searched into the smoke, looking for a lady from his past. Instead, he saw a striking lady in a blue business suit, her hair flowing over her shoulders, jumping up and down with excitement. Karl did not wait for the train to come to a complete stop. Flinging the door open, his boots slid on the concrete. He ran up to Claire and swept her off her feet as he swung her around several times. That smoke and steam would have a different meaning from now on. That haunting image had left and would never return. His thoughts from now on would be only about Claire.

"Darling, you're home. It feels like an eternity since I saw you off last Monday," said Claire, her excitement becoming contagious to Karl. "I told Mama and Freida that I can't wait to become another Mrs. Vita. They both just laughed, hugging me tightly. By the way, she also mentioned you have something to give me tomorrow. Karl, I'm praying it's what I think it is." Claire so wanted to make this permanent, and marriage would give her that closure.

"Yes, sweetheart, I do, but remember, it's only been a week. Can we at least agree on a couple of months before setting an actual wedding date?" said Karl, laughing out loud, thinking, we are going to do this. It's time for me to become Claire's husband, and I am more than ready to make that happen. Back at the house, Claire took him upstairs into the bedroom. Beaming, she opened the wardrobe on the opposite side of the room to hers. There, neatly arranged, were all of Karl's hanging clothes. Then she showed him the chest of drawers with all his other things also neatly arranged.

"What do you think, darling? Freida and I moved all your things over on Wednesday afternoon while Mama took care of Franchot."

"Claire, you are moving faster than an express train, thank you." Karl was a little nervous but really delighted about how things were taking place.

"Let's stay home tonight. It will do you good to wind down after your hectic week. I hope you are up for beef stew. It's quick and very tasty. Why don't you relax in the living room while I set the table?" said Claire, so very happy to be a couple once again. Over supper, they enjoyed small talk with a bottle of white wine that they finished in the living room. Sitting very close on the couch, Karl had his arm around her shoulder. Claire, still talking, could tell Karl was changing his gaze.

He moved with stealth to the top button of her blouse, still without saying a word. Claire was a little nervous to know how Karl could arouse her sexual desires so easily. Talking was no longer necessary. Karl was controlling the inevitable. His hand slid inside her bra; this very movement took her breath away. She turned toward his face and surrendered to his touch and kiss.

Claire stood up and removed her blouse, then her skirt, leaving her underwear and nylons for Karl to view. Sitting back down, she started undoing his trousers, thinking two can play at this game.

"You are a big tease tonight. That friend of yours will be my dessert." Karl laid back as Claire performed her magic on him for the first time, thinking, this lady is no amateur, thank God. With a slow and deliberate motion, Claire would bring him to the brink, then stop. This teasing was driving Karl over the top. She felt his tension mounting and the continuous throbbing. Looking up, she smiled, then lowered her head again as Karl said, "Claire, this is too much teasing." With that, she felt his eruption, followed by Karl totally relaxing.

Claire raised her head with a big smile of success, saying, "You needed that, Sailor. Tonight's dessert was way overdue, was it not?" Claire reached over the back of the couch, grabbing a throw blanket and wrapping it over them. She said, almost in a whisper, "Let's lay here quietly for a while. You need this rest, darling."

Karl responded, almost asleep, by saying, "What about you, Claire? I need to take care of you."

Karl could hardly keep his one eye open. Claire kissed him softly on his forehead, replying, "Tonight was wonderful. As for me, I have a lifetime to make love to you, so don't worry, I'll still be here in the morning." Claire did not need anything else. She had everything she needed right here in their place. Exhausted, they fell asleep, safe in each other arms.

Karl woke first. Looking at his watch, he saw it was past midnight; softly, he whispered into Claire's ear, "Honey, it's after midnight. Let's go up to bed, shall we?"

Claire responded by saying, "Goodness, Karl, I guess we needed that nap. We have to get up early in the morning, so yes, let's head upstairs. We've both had a long day.

Around 2:30 a.m., Claire woke up Karl. He was thrashing around in a nightmare. "Karl, Karl, it's alright. Whatever you're dreaming can't hurt you anymore. Come here; let me hold you until you fall back to sleep." Claire's heart was pounding, thinking, what did they do to you, Karl? Was it so bad that you considered taking your own life? Still holding his head on her chest, she fell back to sleep for the few hours before the alarm clock went off.

Claire moved Karl to his pillow, then rolled over to silence the alarm clock. Then, putting on her bathrobe, she went downstairs to make the coffee. Last night's episode had shocked her to her very core. I wonder how long these nightmares have been going on. We need to get help for him before they get any worse.

Without a sound, she felt those strong arms enfolding her, "Good morning, darling. I did not mean to scare you like that." Karl was thinking now she knows that I nearly took my own life out of despair. I must have yelled that out when she woke me up during the night. Taking their coffee to the kitchen table, Karl reached over, taking Claire's hand before saying, "Claire, that should never have happened; it's only occurred a few times before. I am so very sorry that I scared you like that; please, accept my apologies," said Karl, looking at her with fear written across her face.

"Karl, you poor man. I feel so stupid not having the foresight to see you have been wrestling with this for God knows how long. Share it with me, Karl; it's too much of a burden to carry it all on your own. Please, darling, let me remind you; we promised never to have secrets between us." Claire was pleading with him to share this nightmare of horror, and by doing so, help him face that trauma.

"Claire, what I am about to tell you can never be repeated, so put your solicitor's wig on, which will bind you to client confidentiality, is that right?" asked Karl.

"That is absolutely correct, Captain Vita." Claire was thinking, this is one time that I'm glad to be his solicitor. Taking over an hour and a half, he told her everything, leaving nothing out. As he spoke, the look on her face was one of complete horror and shock. "Am I the only one who knows this outside the military?" asked Claire.

"No, darling, my mother and Freida know as well. I had to tell them; my mother would see right through my lie."

Claire responded by saying, "Karl, we must get you help. You cannot handle this on your own. It's our problem now, so who should we contact?"

Karl, getting concerned, responded by saying, "Claire, it can't be military. That could cost me my commission, so whatever I do, I can't include any military help. Are we clear on that? No military whatsoever."

Claire, with that legal look on her face, said, "I understand, Karl. I will work on that right away. We have very good contacts at the Lister Hospital. Father knew doctors that handle cases like yours. We'll find someone we can trust, my darling. Are you up for breakfast yet? I really would like to arrive at Mama's no later than lunchtime." Claire, the very professional woman, would diplomatically look for the help Karl needed. He had been through so much during the year. Keeping it locked up inside like this was now surfacing in those nightmares.

"Claire, let's take the MG. It's a nice day, and I would like to clean and polish it while Mama gives you those cooking lessons." Whenever Karl returned home to Wien on leave from his ship, the *Tristian*, he always found cleaning his little Amilcar so relaxing that it was almost a ritual, and today, he was on leave, so cleaning the MG was the therapy he needed.

"Of course, we can, Sailor. If I get finished with Mama before you're done, I'll help you clean the inside." Claire had cleaned that little car so many times before with Patrick. Today, however, she would look at that car in a whole new way.

Arriving at the bungalow, Karl removed the polish and leather cleaner that Charlie from the motor pool had given him to take with him. The drive through the back roads to Baldock was the relaxing medicine Karl needed. Claire could see the look on his face. It was one she could see would help him by blowing the ugly thoughts out of his mind—maybe not today, but for sure one day in the future. Turning into the driveway, she reached over to pull up the handbrake. Her heart skipped a beat, looking at Karl's face as he sat there with a big smile on his face, enjoying the warm sunshine. "Servus, where is everybody," yelled Karl.

"Servus, what does that mean? Is it like saying hello?" asked Claire, thinking it must be an Austrian slang word. They all sat around drinking strong coffee in the living room and eating some of Mama's homemade strudel she had made for Karl.

"Claire, this is the first thing you need to learn to cook, and, of course, Mama's Goulash." Karl was happier today than he had been all week. What could be better than family, a new fiancée, and his beautiful little MG? Mama kept looking at Karl in such a way to remind him, while they were all together, should this be the time to bring out the red leather box? Karl smiled back at his mother, nodding his head in agreement.

Ronny, Freida, and Franchot sat on one couch. Mama was sitting next to Claire on the opposite couch. Karl left the room, returning moments later. "Claire, darling, now that we are all together, I have something to give you. Although it's been my mother's for so many years, she would like you to be its new custodian. That is if, of course, you care to wear it on your wedding finger. Claire, in a little over a week, you have won my heart, and whatever I am and what I may become in the future, I will be faithfully yours."

Karl stepped forward. Kneeling on one knee, he opened the box containing Mama's engagement ring, gleaming in the light streaming in from the window. Taking Claire's hand with tears in his eyes, he asked, "Claire McGivern, will you consent to becoming my wife?" Karl was having such a hard time holding back the tears and the emotion he had held back for so long. Mama, for the second time, was gaining a daughter. Freida and Ronny were reliving their own engagement.

"Karl Vita, I married you in my heart the day I first met you. To wear Mama's ring from this day forward will be my honor and pride, always with love for you and my new family. Karl, what are you waiting for? Are you going to put the ring on my finger or not?"

Claire, laughing, with tears of joy rolling down her face, was enjoying this moment of humor. Karl slipped the ring onto her finger, and it fit perfectly. Mama looked at Karl, their eye contact confirming what they were both thinking it was originally sized for Kitty! Claire was so much like Kitty; it's like she was giving them her final blessing.

Karl, from this day forward, would stop the crazy life he had been living. The image of Kitty in his mind was softly fading into a distant memory, always fondly remembered but never forgotten. He continued to hold Claire's hand as she stared at her ring. The last act Claire did was to whisper something into Mama's ear. They embraced each other. Holding hands and smiling at each other, Claire said, "Mama, we should start our cooking lesson, and Freida, can you help me learn German while we do that? No, correct that, show me how to speak like a Weiner."

Karl stood up, staring at Claire; she would be a wonderful wife and an amazing mother one day. Claire Vita! It had a really nice sound to it.

The weekend flew by; Karl and Claire spent the rest of Saturday with the family, then a nice Sunday down by the river in St. Neots. Claire had packed a lunch and a bottle of wine, along with a blanket to spread out on. The sun was warm, and Karl laid back, closing his eye and drifting off into a restful sleep. Claire had her arm under his head as a pillow, perfectly happy reading a novel she had wanted to finish for such a long time.

The following morning, Claire took Karl to the station at 0630 hours, as he wanted to get to the office no later than 1100 hours. "Claire, now remember to book a room for us at the Charter Arms in Slough. Let me know as soon as you are checked into the hotel, alright? Clive will arrange for a pass to be issued in your name, so remember to take the directions to the camp I gave you last night. Try to be there by 1600 hours if you can, so I can show you off, and Claire, remember to wear your engagement ring, alright?" Karl started laughing as he said that; there was no way that ring would ever leave her finger.

"Karl, you are such an idiot at times; you know full well that will never happen."

Claire was enjoying the bantering until the conductor yelled, "All aboard!"

Claire hugged Karl tightly. "I won't sleep well until Friday evening at the Charter Arms, and Karl, keep applying those eye drops, or you will be in real trouble with your future wife." Claire stood back from the door as the train slowly pulled away. Karl, as usual, stood by the window, waving and staring at Claire as she held up her left hand, wiggling her engagement finger. Karl settled down for the quick ride to Kings Cross station. Opening his briefcase, he took out the morning paper. The headline news was yet again bleak. The people of Norway were banned from having a radio in their houses! Changing trains in Paddington station, Karl placed a call to the motor pool to have a car meet him at the station in Slough. This would save time getting to the office.

Outside the station, Karl spotted his car and driver waiting by the entrance. "Morning, Charlie, did you have a nice weekend?" The car dropped him off at the main entrance. Karl thanked Charlie for the ride, then proceeded to scale the steps two steps at a time. Entering the building, he wished the ATS girl on duty a pleasant day, then walked down the hall to his department. Karl was in a marvelous mood.

Entering, he gave a jolly greeting to his staff, followed by a request, "John do I have the wires on my desk yet?" he asked, firing orders in all directions. Bill walked in with a binder under his arm containing the biography on the U-Boat prisoners.

"Morning, you old bugger. Well, did you put that magnificent ring on Claire's finger over the weekend?" asked Bill with an edge of sarcasm in his voice. "Here is the binder that Clive generated over the weekend. I think Sally and John, with the additional help of Peggy, did a superb job of identifying potential Germans officers we can consider using for the mole operation. Their efforts made it possible to have these files ready for you this morning. Don't forget to thank them for doing this," said Bill, sitting down in front of the desk.

"Who asked them to do that? I had no idea they would volunteer to do this," said Karl, somewhat embarrassed that he did not stay to help them. Karl excused himself, going out into the office and saying loudly, "John, Sally, thank you so very much for the hard work you both did. I'm somewhat embarrassed that I did not have the forethought to stay and help you."

John stood from his desk and responded, "Sir, we knew you needed those files for Monday, so after you left on Friday, we decided to pool our resources to have them ready for you. Glad we could make that happen. Excuse me for asking, Sir, are we allowed to brag about your engagement yet?" John and Sally were beaming with the praise they received. "I'll stop by the analysis department to thank Peggy on my way down to the meeting room; thanks again."

Karl and Bill walked down the hall, stopping in to also thank Peggy. Karl was always the gentleman, and Peggy was so happy he had included her in his thanks. She especially liked this because it was in front of her fellow workmates. At the end of the hall, they entered meeting room M-3. Clive and several other officers from the general staff sat waiting with two clerical ATS girls who would be recording the meeting. "Morning all," said Bill, taking his seat alongside Karl.

"I'm assuming you have all read the brief on this operation, so we all know what we are attempting to accomplish over the next couple of days, correct?" said Clive, looking around the room at their faces. He stood and walked over to the big board at the head of the room; with a pointer, he tapped on the harbors they wanted to collect additional information on.

"St. Nazaire was the one Captains Vita and Jerva visited. In his report, Captain Vita stressed that if we could immobilize those lock gates, it would deny access to transient submarines entering or leaving these pens. "So, how do we disable those gates?" asked Clive. Turning his attention to Karl, he said, "Captain, please take it from here."

Karl stood, thanking Major Knight. "Bombing could cause delays but not for very long. Germans, by nature, are masters at building and repairing large structures. But Major, we are not here to talk about specific French harbors. We are here to review candidates we can train to be inserted in with the surviving sailors from the U-Boat, are we not? Do we even know if others are being held in other POW camps who we could interrogate using the same approach? I really believe ordinary seamen could also be another excellent source of information, so Sir, don't let's overlook these in our review process." All day long, they hammered out a profile for the perfect candidates, each file being scrutinized many times over until the list was narrowed down to just five, then eventually down to two.

"Make arrangements to have those two brought here. If they're stationed up north, fly them down. We don't have time to waste on this operation. Are we clear on this? We will reconvene once those agents are here. Gentlemen, thank you for putting this together so quickly," commanded Major Knight.

Karl quickly spoke up, correcting Clive about who really put these files together last Saturday. "It wasn't Captain Lowes or me; it was members of my team, Sally and John, with the help Peggy. We are so lucky to have conscientious people here in the BIS that gave of their own time to make this happen."

The time was now 1700 hours. Walking out of the meeting room, Clive asked, "Up for a pint or two? Or do you have other plans?"

"I'm game," said Bill.

Karl followed by saying, "Hope you don't mind. I must make a quick call first."

Clive and Bill looked at each other. Bill laughed and said, "Isn't love grand?"

Clive joined in by adding, "Tell Claire, we are all looking forward to meeting her this weekend. Oh, before I forget, Julie asked me to have Claire call her any time over the next couple of days. You have our home number, don't you?" concluded Clive.

"Will do," responded Karl as he hurried off to his department. Entering the department, Karl said to Sally and John, "Major Knight sends his thanks for a job well done." Sitting down, Karl looked at his watch, then placed the call to Claire.

"Darling, is that you? I have been waiting for your call all day. How did your day go? I understand you have been in meetings all day, so you must be exhausted. Everyone at the office could not believe how magnificent my ring is, Karl. I keep looking at it and pinching myself in disbelief. I'm sorry. I'm rambling on, and you haven't said one word yet, or are you all talked out?" Claire stopped talking; her enthusiasm was getting the best of her.

"Claire, I'm fine. So much for working on a secure military base. You know what I'm doing every minute of the day." Karl was laughing while saying that.

"Sorry, Karl, I called this morning to tell you we are booked into the Charter Arms for three nights. Now, don't get mad at me. I booked their best suite—only the best for my man. Anyway, that nice Sally on your staff told me you would be tied up all day and could not be disturbed until after 5:00 p.m., so that's how I knew you were unavailable." Claire thought, I guess my excitement is getting the best of me. I need to slow it down.

"Claire, that's wonderful. When you get excited, it's like medicine. Please, never change. By the way, before I forget, write down this telephone number. When time permits, Clive's wife Julie wants you to call her. You will love her; she is a real sweetheart. Time to go, darling. The chaps are waiting for me in the lounge. Sleep tight; only four nights left until I see you. I hope you are ready for dessert Friday night." Karl, laughing, hung up the phone, then headed down to the lounge, thinking, so much to do and not enough time between now and Friday.

As expected, the rest of the week did not have enough hours to achieve the elimination process. Karl still believed he was the best candidate for this operation. However, Clive would have no part of it. Karl got up early Friday, packed his case, then went down to have morning tea with his landlady. "Morning, Mrs. Mann, sadly, I need to inform you that I will be moving out at the end of the month. Right now, it makes more sense to move back into the officer's quarters. I am working longer hours—sometimes late into the evening, so I think this will be for the best. Would you like me to post my flat in the officer's lounge? I really don't think there will be a problem in leasing it."

Karl could tell Mrs. Mann was saddened by hearing this but understood that his line of work would require more of his time. "Sorry to see you go, Captain. I totally understand, though. If you could post the flat, it would be greatly appreciated. Hope you can stop by for a cupper when you can to brighten up my day with that big smile of yours." Mrs. Mann would miss having Karl as her tenant but understood completely his need to be closer to the duties at the camp.

CHAPTER 15

CLAIRE IN SLOUGH

The workload continued to pile up on Karl's desk, no matter how diligently he pursued each project. "Sir, you have a call on two; I think it's your fiancée," said Sally, sticking her head into his office.

"Claire, don't tell me you're already at the hotel, are you?" Karl looked at his watch in shock. *Where did the day go?*

"Yes, I am, dear. I decided to get an early start. Well, that's not totally true; Beverly threw me out. What time should I come over?" answered Claire, her excitement building at the thought of meeting Karl's staff and fellow officers.

"Clive suggested you plan on about 1630 hours, alright? Make sure you have the directions and instructions for getting the pass at the gate. If there are any problems, have the guard give me a call. See you real soon, bye, darling."

Karl hung up the phone, then called Sally to come to his office. "Sally, that call was from Claire. She will be here in about forty minutes or so. Please, make sure that all sensitive documents are covered up or put away before she gets here," asked Karl, thinking, she may be my future wife, but everything in here is highly classified. Next, he called Clive, then Bill, advising them Claire was on her way over.

"Is everything secure in your department?" asked Clive, knowing full well that when it came to security, he never had to worry about Karl. At 1645 hours, the guardhouse called, requesting permission to issue a pass and parking ticket for a Claire McGivern. The guard asked for someone to meet her in the lobby.

Sally stuck her head into Karl's office. "Sir, I'm going down to the lobby to escort Miss McGivern back here to the office. I'll be right back," Sally said with a cheeky smile on her face as she turned and marched out to meet their guest. Claire signed in at the reception desk, receiving a badge to clip onto her suit jacket, then sat down to wait for her escort to arrive.

"Miss, someone is on their way down to escort you. It shouldn't be too long," said the receptionist. Sally entered the lobby. After looking around at the visitors waiting there, her gaze fell on Claire.

"Miss McGivern, pleased to meet you; my name is Sally. I'm here to escort you to Captain Vita's office." Sally put her hand out to shake Claire's, saying, "We have all been waiting to meet you; this way, please."

Karl put his files and documents into a desk drawer, then put his tunic back on before sitting back down at his desk to wait.

Karl could hear people talking boisterously out in the main office as they introduced themselves to his future wife. Karl walked to the door. Opening it, he could see Claire making friendly introductions and winning over everyone. Standing there, he thought she is a genuine solicitor. Look at her winning over these people. Claire caught sight of Karl in her peripheral vision, leaning against the door frame, his arms crossed with an uncontrollable smile that gave him away.

In a loud voice, he yelled, "Who let this civilian in here?" Karl loved how his staff was enjoying meeting Claire, and it was obvious she felt the same.

Claire turned toward Karl, answering him, "Private McGivern reporting for duty, Captain Vita." Karl, laughing loudly, walked over to the group, putting his arm around Claire's waist, then kissing her on the cheek. As the head of the department, he needed to show restraint at times like this.

"Well, now that you met my bunch, let's take a walk down to Major Knight's office, shall we? Sally, would you please call his office to inform him we are on our way down? Also, call Captain Lowes' office and let him know to meet me there; thank you."

Karl turned Claire toward his office before heading out. With the door closed, he turned Claire toward him, kissing her passionately before saying, "What an artist you are; it must be that solicitor training. They all loved you. Am I surprised? No."

Waving goodbye, Claire linked her arm through Karl's as they walked toward Clive's office. "Claire, so very pleased to meet you," said Clive, extending his hand to Claire, followed by Bill kissing Claire on the cheek. "Please, have a seat. Can we get you some tea, or has this Austrian got you converted to coffee?" Clive, being the perfect English gentleman, was giving Claire every courtesy.

"Either one is fine, Major, or may I call you Clive? And is that alright with you also, Bill? I'm so please you allowed me to visit your facilities. Karl is so proud of everyone here, especially when it comes to you two. Meeting you both face to face is the only way I know to distill any doubts that may still be lingering in your minds about Karl and myself. Until this meeting, you may have been thinking I'm another one of his flings, which, by the way, I can't blame you for thinking. Karl and your charming wife Julie have told me all about his wild romancing of the ladies, so let me categorically deny that thought. I am not one of those ladies. Enough said for the time being. Really, it's a real pleasure being here." Claire, saying that, was thinking, I believe that preemptive opening may be what is needed to set our intentions on firm ground.

Karl sat there with that big grin on his face, staring at Clive and Bill, thinking, God, she gets right to the point, and in such a diplomatic fashion. I'm glad she is my solicitor and not one suing me.

Clive was the first to speak, "Miss McGivern, or may I from now on refer to you as Claire? How delighted Bill and I are to finally meet the lady who will keep our friend in line. We think very highly of him, and may I say, he is one of the best officers I have had the privilege of serving with. So, if we initially appeared cautious, it's because we have been with Karl from the first day he arrived in England, wearing the uniform of a merchant marine officer. If we created the wrong impression, it's still a little hard to comprehend that, in less than a week, you two have become engaged. Bill and I are now willing to admit that we are looking forward to seeing Karl slide that wedding ring on behind that beautiful engagement ring."

Clive and Bill knew that ring so very well from when Kitty Johnson wore it. Clive excused himself, picking up the intercom and telling his secretary to hold all calls except for his wife and his commanding officer. Turning to the cabinet behind his desk, he took out a decanter and four glasses, saying, "Claire, I believe we have something really special to celebrate, and may I add, it's been a long time coming." Clive poured four healthy glasses of Scott, then with a raised glass, said, "I give you the future Mrs. Karl Vita, an English Rose if there ever was one. Now, I know it may be premature to ask, but when should Bill and I have our dress uniforms made ready for the wedding? You must also consider, we are fighting a war, so when you plan that, you must remember to keep me in the loop in case it interferes with the plans of the War Department." That comment had them all laughing.

Claire asked Clive if he could show her around the place, not the secure locations, though. Clive took great delight in introducing Claire to each department, Bill and Karl walking behind them. Bill whispered to Karl, "Wow, she is such a catch. I would marry her myself, and may I also say, she's quite the looker, you lucky bugger you." Bill was noticing the form-fitting dark red suit and walking behind her, he was enjoying that view. Karl excused himself while he got his suitcase and briefcase from his office, telling them he would meet them in the lobby. Walking fast, he swung open the lobby door, saying, "Seeing you at Charter Arms at six Saturday evening; have a nice evening."

Clive and Bill watched them leave, saying nothing until they were back in the hallway. Clive spoke first, saying, "Well, Bill, what do you think? Quite the woman, you agree? Smart as hell! Old Karl will have to stay on his toes around her."

Bill sarcastically remarked, "I would venture to say she is built for comfort and lots of speed. I hope old Karl still has the stamina to handle that one." Clive just shook his head, thinking, Bill will never change.

Claire opened the door to the suite, then Karl walked in right behind her. Claire had already unpacked, putting everything away except the new silk negligee and matching light blue sheer robe hanging from the door of the armoire. Karl just looked at it, then back to Claire, saying, "Darling, is that the dessert wrapping?"

Claire approached him, sliding her arms around his waist, saying, "If that's what you want it to be. But we could be wasting time doing that. I had the hotel deliver Champagne while I was at the camp this afternoon. Are you ready for some now, or would you like to wait until later?" Claire crossed the room, pulling down the bedsheets, while Karl just stood there watching her.

Next, she removed her jacket, followed by her skirt and slip but removed nothing else. Karl was in awe of her poise, her deliberate actions, and how she did not take her gaze from him. She had a mysterious fixed smile across her face.

She crossed back to where Karl was standing, still wearing her black high-heeled shoes, thinking, if this doesn't get him going, I need to go back to school. Standing close in front of him in her alluring black lingerie, she was sending Karl a very strong message. She was not leaving this room until he had made love to her. Karl just stood there, playing her teasing game, waiting for her next move. Claire reached up, removing his tunic, then his shirt, kissing his chest as she opened each button. She fumbled with his military web belt, not sure how it unclipped; quickly, she figured it out. With confidence, she pushed him down onto the love seat behind him, removing his boots and socks. The silence continued amplifying the sexually charged desire Claire was generating. She continued by unbuttoning his trousers, giving them a strong tug to slide them down.

Parting Karl's legs, she placed her left hand on his cheek, kissing him slowly, her tongue mingling with his. Karl's eye closed as he felt the sensation of her hands pulling down his underwear. Karl went to speak, but Claire simply put a finger across his lips not to say a word. With a deliberately slow movement, she allowed her hand to stroke his skin all the way down to his erection. In his mind, he was following her every move, and he knew where she was going. She caressed him further with her hand; then, she softly encircled him with her warm, moist mouth.

Karl remained perfectly still, thinking, something has happened to Claire to make her act like this. Not that I'm objecting, but there is a reason she is acting this way. She stood up, bending over him, passionately kissing him again, and in an almost whisper said, "Karl, I love you so much. Let me make all the moves, alright?" Karl slowly nodded, not wanting to break her magic. Claire pulled back from him, still staring at his one good eye, then removed her underwear, stroking his chest with them before she lowered herself onto his erection. Karl could not believe what was happening. This very proper English woman was acting as he could never have imagined.

His mind was scrambling in this web of magic she was creating. Claire quietly moaned as she increased the depth of motion. As much as Karl tried to hold back, it was becoming harder to contain himself. Feeling Claire starting to shake, her moaning increasing, she looked at Karl's face, crying out, "Oh, God, Karl…" She never finished the sentence as they both gave into a magical orgasm. For the longest time, Claire remained perfectly still, straddling Karl's lap, her head on his shoulder, both mingling in sweat. After a few minutes, Claire said, "Karl, once we are married, promise me we can make a baby, and to hell with waiting for this damn war to end. Promise me that, Karl. If anything should happen to you, God forbid, I will have you in that baby. Karl, please make me that promise right now while you are still inside me." Claire had just made her intentions very clear.

Her hormones were racing, and only he could satisfy that maternal desire. Karl, holding her tightly, was processing what she had just asked of him. So, this amazing sexual display Claire just gave me was leading up to that question, and she wants an answer right now? Claire kissed him on the cheek as she climbed off, the spell now broken, saying. "How was that, lover boy?"

At first, Karl clenched his teeth as Claire hit a nerve by saying that, but that tension quickly melted away as he looked at this beautiful woman in front of him. "Let's talk about what you just asked me over dinner, alright?"

Claire nodded her head in agreement, kissing him on the forehead, then walked toward the bathroom, saying quietly, "I hope you realize I meant every word of that, Karl?"

Karl locked the door behind them as they walked downstairs for dinner, feeling refreshed after a nice hot bath. Claire had changed into a fitted bottle-green dress with a standing collar, with a wide matching belt finishing the look. Claire had put up her hair in a

French Twist, so the single strand of pearls adorning her neck would not be covered. Karl was in a tweed jacket with dark blue trousers; instead of a tie, he elected to wear a striped cravat. Entering the restaurant, the *maître D* commented on how handsome a couple they looked. Karl held the chair out for Claire and kissed her on the neck, complimenting her on how attractive and very sexy she appeared.

"Did I tell you I'm head over heels in love with you? Instead of sitting across from you, I'm going to sit right next to you. It will be more romantic that way." Karl wanted to hold her hand when the question of a baby came up again, as he knew it would. The menu was limited due to rationing, but what they had was very tasty. After dinner, they moved to the lounge for a glass of port, sitting on a couch, the baby question came up again.

"Karl, I know what must be going through your head, and I need to apologize for allowing it to come out that way. We have both lost someone special. My darling Karl, I can honestly say I have never met or wanted to make love to anyone like I wanted you today. I didn't mean to surprise you by acting as I did. Something inside me eliminated any reservations about making love to you like that, and I just gave into that sexual desire. By the way, I may have discovered another side to Claire," she concluded.

"Well, darling, anytime you want to reenact that style of love making, count me in." Karl kissed her again on the neck before bluntly asking the real question. "Talk to me, Claire, about having a baby. Where did that come from?" asked Karl.

Claire was blushing; she really didn't want to address that tonight, so she answered by saying, "Karl, we are going to become man and wife. What scares me the most, and darling, forgive me for putting it this way, when Patrick died, there was little left of that wonderful bond between us but memories—some more painful than others, which brings me to us. We are both intelligent and mature enough to accept that you are an intelligence agent and could be killed in your line of work before this war is over. I guess you can say such is the life of a spy. Karl, I can't face this twice in a row. The love we share is strong enough to weather that storm. I pray that day will never come, but if it does, I will have a part of you living and breathing at home with me—a testament to what we made together out of love. Does any of this make sense to you, darling?" Claire sat quietly as Karl gathered his thoughts before answering.

"Claire, were you trying to trick me into becoming pregnant earlier?"

Claire responded right away. "Today, I was. It's something I want us to share together."

Karl, still holding her hand, answered, "If it is meant to be, we will cherish that child with all the love we can muster. It would be nice to get married first, though, don't you agree?" Karl was trying to make light of what his new wife would want first after the wedding. They retired to bed, content and secure that their relationship had just taken another step into becoming a real family, and Karl was alright with that.

Up early the following day, they drove to Great Windsor to explore the sights of this historic city. Arriving back at the hotel, they had an afternoon nap, safe in each other's arms. Karl woke to the room phone ringing, "Yes?" he answered.

"Did I wake you, or were you doing something I don't need to know about?" asked Clive, laughing at what he had just said.

"Clive, you can be such an idiot at times. Didn't you figure out that was the first thing on the agenda when we entered the room? Now, what's on your mind?" asked Karl.

"We will be there at 1800 hours; shall we meet you at the bar, or should we go straight to the table?" asked Clive.

"Why don't we get Claire comfortable by meeting at the bar, alright?" Even as he said that Karl realized that Claire was a very confident lady in any new crowd.

"By the way, old man, Julie can't wait to meet Claire face to face. She said they talked about so much yesterday, and if you are wondering, they did discuss you; imagine that." Clive was enjoying the ribbing he was giving Karl. "See you later, Casanova." Karl sat there on the edge of the bed, thinking, what did these girls talk about? Claire must have been wearing her solicitor's hat again; I can only imagine that discussion.

Karl looked back at Claire, still sleeping soundly. He moved over to kiss her forehead gently, and in a soft voice, said, "Claire, honey, time to get up and get ready for tonight." Karl hated to wake her. She looked so serenely secure in having her man next to her. "Come on, sleepyhead; the gang will be here at 6:00 p.m., including your new pal, Julie."

Claire rolled over, rubbing her eyes. She turned to Karl; lifting her head, she kissed him on the cheek, saying, "Sounds like Clive has been telling you about our ladies chat on Friday." Karl got dressed in his dress uniform, which Clive had requested the three men wear for this special occasion. Karl was getting very fidgety thinking about tonight and the long wait for Claire to come out of the bathroom.

Finally, the door opened, and out came Claire. "Wow!" was all that Karl could say.

Claire answered him by asking, "So, Sailor, how does your fiancée look for tonight's celebration?" Claire had on a form-fitting black dress that showed off her figure so very well. The wide off-the-shoulder neckline made the single strand of pearls stand out in a very classic way. Once again, her hair was up in a French Twist to finish off that look of a very classy, elegant lady. Flashing her engagement ring in front of Karl, she was enjoying the attention he was showering her with.

Karl, with his arm around her waist, whispered in her ear, "I think we should make them wait. I feel like ravishing you right here against the door." Claire was getting Karl's juices going again, and she loved every minute of it.

"Down, tiger, everything comes to those that wait." Claire saying that had triggered a fond memory Karl had of his father saying that.

"Claire, what you just said is an expression I have used so many times in the past. Hearing you say that convinces me we are somehow on the same wave band. God, I love you, Claire. Now, do I rough you up, or will that be later?" Karl, with his arms around her, held her tightly. No more words were necessary; they had what they both needed.

Walking down the stairs, they entered the lounge. Looking around, Karl saw Bill's arm waving at them. Clive and Julie were sitting on one couch, and Bill and Dorothy were opposite them in two armchairs. "Show time, you sexy creature. Are you ready?" asked Karl, holding her arm.

"As ready as I'll ever be," replied Claire. Clive stood, greeting Claire with a kiss on the cheek, then introduced Dorothy and finally Julie, who came around to welcome Claire, putting her arm around her and giving her a cheek-to-cheek embrace.

"Claire, so nice to finally meet you. I enjoyed our talk on Friday afternoon. I feel like I already know you so well." Julie patted the couch for Claire to sit next to her and Dorothy. Clive sat opposite with his fellow officer.

"Dorothy, you are such a gem. I hope Bill appreciates what he has, and Julie, it's hard to believe you have daughters five and seven years old. You look so young; you have quite the figure too, for being a mother. These three blokes are lucky men; wouldn't you agree, ladies?" Claire, the diplomat, had won over two ladies who would quickly become her close friends as the dangers of war increased for the BIS and its agents. They would lean on one another when their men went into harm's way, but not tonight anyway.

Over dinner, they all enjoyed the bantering. There was so much to talk about. Clive eventually stood up with a glass in hand, asking for silence and for those at the table to raise their glasses. "Tonight, we come together as friends to celebrate the engagement of our close friend Karl to his new fiancée, Claire. We have only just gotten to know you. If the term love at first sight can be used, we are all guilty. When Karl announced he had bought an MG sports car, I could not have imagined that also included its owner as well, and may I add, a true English Rose. Claire and Karl, may your lives together be full of love and health, and may your lives always be fortified with the hopes and dreams you both aspire to reach for one another." Clive sat down as they all clinked glasses.

Claire asked, "May I also add to that wonderful toast? A few weeks back, I was a sad and very lonely lady. Then, on a Saturday morning, a dashing intelligence officer changed my life forever. Yesterday, I started making new and lasting friends, and tonight, I can honestly say this may be one of the best times Karl and I will ever have. Thank you again for this special evening." Claire hugged them all, then wrapped her arms around Karl's neck, saying, "Ladies, he's all mine. You have my permission to slap him if you see his eyes looking in the wrong direction. Clive and Bill, if he gets out of line, just call me. I know what gets his attention real fast." Claire and Karl started laughing; it had been a wonderful celebration.

Sunday, Karl and Claire were invited to Clive and Julie's home to meet their daughters and enjoy a wonderful lunch. Driving back to the hotel, there was silence in the car until they parked. "Claire, tomorrow, God willing, I will get good news about my eye, and you will be heading home to Hitchin. Darling, I must tell you, I'm working on an operation that will keep me in Bedford for a couple of weeks. When I return home on Friday, I will use the MG to drive to Bedford. I don't believe I will have any problems driving with one eye. With any luck, I may be able to sneak away for an evening or two during those weeks. How does that sound to you?" Karl was careful about what not to say.

"Karl, are you doing something dangerous on that spy operation?" asked Claire, knowing full well what he did in the BIS.

"Not really; as for tomorrow, when you drop me off, you can take my case home with you, alright?" Karl was guiding her away from her pointed question. That night, they had a quiet dinner; neither was in the mood to make conversation. It had been a wonderful few days and all they wanted to do now was retire to bed in the comfort of each other's arms. Monday morning, they left early to drive to the hospital. The traffic, as expected, was heavy.

Arriving at the entrance, Claire turned to Karl, saying, "Darling, let me come in with you. Otherwise, I'll worry until you call me." Claire could not bring herself to say goodbye, not just yet anyway.

"Claire, we talked about this last night, did we not? It serves no purpose, waiting around this hospital, and let's also remember you have a responsibility to your practice. Now, be off with you. Don't worry; I'll try to call you as soon as the doctor has finished with me." Karl held her arms tightly, looking into her face. He reached over to kiss her passionately before opening the car door. "Drive carefully, and don't fret about me, alright?" Karl stood on the pavement, smiling and throwing kisses as she drove off. Entering the lobby, he registered with the receptionist, then made his way to the waiting room.

A nurse came out of the examination area, calling, "Captain Karl Vita." Karl stood up, then followed her into the room. "Have a seat, Captain, while I take a look at your eye and get it ready for the doctor to look at it," instructed the nurse as she carefully removed the gauze from under his leather patch. "Nice job, Captain, taking care of your eye. It looks very clean other than the ointment in the corners."

Karl responded by saying, "I can't take credit for that. It's mainly my fiancée who changes the dressing and applies the ointment. When she is not with me, she hounds me anyway." Karl was making light of her question. The middle door opened, and in walked Dr. Phillips.

"Well, old man, let's get a look at that eye, shall we? I'm going to recline you, then pull that incandescent light up close." Dr.

Phillips rolled his eyelid up, telling Karl to look up, then down, and finally from left to right. "Well, Captain, you are doing better than I expected. I'm going to raise the lights a little higher; then, I'm going to ask you to look straight ahead and tell me what you see. On the opposite side of the room, the nurse was slowly waving a round target. "What do you see now with your left eye only?" asked Dr. Phillips.

Being his usual self, Karl answered, "A white ring with two red stars on opposite sides being waved by a charming nurse." "That's really good. I believe your vision will improve as it continues to strengthen and as long as you continue to clean it

daily. I'm satisfied the doctor at the camp can take care of you from this point on, unless something goes dramatically wrong. In the next couple of weeks, that nice patch can be returned to its box. Hopefully, it will not be needed in the future." Dr. Phillips shook Karl's hand, saying, "Goodbye, Captain Vita. Take care of yourself doing that undercover stuff. Nurse, would you replace the dressing before the captain is released." Then, Dr. Phillips marched off to the next patient.

"I didn't even have time to thank him, Nurse," said Karl as he stood up from the examination chair.

"He knows how thankful you are. Getting better is all the thanks he needs," answered the nurse as she escorted him back to the lobby. "Goodbye, Captain; God bless you for what you do—please, stay safe." Karl walked outside in the dismal morning drizzle, not caring at all about the weather. There was sunshine in his heart.

Looking around, he saw Charlie standing next to the big Humber with an umbrella already opened at the rear passenger door. "Everything go alright, Sir?" asked the friendly driver.

"Yes, Charlie, we are on the mend. Have you been waiting long?" Karl always liked this Londoner. His questions were truly sincere.

"Not really, Gov, only about forty-five minutes."

Returning to the camp, Karl went right to the wireless room, asking, "What came in that needs my attention?" Karl was back in intelligence mode.

"Only got six, Sir. They are in the locked pouch on your desk. Major Knight reviewed them before I locked them up," answered the operator.

Back in his office, Karl opened the pouch, then read each one of the transmissions. One of them caught his attention. Its closing line read, has Grandmother passed on? Karl kept looking at it before he put it in with the other wires. This is not going to be easy when Hazel returns. Peggy entered, saying, "Well, Sir, how did it go this morning? You are looking very concerned. By the way, we all think Miss McGivern is really smashing. Captain Lowes asked for you to meet him in his office at your earliest convenience." Sally took the pouch from his hand as she said that. Karl grabbed his agent file from the locked drawer in his desk, thanked Sally, and headed for Bill's office.

"Afternoon, Bill, are we going to finalize our pick of agents today?" asked Karl.

"Yes, we are, but first, how did you make out this morning with the eye exam?" Bill, the ever-loyal friend, needed to know his status.

"Better than Dr. Phillips expected, so I'm on the mend, thank God," answered Karl as he opened his file to continue with the planning of the operation.

Claire had gone right to her practice, throwing herself into the pile of folders on her desk. Beverly entered, asking her how the weekend went, her gaze not leaving the ring. "Oh, Bev, it was wonderful. Everyone on Karl's staff made such a warm fuss; I felt like a princess. As for Karl's friends, they also gave us a marvelous time Saturday evening, then Sunday at Clive and Julie's house for lunch. She has two beautiful girls, who are so well behaved. It could not have gone any better. I think I have made lasting friends in Julie and Dorothy, crazy Bill's girlfriend.

"By the way, your sister called looking for you. She said to remind you she has not heard from you in a long time, and it must be that army chap you're over the moon about." Beverly gave a little chuckle when she said that last part.

"Oh, God, Bev. I usually call her every weekend. She must be really angry at me right now. I'm willing to bet she's more interested in all the juicy stuff; she always was the nosy one." Claire shook her head as she said that.

Claire got home a little after six o'clock to an empty house. The first thing she did was call Karl at the camp as she had not heard from him yet, the operator asking her to hold while he located him. "Karl, darling, what did the doctor say this morning? Is he pleased with your progress?" said Claire, her brain going at a hundred miles an hour.

"Everything is better than expected. Dr. Phillips told me there's no real need to see him again unless something goes wrong. The camp doc can take over from here on; isn't that great news? Karl could tell she needed to talk, so he kept it brief.

"I Just got home a little while ago. I'm so bogged down with file reviews; I think I will start real early tomorrow morning, so I'll have an early night tonight. Karl, while I was driving home this morning, I had time to relax and reflect on how I have changed in just a few weeks. When I was married to Patrick, we had a good marriage, and our lovemaking was comfortable but never over the top if you are following me. Friday evening, before going out, something came over me, making me someone else—someone who was forceful and daring in her teasing, and God knows, leaving high heels on during love making is something I would never do. Until I met you, I was more the flannel nightgown type. I swear to God, Karl; it's being with you that's turning me into a nymphomaniac, and that scares the heck out of me. You must be thinking, what on earth am I getting into with this sex-starved woman." Claire, saying all that, thought, oh, my goodness, I've said too much, haven't I?

Karl, on the other end of the phone, was trying hard not to burst out laughing. "Claire, you are so adorable in the innocent way you just described yourself. Darling, it was always there; you just suppressed those feelings, holding them back, maybe too scared or even too aloof to let yourself go and be the person you secretly dreamed of being when you love someone with all your being. You do understand; if I ever see you in a flannel nightgown, I will burn it, don't you? What a wonderful, complex, intelligent, and sexy solicitor you are. Claire, when I come home, you realize I want and will get a repeat performance of Friday night, don't you? Claire, what happened is something you have always wanted to do. I simply opened that door you have always been too scared to pass through."

Karl became serious, realizing that this proper English lady had scared herself and may be a little afraid that the confident upper lip had been slightly altered. Whatever happened, she knew there was no going back, nor would Karl allow her to.

"Darling, I must call my sister, Caroline. She called my office, wondering why I haven't called her; she must be really mad at me about now. I'm willing to bet she wants to come to meet you.

What are we doing this weekend, other than scaring me half to death?" Claire was now returning to her composed self.

"Nothing as far as I know. I'll let you know my schedule tomorrow. Good night, Claire; you make each day a delight—never change." Karl hung up the phone, then went back into Bill's office to continue where they left off.

Claire dialed her sister's number. Hearing her sister's voice, she said, "Caroline, are you mad at me? I'm so sorry; it's been a whirlwind weekend. I drove to Slough to meet up with the people that work for Karl. His close friends gave us an engagement party at this swanky hotel and restaurant called the Charter Arms—what a night. Caroline, I can't wait for you to meet your new brother-in-law. I know you will love him; his personality is so contagious. When I'm with him, I find myself becoming daring in so many ways."

Over the next ninety minutes, she told her sister everything, leaving nothing out. Their bond of sisterhood was such that they always told each other everything, and this phone call was no different. After Claire had finished, she quietly asked, "Well, what do you think of your big sister now?"

There was a pause before Caroline yelled out in laughter, "Claire, you're such a slut. What happened to my stuffy, stuck-up sister, always proper in whatever she does and says? Tell me again about Friday night and what you did to him." Caroline was loving this new side of her big sister.

"Now, let's stop laughing and be serious, shall we? I was thinking of inviting myself for the weekend. I have cleared it with David; he is alright taking care of the kids. In fact, he told me last night, don't you think you should visit your sister, especially now that she is engaged to that intelligence chap? So, should I plan on it?" asked Caroline.

"Yes, yes, yes, my little sister, that would be wonderful. Karl usually arrives late Friday afternoon. He catches the train from Kings Cross, which arrives here in Hitchin about 6:30 p.m. If you plan it right, you could meet up there, then take the same train. It would be so much easier picking you both up at the same time." Claire, the organizer, was excited finally to have Karl meet her younger sister. Feeling really tired, she made herself a sandwich, then went upstairs to bed. Undressing, she went to put on her nightgown. Stopping, she broke out laughing—from now on, I'll have to hide this one on Fridays before Karl arrives home.

Tuesday morning, Karl and Bill sat in the small meeting room, waiting for the German candidates to arrive. The door swung open, and in walked four uniformed BIS agents. "Gentlemen, please take a seat," asked Bill. The four agents took seats across from Bill and Karl. "Your files are very impressive as former seamen for the Kriegsmarine. This morning, we will interview each one of you separately before deciding which two fit our requirements. Do you have any questions to ask before we start the process?"

The four Germans all said no, but they wanted to know the details before going any further. Over the next five hours, each agent was asked the same questions, then cross-questioned until Bill and Karl zeroed in on two. "Bring Fredrick and Walter back in," said Bill to the MP stationed at the door. "Gentlemen, please have a seat. Sorry that it's been a long day for you so far. The mission we are asking you to undertake is right here in England. We need you both to masquerade as shipwrecked German sailors. Your mission is to gain the confidence of other shipwrecked German sailors who are prisoners and, by doing so, get them to disclose certain facts about U-Boat activities, their numbers, strengths, and how they are directed to attack allied convoys in the North Atlantic. This mission will be very dangerous for both of you. It could cost you your lives. Are you prepared to undertake a mission like this?" asked Bill, staring at them both.

"How do you propose we go about doing this, assuming we can gain their trust?" asked the one who had been a senior officer on a destroyer based in Norway. Bill turned to Karl, asking him to take over the meeting, describing the plan's details. Speaking German, Karl proceeded. When they discovered he was a maritime officer for a German shipping company, the look on their faces was amusing to both Karl and Bill.

After hearing the plan, the German agents agreed they were eager to undertake the mission, asking, "When are we going to do this, and where are these prisoners being held right now?"

Karl pulled the thick files out of his briefcase, spreading them out for each prisoner, then said, "Alright, let's get to work, shall we?" Over the next two and a half days, they refined the plan and their cover stories. At 2345 hours on Wednesday evening, the plot was finished. The four of them could do no more; they were so tired.

"Alright, chaps, let's call it a night. Tomorrow, you two will be transported to the Bedford facilities in an armed lorry. We will be arriving later, masquerading as interrogators. Remember, we have never seen you before, so act the part of being rebellious German prisoners of war. Have a good night's sleep; tomorrow will be a long one," said Karl, walking toward the door.

The following morning, Karl and Bill met early at the NAAFI for hot tea and a sandwich before driving to Bedford, Bill doing the driving. Their interrogation cover would commence Monday morning. Only the camp commander knew about what was happening. Fredrick and Walter would be driven to holding cells at the camp; they would occupy a cell together until Monday.

That would give the rumor mill time to spread the news that two more sailors had been brought to the Interrogation Center.

Arriving at the camp, Bill and Karl spent the afternoon with Major Warren Biggles, the camp commander, who later invited them to join him for supper in a very posh officers' club.

"Gentlemen, what role would you like me and my chaps to play in this masquerade of yours?" asked the major.

Once again, they explained their web of deceit. Major Biggles, hearing the plot and how it would play out, sat back, saying. "Bloody marvelous idea. Who did it come from?"

Bill, looking at Karl, said, "from Karl."

"So, tomorrow, you two will start your interrogation of all the German sailors, correct? Will there be any roughing them up, or will that be later?"

"We will have to play that one by ear. Our two moles may have to go along with that idea if it brings credence to them being loyal German Kriegsmarine sailors. The major walked them over to the visiting officers' quarters before wishing them good evening.

"Hope you have a relaxing evening, chaps; see you in the morning."

Karl was tired; he needed to get an early night. Bill was feeling the same, so they both headed to their own rooms. Karl decided it wasn't too late to call Claire, so he walked back to the operations area. "Excuse me, Sergeant, where can I use a private phone?"

The sergeant pointed to an office across the hall, replying, "Right over there, Sir, dial the operator for an outside line."

Karl went in, closing the door behind him. Sitting down, he placed the call. "Hitchin 4567," answered Claire. Without asking, she knew it was Karl. "Darling, I was wondering if you would call me tonight. Are you in that other place tonight?" Claire was careful not to mention locations.

"Yes, I am, Claire. I will be home early tomorrow evening. Now, where do I meet your sister in Kings Cross Station? And what will she be wearing?" Karl took his pocket pad and pen out to write down the information. "Remember, on Monday morning, I will be leaving at the crack of dawn. Sunday, I need to park the MG at the house. That will work out nicely. Then, on the following Friday, I can drive back home again. Now, Miss McGivern, I need to know; do you miss me terribly?" Karl already knew her answer.

"You tease, why do you say things like that? I can't wait to devour you tomorrow, sister or no sister. By the way, we are having Goulash for supper tomorrow. I have invited the family over to meet my baby sister; it should be fun. I'm picking Mama, Freida, and Franchot up at about 2:00 p.m. She wants to help me make dinner; it should be interesting. Karl, how are you sleeping? Any bad dreams I should know about?" asked Claire.

"Not really; I think talking about it like we did has helped me tremendously. I'll see you Friday. By then, your sister will have spilled the beans on your younger days. Good night, darling."

Karl hung up the phone and headed back to his room. The following morning, Karl and Bill reviewed the plan with Fredrick and Walter, making sure they had studied the plot repeatedly until it was engraved into their brains. Both agents were using their cover names. Even when Karl shot a question at Fredrick in German, using his real name, he answered, "I'm sorry; I don't know a Fredrick. Is he a POW in this camp as well?" The plot was as bulletproof as it could be. Bill, satisfied with the readiness of the two agents, turned to Karl, saying, "Time for us to hit the road, Captain. Any last-minute advice you would like to pass on before we leave?"

"Only this, weigh each and every word carefully before you speak. They will be feeling you out at first, so that's the most dangerous part of this plot." Karl and Bill stood up, shaking their hands, then left. They said goodbye to the camp commander in the lobby, saying they would arrive back on Monday morning before 1030 hours. The drive back to Slough was surprisingly quick, with no traffic delays.

Bill took Karl straight to the station. "See you Monday. I'm looking forward to seeing the MG—no speeding with only one eye." Bill drove off, laughing about his last statement.

Standing under the arrivals and departure board in Kings Cross Station, Karl kept looking for a younger version of Claire in a Harris Tweed suit. Looking repeatedly at his watch, he was thinking, she's cutting this really close. Almost ready to head to the platform on his own, Karl spotted an attractive woman walking fast, almost at a jog, and waving as she approached, yelling, "Karl, hold on. I'm here. I'm so sorry for making you wait; are we going to miss the train?" Caroline had made it.

Thank God she was only looking for a military officer wearing a brown eye patch to identify him.

"Caroline, I was almost going to leave without you. Come on; we can make formal introductions once we are on the train.

Here, give me your suitcase and grab my arm. We will have to move fast; how strong are your legs?" Karl laughed as Caroline tried to keep up with him.

The ticket conductor punched their tickets, saying, "Jump into the first available compartment; the train is leaving right now."

Karl opened the first empty door, half lifting and pushing Caroline into the compartment, saying, "Almost out of breath."

Caroline yelled back at Karl as he shut the door, "Bugger, that was close. What a way to meet my new brother-in-law. Thank God for the eye patch. I would probably have missed you amongst all those uniforms. Now, come here and give me a hug and a big kiss on the cheek." Caroline was excited to meet Claire's future husband. "Karl, I must say, Claire picked a smashing bloke to marry. I can see how she fell for you in such a big way. You're quite the lover boy from what Claire has told me." Caroline looked so much like her big sister, but their personalities were so different. She had a devilish side to her, which Karl enjoyed.

"Caroline, I must say; you are a very attractive, bubbly lady." Caroline, with a big smile on her face, answered, "Thank you kindly, Sir. I'm glad you approve. Now, wait a minute; we need to celebrate before we get into Hitchen." From her hand luggage, she retrieved two metal cups and a hip flask containing whiskey. Karl, watching her, was laughing at what she was doing as she handed Karl a very full cup and poured one for herself. Linking arms, she looked up at Karl, saying, "Welcome to the family, Karl. Claire loves you so very much. Please, don't get yourself killed; she has been down that road once already. Now, drink up; we have enough for one more refill." Caroline, the younger sister, was so outgoing and very cheeky; other than looks, the two sisters were utterly different.

"The next stop is ours. Let me get your case down and ready," said Karl, putting his tunic back on. The train's brakes squealed in protest as it entered the station. There, on the platform, was Claire, along with Freida, looking at the passengers getting off.

"Freida, there they are, behind that porter. Karl, Caroline, over here!" yelled Freida as they all came together on that crowded platform. Claire introduced her sister to Freida, then turned quickly to face her one-eyed soldier.

"Claire, kiss him, or I'll do it for you," said an excited Caroline. Karl put down their cases, then, with open arms, wrapped them around Claire, quietly saying, "I'm home." With that, he kissed her first on the lips, then on her neck.

"Freida, it's so nice to see you coming to welcome us." Karl hugged his younger sister, asking, "Where is Ronny?"

"He'll be along after 6:30 p.m. He's driving straight here from the base." Back at the house, Mama hugged her son, then did the same to Caroline. Karl's nostrils were catching the familiar aroma of Goulash wafting from the kitchen.

"Karl, you should be proud of Claire. She made our supper all by herself," said Mama.

"That's not completely true. Mama and Freida guided me on some of the steps." Claire was excited, having her sister there finally to meet her new family.

Sitting in the lounge, waiting for Ronny to arrive, Caroline picked up Claire's hand, saying, "I say, Sis; that's a smashing engagement ring you're wearing. It's quite an unusual design." Ronny arrived in time to join them all for dinner. Claire, with Freida's help, served dinner; Karl and Ronny enjoyed the large portions they were given of tasty Goulash, finishing it off with bread.

Ronny turned to Claire, saying, "I have to wait for Karl to come home to get this treat. Come home more often, will you?" Ronny loved it when they all came together like this. With Karl and himself in uniform, a normal life was out of the question.

The weekend was delightful. Claire and Karl took Caroline to Cambridge, stopping on the way back in Baldock to have a cocktail at the George and Dragon. Their final stop was at the Bungalow for cake and coffee with the family before returning home to Hitchen. That evening, Claire and Caroline told tales of growing up in this house with their parents. "Caroline, before you had children, what did you do for work? Did you also work for your father?" asked Karl.

"No, I did not. I was a Science teacher in Watford. That's where I met my husband, David, and the rest is history. We moved to Oxford after our first child was born. We decided it was the perfect place to raise a family. I wish you both could be closer, though," she said, putting her arm around Claire's shoulder.

"Tomorrow is Sunday, so what shall we do?" asked Karl, wondering what to do with these two beautiful ladies.

"How do you feel about going to church? You both have much to be thankful for," suggested Caroline, eyeballing Claire, then staring at Karl.

"Why not? You are absolutely correct. I hope the roof doesn't cave in when I walk in, though," said Karl, trying not to laugh.

The two sisters dressed in their Sunday best, and Karl wore his dress uniform. Built in the late 1600s, the old church had a musty smell to it—probably from all those candles burning at the back by the entrance. Karl, in an almost whisper, said, "So far, so good."

Claire answered, "Vita, behave yourself." After mass, Claire introduced Karl to the priest. Karl surprised them by telling tales of when he was an altar boy in Vienna. "Father, thank you; we will see you on Sundays from now on," said Claire as they returned to the car.

Caroline added, "Well, I thought if it remains nice and sunny, we could go walking around the streets of Hitchin. We must be boring Karl to death with our stories of growing up in this old town and doing things proper young ladies should not be doing." Caroline enjoyed embarrassing her sister in front of her fiancé.

"Well, if we do, we can stop at your office on the way back to pick up the MG. I must be on the road early tomorrow morning to arrive back at the camp by 0900 hours. How does that sound to you two ladies?" replied Karl, enjoying the horseplay between the sisters. Another wonderful day was spent walking around the old historic farming town. Claire and Caroline explained the history of the old buildings as they walked along. Karl enjoyed it immensely, stopping in at the Bull Public House for a plowman's lunch.

Before leaving, Caroline asked Claire, "May I use the Wolsey later? I would like to stop by to see Pearl, my old school friend, while I'm here in Hitchin. You don't mind, do you?" Caroline knew Claire wanted some private time with Karl before he left in the morning, and this would be a good way of excusing herself.

Karl looked at Claire, a twinkle in his eye as Caroline said that. Leaning over, he kissed Caroline on her cheek, saying, "Thank you; that's such a sweet lie." Arriving at the office, Karl backed the MG out of the garage, Claire locking it behind him. "Alright, let's head home. Karl, park the MG to one side of the driveway, so Caroline can put the Wolsey back in the garage when she returns home later today."

The house seemed very quiet once Caroline had left to see her friend. Claire asked, "Well, now that you have me all to yourself, Sailor, what do you want to do with me?" Claire pulled him closer to her.

Karl, answering with his unique Austrian humor, said, "Well, seeing as I'm leaving early tomorrow morning, I seem to be experiencing some separation tension. I know you could treat that with those wonderful lips of yours. It would be a good way to start the evening, would it not?" Karl gave Claire the stare that unhinged her each time he did it.

Claire knew what he was thinking. Leading him into the living room, she guided him to the couch, saying almost in a whisper, "Lay back, darling. Close your eyes and think only of me. I know exactly how to treat that tension." Claire kissed him, her hand unbuttoning his shirt and then his trousers. To arouse him further, she removed her jumper and slacks, allowing her soft skin to awaken those feelings within him. Claire's lips kissed him all the way down; then, her mouth encircled him. Karl, fully aroused, turned Claire over onto the couch, removed her underwear, and spread her legs to reciprocate with his tongue. Claire was on a cloud. Karl had a way of eliminating her inhibitions, letting herself go in a way she had never done before. Claire's breathing was becoming intense. She was at the brink of exploding. Karl pulled back and immediately entered her to feel her orgasm, which triggered his.

Karl laid on top of her without moving, softly kissing her as she still quivered, totally spent. Claire finally regained her composure, saying. "Karl, you continue to bring something new out in me. I have never felt this type of intensity from anyone else. Unfortunately, that includes dear Patrick. Darling, you know, as much as I love us being this close, there is a part of me that is scared to death of losing what we have. In your line of work, there will always be a part of you that needs to be out doing spy things, and it's that part that scares me so. I would never ask you to change positions in the military. That would be selfish to do that to you. All I can ask of you is, try not to be a hero; will you do that much for me?" Claire needed Karl to know that, in her heart, she knew he would return to the dangerous missions someplace not so safe.

Karl looked at her before he answered her. "Claire, you know I will try to be careful. I can't promise you more at this time. Now, let's get dressed again, so Caroline doesn't get a shock when she walks back into the house."

Claire smiled, answering, "Nothing you could do or say or what we are not wearing would faze Caroline in any way. Whatever you're thinking, she has probably done many times over." Claire was somewhat serious in saying that.

Caroline returned home at 9:15 p.m. As she entered the living room, she cheerfully announced, "That was so nice to spend time with Pearl and her family for a couple of hours. I expected to see your bedroom door closed."

Claire, hearing that, looked at Karl before they both started laughing. Claire eventually said, "Caroline, for once, you are too late." In the middle of a world war, three people were taking the time to enjoy themselves, but for how much longer?

The following morning, Karl, dressed in his everyday field uniform, kissed Claire, then Caroline on both cheeks, giving her a big hug, saying, "Caroline, I am so pleased to have met you.

Next time, Claire and I will come to Oxford to meet your family. That's if you want us to?" Karl gave Claire a last kiss and hugged her like he would never see her again. Backing out of the driveway, he took a last look at Claire and Caroline, thinking, someone up there has given me a second chance, and I will not take this lightly. Thank you, Lord, he thought as he put the MG into gear, driving away back into the intelligence world he lived and survived in.

CHAPTER 16

1941 A TIME OF CHANGE

Claire had given Karl the directions the night before, although her directions would direct him to Bedford's City Center. Realizing his final destination could be some secret location that he could not divulge to her, Claire indicated the secondary roads would be better at that early time in the morning. She told him to look for signs that would take him through the villages of Arlesy, then Shefford, and close to Ampthill. When he crossed the A-421, he would arrive at the outskirts of Bedford. "It's only about twenty-five or so miles, so it shouldn't take you too long," indicated Claire with a puzzled look on her face.

Caroline interrupted by blurting out, "If that's where he's actually going? I'm willing to bet he's going to RAF Cardington. No need to answer that, Karl. I know you won't tell us anyway if that's the case. When you get to the A-421, you need to head northeast. The camp is not too far after you turn right, assuming that's where you are really going." Caroline remembered some years back, when she was dating an RAF warrant officer stationed at Cardington—the electrifying evening she had experienced in the back seat of a Hillman staff car! Karl had his Intelligence face on as he listened to Caroline, who had just given him the actual directions to his location.

This morning, driving through the town of Shefford, Karl was enjoying shifting the gears of his little MG, loving how nifty it handled on these winding roads, wishing it could be nicer weather to drive with the roof down. Maybe, on the way back, he could do just that. Turning right on the A-421, he noticed the traffic volume increasing with mainly military vehicles heading east to who knows where. Getting closer to the camp, he saw several silver-colored Barrage Balloons hovering about fifty feet off the ground in front of an enormous hangar. Their massive sizes looked more like giant tear drops. He presented his credentials to the guards at the gate, then followed a Jeep that led him to the building the BIS was using for their interrogation activities.

Pulling up to the entrance, Karl parked the car close to the big Humber being used by Bill, thinking he's already here. I'm not surprised. Entering the lobby, Karl registered, then proceeded to the room that had been secured for the next several days. "Bill, good morning. Did you arrive last night, or did you drive up this morning?" inquired Karl.

Bill answered, "Karl, did you drive the new MG here this morning? Let's go take a quick look before we get serious about our task for this morning, shall we?" Bill slapped Karl on the shoulder as they went back outside. Bill took one look at the gleaming little sports car, then asked Karl, "So this is the culprit that made you and Claire the success story for 1941?" Bill was elated with joy to see the look of pride Karl had on his face.

Getting behind the steering wheel was a challenge for Bill; his leg injury received back in 1937 was still giving him problems. "Karl, you will let me drive it before you head back to Baldock, won't you? By the way, Clive asked me to have you call him as soon as you can. He did not want to spoil your time with Claire by calling you over the weekend. Why don't you make that call before we start our interrogation session?"

Back inside, Karl asked for a quiet office with a secure phone. The pretty WRAF rating escorted him to an empty office, telling him, "Dial the operator for that secure line by dialing #871. She will secure the line for you."

Karl sat down, taking out a small pad and a pen. The phone rang through to Clive's office with Mary, Clive's secretary, answering, "Major Knight's extension; who is calling, please?"

Karl replied, "Good morning, Mary. It's me, Captain Vita. Is the boss in his office?" Instantly, Mary knew that it was Karl by his distinctive accent.

"Morning, Captain, yes, he is. It's nice to hear from you. I hope all is well, and how is that sweetheart of yours, Claire?" she inquired.

"Thank you for asking, Mary. We are all fine and should be back at HQ soon," concluded Karl, not wanting to give an exact date.

"Hold one minute, Captain. I'll get him for you."

Clive picked up the phone, answering in that controlled voice of his. "Karl, good to hear your voice. Are you on a secure extension?" Clive was making sure their conversion would not be compromised. "When you arrive back, come see me right away. I have some exciting news for you. Oh, by the way, you will need to pack for ten days. We are sending you to Scotland. Remember that camp up there? Well, you will be returning to it."

Karl, stopping him mid-sentence, asked, "Why?"

"Well, Karl, you are to be promoted to the rank of major as the commanding officer of a brand-new Special Intelligence Division. That promotion, by the way, is a battlefield commission. I'm confident that it will be made permanent at some later date. We did this because it was the quickest way to get your rank bumped up. By the way, this was not my idea, although I am delighted to know you are one rank below my new rank of Lieutenant-Colonel! As of this coming Friday, I have accepted a position on General Jacks' staff," explained Clive, knowing all these changes would rattle Karl, who never embraced change that well.

"So, if you're being promoted out of this command, who will be its new C.O.?" asked Karl, now suspecting another bomb to be dropped on him.

"Another new major by the name of William Lowes." Clive could not contain himself. He loved it when Karl got rattled.

"You are pulling my leg. So, when Bill returned to Slough last Friday, all of this happened over the weekend?" asked Karl, thinking, here we go again with all that secret BIS stuff.

Clive simply answered, "Yes, I took it upon myself to wait until you arrived this morning to tell you about the changes that are happening. So, don't yell at Bill too much after hanging up the phone. He is your friend; remember that." Clive, as he spoke, was also deciding whether to tell him that he had spoken to Claire earlier this morning. "Karl, there is something else I need to share with you. This morning, after you left Hitchin, I took it upon myself to call Claire to inform her that you have been promoted to major. Karl, she was so excited; it made me feel really good. One last thing, considering you will be out of town for a while, I told Bill earlier to send you home early—probably Wednesday afternoon, so you and Claire can celebrate your promotion together. Karl, are you still there?" asked Clive, not sure if he had lost him.

"Yes, Clive, I'm still here. I'm trying to wrap my mind around all the changes taking place right now. Thank you for making this happen, old friend. It was so considerate of you to include Claire. I can't thank you enough. If you don't mind, I'm going to give her a quick call before becoming a devious Intelligence officer for the next three days." Karl hung up the phone, looking at his watch to make sure he still had enough time to make that call. Calling Claire's office, he greeted Beverly saying, "Morning, Bev, is Claire busy? This is Karl."

Beverly answered cheerfully, "Never too busy to talk to you, Major Vita. I'll put you through."

Claire picked up the phone, "Karl, darling, isn't this marvelous news? Please, don't be mad at Clive. He is so proud of you and wanted to tell me right away. Darling, you're a flashy new major; when do you think you'll receive your new insignia bars? Hopefully, before you arrive home on Wednesday evening." Claire, being so excited, had told everyone in the office about his promotion. However, she had no knowledge of the dangers associated with this promotion. Karl had been usurped by his boss, Clive, being the last to receive the news on his new assignment and advancement. Just think, one of these days, I will be the one to surprise everyone with some breaking news, thought Karl.

Walking back toward the meeting room, Karl could see five German POWs being escorted down the hall from the opposite direction by four armed military police guards. As they shuffled closer, he heard one of the U-Boat officers speaking in a hushed voice to the officer behind him. Karl recognized that his insignias and white cap meant he was the captain. "Look at this pompous ass; he thinks he has the upper hand. It's a pity the S.S. isn't here. He would be shitting himself to death."

Karl walked right in front of him, poking his finger against the German's chest. Standing there, he glared at him face-to-face, hate and anger in his one good eye. Pointing at his patch, he screamed at him in German, "You conceited, pompous idiot.

Who do you think you are? This eye was the work of those gutter scums in the Gestapo. Maybe I should be doing the same to you. How does that appeal to your sense of survival, you idiot. You are looking at one of your interrogators; yes, that's me. I was forced to leave Austria because of pig-headed maniacs like you who bullied their way into my country. Stand at attention while I'm talking to you and deciding your fate."

Karl had lost his composure over this sailor, and now he was regretting it. However, this sailor was visibly scared at what Karl might do to him. The captain came forward and politely saluted Karl, asking his forgiveness for the insolent behavior exhibited by his junior officer. Hearing the screaming, Bill came out into the corridor, saying, "What on earth is going on out here? Captain Vita, please explain."

Bill was worried that their strategy might have been compromised. "It's alright now. The captain here has apologized for the insolence shown by this classless officer. I really expected more from the U-Boat Service," said Karl as he elbowed his way past the offending sailor.

Lining the five prisoners up in front of the table, Bill asked the clerk to record their names, ranks, and serial numbers, starting with the U-Boat captain, then onto the next, who was the big mouth in the corridor, somewhat less arrogant than earlier. The third did the same very politely, answering in English, to the surprise of Karl and Bill. The two moles were next, expressing that they were not from the U-Boat Service but served on a fast E-Boat.

"So, you are telling us you did not serve together in the U-Boat service? Well, that changes things," said Bill, working up to their cover plot. Over the next three hours, they skillfully laid their trap, focusing on the big mouth to be the one who would spill his guts to the two E-Boat sailors.

"Guards, we're done for the day. Take them away and bring them back at 0700 hours tomorrow morning," said Bill as he stood up.

Karl, on the other hand, walked up to the big mouth, saying in German, "I will have my time with you; count on it. Now, get out of my sight." Pointing to his patched eye, Karl was laying a trap and needed the sailor to think about what his future would hold for him. Walking back to the lounge, Karl congratulated Bill, and Bill did the same to Karl on their new promotions and postings.

Bill added, "Karl, Clive will be moving to General Jacks' headquarters. Thank goodness he will not have to move the family.

The new offices are only twelve miles away, so he is tickled pink about that. As for you, your new division will be formed at our present location unless you request another location." Bill looked at his friend for an answer.

"Bill, I have a lot to understand about what will be expected of me. I'm assuming there will be an in-depth indoctrination on our return to Slough next week, correct?" inquired Karl.

Bill stopped him in the corridor by answering, "Karl, it's counter-espionage—not that different from what you have been doing for us all along. You're the best at this sort of thing. That's why you, over anyone else, were selected to lead this new division."

The following morning, Bill and Karl sat once again at the table, ready to interrogate the prisoners on an individual basis, this time looking for a weak link to focus on. The captain, as expected, was polite but totally uncooperative when it came to providing information. "Guard, put the captain in isolation cell #03 until we need him further. Bring in Lieutenant Wartburg next."

"Come in and sit down." Bill directed the German to take the seat directly in front of them. Karl glared at him, not taking his eye off him. "Now, we have heard from other POWs that you did not want to follow your captain's orders when leaving Brest to attack a British destroyer squadron operating in the channel, is that right?" asked Bill.

"I follow orders. Whatever my captain tells me, I do. I know nothing about challenging those orders. When we left Brest, it was to attack a convoy nearing the Lizard off the southwest tip of England.

I repeat; I know nothing about attacking a destroyer squadron." Wartburg had a confused look on his face, wondering where this was going.

"Guard, take this prisoner to cell #2 until we need him further." Once Wartburg was out of the room, Karl turned to Bill, saying, "Now our moles can commence their fact-finding. Let's now repeat this on the captain with the other mole." Over the next two days, they gathered snippets of information that, when pieced together, would create a harvest of data about how the Germans were directing U-Boat patrols in specifically defined numbered grid patterns, and more importantly, their encrypted communications to those vessels using an encryption device known as the Enigma.

Wednesday, Bill pulled the two moles out of their holding cells. Their work had been done successfully, and a new method of non-aggressive interrogation has been created. "Karl, you asked why you were being given command of this new division. Look at what you have just done with this new head game of yours. It worked, did it not? I'll report back to HQ on our initial findings. Tomorrow, those prisoners will be dispersed to new and different POW camps, never to see each other again until this blasted war is over anyway. Good job, Karl."

That afternoon, Bill and Karl drafted revisions to this new procedure for future interrogation sessions. Their work complete, Bill walked Karl out to his car, saying, "Enjoy your four days off, old man. Monday, you are scheduled for an early morning flight to Scotland. Are you getting excited yet?" Bill was laughing at the look on Karl's face.

"I have a feeling you and Clive are behind all of this," said Karl. "See you on Monday." He then climbed into his little MG.

"Hold on, Karl; I nearly forgot something. You must come back inside with me. I promised Clive that I would change your rank insignias before you left today. Come on; follow me," said Bill, angry at himself for nearly allowing Karl to leave. Entering the supply area, they waited while a WRAF sergeant replaced the badges on his tunic and issued his new identification cards.

"Now, you can go home, Major, and give Claire a big kiss and hug for me."

"Will do, Bill, but I'll decide where those kisses go," laughed Karl as he drove off with the roof down. The traffic was heavier, considering the time of day, but that did not deter Karl from enjoying the drive back to Hitchin.

Karl parked the car to one side of the garage. Removing his house key, he unlocked the door and entered the kitchen to find Claire was not home yet. Draping his tunic over the kitchen chair, he made himself a pot of coffee, then removed several folders from his briefcase and went into the living room to get some work done. He did not get far before the heavy feeling of sleep overcame him. Giving into that feeling, he removed his boots to lay on the couch.

Claire, arriving home, excited to see the MG back in the driveway. Entering the kitchen, she sensed the lack of sound. Tiptoeing into the living room, she saw Karl stretched out, fast asleep. He's probably exhausted; best not to disturb him. Claire climbed the stairs to get out of her business suit and have a relaxing bath. Feeling so much better, she dressed in a casual pair of slacks and a loosely fitted jumper before going back downstairs. Karl was still sleeping, so she went back into the kitchen to make herself a cup of tea. Returning to the living room, she placed her briefcase to one side of the desk, then started working.

A little after 7:00 p.m., the telephone rang loudly. Claire was thinking, oh, God, that will wake him up for sure. "Hitchen 4567, who's calling, please?" asked Claire, upset about the loud ringtone.

"Claire, how are you doing? It's Clive; did Karl make it home yet?"

Claire quietly started to answer him by saying, "He's still sleeping on the couch," when Karl surprised her.

She felt his lips kissing her cheek and heard him say, "Sounds like it's for me, is it?"

Claire turned to kiss him back, saying, "It's Clive, darling. So sorry, I was going to let you sleep; you looked so relaxed."

Karl took the phone from her hand, tapping her on the backside and pointing to the coffee pot, gesturing for another cup.

"Clive, old man, good to hear from you. I guess Bill filled you in on our little scheme. I won't say any more until I see you on Monday."

Clive, listening to him, felt bad that he was cutting his time with Claire short. "Karl, I hate to do this to you, but we have been told to report on Sunday for a general staff meeting. Please, adjust your plans accordingly. By the way, I'm having a secure separate telephone installed on Friday morning. I've cleared it with Claire. She understands completely. I guess you haven't had time to talk about it yet. See you Saturday afternoon. By the way, Julie is inviting you and Bill for dinner about 1800 hours. Sorry to wake you up, cheers."

Karl hung up the phone, thinking, what is going on for the bigwigs to call for a staff meeting this Sunday? "Claire, we have a change of plans. I have to return to Slough Saturday instead of Sunday afternoon. It sounds like something really important is happening." Karl was saddened that, instead of ten days away from Claire, it would now be twelve or maybe more. Thursday, Claire went off to the office, so Karl drove to see his family in Baldock. Mama prepared a wonderful lunch for her son, the new major, while Karl fixed a hinge on the bathroom door.

In the afternoon, Karl, Freida, and Franchot walked up the street to the pasture to see Tug, the big draft horse. This time alone gave them time to talk about Papa and his brothers and Hazel and how to handle that glaring problem. Finally, the question of wedding plans came up. Where would it be held? Probably in the church where Claire attends services.

Sitting on the fence, Karl spoke up by saying, "Claire told me earlier, with all that is going on right now, next June would probably be a good time to plan the wedding. She also thought we could have a small reception at the Letchworth Hall Hotel. The problem will be my work, which could take me away with little to no notice. So, we need to give that a lot of thought. She has already told me we should not let this war interfere with our wedding plans."

On the other hand, Karl would prefer to wait until they knew more about which way the pendulum of this war would swing, but if Claire needed that security, he would be for it. Back at the bungalow, the afternoon was fading fast, and the time to return home to Hitchin had arrived. Kissing them goodbye, he told them he would be going up North for a couple of weeks to coordinate his new command. His parting words were, "See you when I return; stay safe," as he drove off up the Letchworth Road back to Hitchin.

After hearing the car pulling into the driveway, Claire walked outside, throwing her arms around his neck, saying, "Corporal McGivern reporting for duty, Major." Karl could not help laughing at this line she was using.

"Darling, we have been invited to meet up with my partners and their wives later at the Crown and Castle. I told them we would love that. Is that alright with you, darling?" Claire knew he would not object; he was that type of a fellow. The Crown and Castle was a quaint historic public house that had weathered many an uprising since the late 1600s. Karl opened the door for Claire, then followed her into the lounge.

"Over here," called Jeffrey, standing and waving his arms. Karl looked at Claire's two junior partners, thinking, I wonder who they know to keep them out of military service?

"Nice to see you again. Our last meeting was short and chaotic, so we're pleased you could join us this evening," said David, moving over to make room for Claire and Karl. To his surprise, Karl found himself enjoying this gathering. However, that question was still in the back of his head. The British military needed more young men. He wondered what their story could be.

Friday morning, Karl waited alone at home for the telephone service people to arrive, along with a military security chap who would program the encryption for the new telephone. Claire arrived home after 6:00 p.m., carrying a large document case. "Darling, did you miss me? I haven't heard from you all day." Claire could see he had been working as well, then noticed the green phone on the desk, saying jovially, "Is this the only color available? I would prefer white or dark blue. I'm only pulling your leg, you sensitive chap." His facial expression amused Claire. "I'm going upstairs to get out of this suit and have a quick bath.

Care to join me?" Claire was thinking, he's in that BIS mode again. I can see he's already thinking about tomorrow.

Claire came back downstairs, saying, "I'm going to start supper. Will you be ready in half an hour?"

Karl was still writing directions, placing them into each folder. "Almost done, Corporal McGivern," replied Karl.

After supper, they sat in the living room, listening to classical music and enjoying their quiet time together before Karl left Saturday morning. "Let's have an early night, shall we? I'm really tired; I did not stop all day," said Claire, hoping Karl did not want or expect more this evening. Lying in bed, they had that quiet time in each other arms, both thinking about Karl's new responsibilities and the dangers that surely lay ahead.

Rising early, Karl got his things together, then joined Claire downstairs for breakfast at 0730 hours. In his duty uniform, Karl could tell Claire was acting fidgety, probably because he was going North to Scotland on Monday. But what will he be doing, she thought. They sat together on the couch in the living room, continuing their small talk that eventually came around to scheduling their wedding. Karl, on the other hand, was only going through the motions. His mind was already in Scotland. "Time to go, darling. What will you do after you drop me off?" asked Karl as he put on his tunic.

"I'm going to pick up Freida for a girl's day out. She really does need some time away from her daily chores and the baby," replied Claire. From the garage, she backed out the Wolsey. Karl put his things on the back seat, then climbed into the passenger seat. "Ready, lover boy, or should I get you into trouble by jumping you right there in that seat?" Claire laughed, trying to make light of saying that. The train was scheduled to arrive from Cambridge at 1045 hours. Claire insisted she walk him to the platform, her arm firmly locked around his. The smoking train slowed to a stop, discharging and boarding passengers heading to London.

Karl turned to Claire, saying, "Claire, I'm sorry I was not the best company last night or this morning. Please, forgive me. You know how I hate goodbyes. Claire, my sweet, adorable lady, I already miss you." Karl pulled her into his arms and kissed her passionately before picking up his luggage.

Three sailors walking by yelled back at them, "Sir, maybe you should take the next train?" The sailors waved and laughed as they walked down to the third-class section of the train.

"Karl, you know how I miss you. Please, don't do anything silly. In just a very short time, you have become my world, so keep that in mind when you're playing hero," said Claire, that worried look showing through.

"Darling, I'm only going to meet my men and start classroom training. Now, take that worried look off your face, and I'll see you in a couple of weeks." As Karl said that, the PA announced the departure of his train on track number four. "That's mine, darling; now give me a big wet kiss; it's got to last me awhile." Karl turned toward his compartment, waving as he did so.

Claire yelled to him, "I'd rather do something else with that big wet kiss, lover boy." Claire watched as the train chugged slowly out of the station. She remained there until it was clear of the station, taking a big part of her heart with it.

Waiting in Paddington Station, Karl called the camp motor pool from a telephone box on the platform to give them the train number and arrival time.

This second train was always the quickest. In an hour, he was walking down the pavement in front of the station to the waiting staff car. "Afternoon, Sir, are we going to the camp or your flat?" asked Corporal Adams.

"To the camp, Charlie. I gave up my flat. Please, drop me off at the new officers' quarters, alright?" Karl looked at his watch. I have a little over an hour before Bill picks me up, so plenty of time. In his room, he freshened up, then changed into civilian clothes before walking outside to see Bill already waiting.

"Bill, it's good to see you. How are things in the BIS since I left?" asked Karl, making small talk. The ride to Clive and Julie's home took twenty-five minutes. Bill pulled into the driveway, parking next to Clive's staff car.

The front door opened, and out came Clive, saying, "Welcome, you two, come on in. Julie managed to have her mother take the girls for the evening. I thought you two would prefer no children running around while we have dinner," concluded Clive.

"Welcome, you two good-looking chaps. What's your poison to start with?" asked Julie as she came out of the kitchen. "I thought we could have cocktails before dinner is ready. Do you chaps feel like having those cocktails outside in the garden, seeing as it's still nice enough? Oh, Karl, Claire said for you to call her either tonight or early tomorrow morning before you boys start your meeting. You can use Clive's office if you would like to make that call tonight while you're still here."

Julie and Claire, along with Dorothy, had quickly formed a lasting bond of friendship. All three of them would lean on that bond in the coming years, leading up to the climactic end of WW2. "Claire called you, Julie?" inquired Karl.

"No, Karl, I called her just before you arrived. She was having supper with your mother and family," replied Julie.

Clive changed the subject by bringing up BIS stuff, "Karl, all of us here are very close friends; these bonds are what we lean on during difficult times, so keep that in mind. While you two were in Bedford, oh, by the way, superb job of extracting that information from those German POWs, well done, chaps. Now, back to what I started to say, Major Vita. I attended a debriefing of the Delta-1 team in Aldershot at the Hammersley Barracks, and yes, Karl, Hazel was there. She and I had a drink together after the first day's debriefing. She came right out and asked me whether the rumors true about Karl's involvement with someone else.

Karl, I had no choice; I had to tell her it was true. The look on her face was one of defeat and maybe despair. Karl, the following morning, she gave me this letter to give you and told me to tell you she wishes you both a wonderful life." Clive went over to his desk, returning with Hazel's letter. "Here you go, Karl; put it in your jacket. I think after you have read it, you should write back to her, or if you're up to it, call her." Clive returned to the whiskey decanter, asking, "You two ready for a refill yet?"

Karl stood with the letter in his hand and felt terrible, knowing he had broken Hazel's heart. It had to be awful to come back to this after all she had been through.

"Clive, is she still here?" Karl thought he would prefer to confront her to explain how sorry he was that it happened as it did.

"She left right after the debrief to return to her parent's home. She has also put in a request to be transferred to another branch after her leave is over."

Clive looked at the pain in Karl's face, realizing it was a slam to his gut.

"Alright, you blokes, I hope you're hungry," said Julie as she came out into the garden. After a wonderful dinner, they adjourned to the living room, and Karl excused himself to call Claire.

"Hitchen 4567," answered Claire, knowing it would be Karl at the other end. "Darling, are you still at the Knight's house? I talked to Julie earlier. She said you would call from their house. Are you having a nice evening? Everyone here sends their best. I will be thinking of you tomorrow. Don't volunteer for anything dangerous, darling; I know how you get." Claire was fishing for something, but what did Julie tell her?

"Yes, darling, it's nice spending time reminiscing about old times. Tomorrow, we will find out more about changes and new assignments. I just wanted to say hello and how much I miss you. I love you, Claire. I will call you tomorrow evening, bye for now." Karl hung up the phone, thinking, I'm willing to bet Julie has told her about Hazel being back in England. Sitting back down next to Bill, Clive gave Karl a questioning glance as if to say, what did Julie tell her?

Bill stood up and kissed Julie on the cheek, saying, "This was a wonderful evening, but our Austrian friend and I should think about leaving. Sunday will be a long repetitious day of what-ifs," said Bill, looking at Clive for support.

"Julie, let me add to Bill's thanks. How you got that beef is beyond me. Who said you couldn't find things with ration books?" Karl laughed at his sarcasm.

"Oh, Karl, I can always count on you for a knife-edge compliment." With that, they gave Julie a goodbye hug, shook Clive's hand, and gave him a man hug before stepping out into the black of the night. Bill dropped off Karl in front of his quarters, then headed back out to Dorothy's flat. Karl walked slowly up the steps into his building.

In the corridor, he felt his jacket to make sure the letter from Hazel was in his inside pocket. He opened the door. Inside, he poured a glass of whiskey, placing it on the nightstand. Next, he took off his shoes and hung up his jacket. Lying on the bed, he stared at the envelope in his hand, aching at the pain he was responsible for. Removing the letter from its envelope, he unfolded it and started to read.

My Dearest Karl,

First, let me first congratulate you on your engagement. Does she know how lucky she is to be the one who will finally be your wife? That same thought kept me going all those months away from you. How I yearned for that time when I would finally arrive back in England, you waiting to sweep me off my feet.

Karl, every hour of every day, I prayed for that and to eventually wear your engagement ring. All the things we would be planning for our wedding after this crazy war comes to an end, but now that will never happen!

When I arrived back in Aldershot, I was so excited that I would see you in a couple of days. Clive could see my excitement and decided he should be the one to break the news to me. Over a drink, he diplomatically gave me the shattering news that has devastated my world. Clive told me he had sent you and Bill on a field mission. Good old Clive, always making the right decisions when they are most needed. Darling, by the time you read this letter, I will be home with my parents.

I have an extended leave coming to me, so I'm taking this time to apply for an overseas posting, maybe in America or perhaps as far away as Australia. Will we meet again? Maybe, but more than likely not. I don't believe I'm strong enough for that.

So, my crazy Austrian lover boy, my heart will always have a very special place in it for you, securely locked away. Wish me luck, and please stay away from those dangerous missions. That last one nearly cost you your life.

I will always remain truly yours,
Hazel Collins

Karl kept reading it over, then over again, tears cascading down his cheeks. *What have I done? How could I hurt her so badly? The day she left on that mission, she told me how scared she was about losing each other. She was correct in thinking there would always be three in that relationship, two of us and Kitty's memory. Every time I looked at Hazel, I was really seeing Kitty. Why did I allow that to continue when it was doomed from the very start? Once I'm in Scotland, I will write to her. I owe her that and probably much more.* Taking the last swig of whiskey, he undressed and went to bed, completely exhausted.

Sunday morning, Karl and Bill had a quick breakfast at the NAAFI. Bill asked if he had read Hazel's letter yet. "Yes, Bill, I have, and at this particular time, I really don't like myself. I feel like all I do is break hearts. As Gunther once told me, I need to take responsibility for the damage I create." Karl hung his head low as he poured his heart out.

"Karl, let's hope that you have finally released Kitty and given Hazel a chance for happiness while she is young enough to make a new start. That is all you can do right now. Clive and I have been your loyal friends from day one. We both share the same opinion that Claire is strong enough to give you that wonderful life. She loves you that much. Maybe you should consider giving Hazel a call. I know she would prefer that to a letter. Consider doing that, my friend; now, drink up. We have a war to win." Bill, feeling his guilt, was trying to give him a way to help Hazel through her pain. Leaving the NAAFI, they headed down to the meeting room. It was now 0730 hours. Entering the meeting room, they were surprised to find about twenty officers of higher rank all milling around with mugs of tea in their hands.

Clive came over to welcome them, then surprised Karl by saying, "Before we start, why don't you both welcome back your old friends over there with General Jacks?" Clive thought maybe it would have been a better idea to mention last night that Gunther and Herbert would also be attending this meeting. *I'm glad I decided a relaxing evening with these two would be more appropriate. Sunday would come soon enough to mend broken bridges!*

"My God, I'm so pleased to see you two again safe in these surroundings. I'm surprised Clive did not mention last night that both of you would be attending." Karl, delighted to be reunited with his old friends, looked at Bill. He instantly knew that Bill already knew!

"Nice to see you too, Karl. I understand congratulations are in order. I must admit, I was under the impression it would be Hazel that we would be congratulating on getting engaged." On the one hand, Gunther was pleased to see his old friend, but inside, he was seething at seeing Hazel coming apart after Clive broke the news to her about Karl's engagement.

"Karl, I understand you got that wound to your eye from Gestapo thugs, is that right?" asked Herbert, trying to get Gunther away from the firestorm brewing inside him.

"That is correct. If it weren't for the French partisans attacking the Gestapo Headquarters, I was within minutes of cracking that cyanide capsule and ending it all," replied Karl, still looking at Gunther. Like the good German officer he was, he simply shook his head, listening to what Karl had just told them. Moving to Karl's side, he placed his arm around his shoulder, composing himself before responding.

"Karl, you crazy Austrian, I was ready to give you a piece of my mind. Then, hearing you were that close to taking your own life made me realize your loyal friendship takes precedence over my anger. Even though I feel like banging your head again for what you keep doing." Gunther was expressing that their friendship meant more. "When do we get to meet this new lady of yours?" concluded Gunther.

"Gentlemen, please, take a seat; we have much to cover today and let me apologize for taking away from your weekend, but getting you all together like this is very difficult, so that's why it's a Sunday meeting. Colonel Knight, would you first take the roll call?" asked General Jacks. After getting all the trivia out of the way, Clive asked them to refer to the folders in front of them. "Each one of you is here because of your unique abilities that enabled our intelligence service to continuously infiltrate the highest levels of the Nazi Party. This war is so much more than military equipment and armed forces. It's about infiltrating their highest levels of secret scientific developments. Today, we will formulate how we can improve and accomplish those objectives. During this meeting, we will call on some of you to describe your most recent missions and how you met or exceeded those objectives behind enemy lines."

Clive asked Gunther and Herbert to describe their recent mission and how effective the Delta teams were in obtaining information on military movements in the occupied countries. Gunther was the perfect officer to answer that question, describing the many obstacles they faced daily and how they were nearly compromised by one of their own agents who collaborated with the Germans to save his family—a good agent who placed family over duty.

This situation opened a whole discussion on more effectively screening European agents. Clive asked Karl to describe further how he discovered such a glaring problem brought up another question, should they continue using agents who still had family ties in Europe and could be blackmailed into becoming double agents? Another officer asked Karl to take them through his experience, masquerading as a Kriegsmarine Officer, and what went so terribly wrong that it nearly cost him his life. One by one, they told their stories of espionage and how, in so many cases, the partisans proved to be an invaluable underground force that saved their lives, including Karl's own life.

Moving forward, it was agreed that partisan support in all operations should be paramount, providing additional training and assistance in the use of munitions, better field medical supplies, and better distribution of funding so desperately needed to expand their disruption of the German war machine. Another program that would be given a higher priority was embedding BIS agents into larger partisan groups, providing better utilization of newer radio equipment and their operators, effective immediately. General Jacks asked how to improve prisoner interrogation methods now that more POWs were arriving in England.

The biggest problem they faced was weeding out the lies and deception that constantly provided erroneous results. Karl and Bill outlined their recent success, interrogating three U-Boat prisoners by imbedding German members of the free European brigade in with these POWs. Also stressed was the need to expand the number of agents trained as interpreters, capable of determining a prisoner's origin by listening to their language and dialect. Major Knight explained further that a concerted effort was underway to recruit and train agents with these abilities to fill that gap. He explained further that Major Vita's new division was already getting survival training in Scotland before training as interpreters began in Slough, then Aldershot. The meeting concluded at 1900 hours, with everyone mentally drained.

Clive was heading home, so Gunther, Bill, and Herbert decided to treat Karl to a hearty fish and chip supper at a local pub. They refrained from discussing the meeting; too many ears around them to do that. Herbert asked Karl how he found his MG-PB and captured the heart of its owner, Claire. Gunther, making light of the small talk, continued by asking, "When are we being invited to Hitchen to drive the MG and meet Claire? Do you have a photograph we can see?" asked Gunther, grinning.

Karl removed his wallet from his inside pocket, removing a color photograph of Claire. Passing it around, he got a chuckle out of them as he watched their faces with remarks like, "Wow, what a beauty, and will you look at the gams on her?" Karl was feeling good about the acceptance of his friends.

Quietly, he said, "When I return from Scotland, we can arrange a weekend in Hitchen to meet Claire and then Baldock to meet my family." Gunther looked at the others as if to say, I think this is it, but then again, he had said that before.

Bill finally spoke up by saying, "Dorothy and I had the pleasure of spending an evening with Claire, Julie, and Clive not that long ago. She is not only an elegant lady but an accomplished solicitor in her own practice. Karl should never get out of line with this one; she is way too quick for Karl, here." Bill broke out into laughter at that last line. "Seriously, it would be very hard not to adore Claire. We all did and do," concluded Bill. At about 2000 hours, the party broke up.

"Karl, the car will be waiting to take you to the airstrip at 0730 hours. If I don't see you before you leave, I'll be anxiously awaiting your evaluation report on your return," said Bill as he let them all off back at the camp.

Karl, like a clock, was at the curbside promptly at 0730 hours. He had a topcoat over his arm as he waited, remembering the taxing weather conditions at the training camp just north of Glen Nevis and the five-hour drive from the city of Edinburgh. Karl was thinking about the first time they all went to that bleak outpost when he was a mere first lieutenant, the journey to Edinburgh on a train, followed by a coach ride to the camp, which added another five hours, making for a really long day.

Today, it was different. He would be taken to the airstrip in a staff car, then by plane to RAF Kirknewton, just outside Edinburgh, and from there to Glen Nevis in a staff car—how things had changed in just a few short years. The car arrived at 0740 hours, the driver apologizing for not being on time. The flight was noisy but so much quicker than a train. At the airbase, a staff car was waiting to drive him to the camp. Four hours later, the car turned into that familiar driveway. Stopping at the gate, the driver told the guard, "I have Major Vita reporting."

The MP walked back to the open window. Saluting, he asked, "Your ID, Sir? Welcome to camp Nevis." They drove up the hill, arriving in front of the main building. Karl felt a little tense, looking at these drab buildings that were flooding his mind with memories of Kitty, but no black clouds, just fond memories. Entering the lobby, Karl registered with a burly MP behind the desk.

"We have been waiting for your arrival, Sir. I'll tell your second in command, Captain Meyers, that you have arrived," said the guard. "That's alright, Sergeant. I know my way around this camp. I'll head down to the officers' lounge. Have my bags delivered to my quarters, then bring me the key," said Karl, feeling better than the last time he was here as a trainee.

As he opened the familiar swinging door to the lounge, heads turned to see who was entering. Someone yelled, "Attention." Karl was not ready for these junior officers to stand at attention for him.

"Please, no need for this pomp. This is a training camp, not a parade ground. No need to stand on ceremony for me."

A tall officer in his early thirties approached Karl, saying, "Major Vita, so pleased to see you again after so long. Remember me? Captain Hardy Meyers, your second in command. May I be the first to congratulate you on this new command, and please, may I buy you a cocktail?" asked Meyers.

"I thought you would never ask, and, of course, I remember you. We will get on famously," replied Karl, already feeling at ease. Over supper, they discussed their strategy for molding the new trainees into Intelligence interpreters for the BIS.

At 0630 hours, Karl entered training room M-3, his swagger stick under his arm. Meyer, at the front of the room, yelled, "Attention."

Karl approached the stage, turned next to Meyers, then asked everyone to be seated, "Gentlemen, good morning. My name is Major Karl Vita; it wasn't that many years ago that I sat where you are sitting this morning. More than likely, thinking the same as you are doing right now. I wonder what type of bloke this one is? Well, let me put your minds at ease. If we all work together and abide by the rules, things will go smoothly. If you cross the line, I will throw the book at you. Is that perfectly understood?

"This is a new division in the Intelligence Service; your life could well depend on the individual by your side, so pay attention. As new recruits, you have never been exposed nor have any idea how brutal the enemy can be. I have firsthand experience of their barbaric torture methods." Karl pointed to his patched eye, adding, "This was a gift of the Gestapo. The training you have been undertaking these last few months is to prepare you for field operations. This new division will more than likely not be put into those dangerous situations. Our primary function is to provide interrogation support. We are processing more POWs daily; our job is to get an accurate picture of where that prisoner came from and, by deception methods, find out what the enemy is planning. Our concentration probably will not be on the rank and file, but more on higher-ranking officers from the various branches of the German Military Services."

Karl spent about another ninety minutes outlining how the training they were currently undertaking would change from survival skills to classroom studies, perfecting their languages and dialects abilities. The final part of their training would be honing their skills in these new interrogation methods. "Some of you could be asked to volunteer for field assignments outside of England, another reason you are still being trained in survival techniques," concluded Major Vita.

Karl spent the next ten days working with his staff to build a plan that would become their bible for future operations. During that time, he tried to spend time with each of the team's twenty men, encouraged by their enthusiasm and finding their knowledge to be of the highest standards. Each night, he would call Claire, assuring her he was in no danger, always ending by saying, "Wish you could be here to handle those special needs I have. I love you, darling; I will be home real soon."

On his final day, he met with Captain Meyers to discuss the team's transfer back to Slough. "Meyers, when you arrive back, it will be your assignment to settle them into the barracks that has been assigned to this team. As for me, I'll be back in the camp already, so I'll coordinate with the camp commander, Major William Lowes, to officially welcome them and give them his direction for integration into camp life and camp operations," instructed Karl, confident that, as he left, the division would excel in their duties.

Walking Karl to the staff car, Meyers said, "Sir, I am so pleased to be reporting to you. I'll take care of making sure all goes smoothly from here on; see you back in Slough." Stepping back from the car, he saluted his commanding officer. Karl reciprocated the gesture by tapping the edge of his cap as the car drove off. The last leg of the return trip would be to Duxford. With any luck, Ronny would still be there to give him a lift back to Hitchin and Claire.

Karl was exhausted, and sleep came quickly. He did not wake until the pilot announced, "Buckle up, Sir. We are making our approach into Duxford." After a bumpy landing, the old Avro Anson taxied up to the front of the hangar; then, there was silence as the props windmilled to a stop. An RAF private moved quickly to open the rear fuselage door, folding down the ladder from inside. Karl thanked the pilots, then, grabbing his case, he stepped out into the drizzling rain. Walking quickly, he opened the hangar door, hoping to catch Ronny before he left for the day. Inside the enormous hangar, crews worked on battle-worn Spitfire aircraft, one of which was badly shot up.

"Excuse me, can you direct me to Lieutenant Whiting's office?" asked Karl, not sure which hallway to take.

"Right down the middle corridor, Sir. His office will be on the left. Did you just arrive on that Anson outside?" asked the friendly aircraft fitter.

"Yes, I did," replied Karl, walking off to find Ronny's office at the end of the corridor.

Knocking on the door, a voice on the opposite side said, "Come." Karl opened the door to find his brother-in-law buried under a pile of service requests. "What can I help you with?" Ronny said without looking up.

"How about a ride to Baldock in that little Austin of yours?" said Karl happily.

"Karl, when did you arrive? Don't tell me you were on that old string bag Anson that arrived fifteen minutes ago, were you?" Ronny got up and came around to the front of the desk, his arms outstretched, so pleased to see Karl. "I'm having a hard time getting my head around the fact that you're already a major, and I'm still a lieutenant. Let's call Claire. She can come over to pick you up from the bungalow. How does that sound?" said Ronny as he phoned Claire in Hitchin.

"Claire, Ronny here, guess who I have in my office? It's a major giving me the eye to get going. I think he's in a rush to see his fiancée," said Ronny, handing Karl the phone.

"Claire, he's so right. I'm in a rush to sweep you off your feet. See you soon, darling." Karl returned the phone to its cradle. Ronny grabbed his tunic and cap, and they headed to the car park. Arriving back in Baldock, Ronny turned onto Brushnell Way, and there, parked in front of the house, was the Wolsey. No sooner had Ronny shut the engine off when the front door opened, and outran Claire ahead of the others.

"My lover boy, you're back. Come here and kiss me, you good-looking man." Claire was happy as she could be now that Karl was home. Back inside, Mama made them all some strong coffee before serving a light supper and announcing that her supply of paprika was almost depleted.

"Karl, you have contacts in the supply service. Maybe you can be persuasive and try to get us some more?" asked Claire, knowing he could always find things that were impossible to obtain.

Changing the subject, Mama asked, "Well, did everything go as planned?" She knew Karl would not elaborate too much.

"Very satisfactory; glad to be home, though." After supper, Claire could see Karl was tiring very quickly. Standing, she announced, "Karl has had a taxing ten days. Would you mind if I take him home for an early night? Look at him; he's exhausted. Is that alright with all of you?"

Mama smiled and quietly said, "Of course, dear; you are talking about sleeping, are you not?" Mama thought the world of Karl, and now that love included Claire.

"Mama, sometimes you really shock me with the things you say." Claire reached for Mama, saying in her ear, "I love you so much, Mama. It's good to know I have a mother again. Now, let me softly wake Karl. He has a habit of reacting if shaken while he is sleeping." Claire took his hand, gently squeezing it until his eyes opened. "Ready to head home, Sailor? I think you need a good night's sleep, and tomorrow morning, there is no getting up to exercise or go running, and that's a Claire order. Up you get."

Mama's heart was warmed by the way Claire took care of Karl. If only they could've found each other sooner, before that time when they both had their hearts broken by tragic losses. It's their second chance. God, don't take that away from them a second time. Thought Mama as she followed them out to the car. Driving home, Claire looked over at Karl, fast asleep with his head resting against the door frame. She was thinking and feeling whole again, knowing her life and future would be shared by this man sleeping in her car. Considering that, she quietly giggled as she turned into the driveway. Walking around to the passenger side, she removed his case from the back seat, then ever so carefully, woke Karl, saying, "Let's get you to bed, shall we? I'll take care of putting your things away later."

Upstairs, Karl went to the bathroom, then stripped off his clothes and climbed into bed. By the time Claire entered the bedroom, Karl was out cold, so she got herself ready for bed, then stealthily climbed into bed, wrapping her arm around his waist.

Claire woke first. Quietly, she got out of bed, putting her housecoat and slippers on, then she slowly opened the door and went downstairs. After putting the coffee on, she went outside to recover the morning paper. On the front page in bold letters, she read, All Norwegian civilian radios confiscated by Germans.

Another story told about the escalating tension between America and Japan. The article went on to say that America and Great Britain warned that if Japan attacked Thailand, there would be severe consequences. Claire, still standing in the driveway, reading the headlines, shook her head, thinking, day after day, the news is always negative. This world is out of control. Unfortunately, most of this will sooner than later involve the BIS, and that will include Karl's new division.

Back inside, she poured herself a mug of coffee, feeling a sensation of strong arms encircling her waist, followed by a male voice with a very distinct accent announcing, "That aroma of coffee woke me up. Would you pour one for me as well, dear?" Karl turned her around and slid his hand inside her housecoat.

"Karl Vita, behave yourself. I haven't even had a sip of my coffee yet. I think I'm going to start putting you to bed early from now on. You know how I'm a morning person, so remember that, you animal you. Is this to be just a quicky, or should I be preparing myself for a long morning?"

Karl hearing her kidding around like that, kissed her on the forehead, responding, "My sweet Claire, how much I miss our quiet times together. They are the medicine I miss most. Now, come here and kiss me properly." Karl, in high spirits, was over the moon with joy with this woman. Sitting in the living room, they drank their coffee.

Claire reached over to the coffee table and picked up the morning paper, saying, "Karl, look at the front page of the *Daily Mirror*. It looks like the Japanese are saber-rattling the Americans. Do you think the Americans are preparing to enter the war, or are you not in a position to comment on that yet?" asked Claire.

"Correct, darling; however, I can tell you this, the American Navy has already lost several destroyers to U-Boat torpedoes. I can't imagine President Roosevelt would allow that to continue very much longer. What is helping England, Russia, and China is the Marshal Plan, which enables these countries to purchase war material and equipment on a deferred lend-lease basis, just in time for us. Without that, we would have been forced into a cease-fire. As for the Japanese movements, well, their raw materials and oil supplies are being slowly choked off by the American government. President Roosevelt has instructed a freeze on all Japanese holdings in the United States. That move has effectively destroyed their currency. So, it's no surprise they are looking elsewhere for their oil and raw materials supplies. They have no qualms about using force to obtain them, either.

We at the BIS expect reprisals to happen within the next twelve months, but more than likely, much sooner. The British government is hoping these actions will force America to declare war, and by doing so, save England. There, I said too much, but then again, much of this is public knowledge. As for The Axis powers, they think they are invincible. Well, maybe they are, but right now, England and the Russians are fighting them on multiple fronts. Operation Barbarossa back in June put Russia firmly on our side." Karl kept talking and reading the newspaper, totally in a relaxed mode with Claire by his side on the couch.

That evening, they walked to the Cock and Kettle for a light supper and drinks. Sitting at the bar was a place Karl always enjoyed being as it was less formal. Having a very striking lady at his side made it that much more enjoyable. The weekend seemed to evaporate, and now Karl would have to refocus on the many tasks that awaited him back in Slough. Sunday evening, Karl packed his case, ready to leave very early the following morning. Returning downstairs, he entered the lounge, standing momentarily to observe Claire sitting on the couch, engrossed in her book.

Claire looked up at Karl, smiling, saying, "Come sit next to me. Do you want some coffee and biscuits to nibble on before we retire early to bed? We need to get up early for me to get you to the train station tomorrow morning. Karl, I noticed you did not apply your medication last night. You are starting to get sloppy in your medication schedule; don't forget tonight, darling." Claire would remind him of that whenever he was home. She also wondered if he kept forgetting back at camp. Karl excused himself and went back upstairs to apply the medication. Looking in the bathroom mirror, he started smiling, and that turned into a chuckle, thinking, she is like a mother hen—always making sure things are done correctly. Do I object? Not at all; she is the medicine I need most in my life.

Back downstairs, Claire had made a pot of tea, carrying it on a tray with a plate of biscuits to the coffee table in front of the couch. Patting the couch, Karl sat down next to her as she poured two cups of tea, served in elegant bone china cups and saucers with matching plates. "Claire, you are truly a classy English lady. Nothing is ever done incorrectly—never anything out of place—except me, perhaps?" Karl knew by teasing her like this that she would have a comeback; she always did.

"This home needs a little mess to remind me it's a home, not a museum. You're my adorable mess. Don't you ever change on me. Now, why don't you hold me? We only have tonight before you are off again." As she said that, she felt those familiar strong arms encircle her waist and the sensation of Karl kissing her neck. She, of course, responded by kissing him back passionately, her tongue finding his ready. Karl softly laid Claire down on the couch. His hand under her head, kissing her tenderly, he could feel her becoming aroused. With his free arm, he moved her legs up close to him. He could feel the soft skin of her thighs and her breathing becoming shallow as he continued to stroke her.

"Darling, you're driving me crazy. Do something before I explode." Claire was anxious to have him inside of her. Those ladylike manners were gone along with her inhibitions. Karl pushed her skirt up high, then removed her panties, followed by his trousers and underpants. Lying on top of her, he continued to tease her by touching but not entering her. Doing this was making Claire push to make that happen, but Karl simply maintained this contact. Claire could not contain herself any longer. She was about to beg him when Karl slid all the way into her, making her gasp at the sensation. He maintained a steady rhythm until she arched her back and started trembling, crying out, "Darling, I'm going to come. Please, let me feel you inside me, please."

Karl had been holding back until she was close. He felt her pushing into him, and that sensation made him thrust that one more time, giving into a climactic orgasm. They laid there on the couch, trembling in each other's arms until Karl kiddingly said. "Guess our tea has gone cold?" They both looked at each other, grinning like Cheshire cats.

"Let me go make some more, shall I? Then we can go to bed—to sleep, that is, you sex-mad Austrian." Claire stood up, straightened her skirt, and buttoned her blouse. Doing so, she started laughing, saying, "Am I glad I took my nylons and suspenders off when we came home. For sure, they would have runs in them by now. Have you any idea how hard it is to find nylons? And when you do, they cost a fortune." Claire, the ever-proper lady, walked out into the kitchen, leaving Karl lying on the couch relaxing. In the back of his mind, a thought occurred to him. Is Claire trying to get pregnant?

The following morning, Claire insisted on walking him up onto the platform. Holding hands, he kissed her as the smoking monster chuffed into the station. "Call me tonight, darling. I pray this week goes by quickly." Claire reached up to kiss him, then released him to climb into the compartment. Karl waved from the window, silently saying he loved her as the train pulled out of the station. Like those times before, she stayed until the train was out of sight. Only then did she head back to the car and an empty house.

Karl entered the new quarters assigned to his division. Only four clerical staff manned the main area; all the other stations and offices were empty, but why? Looking around, he spotted his corner office with its new shingle; *Major K. Vita* prominently displayed on the door. "Where is everyone?" asked Karl to one of the clerical girls.

"Oh, Major Vita, sorry we have our backs to you. We didn't hear you open the door. May I introduce you to Lora, Beth, Gloria, and my name is Ruth. We are civilian contractors employed to help your command get established. Your staff is at a group meeting in Major Lowes' building. Will you be joining them?"

Karl spoke briefly to the clerical staff, asking questions about where they all lived and how long they would be working for him.

"Ladies, pleased to make your acquaintance. Ruth, would you please hang up my raincoat and put this case in my office? I'm off to join the others." Walking briskly, Karl entered the main meeting room. Quietly finding a seat at the back of the room, he listened to Major Lowes welcoming the new trainees to the camp and telling them what he expected from each of them.

Looking toward the back of the room, Bill pointed his swagger stick at Karl, saying, "Welcome, Major Vita, please, join us up here on the podium. For those who have not met or heard of Major Vita, he is one of our most valued assets in the Intelligence Service. Over the next few months, you will invariably be training with him in the latest interrogation methods, deception techniques, and staying alive while operating in harm's way.

Please, welcome Major Vita to this gathering." Everyone in the room stood up, clapping as Karl made his way to the podium.

"Gentlemen, tomorrow morning, we will start in earnest to understand and learn the many facets of being a BIS agent. Major Lowes, like myself, has suffered under the torturous ministrations of the Gestapo," Karl said, pointing to Bill's leg and his own eye. "That training you received in Scotland was to give you survival techniques that included hand-to-hand combat against the enemy. From here on, we will train your brain and your language skills to second-guess the Hun. See you all tomorrow."

For the next three months, they trained all week and sometimes weekends. Karl's routine kept him at the camp Monday through Friday, then home to Claire for the weekend. Although still a neutral country, America was increasingly becoming involved in convoy protection, its navy protecting Allied convoys, and in many cases, having permission to open fire on marauding U-Boats. President Roosevelt gave that command. As for America's relationship with the Empire of Japan, it was near the boiling point. Negotiations were rapidly deteriorating. In the final month of 1941, Japan made its move by an undeclared attack on the American Pacific fleet in Pearl Harbor.

Prime Minister Winston Churchill, on the other hand, was praying for a political flashpoint to trigger the United States to join forces with England to combat the tyranny being waged across

Europe by Germany and its Axis Powers. Daily announcements were being sent back about the thousands of Jews in all occupied countries being stripped of their possessions and dignity before being thrown into concentration camps to be used as slave labor and worse.

CHAPTER 17

A Day which Will Live in Infamy December 7th

The ingenious lend-lease program signed on October 30th by Franklin D. Roosevelt started paying off by providing over one billion dollars of U.S. aid to allied countries in desperate need of vital supplies.

Unbeknownst to America, Japan, in anticipation of a complete collapse in peace negotiations, secretly dispatched a sizable naval force destined for the American Naval base of Oahu in the Hawaiian Islands. This naval force set sail from Hitokappu Bay in the Kurile Islands, the northern island of Japan, on November 26. 1941. Of the thirty-three vessels in that flotilla, six were aircraft carriers. December 7th started as a typical, sunny day in Pearl Harbor. That would change violently at 0800 hours when the first wave of one hundred eighty Japanese fighters, torpedo bombers, and bombers attacked without a declaration of war, which was not given until hours later. The attack lasted over two hours. When they retired, the Japanese had left behind 2,403 dead American servicemen and women, along with another 1,178 wounded. The mighty *USS Arizona* blew up, taking over 1,000 sailors with her to the bottom. Six other ships were also sunk or destroyed. As for the aircraft stationed in the Hawaiian Islands, more than 169 U.S. Navy and Army Air Corp were destroyed that day.

Fate intervened that day as the U.S. aircraft carriers were out at sea. In the months ahead, that blunder would prove to be a devastating blow to the Japanese Navy. This attack, devised by Admiral Isoroku Yamamoto, ironically a former student at Harvard University and a

Japanese Military attaché in Washington, wrote in his diary: *My fear is that all we have done is to wake a Sleeping Giant.*

The newspapers and radio broadcasts around the world painted a gruesome story of a cowardly sneak attack by the Empire of Japan that would forever brand them as ruthless killers. Karl, along with other officers, sat in disbelief at what was being relayed back to them. Bill stood up to address his staff, saying, "Gentlemen, we are all in shock at this senseless attack. I believe this may be the push America needed to stand by our side as we fight the Germans together. I'm sure the Prime Minister will stand by our friends, the Americans, by declaring war against the Japanese immediately. Our work from here on will be so much more demanding while we wait for developments. As of this meeting, I am canceling any and all leaves. That also includes weekends until we know more." Bill looked at the steel face of Karl as he said that.

"Now, return to your departments to update your people." Everyone stood at parade rest until Bill had left the room. Karl walked back to this department, updating everyone on what to expect in the following few weeks.

Returning to his office, he closed the door behind him and, with a heavy heart, he called Claire's office, asking, "Bev, is Claire in her office?"

Beverly could tell this was not a day for small talk. "One moment, Major. I'll get her for you."

Karl sat patiently until he heard her pick up the phone, saying, "Karl, oh my God, this is terrible. We have just heard a radio commentary by the prime minister on the cowardly attack on Pearl Harbor. Are the Japanese that crazed on conquering the entire Pacific? They are no better than Hitler and his thugs."

Karl listened to her crying, trying to speak to her at the same time. "Claire, this madness changes everything. The Americans have already declared war on the Japanese; we are confident they will declare war on the Nazi regime shortly. Now, to add to that news, we have been restricted to camp, so my darling, it may be quite a while until we see each other. So far, there is no blackout on phone use, but I fear that may be coming very soon. The BIS is the center of our efforts to manipulate the war efforts, so that's why the heightened security. When all else fails, we can at least write to each other. I have to go, darling. Good night and stay positive; I love you." Karl returned the telephone to its cradle; that black cloud had returned for a completely different reason.

Three weeks passed before Karl would be able to return home to Hitchin. Thanks to Bill, Karl could call Claire most evenings, unfortunately, on a monitored line. Karl spent countless hours working with members of the American Military Attaché office from London, coordinating these advance directives. For the most part, he enjoyed their enthusiasm and eagerness toward working together. Karl, being Austrian, was more receptive to this arrangement than his English counterparts, who tended to be a little aloof for his liking. It reminded him so much of his first meeting with officers of the BIS in Aldershot. However, once he gained their confidence, things changed for the better. This would also be the case with the Americans.

By mid-December, numerous branches of the British Intelligence Services were gearing up to establish training programs for the American Intelligence Service, known as the O.S.S. Karl and multiple members of his group would be assigned to the British Security Coordination Group, known as the B.S.C., to undertake training in Belfast, Northern Ireland, commencing in January 1942.

Before that mission, in the three weekends Karl had been away from Claire, his work kept him tied to his desk—sometimes up to 16 hours a day, and Christmas was almost upon them. Bill, with a big grin on his face, entered Karl's office, announcing, "I have a very special mission for you today, Major. You are to proceed early this afternoon to the train station to catch the 1545 hours train to Paddington, and from there to Kings Cross to catch the connecting train to Hitchin, and here is your long overdue pass. Enjoy Christmas, Karl; you have earned it. Please give Claire, Mama, and Freida a big kiss from me. Make sure the one for Claire is a long one."

Bill watched the happy smile expand across his friend's face. Karl had been putting in those long days with his American counterpart, Major Andy Anderson, who had already informed Bill he would be returning to the embassy for the Christmas Holidays, and in his opinion, Major Vita was long overdue for a holiday pass. God knows, we have earned it. "Karl, make this holiday a good one because, when you return, you will be flying over to Dublin to commence the training program for the O.S.S. boys arriving from Washington on January 3rd. I have been advised that you will be there for at least a month, bringing these chaps up to date on our interrogation methods.

Now, there is one sticky area I need to share with you. You're a professional, so I'm sure you will handle it with your usual professional flair. Going over with you will be three radio instructors, the head of which will be Captain Hazel Collins." Karl looked at Bill with a stone-like expression on his face.

An intense moment passed before Karl responded, "Well, that's going to be sticky for both of us. But you're right; we are both adults and officers in His Majesty's Service. I'm sure we will find a way to make it work for the time we are there. How does Hazel feel about this?" asked Karl.

Bill responded by saying, "At first, she was very upset, then she said, "Maybe this is a good thing for us to see each other and part as friends with no hard feelings."

Karl looked at Bill, his facial expression changing to one of relief. "Bill, you realize I will have to tell Claire about this, don't you?"

Bill sat on the corner of Karl's desk. Placing his hand on Karl's shoulder, he quietly responded. "I have already done that, Karl. This was a decision Clive and I had to make before we finalized the team for this operation. Hazel is the very best in that arena, and Clive only wanted our best for this training." Bill waited for the response he knew would come.

"So, you two took it upon yourselves to tell Claire about this operation?" asked Karl, thinking, here we go again with that secret stuff from the bloody BIS.

"Karl, we did the right thing. I told her you did not know yet, and I would tell you before you left today." Bill waited for Karl to process this, which came back very quickly.

"You could have consulted me before you made that call. Wouldn't that have been the right thing to do?" responded Karl, holding back a very sarcastic remark.

"Karl, give Claire credit. She was perfectly fine with the explanation we provided. She paid you a big compliment by telling me, 'Karl will be the perfect diplomat when he interfaces with Hazel. I'm sure she is a very professional officer who knows how to handle herself in difficult circumstances like this.' Claire closed by saying, 'Now, send him home, Bill. I'll work him over enough that he'll be too scared to think of anything other than his assignment.'" Karl felt better about the whole situation, thinking, with a smirk on his face, she thinks I scare that easily?

Before departing, Karl took the time to wish everyone a very Merry Christmas with apologies for not sharing more time with them. Finally, he stopped into Bill's office to wish him a wonderful Christmas and tell him to kiss Dorothy for him. Bill hugged his friend, saying, "Don't forget to go see the doctor so he can remove that eye patch. That's going to be the greatest Christmas present for Claire." Karl had almost forgotten about his left eye and almost forgotten he had an appointment with the doctor at 1330 hours. Karl put his officer's topcoat on, then reached for his case. Heading for the door, he placed his cap under his arm. Out in the main office, he again wished everyone a safe and happy Christmas, then proceeded to the medical center.

Dr. Phillips dimmed the lights, then removed the patch and gauze dressing. "How does that feel, Major? It will take a few minutes for your eyes to normalize, so don't get alarmed at seeing double. It will pass quickly," said the doctor.

"Thanks, Doc, for once, everything is in proper focus. What a great Christmas gift. Thanks again, and please, have a Merry Christmas with your family."

With that, Karl headed out through the lobby to the cold weather of December. Waiting in front of the main door was Charlie, standing by the Hillman staff car with the rear door open. At the station, he got out, wishing Charlie a Merry Christmas, then he went into the familiar station. Karl found a compartment with four RAF members sitting inside. Seeing a major's uniform, they immediately stood, saluting the superior officer. Karl waved his arm in a downward motion, saying, "Thank you, boys, no need to stand on ceremony. We are all military in this compartment." The trip to Paddington seemed to go quickly. Karl enjoyed the stories being told by the young RAF chaps. Changing trains in London, Karl stopped to buy a card for Claire. Then at a corner florist, he stopped to buy some flowers, asking the happy florist, "Will these flowers be alright for about an hour train ride?"

"They will be fine, Sir. She's a lucky girl to receive these from such a handsome chap. Merry Christmas, Sir, and a very Happy New Year," said the older lady as she wrapped the flowers in extra paper, then put a colorful green and red ribbon around the top. Karl walked along the platform, and, finding a half-empty compartment, climbed aboard for the last leg back to Hitchin. Karl waited patiently for the familiar braking from the engine as the train slowed into the station.

Wishing everyone in the compartment a Merry Christmas, he climbed down onto the platform. Turning toward the tunnel, his breath was taken away by arms around his neck and soft lips kissing his cheeks, then his mouth. It was Claire, her excitement obvious, and everyone passing them by was laughing at the attention this striking lady was giving her man.

"Darling, how I've missed you so very much. Beverly threw me out early because, in her opinion, I was useless thinking about you arriving back home. My God, Karl, you look so different without that eye patch. Now you can see me with two eyes; still like the picture?" Claire was over the moon, thinking, it feels so good to once again meet someone special at the station. For so long, that privilege was taken away from me. A shiver went through her as she suppressed a feeling it could happen again.

Walking toward the tunnel, she blurted out, "Darling, let's stop at the Copper Kettle for a drink and a plowman's sandwich; how does that sound?" Claire just wanted to be out and about with her man.

"If that's what you would like, it's fine with me. Which car are we using?" Karl said, knowing she would not take the MG out, so the Wolsey it would be. Entering the bar, they found a table by the fireplace. Holding hands, they sat side by side and talked about the things that occupied their time while apart. In the back of Karl's mind, he wondered, when will my solicitor ask me about Hazel? Won't be long by the look on her face.

Claire, still in her business suit, looked wonderful. Her hair was tied back in a French twist, always the professional conservative business lady in that dark burgundy fitted suit. Karl kept looking at her as she rattled on, her nervous energy keeping her going.

Karl turned in toward her, finally asking, "Claire, you're nervous because Bill called you concerning the upcoming operation in January. He also included that Captain Collins would be on that team, am I correct? Let's get it out of the way so that we can enjoy our time in front of the fire with our drinks, shall we?"

"Karl, you always can read me like an open book. I did not want to mention it in case I hit a nerve. You've had a strenuous three weeks, from what Bill told me. You and your new American friend have been working almost around the clock, but since you brought up the topic of Hazel, let me say this once and only once, then it's over. Look, we both know you and Hazel were close. I also take responsibility for the demise of that relationship. Karl, if I thought for one minute that relationship was strong, I would not have made the first move.

"You were lost, looking for something you couldn't find. I believe you and I have found that. When the time comes for you to interface with Hazel, I expect you to be the friendly and diplomatic professional officer you are. What we have is that strong. I would trust you in a room full of beautifully dressed women, flashing their long legs at you. So, don't worry anymore about Hazel. Everything is alright with me. Are you listening to me, Sailor? Now, give me a big wet kiss, you sexy man. Wait until I get you home. For the record, and for the thousandth time, I'm madly in love with you, Major Vita, and you are madly in love with me, correct?" Claire's nervousness was no more. Her confidence was back, stronger than ever.

Karl sat there, slowly shaking his head, listening to her. "Claire, what did I do to deserve a lady like you?" asked Karl as he pulled her in toward him, feeling her energy that meant only one thing. "Drink up, lady; you have a show to put on for this tired soldier."

Claire's response was immediate. "I thought you'd never ask," she said, showing her not so proper side. Back home, Karl stripped off his uniform, removing the various insignias, ready to send it to the dry cleaners in the morning. Claire poured two glasses of port, taking them upstairs. Karl was sitting up in bed, reading an old local newspaper.

"Well, look at you; are you waiting for something, Your Highness?"

"You could say that, but you are still dressed," replied Karl.

Claire got the message. Sitting next to him at the side of the bed, she tossed the bedcovers back, then slowly proceeded to unbutton her blouse, starting the show Karl had asked for.

The following morning, they went shopping for last-minute gifts and then headed to Baldock for the rest of the day. Christmas Eve, they all came together in Hitchin at Claire's and Karl's home. With the fire going, they all sat around the Christmas tree, opening gifts and enjoying young Franchot, playing with his new toys. Freida had expressly asked that no soldier or toy guns were to be given. The family departed at 9:00 p.m. Ronny had an early morning duty call, and Karl needed to spend Christmas Day alone with Claire. They both knew when he boarded that train, he would be gone a long time, so this quiet time would have to carry them through those long days of separation.

Boxing Day, they dressed warmly, walked through the Western Hill that overlooked Baldock, and finally returned to the bungalow for lunch. As the sunshine gave way to dark skies, Karl and Claire said their goodbyes to Mama and family, heading home for their last evening in December of 1941.

Claire, like so many times before, took him to the station on December 27th. Waiting on the platform for the train to arrive, they both started to speak simultaneously. Claire chuckled, saying, "You first, darling."

Karl, with his arms around her waist, looked into her eyes, and with a calming voice, he spoke, "Claire, this is a difficult goodbye. I'm not sure when we will see each other again. The New Year will present so many hurdles for us in the BIS. Keep writing those letters, and if you call me, assuming you will be able to connect, please use the secure phone, just to be on the safe side, alright? If you're still up on New Year's Eve, toast me, and I will do the same to you, Claire. Who would have thought last New Year's Eve that we would be here now? I did not know you, although I prayed one day, I would find you. Fate changed that, thanks to our little MG car. The next few years will be extremely challenging for both of us; we must remain strong and keep that flame brightly lit until this war comes to an end, and I can come home to you, never to part again." Karl was preparing her for the long months she would not see him and would rarely receive a letter or a telephone call.

"Karl, I have been preparing myself for over a month that you would shortly be entering a new phase of your command. I need you to know, as much as my heart will ache for you, you needn't worry. I will be waiting for this smoking monster to bring you back to me one fine day. Kiss me, Karl; I need that fresh in my mind." Claire, reaching for him, tried very hard to suppress the tears she was holding back. Along the platform, other soldiers, sailors, and air force chaps were saying their goodbyes.

The conductor blew his whistle, yelling, "All aboard, this train departing for Kings Cross Station."

Karl squeezed her tightly for one more brief minute. "Claire, I love you so much. Heaven knows I don't deserve you, but I can't imagine life without you." One more kiss before he broke away, climbing into the compartment of the train. Claire stood by the door, shedding tears, her emotions flowing freely as her man was leaving, returning to the dangerous career of an Intelligence Officer. Like those times before, Claire stood, watching as the train disappeared in a stream of smoke. Feeling completely lost and alone, she walked slowly back down the tunnel and out of the station. She returned to an empty house, feeling saddened by Karl's departure. She picked up the phone and dialed the bungalow. Mama answered.

"Mama, it's Claire. I'm feeling so lost and alone; would it be alright if I come over today? I really don't want to be alone, feeling like this. I need to be with you all." Mama could sense Claire's sorrow and the need to be around others in a similar situation.

In her broken English, she replied, "Claire, get in your car and come over right now; you need to be with your family." Claire, hearing this, started feeling better. Then, grabbing her coat, she locked the front door, climbed into the Wolsey, and headed for Baldock.

Mama was standing by the front door, and as she looked at the red eyes and damp cheeks, she opened her arms, saying, "Come here, child. It saddens me to see you this upset. Let's you and I have a cup of coffee together, shall we?" With her arm around Claire, Mama could not stop thinking; she must get used to this and remain strong. Karl will more than likely be spending less time here at home; his job will demand more of him now that the Americans have joined us.

On the train, Karl was feeling melancholy and probably about the same as Claire was feeling about now. Disciplining his mind, he refocused his attention on the upcoming operation. Arriving back at the camp, he met up with his American counterpart, Major Anderson. "Andy, old man, how was your Christmas? Did you get your packages from the States alright?" asked Karl, pleased to see his new friend.

"Yes, I did, pal, and I kept some food items back for you to have on the flight over tomorrow, okay?" replied Andy, a big smile on his face. Walking over to the main hall, they met up with other members that made up the joint task force flying to Ireland.

One junior officer asked Karl, "Sir, do we have a specific date when we will be returning to England?"

With a stern look on his face, Karl simply replied, "No, I wish I could tell you more. I will get you that date as soon as I find out myself, and as our American friends say, okay?" Arrangements were in high gear, getting ready to leave for Dublin the following day. The sky was still dark when Karl and his team boarded the vehicles that would drive them to RAF Northolt. The flight over to Dublin was bumpy and noisy, so Karl propped his head against the side of his canvas seat and tried to get some sleep. Instead, he started to think about the challenges they would face in the upcoming year and beyond.

Arriving in Dublin, they traveled by road to the secret camp, hastily constructed by the Royal Engineers outside the rural farming town of Shanganagh. Settled in, they gathered in the large main room to meet others that had arrived from England earlier that morning. The introductions were uplifting as they all shook hands. Karl, from the corner of his eye, caught sight of Hazel looking at him intensely. Walking over to her, he politely said, "Hazel, I am really pleased to see you. I never imagined we would meet here in Ireland, though. Before you give me a mouthful, may I say, I have been looking forward to a time when we could meet face to face. Can we talk privately?

"Hazel, I owe you an explanation more than an apology, but no excuses for how I handled myself and the shock you got when you met up with Clive. Your letter touched me deeply, and I pray we can work together without any additional tension between us. I understand it's up to me to make that happen."

Hazel, her arms crossed and her head lowered, stood silent for a few minutes, then looked up, eyeballing Karl, "Well, Major Vita, it's not like I haven't been in a similar situation before, is it? But you're right; we have a big job ahead of us, and we are both professional enough to make this work. Karl, I won't lie about how I feel about you. It still hurts so very much and probably will for a very long time. Now, you two-timing Casanova, why don't you buy me a double whiskey and tell me all about Claire?"

They both smiled at that statement. The fear they both carried at confronting each other had passed. Hazel and Karl had found a common ground they both could coexist and work in.

Sitting at the makeshift bar, Karl, in his own special way, asked Hazel a comical question. "Hazel, in a couple of days, it will be New Year's Eve again. It reminds me of that time up in Scotland some years back, please, no repeat performances on the dance floor." They both looked at each other, remembering that evening so very well.

Hazel, looking at him with a stern face, responded by giving Karl a 'V' for victory sign with her left hand, then a mischievous smile. With time and the proximity of working together, they would forge a true lasting friendship. Hazel finished her drink, kissing Karl on the cheek, then excused herself, returning to her group. The sorrow in her heart remained each time she looked Karl in the eyes. Karl found a quiet place. Sitting alone, sipping his whiskey, he started to smile, thinking again about that New Year's party in the Scottish training camp. Under the influence of too much whiskey, Hazel Collins had tried to put the moves on him, only to be politely dismissed by his fiancée, Kitty Johnson, the beautiful, intelligent officer who would never live to see another New Year's Eve or England again.

Karl was now thinking about the challenges that lay ahead in this senseless war that would leave so many countries in ruins, its people left homeless, their lives shattered, and so many relationships forever lost. Millions of innocent civilians would be killed because of their religion or political beliefs. Some would face torture; others would be forced into slavery, only to be killed when their bodies could no longer serve their Nazi masters. His final thoughts would be, we must destroy this tyrant and his senseless tyranny. With our new American allies, our chances of being victorious are getting better with each passing day. Standing up, he swigged back the last of his whiskey, then returned to his group.

From here on, England and its new allies would take the war directly to the Germans, sealing their fate and the final victory in Europe for the Allies.

EPILOGUE

1942 would change everything. On January 26th, thousands of American servicemen arrived in Belfast, Ireland, to commence training, followed by the massive build-up in England of over 1.5 million additional troops. New camps sprung up from Scotland to Cornwall and every county in between to accommodate all of them.

In February, the American 8th Airforce started ferrying over 3,650 aircraft from bases in America to existing bases and many new makeshift bases springing up throughout England. To add to this buildup, huge convoys of ships started offloading mountains of supplies to support the American military buildup as well as replenishing the English and Russian stockpiles of food and military hardware, including tanks, trucks, all types of weapons, and aircraft severely depleted during the last two years of fighting.

For the most part, the English people adapted quickly to the free-spirited Americans, who arrived with full bellies and plenty of money in their pockets, creating some animosity within the English military forces that had been fighting for over two years, tolerating, amongst other things, poor wages, limited food, and many other basic needs. These differences would slowly fade away as the forces started helping each other. However, many a fight would start over some pretty girl who took a liking to a U.S. soldier dangling real nylons as an enticement.

In June of 1942, Claire and Karl made their matrimonial vows. Their lives from here on would forever change for the better. The service was held in the Catholic church of St. Mary's in Hitchin.

Karl's next assignment would be with the British Security Coordination (B.S.C.) to Canada. Accompanying him would be members of his interrogation team to train additional members of the American Office of Strategic Services (O.S.S). Claire would not see him again until March of 1943. Hazel would also be assigned to that British Intelligence contingency. The new relationship with Karl made working together tolerable, but with time, the proximity of their working together became more comfortable but always at arm's length.

1943 would bring another surprise for Karl and the family when Claire announced she was expecting a baby. At first, there was shock, then belated joy. Holding Claire tightly, Karl could not hold back the tears at being a new father.

In 1943, the allied forces were hard at work preparing for the invasion of Mainland Europe. Operation Overlord had a tentative schedule for June 1944, the actual date yet to be assigned, and therefore, was given the code name D-Day. This monumental undertaking would be the most extensive military undertaking in World War II. Karl and ten of his top agents would be assigned to the Americans for this operation. Their background and language abilities would be vital in determining where German prisoners originated from. Their dialect would usually give them away.

In 1945, the German military was almost finished but not quite yet. Intelligence reports were coming in with alarming information about the German development of a device that could annihilate cities with just one atomic bomb. The Allies, recognizing the extreme danger of this new bomb, started planning a daring elaborate scheme to steal the ship transporting heavy equipment to the secret location in Norway after it had left the German harbor of Keil. For Karl, this mission would be the most dangerous he had ever been involved in. Leading a team of specialized merchantmen, protected by elite S.A.S. commandos, they would take over the ship with the help of its captain and members of the crew who were prepared to die to stop any further development of this new weapon.

The war in Europe would come to an end on May 7th, 1945. Hitler committed suicide with his new wife Ava Braun, taking the coward's way out. What he left behind was a devastated Continent. General Alfred Jodl of the German High Command signed the unconditional surrender in Reims Northern France for all German Forces.

On the other hand, Japan would face the awesome might of the American forces and its allies, seeking revenge for the attack on Pearl

Harbor and so many other places throughout the Pacific. Defeat would be forced on them by the devastating destruction of the world's first Uranium Atom Bomb (Little Boy), dropped on Hiroshima on August 6th, 1945 by a single B-29 bomber, commanded by Paul Tibbets.

As for Hazel, she would finally get her posting to America. Finding a new love, she eventually married, making her new home in Rhode Island. She would not see any of her friends in the BIS again until Clive had a reunion at the Charter Arms in Slough in July 1950.

In September of 1951, Karl, Claire, and Nicholas, their son, drove to Vienna to see Mama and the family. Papa was buried in Italy; they would visit his grave the following year. Before arriving in Vienna, they had made a diversion, stopping in the small village of St. Sebastian in upper Bavaria in Germany to find Kitty's grave. Staying for two days, they had a new headstone made that read:

Here lies an English Rose who left this
world too early for her years.
October 1938
Lieutenant Kitty Johnson
of the British Intelligence Service.
Rest in Peace

Karl and Claire would remain in Hitchin, raising their son in the post-war peace that would be worldwide, but for how long?

Karl could not give up his dream of returning to the sea. It had been fifteen years since he said goodbye to his ship, the Tristian in Marseille, France. In her infinite wisdom, Claire made Karl a deal to once again pursue that dream with the condition it would be for only three years. The circle was almost complete.

THE END

This is the second book in this series.

ABOUT THE AUTHOR

PETER A. MOSCOVITA grew up in England and had a love for exploring different countries, sparked by exciting family trips across Europe. His Dad's adventure stories from his early years as a ship's officer made him dream about discovering new lands far beyond.

In 1966, his dreams came true, when he emigrated to the United States of America as a design and development engineer. In later years he would enter medical device manufacturing.

In 1982, he met Martine, who shared his passion for travel, sailing, cruising, culinary clubs and the love of history.

In 1986, alone with two fellow engineers they founded a startup company that designed and developed a line of advanced Medical Vascular Diagnostic instruments. Once the instruments were ready for market he turned his attention to creating a National Sales and Marketing Division. As the company grew he convinced his wife Martine to join the company as its event coordinator.

When time permitted the couple continued their long distant traveling all over the world, exploring was in their blood.

In 2010, the partners agreed they would sell the company, now traveling and exploring had no boundaries.

In 2011, The couple moved to Florida in their boat, living on it in Sarasota before settling ashore in Lakewood Ranch. Since then, they've continued to explore distant lands and enjoy life to the fullest.

In 2018, the author wrote his first book, *The Following Storm* which readers loved, that first book turned into a series. The four thrilling books follow the life, loves and dangers of Karl Vita throughout World War II into the early 1950's. *The Last Train Home* wraps up Karl Vita's story.

Since then, his books continue to receive five-star reviews.

To review additional titles and updates please visit the authors website:

www.petermoscovita.net

Note: *'The Ultimate Sacrifice'* from the same period but not associated with The Following Storm series is available through various outlets like Amazon and Barnes & Noble and other online retailers. *'The Unexpected Encounter'* takes place in the 1960s during the cold war between America and Russia. This gripping story of espionage, romance and commitment will keep you guessing with its never-ending twist through numerous continents. Another book available during the first quarter of 2025 takes on a completely different story.

'My Journey To You' centers on two major characters, a high powered American advertising executive and a German superstar. Both very successful in their chosen careers but in their private lives they both lack that relationship they both crave to find. This story starts off with an online relationship you will embrace but don't get comfortable with. It will take you by surprise as you read on.

Am I considering another series? Stay tuned to find out!